Anita Faulkner writes warm and fuzzy romcoms from her upcycled bureau in the south west of England. She grew up sniffing books and devouring stories. And she insists it was perfectly normal to squirrel boxes of pretty stationery that felt far too magical to actually use. She's also accumulated a brave and patient husband and a strong-willed little boy who brighten up her world.

Keep in touch with Anita by joining her Facebook Group (chicklitandprosecco), subscribing to her mailing list (bit.ly/anitafaulknernews) or by following her on Twitter and Instagram (@anita_faulkner_).

Also by Anita Faulkner

A Colourful Country Escape

The Gingerbread Café

Anita Faulkner

SPHERE

SPHERE

First published in Great Britain in 2022 by Sphere

3 5 7 9 10 8 6 4 2

A CIP catalogue record for this book
is available from the British Library.

ISBN 978-0-7515-8438-7

Typeset in Caslon by M Rules
Printed and bound in Great Britain by
Clays Ltd, Elcograf S.p.A.

Papers used by Sphere are from well-managed forests
and other responsible sources.

Sphere
An imprint of
Little, Brown Book Group
Carmelite House
50 Victoria Embankment
London EC4Y 0DZ

An Hachette UK Company
www.hachette.co.uk

www.littlebrown.co.uk

*To Gina, who never got the chance to write
the wonderful books she'd planned.*

Thank you for everything – this one's for you. Xx

Prologue

Eleven months earlier

Gretel Rosenhart's world was as fragile as a snow globe. That was the thought that swept into Nell's head as she moved towards her with a mug of cinnamon hot chocolate. She placed it down gently on the wooden café table where Gretel was working. *Don't disturb her peace.* It was the approach Nell took when the young woman was crafting with glass. And, in fact, always. Had that been the right thing to do over the years? The poor soul had surely been through enough turbulence.

Gretel looked up and smiled; a beautiful smile that didn't always reach her forest-green eyes. 'Thank you.' She put down the iridescent glass fairy she'd been working on and tucked a few tendrils of hair back inside her knitted Christmas hat.

Nell's heart felt as warm as the chocolate as she watched

1

Gretel blowing the vegan mini marshmallows on her drink for the simple pleasure of watching them bob. She'd always done it, ever since she was a little girl visiting The Gingerbread Café with her mother. Nell looked upwards and blinked a few times. Getting sad wouldn't change things.

'You didn't need to bring me extra gingerbread people,' Gretel admonished softly. 'You spoil me.'

'No one else to spoil.' Nell took a deep breath and wiped her hands on her candy-striped apron. 'Anyway, you've been here all day making those Christmas decorations. You must be hungry.'

Gretel shrugged and gave a little smile. 'Nowhere else to be.'

She was always so matter-of-fact about it. Never doleful. And she seemed happy enough in her safe little world of glass trinkets, didn't she? Nell gave her a delicate touch on the shoulder and retreated behind the counter, its string of festive lights flickering like they weren't quite sure.

It was probably just as well Gretel had been here all day, Nell thought, as she pinched one of her favourite gingery lebkuchen biscuits from under a cloche and began munching. There'd been hardly any other customers. But trade would pick up soon; it was nearly Christmas, after all.

Not that a person could tell, in this place. Nell's eyes bounced from the holly wreaths in the windows to the winter-spiced candles which glimmered from every table. The novelty of keeping The Gingerbread Café festive all year long had worked a treat in years gone by. The crowds they used to get. But now . . .

No. This was no time to change things. She sank backwards onto a stool, her bones audibly creaking. Every part of her body was feeling its age. And now it was more than age: she was ill, and she wasn't getting better. At first she'd kept it a secret because she didn't want anyone to worry. Then when the worst was confirmed, Nell had been determined to live normally for as long as possible – and that meant keeping the café going, too. Most folk would have retired years ago, never mind messing about with new business ideas. She'd have to leave all that creativity to the youngsters. Talking of which, Nell checked her watch and smiled. Not long now.

'Would you look at her!'

Nell shook herself back to the present. Gretel was standing near the doorway, holding her Christmas fairy up to the spotlight and spinning gently with it, its rainbow colours dancing. She'd taken off her knitted hat and her milky blonde hair tumbled around her pale face and down the back of her blue snowflake pinafore dress. In that moment, caught in the ray of light, she was the very essence of a Christmas angel.

Caught? Or was she well and truly stuck? Nell swallowed down the lump in her throat. If she was honest, that's why Gretel was always here.

The poor woman was stuck in Christmas.

And who could blame her, after all that had come before? But perhaps it was time to move on; at least for one of them.

The bell above the café door tinkled, and the quivering tip of a Norway spruce emerged, exactly as ordered. Always a real tree for Christmas. It was being carried by her only nephew, Lukas. Nell gave a wry smile as his handsome face appeared, even though his expression was distinctly narky. She knew he'd rather stick pine needles in his steely grey eyes than embrace the joy of Christmas, but here he was, just the same. He was a good lad under the chef's whites and huffy persona. And he hadn't *always* hated Christmas.

'Damn this thing.' Lukas sighed. 'Bloody Christmas. What a load of faff.' He gave the tree an angry shove, its bushy branches sticking in the doorway.

Gretel pulled a face at his words. Then hearing Lukas's final heave, she spun to face the door just as the tree unwedged itself and came hurtling towards her. As she contorted her body in an attempt to avoid being speared, her arms flew forwards.

'Oh no!' The cry left Nell's panicked throat as the iridescent fairy flew through the air from Gretel's hand, catching the light and shimmering all colours of the spectrum as it spiralled.

Lukas looked up as he saw the glass object hurtling towards him. He could have ducked to save himself from it, but instead he shot his arm upwards and caught the fairy, steadying the tree with his other.

Nell heard Gretel stifle a sob as Lukas saved her prized creation from being smashed to glass confetti.

The flash of gratitude quickly passed.

Gretel cleared her throat and met his eye. 'People should be more careful.'

Nell blinked. Gretel would usually shrink away rather than speak out.

'Says the woman dancing around in doorways waving shards of glass,' retorted Lukas.

'She's not . . . ' Gretel exhaled. 'You wouldn't understand.' She thrust out her hand for the fairy.

Lukas held Gretel's gaze for a moment. When he moved his hand slowly towards hers and Gretel reached to close the gap, their fingers touched. Just lightly. A less keen eye may have missed it, but Nell hadn't spent a lifetime tending to fragile hearts with sweet drinks and gingerbread not to spot the slight blush of two faces.

But before either could dwell on it, the old-fashioned juke-box chimed in with a gratuitous rendition of 'Underneath the Tree'. Nell had always suspected that machine of tom-foolery. Gretel shook herself down and retrieved her delicate creation, with a hostile *thanks*. Lukas cleared his throat and returned to battling with the spruce, a little flustered.

As an exquisite voice in the background sang of loneliness and being lost, a thought began to fuse like a snowflake in Nell's mind. She'd been wondering what to do, hadn't she? This seemed like the perfect plan. Not only did it settle her musings about what should happen with the café when the time came, but maybe she could encourage a few more moments of magic in Christmases to come too.

Having someone to catch you when you fell was a beautiful thing.

Chapter 1

There were worse things to be doing on a dull November day than sobbing into your apple strudel whilst a ferret nipped holes in your slipper socks. Weren't there? And anyhow, Gretel Rosenhart knew that just like before, she would pull herself up like a *Sound of Music* string puppet and get on with things. She poked the bowl of congealing pudding with her spoon and sighed. It was a poor excuse for a microwave pastry anyway.

'Angel Gabriel!' Gretel yelped as her pet's spiky little teeth found flesh. It was an occupational hazard of being maid to an albino ferret with a penchant for toes. Good job she'd never wanted to be a ballerina. But her little man was right: it was time to get up and stop sulking. It had been two weeks since Nell had died. The dear, stubborn thing hadn't even mentioned the illness until she could no longer hide it. Terminal. Such a loaded word, but her friend wasn't just off on her travels. She could only wish Nell's soul had flown somewhere lovely.

Gretel blinked back a tear. At least there was no danger of her feeling this dreadful again. There were no more people to lose, and that was just fine. Really it was.

She jumped up on one leg, trying to gently wriggle Angel Gabriel off the end of the other. When she'd reclaimed her nibbled limb, she padded across her tiny maisonette to the kitchen in her reindeer onesie. Moving aside a small mountain of tissues, she plonked her half-eaten mid-morning snack on the worktop and exhaled. What she really craved was one of Nell's gorgeously iced gingerbread people, all frilly and smiling, smelling sweetly of nutmeg. But like all of the loveliest things, they would live only in her memory now. She couldn't even bake.

Gretel shook her head.

'We must crack on,' she announced to Angel Gabriel, who probably wasn't even listening.

It wasn't her thing to dwell on what she couldn't do or didn't have. What she *could* do was craft. So she should get dressed and get on with it. Creating stained-glass Christmas ornaments had seen her through the darkest of times; those creations were her light.

She picked up her iridescent glass fairy and smiled at her. Brigitte had become her favourite. She'd named her after her Austrian mother, who, like Nell, now hugged only in memories. Then there was dear little Rosa – for ever frozen in Gretel's thoughts wearing pigtails and a hand-me-down Christmas jumper. A tightness clutched her throat. They said grief was a journey, but when would she be allowed to step away from the path?

Thud, thud, thud. Angel Gabriel arrived at her feet, dragging a pair of crafting pliers in his mouth. She bent down to save her tool and give his snowy white fur a fuss. His warm, fluffy body always felt like a little bag of calm.

'Thank you, small guy. You're all I need, huh?' He didn't answer, but then he never did say much other than the occasional squeak. She didn't take it personally. 'Although a bit more space wouldn't go amiss.'

Since Nell had passed, her life had suddenly felt so much smaller. Gretel generally steered clear of people, but Nell had been her lifeline, and she'd loved every squishable inch of her. Spreading herself out on one of Nell's old wooden café tables to craft had become her life. She closed her eyes. The café had been shut since Nell had gone, but she could picture every detail. Its twinkling lights and sweet, spicy smells. Even that cantankerous jukebox. Would she ever get the chance to visit again? Or perhaps Nell's lifework would be gobbled up and regurgitated into a faceless franchise, selling bitter coffee and factory-packed cakes.

Angel Gabriel tried to grab the pliers again. Gretel rolled her eyes. They didn't say ferret meant thief for nothing.

'You think I should commemorate Nell and the café with a glass ornament? I bet you're missing them too.'

Strictly speaking, ferrets hadn't been allowed in The Gingerbread Café – something about Environmental Health having a field day if he escaped into the kitchen. In fairness, he had form. But Nell had often turned a blind eye when Gretel snuck him in and left him sleeping under the table in her bag. He seemed to need company a lot more than

Gretel did. She couldn't pretend to understand much about ferrets, although she muddled through. This one had chosen her by looking particularly sorry for himself in an abandoned cardboard box on her way home from the café one blustery night. She'd brought him home and knitted him a fetching snowman jumper and the rest had been history. As much as Gretel tried hard to avoid becoming attached to living creatures, the odd one had the habit of sneaking in. She must keep a stricter eye on that.

Angel Gabriel sniffed his way over to the bags and boxes of craft equipment and handmade ornaments that flanked the room like sandbags. She sold the ornaments in her online shop, and Nell had been great at pushing them onto café customers too, when there'd been any. Maybe if Gretel was brave enough to face selling at markets, she could upgrade to a slightly less crummy home. But unlike her late mother, she wasn't good with people. She got nervous.

'We should make a start.' Gretel climbed over ferret tunnels, empty tissue boxes and bits of discarded knitting projects to reach her crafting stuff. She gave her head a contemplative scratch before pulling open box lids and having a poke. 'Pencil and paper . . . ?'

Like all good designers, she'd start with a sketch. She could see it already – the perfect stained-glass gingerbread house to remind her of Nell and her heart-warming café, though she had no idea where she'd display it in this shambles of a maisonette. When ideas came, they flowed quickly. She needed to get scribbling.

'I'm seeing coloured lights around the door.' She pointed

to Angel Gabriel as though expecting him to find the pad and take notes. 'And candy canes.' Gretel remembered Nell's trademark stripy apron with a pang. 'A snow-topped roof.' Was her ferret nodding now? Well, he did love to play in the snow. 'And a Christmas tree!'

Angel Gabriel gave a small yelp and went to bury his face under a sofa cushion.

Gretel stood up and blinked. Although Nell used to keep the café festive all year long, having a real Christmas tree had been a once-a-year treat. She'd got her nephew to drag one in last year, even though he'd pulled a grumpy face and had sworn a lot. What kind of person didn't love Christmas? No wonder he'd made her armpits clammy and her face all hot.

'No Christmas tree,' she confirmed to Angel Gabriel's furry bottom. 'Especially after a certain person nearly murdered my Christmas fairy with one.'

She shivered.

'Ta-daaaaah!' Gretel finally rescued her sketchpad and pencil from one of the boxes, which was quite a feat, considering how many there were. They'd surely been sneakily breeding.

Angel Gabriel popped his snowy head up, and apparently noticing Gretel's tasty pencil, made a leap from the sofa onto the nearest box. Gretel gasped at the sound of tinkling glass beneath him.

'People in glasshouses shouldn't have ferrets.' She scooped him off the box before it caved under his wriggling. That was one less job lot of glass snowmen to worry about.

Rat-a-tat-tat.

Who could that be? Gretel narrowed her eyes at the potential intrusion. With a heaviness, she realised she ought to face it. She made her way through the maisonette jungle to the front door, depositing Angel Gabriel safely in his cage as she went. If she'd learned one thing about ferrets, it was that they liked to escape, and it was a Herculean task to find them.

Gretel inched open the front door and a gust of wind blew in. The glass decorations on her plastic Christmas tree shivered in protest. She never had visitors, which was probably just as well. There was barely enough room to swing a ferret as it was; not that she'd ever be so cruel.

'This one needs to be signed for, miss, if you've got a moment.'

It was a young elf of a postman, waving a letter with his red-sleeved arm. She gulped. It looked kind of official. Had she paid that electricity bill? She made a mental note to turn the tree lights off and stop being so frivolous.

As she tried to scratch her signature onto the postman's tiny screen with a plastic pen, she could sense him gawping over her shoulder.

'You're ready for Christmas early. We're only two days past Halloween.'

Gretel pursed her lips. Who'd sent this cheeky guy? She wouldn't get this kind of chat from her ordinary postwoman, who knew full well she kept the place like this all year round. And why not? She had her reasons.

But Gretel gave a faint smile and hoped that was the end of it. That was *people* for you. They rarely meant any harm, but it was simpler not to befriend them unless you had to. It invariably ended in awkwardness or feeling exceptionally sad. She handed back the screen and took the letter.

'Mistletoe too. Who are you planning to kiss this year?'

'No one!' She hadn't meant for it to come out like a bark. She muttered an apology.

The postman took a step back and held his hands up. 'OK, miss. Just joking with you. Didn't mean to hit a nerve.'

He hadn't hit a nerve. Had he? She'd chosen this quieter life, after all. She looked at him, all Bambi eyes and bum-fluff beard. He could only be about seventeen. When she was that age, she'd lost her mum and Rosa. Nearly a decade had hurtled past, and yet most days she still felt stranded in her late teens too. Most people mistook her for younger than her twenty-six years, although if she did insist on dressing like a reindeer . . .

She cleared her throat and found a faint smile. She wasn't a natural with people, but she couldn't stand to make any creature feel bad. She wasn't the Grinch.

'It's fine,' she told him. 'I'm not offended. Anyway, the mistletoe's made of glass. It just . . . lives there.' It hung from the rickety light fitting and looked kind of sparkly when the lights were on. Not that it was her job to educate him on pretty decor.

And she didn't need to explain why her life had no space for smooching under parasitic plants, even if they did look cute in winter. Tradition had it that you had to pick off one berry for every person you kissed. She had no time for sharing her berries.

'Awesome,' he replied, looking relieved that his runaway mouth hadn't got him into trouble. 'Hope Santa's sent you something nice.' He pointed to the envelope in Gretel's hand.

Did nice things arrive by official-looking letter? It was no Christmas parcel with sweet little robin paper. Wouldn't Santa have at least added a bow?

'Merry Christmas,' she wished him as she closed the door. It might have been a bit early, but you never could be sure when you'd see people again. If at all.

And you never could tell when the contents of a letter, hand-delivered by a red-coated elf with bum fluff, could change things for ever.

Chapter 2

Duckman & Birdwhistle Solicitors
18–20 Bell Lane
Mistleton
Gloucestershire

1st November

Miss G. Rosenhart
42b Holly Road
Mistleton
Gloucestershire

Dear Miss Rosenhart,
Re: The Estate of Mrs Eleanor Ellbridge
　We confirm that we have been appointed as executors
of the will of the aforementioned Mrs Eleanor Ellbridge
(who we understand to have been known colloquially
as 'Nell').

As such, we are instructed to request your presence at the following time and place, in accordance with our late client's wishes.

Date: 21st November

Time: 11 a.m.

Place: The Gingerbread Café, 8 Green Tree Lane, Mistleton

We trust you will be in attendance unless we hear from you to the contrary.

Condolences, et cetera.

Yours sincerely,
Mr Birdwhistle (Junior)
cc: Mr L. Knight

Chapter 3

Condolences, et cetera. Really?

As much as Gretel had promised herself not to get too judgey before she'd even arrived at the mysterious meeting, she was not convinced she'd find much love for *Mr Birdwhistle (Junior)* and his funny formal lingo.

As she trotted the short distance to the café on that fresh November morning, she wondered for the one millionth time what this gathering was about. Why would Nell's last wishes involve her? And who was this Mr L. Knight who'd been copied in on the solicitor's letter? Would he be there too?

She reached Green Tree Lane and found herself stepping into the cobbled road to avoid an arm-in-arm couple. The quaint streets were beginning to get busier in the run-up to the Christmas shopping period, even if it never seemed to be as buzzing as years gone by. She realised she'd barely been out in the month or so since Nell had died. The sight of other humans made her want to shrink into her own skin a little at the best of times.

Oh, but Green Tree Lane. Though the day was chilly and the breeze nipped in through the hand-knitted stitches of her penguin jumper dress, in years gone by, this cosy street would have effortlessly warmed her heart. It used to be decked out for Christmas with red and green lights strung between the old-fashioned lamp posts and dotted through the trees like berries. The shop owners would fuzz up the panes of their casement windows with fake snow. And the trademark Christmas tree, which stood proudly in the centre of the pedestrianised street, would be resplendent in a blanket of twinkling silver lights. When did all of that slip away? Now all that remained were a few sorry lights on the tree.

Gretel noticed the pace of her furry snow boots slowing as she reached the front of The Gingerbread Café. She almost couldn't bear to see it. The warm glow of Nell's year-round festive lights used to radiate onto the street like the glimmer of toasty embers, but today Gretel didn't even want to take her mittens off. Every inch of the Cotswold stone felt cold. Even the holly wreaths in the windows now looked like a sad tribute to times gone by, rather than an evergreen celebration of Gretel's precious yuletide. Underneath the café's name, the sign promised *Festive Cheer All Through the Year*. Where was that cheer now?

She stole a look through the window, eager to get a preview of what might await before the street's clock struck eleven. But all she could see were . . . *ghosts*? No, wait. They were stark white dust sheets, covering the furniture like time was on hold. She took a deep breath and blew it out hard, knowing the simple process would help calm her. As she used her mitten to circle off the patch of her own steamy breath on the window, she strained to get a better look. The haunting apparitions were moving now, as a tall, thin man snatched them up and bundled them under one arm, contrasting against the black of his too-large suit.

'Is there a Quickie Café around here, love? People need coffee.'

Gretel jumped, a hand flying to her chest. It was just the shopping couple, bundling in close to the window. Gretel inched away, keen for some space.

'Erm. None of those around here. Sorry!' And she hoped there never would be. It was her least favourite chain, and definitely not what her precious street was all about.

She stepped around them and knocked briskly on the door. Maybe she was overreacting. She just needed to get inside and take a deep breath of something familiar, even if nothing in her world would ever be quite the same again.

To her relief the door opened quickly and she stumbled inside. She pulled off her festive owl hat, strands of her pale blonde plait flying wildly.

'Were those people bothering you, madam?' The man with the dark suit began securing the door behind her.

'No!' Had she said that too quickly? 'Not at all. They were just being . . . *people*.'

He turned to look at her, pushing his glasses back up his nose and squinting. She gave him a weak smile and hoped it would do. How could she explain there was generally nothing wrong with *people*? It was simply her knee-jerk reaction to avoid them, because when she let them get close it ended in sadness. Since losing Nell, who'd been the only non-relative she'd let wriggle in since for ever, her sensors were on high alert. If she let her guard down – even for a moment – she was terrified the temptation of kindness or company would lure her in.

As though the universe was trying to test her, the man extended a hand. 'Birdwhistle Junior,' he confirmed. 'Pleased to make your acquaintance.'

Well, at least he hadn't said *et cetera*. Feeling safe that this bird man wasn't going to bowl her over with compassion, Gretel shoved her hat into her crochet bag and gave his hand a limp shake.

'I was endeavouring to set things up to look ...' – he scratched his head, disturbing his feather-like hair – '*inviting and atmospheric.*' It sounded like he was quoting something. 'The deceased's wishes.' He gave a pleased nod.

The deceased. Was that why his language was so overly formal – because it was the easiest way to deal with death?

'Her name was Nell.' Gretel cleared her throat and put her bag down, grabbing hold of a box of matches on one of the uncovered tables and lighting a winter-spice-scented candle. She moved around the room doing the same on each table, the simple ritual bringing with it a wave of calm. She'd helped Nell set up on countless occasions. Useful talents like baking or working a till were beyond her, but she knew how to make things look pretty. She gulped back a sob, concentrating on the comforting flicker of each tiny flame as it danced to life.

Mr Birdwhistle hurried around sweeping dust sheets from tables, as though worried an anxious woman in charge of a matchbox had *blazing disaster* written all over her.

Just as Gretel finished her rounds with the last satisfying strike of a match, she heard a key in the door and the frustrated shaking of a lock. Was it usually so reluctant to let people in? Maybe it was taking a leaf out of her book. She tried to slow her quickening heartbeat with a few deep breaths. But Mr Birdwhistle was checking his watch and nodding. He didn't seem alarmed.

When the door finally shoved open, it sent a draught through the room that extinguished every carefully lit candle. As she caught a clear eyeful of who had just stepped through it, her skin went equally cold.

Chapter 4

So *that* was who Mr L. Knight was.

Although no shining armour today. Or ever, Gretel wouldn't mind betting – unless the pristine white chef's uniform she'd seen him wear counted. Nell's nephew Lukas gave her a visual sweep with his stern grey eyes, raising an eyebrow as his gaze landed on her penguin jumper dress. Well, he could just get lost if he didn't respect good knitwear. She blew rogue strands of her hair from her face and tried not to look like a flustered idiot.

'Gretel.' His voice was huskier than she'd remembered from that day he'd nearly knocked her head off with a Christmas tree. Was he feeling the sadness of this place too? Surely not, Mr Steely Stone-Face.

His voice seemed to bounce around the room, mixing with the echoes of what used to be. There was no toasty log fire today. No dancing fairy lights or gingery treats under glass cloches. Silence had taken over where tinkling tunes had once reigned, and no matter how deeply Gretel breathed, she couldn't smell the sweet comfort of hot chocolate. How she longed for a cup to warm her heart right then. Was all of that now lost for good?

Lukas ran a hand through his stylishly slate-grey hair and she watched as it resettled itself on roots that were as dark as his stubbly beard. Not that she was studying his face. She shook her head and wiped her clammy hands on her woolly dress.

Lukas looked down at the patch of floor he was standing on. 'It can only be about a year since . . . ' His voice trailed off.

'Since you nearly impaled me on this very spot.' She winced. This was why she should stay safely tucked up in her maisonette and only ever speak to ferrets. 'I mean, with a Christmas tree.' Oh brilliant. That was unquestionably worse.

'The whole season is a waste of good trees.' He batted angrily at a dusty length of tinsel which had become partially unstuck from the ceiling and was wafting dangerously close to his face. Dust motes teased the air around him.

Gretel opened her mouth to protest about his season-bashing, but thankfully Mr Birdwhistle stepped forward, pulled down the unruly tinsel and shook Lukas's hand.

While the other two introduced themselves, Gretel thought back to the day of the near impaling. Nell had been a friend of her mother's, so Gretel had known her since she was a girl. Nell had definitely mentioned Lukas before, somewhat adoringly, and Gretel must have seen him in passing. But that day last Christmas was the first time Gretel could recall really *seeing* him.

She dared a glance at the two talking men. Did Lukas's

eyes keep darting back to her? She could have sworn he was scowling at her poor, defenceless penguins. Mean old festive-bird-hater.

Yes, that was why Lukas Knight unnerved her. It was those flinty stares and his disconcerting animosity towards the one and only season where Gretel wanted to exist. That kind of attitude just wasn't *normal*.

At last, the solicitor settled them both down at one of the café tables, wrestling the tinsel under one of the dust sheets as though its presence might cause a fight. Gretel scraped her chair as far away from Lukas as she politely could. She had no desire to be choked by his spicy aftershave and abrasive words.

'So, you two are already . . . *acquainted*?' Mr Birdwhistle looked over the top of his specs at them.

'No, we're not,' Lukas said firmly, clearly put out by the unnecessary emphasis. Well, good. She was glad he didn't want to be *acquainted* either.

Gretel and Mr Birdwhistle jumped as the old-fashioned jukebox spluttered to life and spat out the words '*Laaaaaast Christmas*'.

'I'm sure I didn't switch that thing on.' The solicitor twitched his head around.

'That machine needs to go. The wiring has always been faulty, like it's stuck in a bloody time warp.' Lukas's jaw was tight.

What was wrong with a familiar festive tune? If he wasn't so scary, she'd have shot him a look. Although she had to admit it was spooky how the jukebox often chose songs that were oddly close to the mark. Not that anybody had been giving away any hearts last Christmas. Hers was safely pad-locked, thanks all the same, George Michael.

'Look, why are we here? Don't you know I'm busy?'

Gretel could hear Lukas tapping his foot under the table like he needed to rush off and sauté some shallots, or whatever fancy chef people did.

'I know you're in charge of administering the estate, but presumably you don't need to gather us here for some grand will reading,' Lukas continued.

'Quite,' Mr Birdwhistle replied, shaking his papers as though not appreciating having the wind knocked out of his bird wings. 'But it was the deceased's wishes . . .'

'Nell. Her name was Nell.'

For once, Gretel didn't feel the urge to roll her eyes at Lukas's words.

The solicitor gave a small sigh. 'Apologies, Mr Knight. Your Aunt Nell. It was her wish that we give you both a few weeks' space after her passing and then gather you here to break the fortuitous news.'

Why would you need to *break* news if it was fortuitous? Surely breaking was something you reserved for bad things. Gretel screwed up her nose.

'Eleanor . . .' The solicitor cleared his throat. '*Nell* wanted you to receive the message simultaneously.' If he shuffled his papers any more, Gretel might be pushed to jump up and snatch them off him. It was doing nothing for her nerves. 'You're to inherit The Gingerbread Café together, with the flat above too, of course. As joint owners. Congratulations, Mr and Mrs . . . erm, Mr Knight and Miss . . .'

'Rosenhart?' Gretel added, unsurely. Did he really mean her?

'Indeed.' Mr Birdwhistle nodded, looking as pleased as if he were handing over the premises out of the goodness of his own heart. 'Exemplary news, wouldn't you agree?' His head pecked the air in both of their directions.

Lukas swivelled his body around to look at her, his expression somewhere between confusion and mild annoyance. She guessed she couldn't blame him. Lukas was Nell's only close living relative. She'd been widowed young with no children, and her only sibling, Lukas's mother, had moved away years ago and had barely kept in touch. He must have been expecting to inherit everything.

But Lukas merely shrugged and looked back to the solicitor. 'Understood. Nell always had a strange soft spot for her, so I kept hearing. We'll be selling up anyway, and neither of us will want to move into Nell's old flat. Tell me when the legal transfer will take place.'

'Ahh.' Mr Birdwhistle rustled more papers. 'That's the thing.'

'What thing?'

Gretel sensed Lukas's tension to the side of her. She couldn't wait to get away from the moody man.

'It was ... *Nell's* wish that after your designated period to get over things, you would jump to it and get the café up and running. *Together*.'

Lukas shot a furrowed-eyebrow look between Mr Birdwhistle and Gretel, as though this was all some elaborate joke.

The solicitor consulted his papers. 'You're a chef, no?' He looked over his glasses at Lukas before sweeping his gaze to Gretel. 'And Nell insisted you were her dearest and most loyal customer who worships Christmas just like she did. You're part of the cloth.' He waved an arm towards the red and white gingham curtains which framed the windows like puffball skirts.

Lukas's face was an angry shade of red. 'I'm a full-time head chef at La Carotte Rôtie. I don't have time to be messing about with pathetic gingerbread people or serving up cute marshmallow drinks to the occasional passing teenager. As for *Festive Cheer All Through the Year* . . .' He shuddered. 'No thank you. I can't even stand to be festive at Christmas. Surely we can just sell up?' Lukas looked at Gretel, his smoky eyes fuming.

Gretel felt her heart hammer against her chest, her eyes suddenly brimming with tears. If she'd disliked Lukas Knight before, she was beginning to hate him now. How could he slag off the sanctity of Christmas and Nell's café – the one place that made her feel safe? And how on earth could Nell have thought it was a good idea to shove them together like this?

But she blinked back her emotion. She couldn't bear for him to see it and it surely wouldn't change a thing. He'd made it clear he was in charge here. The grown-up. And she was too scared to make a fuss. 'I guess,' she said, reluctantly.

They looked at Mr Birdwhistle.

He leaned back in his chair and shook his head, the voices of Wham! picking up in intensity around them. 'Selling up? No, no, no. I'm afraid it's not as simple as that.'

27

Chapter 5

'So why can't we just sell The Gingerbread Café and get on with our lives?' Lukas was eyeballing the solicitor, and he didn't look amused.

But Mr Birdwhistle was apparently just warming up. 'It's likely to take six months or so to get the grant of probate. And that's just the beginning of the work I need to do. Then there's taxes to be paid . . . '

Lukas winced. 'OK, OK. But there's no stipulation that we have to run the café in the meantime? We can just shove the dust sheets back on and wait?' He pointed to the ghostly mound on the floor.

Mr Birdwhistle embraced his role and pursed his lips.

'What?' Lukas waved his hands impatiently, palms upwards.

'It was your dying aunt's wish that as the only two people she loved and trusted on this mortal coil, you take the helm. Although she did express concerns that at least one of you would want to sell it.' If looks could be pointed, Lukas was on the receiving end of a dagger right then. 'But she wanted you to at least try. No *stipulations*. Just a deceased woman's last hopeful wish.'

Lukas let out a frustrated huff.

Mr Birdwhistle gulped. 'If you want to look at things with a practical head, the business will be far easier for you to sell at a healthy price if you keep it running and make it a success.'

'A success?' Lukas scoffed. 'Auntie Nell, God rest her, could be a bit of a dreamer. She kept this café as a shrine to Christmas all year long. Even in bloody July! It was pretty weird, and the rest of the world seemed to agree. As evidenced by the distinct lack of customers. I mean, who wants to sit round a log fire drinking spiced latte and munching festive gingerbread snowmen during a sweaty heatwave?'

'Me?' Gretel heard herself say. Who didn't love a crackling log fire? was the more sensible question. 'Christmas is special to *me*.' Gretel's voice wobbled. 'And this café was always a safe space for anyone who felt the same.' She realised she'd jutted out her bottom lip and pulled it back in. She didn't need sympathy, especially not from a man who made Scrooge look relatively jolly.

'All one of you?' Lukas seemed amused, although that didn't make his words feel any less harsh.

'The festive period got quite busy, actually.' Which he'd have known if he'd bothered to show Nell his support, other than his starring role when he *carried a Christmas tree*, like he was the inimitable Baby from *Dirty Dancing*. But she didn't dare say that. She tried her best cross face instead.

Lukas held his hands up. 'Look, I didn't mean to make you feel defensive. You obviously have your *stuff*. I'm just saying that a year-round sleigh-belling Santa fest is a stupid-arsed business plan. And it's most people's idea of hell.'

What did he mean by *stuff*? Was he poking fun at her when he didn't know the half of it? Well, he could bugger off.

'Actually, no. It's not most people's idea of hell. Most people love Christmas and knitted stockings and fairy lights.' She could feel herself beginning to shake, but he'd hit a nerve. 'They adore little gingerbread people and cosy-ing up with a hot chocolate and the smell of nutmeg and spice.' She knew she should end it there, but she was on a dangerous roll. 'It's only people who carry around their *stuff* like a big old grumpy sack who can't find a smile for the most wonderful time of the year.' By the time she'd finished, she was positively trembling. It was the most she'd said to anyone in weeks. Or maybe months.

'Wow. OK.' Lukas turned away from her and crossed his arms on the table. 'You're right – Christmas is not my bag. I hate it. So I guess we all have our *stuff*.'

There he was with the *stuff* again. Gretel felt her hackles rising.

'Anyway, even if I could embrace this ridiculous festive merry-go-round, I'm far too busy running an extremely popular kitchen at La Carotte Rôtie, on the outskirts of the village. We're hoping for a Michelin star next year so I'm busy doing *real* cooking. I haven't got time to be icing pink toenails on gingerbread people.'

Gretel was glad he was talking to the table with his condescending speech, because if she could see his silly grey eyeballs, she might just poke them out. She took a deep breath to steady her nerves. Confrontation was not her thing, but right then she felt like she was speaking up for Nell. And she'd flipping loved that woman, even if certain others couldn't find it in themselves to care.

'And is a twinkly Michelin star the only thing shining on your tree? Because I thought the star belonged to the restaurant, not the chef, and as far as I know that Rotten Carrot place belongs to some French guy. Maybe your Auntie Nell wanted you to create a legacy of your own. Like she did.'

He turned to look at her slowly, as though the cogs in his brain needed extra time to compute what she was saying. She needed time to process her own words too. Where was all of this coming from? The words were almost pouring out of her when she normally barely dared to speak.

'The translation is *roast*, not *rotten*.' He spoke to her like he was addressing a child, although in fairness, that happened a lot. It came with the territory when you were a Santa superfan. 'And if you must know, I do plan on having my own restaurant in the future. When we sell this place, I'll be well on my merry way.'

It surprised Gretel to sense herself deflating. At the beginning of this painful meeting she'd been willing to let the café go. Dealing with all those customers would be terrifying, and she didn't have the first clue how to run the place. Yet all this standing up for Nell was making her feel a sudden determination to honour her late friend's wishes. How could she give up on Nell and Christmas without a fight?

'Couldn't we try and reopen for a short while? For Nell?' Gretel's voice was so quiet she couldn't be sure she'd even said that out loud.

Lukas's quizzical look suggested she had. 'You want me to try running a year-round yule-athon with a Christmas lover who hates me?' He glanced towards the street as a group of hopeful shoppers stuck their cold noses to the window.

'It looks like we'd get some trade, at least at this time of year. People need this place.' Her more than most. 'And Nell worked too hard on it to go out without one final fling.'

Lukas gave a long exhale. 'I accept that opening for Christmas might assist in funding this guy's hourly rate.' He waved a hand at Mr Birdwhistle. 'And it might help one old girl to rest in festive peace.' He flicked his eyes skywards.

'Sooooo ... we're doing it?' Gretel asked, almost too scared to breathe in case she blew her chance.

He looked at her, eyes narrowed, as though making his final assessment. 'No, not *we*. I work ridiculous hours at The Rotten Carrot, remember? But if you're so desperate to prove your festive point, then I won't object to you opening up and getting on with it. I assume you can bake gingerbread and you know your way around a milk frother?'

Oh. Well, none of the above. She couldn't bake a potato unless it came with microwave instructions, and as for those complicated frothing gadgets ...

'Erm ... no? But I guess I could learn. I mean, how

hard can it be? Did Nell leave us cookbooks and things? Instruction manuals? I know how to set up the tables ...'

On second thoughts, this was petrifying.

Lukas was rolling his eyes now and she almost couldn't blame him.

'Don't chefs work funny shifts? Surely you could pop in and help?' Lukas was a scary old Scrooge-face, but she couldn't go this alone. Even Father Christmas didn't fly solo.

'Oh, you mean that unpaid snatch of time in the middle of the day when I try and catch up on sleep so I'm less *grumpy*?'

'Hmm. Most interesting. So what do you get when you cross a Christmas lover and a Christmas hater?' Mr Birdwhistle piped up, as though reading a joke he'd just pulled out of a cracker. 'Well, I think we're about to find out. What fun.' He clapped his overzealous hands.

And then the insolent jukebox exploded into 'Happy Xmas (War Is Over)'. But Gretel was certain it had only just begun.

Chapter 6

Ho sodding ho – she may as well give up now. She was as bad with gingerbread people as she was with actual people. And that was saying something.

Gretel was elbow-deep in flour and burnt batches of gingerbread in the kitchen of The Gingerbread Café. A week had passed since the meeting with the curious Mr Birdwhistle, when he'd revealed the astounding news that Nell had entrusted the festive-themed café to Gretel in her will. Alongside Lukas Knight, the self-proclaimed Christmas hater.

The week following the meeting had been a rollercoaster. What did Gretel know about running a café? She was no *people person* and she could barely bake a bean; and she'd had no intentions of fixing either.

So Gretel had laughed in shock. She'd cried a small river in fear. And she'd almost certainly hidden in her wardrobe eating pretzel doughnuts at least three times. But that kind of behaviour was messy, and she was getting ready to open the café again – for Nell. Yes, it was all kinds of terrifying – but so was the thought of never seeing her precious Christmassy café just as it used to be. So finally, Gretel had brushed herself off and got on with it. If nothing else, she'd always been good at that.

'Oh *baubles*.' She cursed as the oven sent her a smoke signal. Three puffs for *another batch incinerated*. She grabbed them out with an oven-gloved hand and threw the tray on the side.

Her first job, when she'd received her shiny new café keys, had been to clean. She'd removed the ghostly dust sheets and had freshened things up. Tending to the place with Nell's red feather duster and traditional string mop had been strangely cathartic. It had almost felt as though Nell was there cheering her on in her candy-striped apron, sending celestial messages of support through the haunted jukebox. 'I Wish It Could Be Christmas Everyday'. Who was she to argue?

Though Gretel still hadn't had the courage to go up to Nell's old flat. It would have made her sad, and she couldn't help remembering that all of this was probably temporary. Grumpy Lukas wanted to sell Nell's soul to the highest bidder in just a few months' time.

Then, using funds which the solicitor said Nell had set aside to help them get going, Gretel had stocked up on ingredients. Not that she had any idea what she was doing. She remembered Nell making different types of gingerbread from around the world and keeping them under shiny glass cloches on the counter. There had been everything from thin and delicate cookies to soft and crumbly spiced breads, each with distinct textures and their own delicious flavours. But there was no way Gretel was ready to turn herself into Mary Berry just yet. She was trying her best to make simple, no-nonsense gingerbread people.

Trying, and failing. Perhaps she was only cut out for the tasting bit, and maybe the decorating, if she could only make a batch worthy of icing. She looked around at the mess. When she'd arrived in the kitchen, everything had looked promising. The marble-topped island had been as clear as a blank canvas, holly garlands draped happily from shelf to shelf and the red gingham curtains were almost winking their support. The kitchen was surely just a lovely extension of the café, but with more scary gadgets. The radio was all set for festive tunes and she'd felt ready to create.

But now there was devastation. A sea of broken eggshells. Sticky golden syrup oozing over everything it touched. And the whole kitchen smelt *burnt*. She grabbed a dismembered gingerbread leg and bit down on it with a sigh.

'Ouch!' She spat it out and put her hand to her jaw. She'd need a trip to the dentist if she tried to get her teeth through that. What was going so wrong? She'd been hoping to open up next week to welcome in the December Christmas shoppers, but seriously? Didn't a gingerbread café need gingerbread? Was it cheating to just bloody well buy some? She imagined Nell turning in her grave and put up an apologetic hand.

Letting out another long sigh, she sank onto a tall wooden stool and put her hands over her face. She was past caring that they were covered in flour and butter; she'd be going home to hide in her wardrobe again at this rate anyway. Her selection of home-knitted Christmas jumpers did not judge.

'Sorry, Nell. I know I'm letting you down.' She mumbled the words into her globby hands, only slightly tempted to lick the butter off. 'What made you think I could do this? You know I'm hopeless around people and I've got the baking skills of Angel Gabriel.'

'I didn't know angels baked.'

Gretel looked up sharply, her flour-dusted mouth dropping open. It was Lukas, and he was giving her one of his long starey looks that made her feel completely ridiculous. Well, his timing was immaculate.

'Angels *don't* bake.' She rubbed her hands down Nell's old red and white striped apron. 'Angel Gabriel is . . . ' Her eyes darted to her crochet bag under one of the counters where her ferret was quietly sleeping. On second thoughts, she did *not* want Lukas to set eyes on him in this kitchen. 'Nobody.'

Lukas raised his eyebrows, but he could do what he wanted with his facial hair. She didn't have to share her life story, even if his stony silences did make her want to gabble something out to fill the void. When Ariana Grande began warbling 'Santa Tell Me' from Nell's tinny old radio, Gretel was actually pleased when Lukas stomped over and turned it off. He scratched the back of his neck as though Christmas really did give him hives And was that a spoon in his back pocket? The man was weird.

'What are you doing here, anyway?' she asked instead, as he started inspecting the mess on the worktop with a disapproving look. 'I thought you didn't want to help?' When she'd messaged him a few days ago to say she'd try to open up the following week, his response had essentially been *good luck with that*. Only she hadn't sensed much emphasis on the *good* bit.

'I was passing on my way back from a shift at the restaurant. I saw the lights. Do you need the multi-coloured flashing things on out there when the place is closed? And that bloody jukebox is at it again.' He pointed back towards the café.

She pinched her lips to avoid singing along to 'Frosty the Snowman', which she could now hear in the background.

Lukas scratched the back of his neck again, his chef's whites looking annoyingly impressive over his broad shoulders. It gave him an air of *in chargeness*, which Gretel was finding both aggravating and oddly compelling in equal measure. She wondered if she could manage to splatter something on them.

'Anyway, what the hell have you been up to?' His gaze bounced between the various piles of broken biscuits and goo, and landed disconcertingly on her face. She remembered it was still sticky with buttery gunk and tried to wipe it discreetly with her sleeve. He threw her the kitchen roll. 'This place is a tip.'

She shrugged, feeling like a little girl being scolded. 'At least I'm giving it a go. It's not like you're lending a hand.'

'Is that why you're talking to Angel Whatshisface and it's not even December?'

Gretel gulped as she saw her crochet bag begin to quiver. If people kept saying Angel, he was going to appear at some point.

Chapter 7

'Why do you actually hate Christmas so much?' As distraction techniques went, it was a risky one – but Gretel needed to keep Lukas's attention away from the bag where her dozing ferret seemed to be fidgeting. Anyway, she was curious.

Lukas turned around to face her. 'I . . . Christmas is just too busy. Too hectic. Like a pressure cooker.'

She was sure he'd been about to say something different and she felt her curiosity twitching even more. What wasn't he saying? But she wasn't one to pry. Her crochet bag stirred. She winced.

'Erm . . . so what is a pressure cooker? One of those funny pans for boiling carrots?' She played the hopeless cook card and made a show of scratching her head, to keep his eyes from the floor.

'Yes, that's right. Rotten ones.' His mouth curved into the smallest smile. Then after seeming to chew something over, he blew out a long stream of air. 'People are hard work, Gretel. Even more so at Christmas. The restaurant gets frantic, emotions are heightened, drunk people get more demanding, everyone expects more, more, more . . . ' His voice trailed off. 'Nothing feels good, OK? No doubt you'll get a slice of it if you decide to open this place for the Christmas rush.'

He gave her another one of those fake half-smiles that told her he'd said enough. It unnerved her that she was beginning to decipher his subtleties.

Not that she would push him to say more, as interested as she was. She knew what it was like to have secrets you wanted to keep to yourself. Besides, as a girl who needed any ounce of help she could get around here, it would be reckless to tip the scales against herself.

'So what about you, Gretel Rosenhart? Why are you such a year-round tinsel-wielding festive superfan? I've seen you wearing those hideous Christmas jumpers even when it's spring.'

And there it was. He was going to turn the conversation onto her, and poke fun too. Well, she wasn't in the mood to embrace *caring and sharing* either. A jiggle from Angel Gabriel's bag told her she needed to get Lukas out of there soon.

'Christmas is ... special for me.' As she thought back to everything it symbolised, she felt her own internal shutters slam down. She stood up. She should tidy. This place was a muddle.

Gretel snatched up the packet of flour she'd been uncomfortably perching on and watched with a gasp as some of it cascaded around the stool in a snow globe effect.

Yet it felt so oddly calming – both the blanket of newness

and the extra mess it caused. She poked the delicate powder with the toe of her snow boot. There, wasn't that magical? 'Maybe the pressure cooker bit is everything outside of Christmastime,' she said.

'What, real life?'

Lukas was at her side now, trying to stop her hands from sprinkling even more of the white flour around her feet like a tiny snowstorm. She'd barely noticed she was doing it. It just looked so . . . lovely.

'If I worked with you, it would be like supervising a child,' he muttered.

He went to grab a damp cloth and crouched to clean her pretty snowflakes from the floor, moving around the kitchen with his funny rubber chef's clogs getting ever closer to Angel Gabriel's sleeping place. As the bag kept gently twitching, a fresh panic began to rise. But before she could think of a plan, Angel Gabriel poked his innocent white head out of his hidey-hole. He gave one of his trademark squeaks, catching Lukas's attention.

Lukas's mouth dropped open. 'A rodent. You brought a bloody rodent into this kitchen!'

He was glaring at Gretel now. She hated being shouted at, and no one should be mean to her ferret.

'Ferrets are not rodents – not that there's anything wrong with a rodent. Angel Gabriel would quite happily eat one for his breakfast if I let him. He's more like a domesticated weasel. Or a very small dog.'

'Tell that to Environmental Health! You'll have this place shut down before it's even open, you reckless . . .'

Though her heart was racing, she found herself glaring straight back, daring him to finish his sentence. Angel Gabriel, not accustomed to conflict or even too much human company, had clearly had enough. He jumped out from his cosy nest and darted across the kitchen like a wild thing.

Lukas shook his head and strode across the room towards the exit.

'And you wouldn't get a rodent into a Christmas jumper,' Gretel added quietly. She let the thought hang in the fractious air.

He turned. 'I actually came to check if you needed anything. But . . . No. I cannot do this.' His words came through gritted teeth, his face hardening like the marble worktops.

She took a deep breath. She was doing this for Nell and it wasn't her fault she didn't have the first clue. 'Yes, you've said that.' Her voice was wobbly, but she was past caring. 'I know where I stand. It's a festive party for one. What's new?'

'A weasel in a knitted outfit, apparently.'

As he eyeballed her, she thought she saw something resembling regret flicker across them. Had he been entertaining the possibility of helping her before Angel Gabriel had appeared? No, surely not? Anyway, he could keep his fickle sentiments. Quite frankly, she'd rather have a troublesome ferret by her side than his thunderous face.

'I'll manage,' she said, lifting her chin and hoping she sounded bolder than she felt. She still had three days, two handfuls of hope and a whole lot of ginger and spice.

Chapter 8

'Excuse me, I ordered my flat white at least ten minutes ago. Why isn't it here?'

'Don't you even have any of those little German lebkuchen biscuits? It's the only reason I came.'

'Sorry, madam, but my gingerbread lady seems to be missing a leg. Can I have my money back?'

So many questions. So many people! She didn't know Mistleton even had this many residents. When she'd zipped around the village putting up posters to say when they'd be opening she hadn't expected anyone to actually read them.

Gretel's thin shoulders tensed as voices yelled at her from all directions. Some were at the side of her, making a writhing, snake-like queue along the counter. Others gesticulated from tables. The café was almost bursting at the seams with hungry, disgruntled customers and every part of Gretel's cowering skin just wanted to run and hide.

A ginormous sob rose up her throat. Nell had trusted her

to take over her pride and joy of a café, but she was seriously letting her down. Gretel had known she wasn't great with people, pressure or chaos ... but *this*. She flicked her eyes to the heavens and prayed for a miracle; and yet she knew it wasn't coming. How could it be?

She pressed more buttons on the complicated beast of a coffee machine, but the evil thing just blinked and hissed at her. It seemed to know she couldn't make coffee and she had no idea what a flat white even was. When she'd tried to serve it up to someone as coffee with a glug of milk earlier, they'd sent it back in a huff. That was certainly the theme of the morning so far.

Over the last few days she'd been so busy trying to bake gingerbread people, ice their broken body parts back on and make up gooey batches of cinnamon hot chocolate that she hadn't had time to master the *coffee beast*. Who knew that decoding a pedantic coffee machine would be trickier than gaining entrance to Takeshi's Castle?

The bell over the door chimed and yet more people bustled in.

'Hey, lady, can somebody clean this table? And why can't we find a highchair?'

'Miss ... ?'

Gretel shook her head. What? There'd been so many questions, she had no clue where to start. *Did* the café have a highchair? When would she have time to learn to bake lebkuchen? And would that stupid, clunky till even do refunds?

Questions and answers glugged around her head as the beast continued its taunting hiss. Lukas was right: this was

44

like being inside a pressure cooker. Boiling alive like one of his useless, rotten carrots.

'Oh God.' She stepped back from the machine, her face hot with steam. 'I just can't ...' She held up an apologetic hand to the impatient queue and scurried towards the kitchen. She slammed the door behind her and ran instinctively to the sink, terrified that her churning stomach was about to empty its contents. She leaned over the stainless steel, the stark surface wobbling to a blur as her eyes glazed over with tears.

In the distance, she heard the café's front doorbell tinkle again, presumably as more people crammed themselves in. Or perhaps some of them were storming out, fed up of crappy service and the hopeless loser in charge. Maybe the marauding crowds were busy nicking broken biscuits and emptying the till, if they could work out how to open the sodding thing.

She stepped back from the sink and untied the strings of the apron, which suddenly made her feel clammy and constricted. 'I'm so sorry, Nell. I'm not worthy of wearing this.'

Her eyes dared to lift to the windowsill, where her latest creation sat. It was her stained-glass gingerbread house, complete with little glass Nell on the doorstep in her candy-striped apron. Well, Gretel needed somebody to talk to, now Angel Gabriel was banned.

'This place used to be my sanctuary, Nell. Since Mum ... *you* were my sanctuary. But now you're gone, and the café's becoming my worst nightmare. I can't deal with all those people. Where did you find the smiles, the patience, the love? I don't have any of that. Do you think I wasn't born with it? Or that I just need practice, like when Angel Gabriel was hopeless at peeing in his new litter box?'

Sometimes she was almost sure her little glass figures uttered wise words in return. But other than the background rabble, there was silence. She rifled up her sleeve for a tissue, suddenly conscious that warm tears had been streaming down her cheeks. At least a good crier was always prepared.

Not even annoying Lukas could be bothered to barge in on her today, although she guessed that was fair enough. She'd always known where she stood when she'd set out on this doomed expedition. Alone, in sad Christmas knitwear. Wasn't that just how she liked things? She began pulling the apron off over her head, but the strap caught on one of her plaited pigtails and she was left wrestling with it like a child stuck in a deckchair.

'Why doesn't it want to come off?' she groaned, her limbs flailing.

Her elbow knocked against something and she yelped. Fighting her face free, she saw a sign. One of those metal hanging things with cute messages, that Nell used to like. *Keep Calm and Wear Candy Stripes*. She couldn't remember seeing it before, but surely it had been there. And hadn't she just asked for some guidance? Perhaps it would be rude to ignore it.

She huffed and wriggled her way back into the candy-striped prison – but only because it was marginally easier than losing half a head of hair.

'Well, be careful what you wish for,' she warned little glass

Nell. 'I'm dreadful at this. I can't even serve up a flat white because I've no sodding idea what the *flat* bit is. And people are probably running off with the takings as we speak.'

She fiddled with the apron strings which drooped sadly at her sides.

'I can't run the show by myself, you know.' Her glass ornament was probably listening. 'And mean old Lukas is hell-bent on selling it as soon as the ink is dry. What hope do I have of honouring your wishes?'

Little glass Nell was silent again. Gretel exhaled.

Then from somewhere in the background, she heard it – the interfering jukebox. It was playing 'The Christmas Miracle'. And was it a trick of the fairy lights, or did her glassy companion just wink at her?

'So that's your answer?' Gretel tried not to roll her eyes. 'Tie the apron back up and hope for a miracle?'

'Miss. *Miiiiiiisssss?*'

A voice shouted through from the café. She barely knew her own mind any more, but those people weren't going away. Perhaps the *miracle* plan was the only thing she had. She tied her apron and took a deep breath. It was time to keep calm and face the mayhem and mochaccinos.

Chapter 9

When Gretel stepped back out into the café, things had gone from bad to worse. The place looked like a zoo with no zookeeper. The tables were a disaster where she hadn't cleared them, children were catapulting her shoddy excuse for gingerbread to see how many more limbs they could break off, and she was sure people had been behind the counter serving themselves and leaving a trail of sticky-fingered destruction.

As though she didn't feel jittery enough, the delinquent jukebox seemed to be stuck on the stressful crescendo part of 'Carol of the Bells' from *Home Alone*, where Kevin frantically prepares for the baddies. *Da da da da, da da da daaaaaa* ... Well, at least he'd had a plan. All she had were sweaty palms and a stomach full of dread.

'This gingerbread is simply awful. I won't be coming back.'

Oh, and she also had people complaining about her hard bloody work. If only they knew the internal battles she'd been through just to open that café door this morning, not to mention the physical strife. Now she couldn't wait to slam the damned thing closed – and December was meant to be her favourite time of year.

'You OK?'

It was only when the stranger spoke that Gretel realised she'd been visibly shaking. 'Erm . . . '

Gretel took a moment to assess the girl, who was sitting on a high stool at the end of the counter, sipping a hot chocolate like she'd always been there. Had she helped herself to a drink too? Her long fire-red hair was poker straight with a blunt fringe that only a kooky girl could carry off. As though rebelling against any more colour, she was dressed only in black and white, with a white shirt, short black pleated skirt and black DM boots. Even her pale skin was etched with black drawings of birds and angel wings, though they looked strangely more like Biro than tattoo ink. How old was she? It was difficult to place her with the thick black eyeliner and lipstick. Late teens, perhaps? Although Gretel was conscious she still looked impishly childlike herself.

The girl raised her eyebrows at Gretel over her steaming mug as though she was bored of being stared at. Gretel had the feeling she probably got that a lot hanging around in a traditional village like Mistleton. She felt a pang of guilt.

'I left my money behind the counter.' The girl pointed to a pile of coins. 'People seemed to be serving themselves, although I'm not sure everyone bothered to pay, so you might want to sort that out. And some people tried asking me for refunds, but I told them it wasn't my job.' She shrugged.

Gretel usually felt extra nervous around new people, yet she was sure she was beginning to shake a little less now. Not that she wanted to be lured in by the kindness of strangers. Her heart preferred its distance, even on a bad day.

'But if you ever do need a hand . . .' Was that a look of concern on the girl's face? 'My name's Amber, by the way.'

Realising that introductions were probably the polite thing, Gretel awkwardly gave her name.

'Are you a . . . waitress?' Gretel nodded at the girl's black and white outfit.

Amber gave a quick glance over her shoulder. 'Umm, yeah. Of course.'

Did she seem unsure about that? Or more likely she didn't want everyone knowing her business. Gretel could relate to that. Not that Gretel was in any position to take on staff, mayhem or no mayhem. By the time she'd accounted for refunds, burnt batches of gingerbread, hissy coffee machine wastage and people not even paying, the café would probably be making a loss. And anyway, sharing her cramped counter space with another human was not on her list of priorities. She would probably be throwing in the towel.

'You know, you might find things a little less hellish with staff.' Amber shrugged. 'Just saying.'

She wasn't wrong about the hellish bit. 'Lukas would go mad,' she heard herself blurt out, by way of an excuse. 'He owns half of the place and will probably burst in and lecture me at any moment.'

Gretel clamped her mouth shut and turned away, busying herself with the dirty crockery. She'd already said too much.

She half registered some scrabbling on the other side of the counter, and when she next looked back, her red-haired confidante had gone. Was it something she'd said, or did the thought of Lukas send everyone fleeing? Gretel never did understand people. She sighed. There'd been something about the girl she'd liked, even if she hadn't planned on doing much *liking*. There was no room at the inn for friendship, or anything silly.

The next few hours felt like days. Gretel plastered on her best polite grimace and hoped no one could tell she was bursting to cry. Pretending to be sociable and assertive was tough for her at the best of times, but when she was rushed off her feet and people were *still* cross at her incompetence, it was even more of a struggle. Even her silent *do it for Nell* mantra was wearing thin. This was nothing like the joyous scenes she remembered from the café in years gone by. Even though most of the year was admittedly quiet, Nell used to handle busy periods with grace, the background bustle feeling somehow peaceful.

Gretel let her thoughts wander back, remembering chatting faces lit up by candles which flickered on tables, and rich smells of hot chocolate and ginger dancing on the air. Children snuggled up with red knitted blankets on leathery armchairs, their little noses pressed into festive books. That dark and cosy feel, with twinkling lights giving the place a special warmth. Amidst those silvery lights which dangled on cords from the ceiling like magical flakes of snow she used to half close her eyes and pretend she was in a snow globe. Protected and safe.

Where was all of that charm now? That sanctuary? Because this bedlam was not what she'd signed up for. Or maybe it was her – she was ruining the place.

And Lukas had warned this circus would be the least of her worries, with the trade on Green Tree Lane now being dire outside of Christmas. The place would be miserably deserted come January. She'd be buried alive by uneaten gingerbread and wondering why she'd bothered, so he'd told her. *You'll throw a party when I find a buyer and we can pretend this Christmas nightmare never happened.* His words rang annoyingly true.

Before Gretel's thoughts could continue on their downward spiral, the bell over the front door jangled and a woman strode in. Even without the bell, Gretel couldn't help noticing her presence. The woman was about thirty, but looked completely out of place in the Christmassy café, all towering and tailored, with a black swingy bob that shone like a mirror. Her ice-blue skinny cut suit looked like a person would need a loan to fund it, yet she was wearing it with black and gold trainers with the initials FW emblazoned on the sides.

Chapter 10

The woman with the swingy bob, who'd just strode into The Gingerbread Café, had her phone glued to her ear and was squawking into it at warp speed. She didn't seem to care about the chaos going on around her as she made her way to a leather armchair. She inspected it before perching on the edge like a great blue heron.

Gretel wondered if she should go over; the woman looked kind of important. Had she seen her loitering around the place before, trying to talk to Nell? She pictured Nell crossing her arms and shaking her head, but she wasn't sure where the image was coming from.

The jukebox burst into the opening bars of 'Run Rudolph Run'. Chuck Berry started warbling something about a mastermind and Gretel decided the woman did look too intimidating to approach, so she busied herself behind the counter. The queue had disappeared, but she still had a major clean-up operation to deal with after the coffee beast's latest hissing fit. Just as Gretel gave up hope and slapped an *out of order* sign onto it, a shadow cast over her view. She looked up and jumped, realising she was languishing in Swingy Bob's shade.

'Miss Whimple.' The woman smiled at her surprisingly sweetly and thrust out a hand.

Gretel blinked a few times and then shook it, wondering if there was a button under the counter to call for moral support. But there was nobody, and she'd better get used to it. She pulled her hand back, dug her nails into her palms and tried a smile.

'Do you own this place now?' the Whimple woman asked, before Gretel had the chance to give her own name.

'Erm, kind of. I will. Jointly.' Swingy Bob seemed charming enough, yet after such a rough day Gretel still had the jitters.

'This place is *on fire*. I love what you've done with it. *Uber* individual. I'm all about individuality.'

Was she? Well, she had to give her credit for carrying off those trainers with a suit. She was obviously one of those *trendy enough to rock anything* people. Gretel tried not to feel ridiculous dressed like a festive eight-year-old.

'So are you selling, now the old woman has ... *you know*? I mean, running a café can be a freaking slog. People in your face all day, blisters on your blisters, *aaaall* those filthy plates.' Miss Whimple pulled an almost imperceptible *gross* face before apparently thinking better of it. 'But if you'd rather move on to save your sanity, we should chat.' She placed a glossy black and gold business card on the counter, which matched her custom trainers down to the swirly FW, although Gretel wondered who the sons were, in the name Whimple & Sons.

'Our family business has turned Lower Paddleton around.' The swingy bobbed woman waved an arm vaguely in the direction of the neighbouring village. 'The whole place was dying off until we bought up the decrepit shops on Penny Road and brought in new tenants. We basically saved it from the scrapheap.'

Had they? Not one to get about much, Gretel hadn't been there for years.

'And from what everyone is saying, Green Tree Lane is on a speedy downhill slope too. Sure, the Christmas period gets busy. Everyone loves the gimmick of that decades-old Christmas tree out there, and getting their cosy Gingerbread Café selfies for Insta. But the rest of the year? Trade here is *slooooow*. The whole street needs an urgent injection of money and life, or it'll become a dusty old relic. How heart-breaking would that be?' Miss Whimple let the question hang, before continuing.

'But more about *you*.' She pointed an ice-blue polished nail at Gretel. 'If we bought this place from you, imagine taking the money and flitting off to live your *hashtag best life*. I'd make sure things stayed exactly the same here, of course. We'd give you an awesome price for the place and we have tenants lining up. I know they'd just love to take over and honour this festive shrine.'

Oh. Well, that sounded nice. Didn't it? Gretel eyeballed the card, which was nearly blinding her under the counter's spotlights. 'I . . . erm . . .'

Miss Whimple's eyes flitted around the mess of the café before landing back on Gretel. 'Girl, I'm not going to lie – it looks like you've had a hellish day. Devoting your life to serving biscuits and being a social butterfly?' She gave her a pitying look as though she just *knew*. 'It's not for everyone, huh?'

Gretel heard herself let out a little whimper. She wasn't proud of it, but she couldn't help being human.

'And I'm guessing you feel a sense of duty to that sweet old lady, but can I tell you something? True friends only ever want you to be happy. I haven't yet seen you smile since I walked into this place.' The swingy bobbed woman gave Gretel's hand an awkward squeeze. 'I'm sure Nell didn't lumber you with the café to make your face all droopy. She loved you, right? She wouldn't have wanted you to suffer like this.'

As tears stung Gretel's eyes for the umpteenth time that day, she had to admit the woman had a point. Even the broken coffee beast seemed to be spluttering its agreement.

'And like I said, the Christmas theme. Love it. Fierce jumper, by the way.' Swingy Bob pointed at Gretel's knitwear. 'Pandas are totally my favourite.'

'They're polar bears ...' Gretel began to explain, but Miss Whimple was checking her phone.

'So sorry, important message.' Swingy Bob woman was already off towards the exit, her eyebrows knitting an apology. 'But call me, yeah?' she yelled to Gretel across her shoulder, doing the hand-to-ear signal thing as though Gretel might not know what that meant. And then she was gone.

It was silly to dwell on the fact the woman couldn't tell a polar bear from a panda, so Gretel told herself not to. It was an easy mistake. Instead, she pondered Miss Whimple's suggestion whilst she sloped around the café gathering dirty plates, feeling sad at the half-chewed leftovers and barely touched questionable coffees. There hadn't been so much wastage in Nell's day. Maybe it would be easier to say goodbye to the faff and go off in search of her *hashtag best life*. Surely her only true friend Nell would have wanted that for her?

In fact, deep down Gretel knew the harder she worked at trying to make this place a success, the more Lukas Grinch Face would be rubbing his hands, ready to sell it to the highest bidder. She'd be running herself into the ground for nothing. And Miss Whimple hadn't been wrong about the blisters.

Gretel plonked the plates down and slumped against the counter. Was there some sense in speaking to this Whimple woman properly? She shook her head. It was just tiredness speaking and she'd had a lousy day. *You'll feel better in the morning.* That's what Nell used to say and that was surely the spirit. She couldn't give up on Nell's wishes just yet. She grabbed a broken biscuit from under a cloche, its gingery fragrance sweeping up to meet her like an old friend. Miss Whimple's words had been food for thought, nothing more. Everyone needed a back-up plan.

Chapter 11

Why was it so aggravating when people were right about things? Especially when *people* meant Lukas *I'm such a grown-up* Knight.

As Gretel sat on the slow, chugging bus to Lower Paddleton in her woolly dress and penguin cardi, a sleeping ferret in her pocket, her thoughts tripped over her first week in charge of The Gingerbread Café. She'd been desperate to cling on to her memories of the place – all that peace, joy and the smell of sweet ginger. When Nell had been in charge, visiting the café had been like walking into a big warm hug. Those cosy corners where she could settle in and heat her chilly hands with a warm mug, forgetting the outside world and feeling a little less alone. Nell's love and care had simply radiated, through her kind words, gentle shoulder touches and lovingly crafted bakes. It had been Gretel's haven.

But in just one week, she was starting to see that Lukas was right. Running the café just as Nell had *was* hard work.

Especially for someone as shy and inexperienced as her. Far from a cosy refuge, being at the café was now like waltzing into her own worst nightmare. It was hot and hectic and she felt like a bumbling nitwit. Customers invariably seemed cross with her, she was always breaking or burning things, and she'd never felt more alone. Worse still was that for all her efforts, the café was barely breaking even, and she certainly wasn't spreading or receiving any festive cheer. Her favourite time of the year was being ruined.

Well, it just couldn't go on, so she'd gritted her teeth, made a phone call and forced herself to take the sluggish ride to Lower Paddleton, home of the offices of Whimple & Sons. When the woman with the swingy bob had handed over her flashy business card a week ago, the idea of selling the precious café to the Whimples had felt like an unlikely fallback. But now . . .

Gretel took a deep breath and tried to ignore the squirm of guilt in the pit of her stomach. It was surprising just how quickly a back-up plan could become a girl's A game. It was time to see for herself whether Lower Paddleton's high street was thriving now that the Whimples had bought and rented out most of its shops. She'd made an appointment with Miss Whimple, to get to the heart of what she would offer for The Gingerbread Café. She knew Lukas was still keen to sell, and whilst Gretel may not have the power or inclination to keep the café after her atrocious week, she could at least try to ensure Nell's legacy wasn't trampled on and the café was kept as Nell wanted it. And the Whimple woman had seemed keen on that too – far more so than Grinchy old Lukas. Who knew what kind of Christmas-hating Scrooge Lukas would sell to, if he was left in charge? No, she was taking some control. For Nell, and for Green Tree Lane.

Gretel watched as the stark, wintery landscape swished past her rain-splattered window. Just one more trip out of her comfort zone, and her café pains may be on their way to a swift patching up. Maybe the Whimples could even move their tenants in before this silly six-month probate waiting period, or whatever that legal word was.

'Next stop, Lower Paddleton!' the driver announced, like he was introducing Disneyland Paris.

As the bus came to a noisy, huffing stop a couple of roads away from Lower Paddleton's little shopping street, Gretel felt a wriggle inside her red duffle coat pocket. Angel Gabriel was waking up. She pulled him out and kissed his snowy white fur before popping his harness and lead on.

'There, don't you look dapper in your matching penguin jumper?'

Gretel stood and walked to the front of the bus, letting Angel Gabriel bounce in front of her on his lead.

'Watch the step, madam. It's a long way down,' the bus driver said as the doors hissed open.

Gretel and Angel Gabriel squeaked their thank yous and made their way to Penny Road – Lower Paddleton's main shopping street. It had probably been ten years since she'd visited, but she remembered it as being much like Green Tree Lane – quaint and picture postcard perfect – but with a honey-coloured stone fountain in the centre, instead of a Christmas tree.

'There, isn't this lovely?' Gretel felt her body relax as they walked past the Cotswold stone cottages with their perfectly manicured hedges and cosy thatched roofs. Chimneys puffed happily and even the rain had stopped its drizzling. Perhaps the Whimple people had worked wonders on the village, after all.

'Ooh, there it is!' She pointed out the end of Penny Road to Angel Gabriel, as though ferrets were partial to a bit of shopping. 'Let's take a look.'

As Gretel reached the top of Penny Road, she stopped. 'Oh.' She scratched her head, double-checked the road sign, and then blinked. This couldn't be right? It didn't seem familiar at all. The beautiful stone shop buildings were still there, but instead of their prettily painted wooden signs in complementing heritage shades, there were a whole lot of clashing colours and plastic. 'But . . . '

She stepped into the street and began a slow pace, hoping the initial shock would subside. The street still seemed busy enough. Much busier than Green Tree Lane. She wasn't keen on having so many bodies close to her, but busy was good, wasn't it? A healthy buzz was surely . . .

'Shhhhhhhhhttttttt.'

Gretel looked down sharply to see Angel Gabriel hissing and hunching his back. Realising with a pang of guilt that people weren't giving him room, she scooped him up and gave his fur a fuss. She was so used to people smiling and respecting his space, but Lower Paddleton had a strange sort of hustle. She stepped back and huddled into an empty shop doorway, soaking in her surroundings. It was so different to the friendly bustle of other nearby villages. People were laden with plastic bags, on a mission rather than stopping to wave or chat. Gretel wasn't a small-talker, but this felt so . . . *impersonal*.

Surely it didn't used to be like this? Hadn't it been just as charming as Mistleton once? She scanned the street for clues. There. Wasn't that the old hardware store across the road, all boarded up and deserted? She turned around in the doorway she was standing in. Aha! The old-fashioned sweet shop. She definitely remembered that and the lovely older lady who'd owned it, with her generous portions. And where was the bakery with the delicious Victoria sponges? There was no sign of it now.

Dotted between the odd relic of a closed-down independent shop were faceless franchises. One of those bargain basement shops. (Go in for two things, come out with twenty.) A 99p shop. (Just in case you didn't already buy a bunch of stuff you didn't need.) A vaping shop. (What was in those things, anyway?) And her own personal worst – a branch of Quickie Café. Loveless refreshments, horrible coffee and staff too overworked to muster a smile. How could this be?

Gretel shook her head and took a moment to calm her thoughts. Perhaps she'd got the wrong first impression. It couldn't all be this bad. Giving a swift look around, she inched out of her hidey hole and tried to filter herself back into the bustle, this time keeping Angel Gabriel tucked under her arm. She continued along Penny Road, breathing deeply and trying to assess the situation. It wasn't that she hated a chain or franchise; she admitted they were useful. Everyone needed to stock up on toiletries or browse the best ever range of weird health foods now and again. But they had their place in the bigger towns and cities.

How would their little villages continue to attract tourists if the quaintest thing they could buy was a 99p family pack of Jammie Dodgers? And how would the independent shops survive if chain stores turned up next door, piled things high and sold them for a steal? They wouldn't, she realised with a sad gulp, as she dusted off a cobweb that must have attached itself to her in that old shop doorway. Lower Paddleton was paddling down the drain, and if the chain shops inched their way into Mistleton, maybe their village would encounter the same faceless fate. It always started with one, didn't it? If they ended up selling The Gingerbread Café to the Whimples, what if it became the wobbly link that sent the other dominoes toppling?

As Gretel's eyes became heavy with the threat of tears, the grey expanse of clouds seemed to feel her anguish. Sharp bullets of rain began shooting down from the sky, stinging her face and attacking the shoppers around her. There were flurries of cursing and umbrella shaking as disgruntled people tried to stake their claim to brolly space. Gretel pulled up her hood and moved out of their way, gravitating towards the fountain in the centre of the pedestrianised street. She remembered it as a place where friends would sit and chat on the benches around it, but there were no friendly faces now. In fact, despite all the water that was falling from the sky, not a drop flowed from the fountain's fish mouth. Its spout looked rusty and the only water in the stone basin was murky and as green as a frog. It was *stagnating*.

And then she saw it – a flash of orange light catching her attention from across the street. It took her eyes a few seconds to adjust to the hideousness of it, but when she did, she was almost transfixed. Just when she thought she'd seen it all around here.

Chapter 12

The sight of the Whimple & Sons office blared at Gretel from across Penny Road. Its signage and street hoardings were a monstrosity of black, gold and huge images of Francesca and her family's fake-smiley faces, with flashing orange lights blazing from the window. It couldn't have looked more out of place in a Cotswold village. How was that level of garishness even allowed? Yet, much like an ugly wart that your eyes were inexplicably drawn to, she couldn't resist a closer look. She checked around her. Nobody she knew. No sign of a swingy bob or a pair of black and gold trainers. Gretel was early for her meeting.

Gretel pulled her hood tighter around her head and moved across the street, stepping as close to the screaming window of the office as she dared. Surely with all that advertising junk in the window they wouldn't notice her having a poke around outside? The posters seemed to shout *we buy any shop* (by pouncing on your struggle) and *we rent or sell on to the highest bidder* (extra points if you're a tacky chain). Or was Gretel just being pessimistic? Even Angel Gabriel was hissing again, and the slow churn in the pit of her stomach warned her this was anything but jolly news.

She slunk back to the benches by the dingy fountain and plonked herself down, giving Angel Gabriel's fur a rub to calm them both.

Just as she was debating whether to flee she heard a series of splooshes coming her way. A woman hidden by a ginormous black and gold umbrella marched past the benches, her matching trainers slam-dunking into the puddles. Gretel gasped as the puddle spray fanned out over her suede snow boots, but the woman was too engrossed in her phone chat to notice. She stopped just beyond Gretel to take a puff on her golden vaping thingamy and cough out a cloud of cigar-scented steam. Then she shook the rainwater off her umbrella before hiding her head back under it. Even from the back view, Gretel would have recognised that swingy bob anywhere. Not to mention those trainers. Francesca Whimple.

'Yeah, so I'm meeting that dippy gingerbread woman in about fifteen.' Miss Whimple checked her oversized gold watch. 'But whatever, she can wait.' She gave a shrill laugh that could probably have shattered windows. 'No, not that old bat – she snuffed it. I mean the mouse girl she left the café to. Looks like a hopeless pale fairy, dresses like a poor kid at Christmas. She's doing a shit job of running the place all by her sad self, and looks like she might burst into tears every time a customer comes near her. Yep, seriously.'

Gretel was sure she felt an eardrum split as the high-pitched laugh came again.

'Talk about no social skills, right?! On the awesome side, at least no one else will be sniffing around to buy the place. Did I tell you they keep it looking like the arse end of Santa's grotto? All. Year. Long! As if anyone else would be willing to take on that festive puke disaster. She and Lukas Knight will be begging me to buy them out as much as Quickie Café are desperate to move in and tear out all that Christmas turd. Lukas needs Christmas like a hole in the head after all the heartbreak it's brought him.' She spun her umbrella, rain flying from it like fat tears. 'And once I get my hands on one of those shops, the rest of the sheep will give up their half-hearted bleating and follow the herd. Ker-ching! It's too freaking perfect.'

Gretel wasn't sure how long her mouth had been open. When the woman turned and squeaked off along the street, every modicum of common sense in Gretel's brain was telling her to storm after her and stand up for herself; but the thought of all that confrontation made her feel even more nauseous. A hopeless, snivelling fairy trying to run a *festive puke disaster*. Was that what people thought of her?

She put Angel Gabriel in her pocket and stood up, leaning against the fountain as she tried to summon strength in her legs. As the dry fish mouth seemed to gawp with her, the answer swam up from the murky depths of the basin. She might not have the guts to chase after the woman and put her straight, and if she did, she'd probably be laughed straight back to the bus stop. But the best way to get to the Whimple woman would be to prove her wrong.

Because Francesca Whimple *was* wrong that no one else was willing to take on the festive café. Gretel was. And as she leaned with one arm against the sorry fountain, one foot already pointing in the direction of her bus, she realised that until now, she had only had one foot in the game, as far as The Gingerbread Café had been concerned. She hadn't really believed in herself or given it her all, because putting your heart into things meant life might trample on them. But if she was going to have a ferret in hell's chance of making the place a success – either for herself or for a buyer infinitely more worthy than Swingy Bob Smoke Breath – she was going to have to go *all in*. No more half in half out, like she was doing the Hokey sodding Cokey. It was time to prove to herself and the Christmas Grinch doubters that she wasn't a lost cause and neither was her precious Christmas-themed café.

Did she know exactly how she would make the magic happen? Not just yet. But she did know where she would start.

Chapter 13

Were Christmas miracles really a thing, like little glass Nell had once sort of promised? Because for the first time since she'd opened the doors of The Gingerbread Café nearly two weeks before, Gretel felt like she might actually be on the edge of one.

It was mid-December, and after overhearing Francesca Swingy Bob Whimple poking fun at her, Nell and the Christmas-themed café earlier that week, something inside her had snapped. She was going to show people she could absolutely do Nell proud and run this place like the wonderful, gingerbread-inspired sanctuary it deserved to be.

As mean as Swingy Bob's words had been, Gretel had forced herself to digest them. The woman had had a point. Gretel couldn't keep battling on like a *hopeless fairy* by her *sad self.* The thought of being in charge of another person felt terrifying, but the café was frantic at this time of year. Gretel knew she'd need someone to help serve customers rather than lose them through the door. She couldn't exist in a bubble, or even a snow globe, as safe as the glass walls she'd constructed around her world had felt. Even Santa needed helpers.

It was clear Lukas wasn't going to step up. He was too busy and important in his rotten carrot of a restaurant, and he only ever showed up to scowl and say *na na, I told you so*. As soon as she'd got home from Lower Paddleton she'd marched back to the café, put up a notice advertising for casual help, and sent out a silent prayer to the elves of festive wishes.

It seemed like they were on her side.

Swiftly enough Amber with the kooky red hairdo breezed in. Of all the people Gretel could imagine trying to nervously work in tandem with, this girl had seemed the least daunting. There was something reassuringly standoffish about her and Gretel wasn't one for getting matey.

'Fancy a job?' The words tumbled out of Gretel's mouth as though conscious she'd swallow them given a second longer. The poor girl had barely set foot through the door.

Amber looked surprised, even though she'd said before that she did waitressing, and she was wearing the black and white uniform for it. 'I'm meant to be at ... ' She gave a suspicious look around. 'My other job.'

Gretel asked her where else she worked, wondering why she wasn't there, but Amber was strangely evasive.

'Oh. It's not La Carotte Rôtie, is it? That place on the outskirts of the village.' She recalled the weird way Amber had disappeared after she'd mentioned Lukas the other day, and there weren't many other places to waitress at nearby.

Did Amber's eyes just widen? But she was quick. 'Nah, no way. I live in Lower Paddleton, anyway. And that guy's far too terrifying to work with. So I've heard.'

Gretel couldn't argue with that, so the name *Scary Lukas* was born.

'Look, I don't want anything formal. But if you're stuck, I don't mind helping out here and there. I can see you seriously need it.' Amber looked around the place, which hadn't filled up with customers yet but still showed signs of devastation from after the last shift, when Gretel had run out of steam and had gone home to sob into her ferret.

Gretel, beyond caring about being offended, gave a grateful bob up and down in her snow boots, before stopping herself, feeling a little self-conscious next to cool and collected Amber.

Amber put up a hand like she was calming a child. 'And don't put me on the books or tell that scary guy about me, yeah? Just keep me fuelled with hot drinks and gingerbread and I'll do what I can when I'm around.'

Don't put her on the books? Well, Gretel didn't even have any books, whatever those were. She was happy enough with limited commitment, knowing she'd want to leg it most days too. And so the footloose agreement was made and Gretel scuttled to the window to whip down the notice before Lukas saw it. Amber was quick enough at disappearing and he didn't have to know everything. It would suit her last scraps of pride if he thought she was getting on top of things without admitting she needed help.

As clunky as it had felt at first, trying to work alongside

another person when Gretel was only used to the company of apple strudel and her angelic ferret, after a while she and Amber clicked into a routine of sorts. Nobody would be giving Gretel the café owner of the year badge anytime soon, but customers were arriving, being served with something vaguely resembling what they'd ordered and not leaving in a huff. She'd take that as a tiny win.

Gretel and Amber zipped about, clearing empty gingerbread plates and taking more orders for cinnamon hot chocolates with all the frills. Nobody needed to know that Gretel had given up and bought in the mouth-watering selection of gingerbread at a not insubstantial cost. Not all miracles could happen in a day, and at least people were nodding and smiling again.

As she and Amber chatted in short bursts as they moved around the café, its tinsel twinkling in the glow from the candles and string lights, Gretel could sense a strange warmth filling an empty part of her. What was that? It wasn't the usual hot panic she felt as she rushed around by herself, fighting to stay on top. It was more like … a sense of purpose? Being part of something? Maybe that was why Nell had loved this place so much.

'So you inherited this café from the lady who used to own it?' Amber asked, when they were out of earshot of customers.

Gretel felt a tightness in her throat, her initial impulse to clam up. Yet as she looked at Amber, busy wiping down the previously uncontrollable coffee beast that they'd mastered together, she felt a strange affinity. And Nell had always approved of a little chit-chat.

'Yes, Nell left half of the café to me. Our little family moved to the village when I was nine, and Nell and the café became our place. You know, it's hardly changed a bit. Still so Christmassy all year long. Nell was friends with my mum, and then . . . ' Gretel swallowed hard and busied herself with her notepad. 'Then she became kind of like a replacement mum.' She wasn't used to talking about it, or about anything much, since Nell had shimmied off and left her. Yet it felt strangely easy to chat to Amber.

'Oh shit. Did you lose your mum?'

'Yes,' Gretel heard herself saying. 'And my . . . '

But Gretel got pulled away by a small girl asking for a gingerbread lady and she was glad of the distraction. It was always hard to talk about Rosa.

By the time Gretel and Amber had a breather to reconvene by the wayward jukebox, the *and* part of the conversation had been forgotten. It was often the easiest way. Gretel sent a silent apology to the heavens.

'I'm sorry about your mum.' Amber reached out and squeezed Gretel's arm. To Gretel's surprise, she didn't experience her usual compulsion to shrink away from the kindness. She swallowed the tightness creeping up her throat and tried not to feel pathetic at how much the simple gesture had warmed her.

'Thanks.'

'You probably don't want to say too much in the middle of a hectic café, but if you ever need to talk . . . ' Amber shrugged.

'You too,' Gretel mumbled quickly.

Amber leaned back against the jukebox and eyed Gretel briefly like she was tempted to share something, then shook her head. The bright red and green jukebox lights flashed against her black and white exterior, making Gretel wonder if she really was one of Santa's helpers.

'So, are you planning to keep this place and make it good?' Amber looked around at the bustling tables. 'No offence, but it's only busy once a year. Christmas in January always seems pretty lame. Although the whole of Green Tree Lane is freakishly quiet for most of the year. They say it's not what it used to be.'

Amber spoke the words like they were obvious, rather than like a person who was trying to be mean, but Gretel couldn't help feeling defensive. The little robins on her hand-knitted jumper were all but pecking in retaliation.

She knew twelve months of Christmas, year in year out, seemed weird to most people. It was only meant to be twelve days according to the song, and there'd been times when she'd tried to break free. Really there had. But that was another reason having people in her life was never going to work out – too many questions and a whole lot of funny looks. Gretel's childhood had been full of both and she'd promised herself that as an adult she would keep them at bay. She was a partridge in a pear tree flying solo, after all. Nobody needed all of those drummers drumming or any amount of calling birds.

Though as the jukebox lights turned Amber as golden as her name, Gretel felt strangely moved to share a few nuggets of truth. So as they resumed their tidying mission around the café, she continued, at a whisper. 'I just want to keep things as they are. For Nell. But I've got no clue what I'm doing, and Lukas, who's inherited the other half, just wants to sell once the legal stuff is sorted. That'll probably take six months, but until it's decision time, I want to do Nell proud.'

'And when it's decision time?' asked Amber.

A customer came past asking for extra mini marshmallows and Amber grabbed Gretel's pad and wrote it down. Her hand felt empty without the pad she'd forgotten she was clinging to.

'I hope he decides he doesn't want to sell,' said Gretel, and as soon as she said it, she realised it was true.

'What, you actually want to stay in business with that scary guy?'

'Erm, no!' Gretel fiddled with her apron strings. 'I guess I'm just afraid to lose the café because ... I've already lost enough.'

Amber shrugged. 'Then you have to make the café such a success he'd be an idiot to sell it.'

Gretel exhaled and slumped onto a stool, the weight of it all suddenly too much. 'I wondered. Although if I put my heart and soul into trying to make it work and he sells up anyway, am I just setting myself up for more sorrow?'

'So buy him out.'

Gretel winced. 'I've got no money, and I'd never get a business mortgage or whatever.' It sounded far too grown-up. She'd been just about staying alive by selling glass creations in her online shop and savings had never been a thing.

'What's the other option. Hiding away and not trying?'

Gretel scratched her head. That strategy had always worked for her before.

'It's better to have loved and lost.' Amber sucked in her breath and gave Gretel's arm another quick squeeze. 'Soz. I forgot about your mum, and now Nell. Maybe it's not so easy to feel that way when you've actually lost stuff.'

Gretel silently added Rosa to the trinity. Maybe one day it wouldn't be so hard to talk about her.

Chapter 14

The day whizzed by, Gretel and Amber doing their best with crowd control and keeping complaints to a minimum. The café was busy and Gretel wasn't sure she'd ever feel *in control*, but for once, she wasn't dangerously sinking. That in itself felt huge.

They scurried around behind the counter, trying to get on top of things after another snaking queue of people had been served and seated. Gretel stirred the next batch of hot chocolate with one hand and cleaned the worktop with the other. Amber refilled the glass cloches with fresh gingerbread.

As a certain flashy business card dug into Gretel's side through the material of her pocket, something began playing on her mind.

'Do you know Francesca Whimple?'

'No!' Amber barked, almost dropping the lid of a cloche. 'I mean, yes, obviously. I live in Lower Paddleton. Everyone's heard of her. But I don't *know* her.'

As Gretel contemplated whether to ask more, the jukebox blasted through the awkwardness with a song about thorns in the hay. Amber glared across the room. 'Is that thing for real? Nobody ever even touches it.'

'It does that. Sometimes I feel like it knows too much.'

Amber eyed the jukebox suspiciously and went to stack the dishwasher.

'So what do you know about Miss Whimple?' Gretel knew she should arm herself with knowledge, because the swingy bobbed woman would surely be back. She pulled the black and gold business card from her pocket and saw Amber shudder.

'FW,' she muttered, thrusting a dirty coffee cup into the washer. 'Should stand for Fuckwit. The Whimples own half of Lower Paddleton. They buy up stunning old commercial buildings and rent them to soulless chains.' Amber's jaw tightened. 'They've ruined the place.'

Gretel gulped. 'She's keen to buy the café. What if Lukas agrees?'

'Yeah, he might. They go way back, so . . . ' Amber stopped herself and coughed. 'I mean, so people say.'

Way back. She'd had no idea. She felt herself deflating. 'Miss Whimple tried telling me that if she bought the café, she'd keep it exactly the same. I just found out that was a lie.'

Amber spat out a laugh, her crockery clanging becoming more frantic. 'If Fuckwit wolfs it up, it'll be spat out into something soulless, with cheap coffee served in polystyrene. And she likes to get her own way. Once she gets her hands on one place, the Whimple effect is contagious. Have you spoken to the other shop owners on the street? Is she bothering them too?'

Gretel felt herself tense. 'No. I don't know them.'

'We should . . . '

'No.' Gretel hoped her quiet voice sounded firm enough. She wasn't sure she could cope with even more people in her life. She flicked off the flame under the hot chocolate and shoved her hands into her apron pocket. She wished Angel Gabriel was in there to keep them warm and steady. 'Anyway, maybe I'm not the best person for any of this. Most days, all I can create around here is a flat white disaster. I'm not even good with people.' She looked out across the room of bobbing faces, which often still made her want to hide in the loo.

Amber pulled a face. 'What does *good with people* actually mean? Is that even a thing? Like you've got to be some kind of shepherd rounding up the hungry sheep? You're nice. That's all it takes to be good with people; just be yourself.'

'Oh.' Gretel doubted it could be that easy. Or maybe Amber was wise for her years. 'How old are you?'

Amber paused for a moment. 'Eighteen, obviously.' She pushed the dishwasher door shut, gave Gretel a quick smile and scuffed off in her black DMs to clear more plates.

Gretel wasn't sure what the *obviously* bit meant, but however old Amber was, she seemed pretty switched on. And good with people too, even if her no-frills approach was the opposite of Nell's nurturing. Gretel watched Amber as she moved around the café, gathering and organising so unobtrusively that people barely noticed. Gretel hoped she would soon settle into her own style of hostessing too.

By the end of the day, Gretel was exhausted, both from rushing around and from carrying the weight of all her thoughts. Amidst the rush, she realised with a pang of guilt she'd hardly had time to miss Nell, or her mum and Rosa. But they were surely still firmly there. This place was the epitome of Christmas, after all.

When she finally stopped to take it all in, she had to admit the café looked like a different place to the pressure cooker it had been over the past couple of weeks. Yes, there was still some mess and mayhem. She wasn't going to deny children the odd marshmallow fight or froth-blowing competition, and there wasn't always time to clear tables before the next customers descended. The coffee beast still had its moments and she'd probably never understand all the buttons on that binging till. But it nearly resembled The Gingerbread Café she knew and loved. She almost wished Lukas was there to witness her small success.

Gretel smoothed down her apron and took a deep sigh. She wasn't stupid. Of course she realised Amber wouldn't always be there to play tag team. She also knew customers wouldn't often stay tidily at tables, rather than waving their arms, demanding things and getting cross. Yet for that moment, things were just about *bearable*, even if the word wasn't quite indicative of *living your best life*.

Although now she had two more things weighing on her mind. Should she be worried about the link between Lukas and Francesca Whimple? And for all this Christmassy-ness, how was she going to get through her first Christmas Day by herself, now that Nell was gone too?

Chapter 15

It was just one day to get through. Just. One. Day.

Gretel puffed her way up the frosty hill, Angel Gabriel tucked safely under one arm. Her ferrety companion looked extra cute in his snowman jumper, even if she did say so herself. Some might find it odd that she was wearing a matching version under her green fluffy coat, but what did that matter? She wasn't planning on seeing anyone that day. Not a soul. Because it was officially Christmas Day.

Having been out for their festive morning walks and done their rounds of visiting, most of the village would be tucked up in their Cotswold stone houses. Gretel imagined them warming their faces around cosy lit fires and unwrapping presents around twinkling Christmas trees, soaking up the love of family and close friends. She plastered on a jolly smile even though there was no one there to see it.

There was also no one to witness the flashing snowflake deely boppers she'd decided to wear to remind herself to stay cheery. Surely no one could be sad in deely boppers? Every time she moved her head the springs jiggled like an alarm to her brain. *Be merry. You've got this.*

She hadn't been expecting to feel this way, on what was meant to be her ultimate time of year. But this Christmas, with Nell gone too, the day was like a stark reminder that now she had precisely no one. She shook her head and blinked back a tear.

Since she'd lived in the village, her Christmas Days had always been spent at The Gingerbread Café. The place stayed closed on that day, but in the early years, with her mum and Nell having been so close and Nell never having remarried, Gretel, Rosa and their mum would pile in and eat their Christmas dinner with Nell. Nell would cook up a delicious feast and spoil them with gingerbread Christmas pudding. In return, the three of them would shower Nell with homemade gifts and trinkets, breaking with the usual Austrian tradition of giving presents on Christmas Eve. In fact, they'd come to embrace the English ways more and more, especially Gretel. She never would forget Nell in the knitted gingerbread man cardi her mother had lovingly made. It had suited her to perfection.

After Gretel's mum and Rosa died, the Christmas Day tradition had continued, albeit a more sombre affair at first, and with less impressive knitwear. But now, there was no Nell either. She looked up to the sky and wondered if they were watching on. Well, at least there was no one to make her eat sprouts today. Tomorrow would be better.

Angel Gabriel wrestled under her armpit and she gave

in with a sigh that made the air steamy. 'I know, I know. You want to play in the frost, you rebel.' She placed him down gently in the glittering grass, holding his lead whilst he sniffed and wriggled. 'We might even get a few flakes of snow today, boy. What do you think?'

Rosa had adored the snow. She remembered them both lying on their backs on this same hill, making snow angels, their mum chiding them about their damp woollens. *When will I get to be a real angel?* Rosa had asked, her eyes alight with the thought of it. Little had they known. Gretel fought up her sleeve for a tissue, the hot tears falling.

'Enough.' She shook her head, the deely boppers flashing in support. Rosa would have loved those too.

At least she had Angel Gabriel, and he enjoyed the snow, even though it only took a few inches of the stuff for his snowy white body to disappear. She blinked away the thought. The little creature was the only living thing in her world this Christmas. Which was fine, of course. It was a crisp afternoon, and as a person who wasn't into company, she would embrace this peaceful walk. It would be quiet. Refreshing. Some time to herself without all the *noise* people brought.

The cold air felt bracing and with Angel Gabriel bobbing along at her side, the pair continued their route up the hill. Their crunchy footsteps were heading towards the bench with Gretel's favourite views of the village. The patch of pine trees at the top of the hill beyond the bench glistened with frost like iced decorations on a Christmas cake.

Every now and then Gretel stopped to turn around and

take in the sight below. It never failed to amaze her how tiny the houses looked from there, nestled in the valley of the hills, windows twinkling and chimneys puffing out woodsmoke.

It wasn't until they reached her favourite bench that Gretel let her eyes search out Green Tree Lane. It stretched out unassumingly in the centre of the village, a huge light-speckled Christmas tree sitting proudly at its heart. Gretel hadn't grown up in the village, but since she'd arrived when she was nine with her mum and baby Rosa, that majestic tree and the quaint little street had felt like the deeply rooted core of everything.

The tree had been planted there decades ago and pre-sided all year round, even though it had considerably fewer working lights than in years gone by. But even without its full display of lights it felt symbolic. Angel Gabriel ferreted around her snow boots and she scooped him up, snuffling her nose against his.

'Just me and you this year,' she said as she found the part of the bench which would do the least splinter damage to her mistletoe-patterned woolly tights.

Gretel placed Angel Gabriel on her lap and put her cro-chet bag on the bench beside her, pulling out a tissue to dry him off. She let him burrow under the hem of her fluffy coat to keep warm whilst she double-checked that she'd packed the food. A paper bag full of broken gingerbread body parts, being the sad rejects from that morning's unsuccessful baking – she was still trying to master the art of making gingerbread people. She shuddered at the memory of all that mess she'd left behind in the café's kitchen. After another ruined batch of baking and a few tears and tantrums, she'd lost the will to tidy. Not that she'd ever had it. Well, at least she'd thought to bring leftovers, and Angel Gabriel's favourite ferret treats too. Some would say all was not lost.

'Tea for two, little man. What more could a girl need?'

The question hung in the still, dewy air and Gretel wished she could take it back. It was a silly thing to say when there was surely nothing more that she could want for. She shook her head, the snowflake deely boppers twanging to remind her of her quest to stay jolly.

'Sugary Christmas leftovers for two is just fine! Nothing sad about that.' She let out a high-pitched laugh that seemed to echo through the trees behind.

'Nothing sad at all,' a deep voice replied from above her head. 'Could you make it three?'

Gretel squealed and jumped up, spinning towards the noise and catapulting Angel Gabriel from her lap. The ferret writhed in the air and was swiftly caught by a strong pair of hands, which she assumed had been attached to the voice.

'Geeeeeeez, Lukas! What the hell are you doing sneaking up on people on deserted hillsides?' Gretel gasped for air and patted herself down frantically, making sure her skirt hadn't flown up around her knickers. She could feel her deely boppers pinging and flashing like an intruder alarm.

'I was taking a walk in the wood. What the hell are you doing floating about by yourself on high, with gigantic flashing snowflakes on your head? You do know planes might mistake you for a runway and come in to land?'

She opened her mouth to defend her headgear, but realising they probably weren't her most solid fashion choice, promptly shut it again. His dark jeans, hiking boots and green parka with furry hood combo looked annoyingly stylish. She couldn't even have a secret laugh at his stupid rubber chef's clogs today.

'I wasn't hanging about by myself,' she replied.

'No, of course. You brought your trusty guard dog with you. Wise choice.' He held Angel Gabriel up to get a better look at him. Gretel noticed with mild irritation that her usually fidgety ferret seemed perfectly calm in his hands. 'He's actually quite cute. Did you knit this?'

'He's not a dog, he's—'

'The knitting's good, but your ribbing's a bit tight here.'

She narrowed her eyes and snatched her ferret back. 'What do you know about rib stitch?' Hers wasn't the best, but knitting wasn't her craft. At least she gave things a go. 'Are you a Michelin-starred knitter now too?'

He held his hands up. 'Hey, no Michelin stars here. And you're right. I know nothing about knitting. Just a wild guess.'

Lukas moved around to the front of the bench and took a deep breath as he looked at the view. Gretel watched his torso expanding and vowed to completely ignore the wobbly feeling in her legs. It was clearly just some subconscious womany thing because he was looking all primal, but she had no space in her life for that madness. Mother Nature would have to jog straight past – her poor fragile heart was firmly closed for business. That was a fact. She hugged

Angel Gabriel to her chest, then shimmied him into her pocket, sensing he was peaceful enough for a nap.

'Stunning, isn't it?' Lukas pointed to the view, looking wistful. 'Do you come up here a lot too?'

She resisted her initial impulse to bat his question away. 'It's one of my favourite spots, though I only come here when it's likely to be quiet,' she ventured.

As she looked at his profile she could see the corners of his eyes creasing into a smile. 'You don't like sharing a bench either.' He nodded slowly, like that was perfectly natural.

'Not really.' Did that sound harsh? He'd been riling her since he'd arrived and yet somehow she didn't want to send him fleeing from her precious bench just yet. She remembered the Whimple woman saying Christmas had been a time of heartbreak for him, although Gretel still didn't know why. Maybe he needed some kindness today too.

'Fair enough, you got here first. Should I go?'

'No! I mean ... stick around for a bit if you must. It is Christmas Day. I'm not the Grinch.'

He turned to look at her, his cool grey eyes seeming to take her in. Her breath caught in her throat for a moment. The lightest of smiles played across his lips. As she subtly rubbed her oddly clammy hands against her coat, she realised what he was probably smirking at. She'd said she wasn't the Grinch, yet there she was padded out in a fluffy green coat that looked not unlike Grinch fur. Class. Clown. If he dared point it out ...

'No, of course you're not the Grinch. That's me. Can I park my grouchy self here?' He nodded at the bench and she felt touched that he was treating her like she was in charge for a change.

She nodded and they sat, perching tentatively on the edge. Gretel was also aware she wanted to quiz Lukas about Francesca Swingy Bob Whimple, but she couldn't face that can of worms just yet. There was something intriguing her more.

'You never did finish telling me why you're so Grinchy about Christmas.'

He blew out his cheeks and raked a hand through his steely coloured hair. Was it odd that she found it fascinating to watch the thickness of it stir and then settle again?

'Didn't I? Then it's a long story.'

Why did people always say that and how long could a story be? But she understood the desire to keep things to yourself.

Lukas undid the zip on the backpack that was at the side of him and eased out a small tin. 'Talking of matters of the heart, maybe I can share something else instead.' He looked around, although they were the only ones left on that darkening winter's afternoon. 'Shh, just this once. Or people will think I'm going as soft as these.'

Chapter 16

Lukas opened the box to display the most beautiful gingery lebkuchen biscuits Gretel had ever seen. They reminded her of the ones she used to eat with her mum at Christmas markets around Europe, and Nell had loved to bake them for the café too. Lukas's were little hearts and stars, some dipped in the darkest chocolate, others coated in a sugary glaze and the rest laced with delicately piped icing. But oh, the smell. Even on a cold winter's day on the side of a Cotswold hill, the fragrance from the small box was just divine: like honey, orange and a mix of spices twirling together in a dance. Gretel closed her eyes and breathed it in, almost wanting to stick her tongue out and taste the memories on the air. Love, family, friendship . . .

A wave of sadness rose up from her stomach and threatened to burst from her throat. She squeezed her eyelids together, desperate not to break into a sob. What was wrong with her suddenly? They were just biscuits.

'Are you OK?' Lukas placed a hand on her arm, his voice uncertain.

Gretel took a deep breath and held it in for a second, willing her body to calm itself. When she thought she was safe, she pulled her arm back and opened her eyes. 'Yes, I'm fine. Sorry. I don't know what came over me. Memories, or something silly.'

She stood up, not wanting to be under the dangerous spell of gingerbread and history. This rush of confusion was exactly why her heart had no space to share a bench.

She put a hand to her head to still the twanging deely boppers. Until then, she'd completely forgotten her need for their *stay cheery* alarm whilst sitting with Lukas.

'Did you bake them?' she asked, putting her errant hand into her pocket to feel the warm comfort of Angel Gabriel, her eyes seeking out Green Tree Lane below. The leb-kuchen looked just like Nell's, if Nell had suddenly got excessively meticulous and started measuring her icing with a ruler. 'Did Nell teach you?'

'No, I . . . ' His voice trailed off, as though sensing now wasn't the time for his sidestepping games. 'Yes.'

She wondered if he knew all of Nell's old gingerbread recipes from around the world. Even if he didn't, wasn't he a fancy, star-seeking chef? He could research the best recipes or make up even better ones. He could teach her. But he hated Christmas and he'd decided to leave her struggling. Another reason they could never truly make peace.

'I thought you were too busy and important for silly gingerbread.'

He sighed. 'You really don't have the best impression of

me, do you? Actually, don't answer that.' He shifted on the bench. 'No, I don't bake gingerbread people any more. You won't catch me making Nell's trademark ladies and gents or faffing about icing top hats and frilly skirts. Don't ask. It's just ... not my scene now. But that doesn't mean I can't bake a bit of lebkuchen as a one-off festive offering to Nell, even if Christmas does suck. At least I didn't have to break my back dragging in a dead tree for her this year, and nearly bowling you over in the process.'

They were silent for a moment, Gretel conscious she hadn't been able to face the emotion of Nell's annual real tree ritual this year. Maybe in January, and she didn't care if most people would find that odd. Thinking of *odd*, there was something else she needed to raise with Lukas. As she looked down onto Green Tree Lane and the tree she hoped would always be twinkling, she felt a small burst of courage.

'Do you know ... Francesca Whimple?'

'Yes.' Did his voice seem cautious?

'She's been sniffing around the café. I think she's keen to buy it.'

Lukas stood up now too, spreading out his chest again, like he needed to take up more space. 'Well, that's ... *great.*'

'There's no need to sound quite so upbeat.' She crossed her arms. 'Apparently Miss Whimple and her family buy places up and rent them out to soulless chains. I heard the little independents in Lower Paddleton couldn't afford the Whimples' rent prices so the cute shops and cafés got strangled out. If we're not careful, our village will go the same way. Green Tree Lane could be destroyed.'

'That's not true. It's just … progress. Change is good – we shouldn't stagnate. Anyway, Franny's just a pawn in the family business. Her dad and brothers call the shots.'

Gretel took a sharp intake of breath, the words piercing her like spikes. Progress? Change? And he needn't get her started on that murky, stagnant fountain in Lower Paddleton. 'Once the Whimple woman gets her silly golden trainer in one door, the landscape of Green Tree Lane would change for ever, with Nell's café being the first domino to fall and put the others at risk of tumbling. Do you think that's what Nell would have wanted?'

She stepped around to face him, hands on hips; but with the rise of the hill she was now on a lower footing, forced to look up at his chin.

'Change the landscape? That's a bit extreme. It's not like Franny's going to tear up your precious Christmas tree. The hefty thing's at least three times the size of her.'

Franny? 'Well, it sounds like you're *great* friends already.' She could just imagine the woman chugging through the village in a bulldozer. Maybe Lukas would be hitching a ride.

He raked a hand through his hair again, but this time Gretel had no interest in watching its rise and fall. 'We know each other quite well, yes. And Franny's family owns the building I'm keen to buy for my restaurant in Lower Paddleton. It's part of an old water mill on the river. It's coming up for sale soon and the wheel room is something else. Turning that place into my first restaurant has been a dream for years.'

'Don't tell me. If you sell her the first domino in Green Tree Lane, she'll be more likely to let you have your stinky old mill.'

'It's only when you let things stagnate that they get stinky, Gretel. Life moves, seasons change.' His voice was lower now, as though explaining something to a small child. 'Staying stuck in Christmas is not sustainable and it's not doing . . . the café any good.'

The café. But she could tell from his pause and the cloudy look in those grey eyes that he'd meant her too. He was comparing her life to a sludgy old pond and her deely boppers were extremely cross about it.

'So if Miss Whimple got her hands on the café, you'd be happy for her to turn it into something completely different from Nell's legacy?'

'Look, she told me she'd respect the general theme of the café and she's mostly a woman of her word. I expect her vision for the future tenants still involves gingerbread and hot chocolate. But saying goodbye to the never-ending Christmas thing? That's just common sense.'

Gretel shook her head and tried not to scowl as the corners of Lukas's mouth twitched upwards. 'I'm glad you find this whole situation funny.'

'I'm sorry. It's just that those flashing snowflake things on your head are quite distracting. Honestly, though, change can be a good thing. Maybe a bit of a shake-up is just what Green Tree Lane needs. Business hasn't been buzzing there for a while. Franny has some great tenants . . .'

'The village doesn't need a bunch of greedy chain stores.'

'Like you do so much socialising with the villagers.'

Ouch! She pulled the stupid deely boppers off her head.

'Life is transient, Gretel. Even the weather.' Lukas put a

hand out as the lightest flakes of snow began falling around them. 'Nothing is ours for the keeping, except memories. Sometimes we've just got to roll with it.'

She didn't notice how tightly she'd been gripping the headband until the sharp teeth were biting dents into her palm.

'Look, I'm not trying to railroad you, I promise. But I do think selling the place to the Whimples would be for the best. I guarantee that once Christmas is done and the café's a ghost town you'll be itching to get the place off your hands too.' He gave a quick look towards the sky as the snow picked up its pace. 'The money from the sale would give you a completely fresh start.' He rustled her bag of broken biscuits and placed them under her crochet bag to keep dry. 'From the usual state of the kitchen, I'd say you're probably making more mess than money.' His voice sounded fake jokey but she wasn't in the mood. 'And on the plus side, you didn't actually move yourself into the flat above. So there you go. It will be painless enough for us to cut the ties as soon as probate is sorted in a few short months.'

As much as it bugged her, she couldn't help wondering if he was the voice of reason. He was the sensible grown-up, after all. But when she remembered the progress she'd been making in the café – that sense of purpose and those tiny moments of success with Amber by her side, she was sure she wasn't out of fight just yet. Maybe she didn't have all the answers, but she'd decided one thing. She was going to try harder to learn to bake. And to apologise for his hurtful mouth, Lukas was going to help her.

Chapter 17

It had been easier than she'd expected to talk Lukas into coming back to the café with her to give her some pointers on her disastrous baking. It being Christmas Day, his most hated occasion of the year, she'd been expecting more of a fight. Maybe he'd taken pity on her, or perhaps he was secretly craving a distraction as much as she was.

She wasn't sure if she'd talk him into actually baking gingerbread, with the fuss he invariably made about it being beneath him. And she anticipated he'd have even more to huff about when he saw the state of the kitchen after her morning of failed festive baking, but they were on their way, and that was an impressive start.

They trudged side by side down the hill, Angel Gabriel bouncing along in front of them on his lead. Gretel had swapped her deely boppers for her festive owl hat and Lukas had pulled up his hood.

The snow was picking up its pace, swirling tentatively

around them, landing on noses and melting into coats. Church bells rang in the distance and the few lights that were still working on the Christmas tree in the lane shimmered below them in the half-light. They hadn't yet spoken on the descent, but Gretel could almost sense Lukas tensing as they got nearer to the village. It was easy enough to pretend it wasn't the big day out in nature, but the village beamed Christmas, with tinselled trees in windows and cottages decorated with string lights.

As they reached the bottom of the hill the smell of log fires and wholesome roasts filled the air, the sounds of laughter and Christmassy TV escaping through windows. They dodged a troupe of carol singers and Gretel thought she heard Lukas swear. She wanted to tell him off, but stopped herself. Perhaps he was struggling too. She knew all too well how heartache felt, even if she still didn't know why his heart was hurting.

'Not working today?' she asked, hoping to distract him.

'I did a shift earlier. Back in tonight.'

'Wow. The fun never stops.'

'Keeps me busy,' he said gruffly. The sounds of 'Good King Wenceslas' and his feast did not appear to be cheering him up. He pulled his hood tighter.

'What do your fancy diners eat on Christmas Day?' she felt brave enough to tease. 'I can't imagine them accepting sage and onion stuffing with instant gravy.' He didn't need to know that was the sum total of her Christmas dinner efforts earlier. There had been no point in burning a nut roast for one.

She hurried to keep up with him as he marched past the festive-looking houses.

'Partridge and pan-roasted pear has been our most popular. The port and dark chocolate sauce finishes it off nicely.'

Gretel laughed before realising he wasn't joking. 'Oh, sorry. People really eat that?' She could live with the chocolate part, but what a bizarre mix. 'Please tell me they at least get a huge blob of Christmas pud and cream for dessert.' Preferably just after the yule log and just before the mince pies and After Eights. Nell had really got her into a traditional English Christmas.

'Deconstructed medjool date cheesecake,' he said, matter-of-factly.

'Which is what? A biscuit with a date on the side?' She'd never been a fan of those chewy little things.

He shrugged. 'Basically.' Was he trying not to smile now? And it definitely wasn't 'Ding Dong Merrily on High' that was tickling him.

As they reached the cobbles of Green Tree Lane, Gretel's heart sank a little to be reminded that it didn't look nearly as festive as in years gone by. When the little shopping street had been more prosperous, the shop owners had made more effort to decorate it with red and green festive lights and fake snow, like something from a film set. She remembered huge candy canes outside the door of The Gingerbread Café, and piped music spilling out onto the pavements. The old-fashioned lamp posts looked far too solitary without the strings of lights connecting them. Not all of the lamp posts even worked now.

'We should fix some of these lights,' said Gretel.

'Not our job,' Lukas replied, and she sensed his mood sinking.

Was it too much to hope he'd cheer up again soon?

Gretel had picked up Angel Gabriel to save him struggling across the wet cobbles now that the snow was trying to settle. The thought of looking out of the window later to see a snowy Christmas card scene made her heart bounce. Surely she deserved one good thing this Christmas?

Passing the other shops in the street, she noticed that most of the shopfronts looked as though they needed some love. Paint was flaking and some of the window displays could do with a touch of life. Was it sad she didn't even know who the other shop owners were, beyond recognising their faces in passing? Amber had mentioned trying to talk to them ... but no. She'd never been one to mingle.

As they reached the front door of The Gingerbread Café, she noted their paintwork could also do with a freshen-up – but there was no point in mentioning it. He'd shrug her off about that too. Not that she was into change.

Lukas pulled out his keys and then frowned at the ferret in Gretel's arms.

'What? I can't leave him out here in this weather, he'd freeze. He'll be no trouble if I pop him in the crochet bag for a nap under one of the tables. I promise we won't let him near the kitchen.'

Lukas looked down at the crochet bag, which was now sodden from the snow that had been wisping around them and seeping into their outer layers, including Angel Gabriel's little festive jumper. 'We'll find him some dry towels. But afterwards, you take the towels home and keep them. I don't want to see them back near a kitchen.'

Even if the snow didn't settle, that small gesture was a Christmas miracle in itself.

Chapter 18

Once they'd settled Angel Gabriel in his warm towel nest in a corner of the café, Gretel braced herself and followed Lukas into the kitchen. His borderline OCD need for order was not going to enjoy the shambles she'd left when she'd tried to make gingerbread people that morning.

But he simply sighed, and began moving around the marble-topped island, grabbing dirty cooking equipment and lining it up with military precision near the sink. He flicked the radio off at the plug in case she'd had any notions of a festive singalong. She wondered if the wayward juke-box was storing up a treat for him. 'If you want my advice, the first rule of working in a kitchen is to keep your workspace tidy.'

As much as Gretel wanted to pull stupid faces behind his back, she was silently glad to see the chaos clearing.

Their red cheeks deserved something warm after that chilly walk, so she went to the cooker and put the flame under the *Glühwein* she'd been tasting earlier. She remembered her mum warming her hands around a glass of it at the Christmas markets, or *Christkindlmärkte*, where they'd spent many of her early Christmases – although Gretel had always loved the non-alcoholic *Kinderpunsch*. She couldn't help a touch of disappointment when Lukas gently shook his head. If *Glühwein* was far too Christmassy for him, she'd have to sip his too.

The smell of red wine, orange and spices began to intoxicate the air in the kitchen, making Gretel feel heady enough for a little sass. 'So you didn't tell me the second rule of working in a kitchen. Anything to do with keeping a spoon in your back pocket?'

He turned to look at her and she felt her icy cheeks fire up like an oven. Although it wasn't there today, she'd often wondered about that spoon she'd seen sticking out of his back pocket. Now it seemed like she was into checking out his bum – which she obviously wasn't. It wasn't her fault if shiny things caught her eye.

She was sure she noticed the shadow of a smile accompany his slightly too long stare.

'It's my tasting spoon.' He moved to his backpack and pulled it out.

She pressed her lips together to stifle a laugh. It had a spoon bit on each end, like a two-headed monster. It pleased her that she wasn't the only one with odd quirks.

'Yes, very funny. It's double-ended. Some might say two heads are better than one.' He shook his head and busied himself, filling a clean food waste bag with cremated gingerbread limbs. 'Not that there's much worth tasting around here. How have you got this so wrong? It's just basic gingerbread.' Yet his tone was gentle.

Gretel sighed as she gave the *Glühwein* a last stir and poured it into one solitary glass mug. 'But it's not, though, is it? Nothing Nell ever made tasted *basic*. Even her standard gingerbread people had *something else*. I've been trying so hard to recreate that, even though I have no idea what the *something else* was. She didn't leave a single recipe. I just want to try and do her justice.'

Lukas stopped what he was doing. 'I can't pretend to understand what the hell Nell was thinking, the dear old girl. She knows I can't stand Christmas, for a start. But I'm guessing if she wanted you to morph into her, she would have left you instructions. Maybe there's some merit in trying things your own way. Whatever Nell was doing, it wasn't exactly working for her. This place was a ghost town for most of the year.'

'My own way? I seriously don't have one.' Her eyes found the floor.

'So did you follow some sort of recipe?' He waved an arm over the murdered biscuits.

She shrugged. 'I found something online. But I was trying to use some artistic flair to make the gingerbread people taste like Nell's. They were always so ... sweet?'

Lukas winced. 'The second rule about working in a kitchen is that cooking's a science before it becomes an art. Until you know what you're doing, just follow the recipe. You can get creative once you've mastered the basics.' He went back to clearing up incinerated body parts.

'I don't come from a background of cooking or baking,' she admitted. They'd rarely had a proper kitchen to call their own, until they'd settled in the village. 'The way I grew up didn't really allow for it.'

He raised an eyebrow.

She didn't usually share things about her childhood, but she missed her family more than ever today. She took a few sips of the spicy warm *Glühwein*. 'Before we moved to Mistleton I travelled a lot around the Christmas markets of Europe with Mum. I lived on waffles and pastries and doughnuts dunked in chocolate. And the special treats from the Austrian markets. Like these.'

Gretel was making her way to the cupboard before she could think better of it. Did she really want to share her last few biscuits? She'd ordered them for herself and she wasn't used to sharing. '*Vanillekipferl*. They're Austrian biscuits. Mum always said it wasn't Christmas without them.'

He walked over, peering inside the packet. 'Can I?'

She nodded, quietly thrilled she was introducing him to something new and strangely keen for him to like them.

Lukas assessed a crescent moon-shaped biscuit and took a bite. 'Mmm. Buttery, like a shortbread. Somehow infused with vanilla, and something else ...' He held a finger in the air. 'Ground almonds? Yes! With a melt-in-the-mouth texture and a generous dusting of vanilla sugar.'

He had some of it around his mouth. She tried not to giggle.

'Delicious. Right. I think I've got this.' He began moving around the kitchen, gathering ingredients, stopping at times to tap the worktop whilst he thought, and then weighing things into glass bowls, ready to do who knew what.

She wanted to feel annoyed at him inviting himself to recreate her favourite biscuits, and at how effortless he made his baking preparations look, even without a recipe. She always struggled to get Nell's funny old-fashioned scales to stop wobbling about and actually balance, and she couldn't go near a packet of flour without a full-scale snow disaster.

Yet for all the panic she usually felt in a kitchen, there was something cathartic about watching him work. He was peaceful, creative and . . . happy?

'Mind if I mix things up and add a touch of ginger and spice?' He looked up from the work he'd been immersed in, his eyes genuinely questioning.

'Erm . . . if you like?'

Gretel found herself watching his hands as he worked. She blushed, realising she'd be mortified if someone was observing her so closely whilst she was trying to create. But he simply looked up absently and apologised, saying he ought to explain things, in case she wanted to make more of her own.

'I'm kneading the mixture into a dough,' he said, one corner of his mouth twitching upwards, his hands working the floury, buttery mixture in the bowl. 'It takes a bit of time. Respect the dough, but be firm with it.'

Gretel usually found this part, when the ingredients looked like a load of crumbs that would never stick together, frustrating and gungy. She often gave up and chucked it into the mixer, sometimes adding more liquid so it would just hurry up. Against everything she would have expected of Lukas, he was remarkably patient with his work. For once he seemed at peace.

'Then the dough needs to rest in the fridge. Don't miss out that bit,' he explained, as though guessing the impatient child in her didn't usually bother. 'The chilling process will cool the fat, and give you depth of flavour and a more even bake. A simple step, but trust me, it's worth it.'

It *was* a simple step, other than the trusting bit.

Ordinarily, his mini-lectures made her want to roll her eyes. But today she sensed it was more like gentle coaching, and she could tell it came from a genuine place. Leading people in a kitchen was what he was trained to do – and it suited him.

From somewhere in the darkened café the errant juke-box whirred to life and the sound of 'Silent Night' poured through. It was the carol she used to sing with her mum, and then Rosa too, on Christmas Eve when they lit the Christmas tree. It was an Austrian tradition, and her mum used to say soldiers had sung it in the trenches. Opposing sides, letting their guards down for one sacred moment. A single night of calm, amidst the conflict. Perhaps this was theirs.

Chapter 19

Whilst Lukas tidied some of his equipment, Gretel sat on the worktop, her legs swinging. She ran her finger around the rim of her glass, letting the blissful ringing entrance her. The sound made her feel like something inside her was peacefully unfurling. Or maybe that was all the *Glühwein* she wasn't used to.

'You know, I haven't always been a Christmas freak,' she found herself saying.

Lukas turned to look at her. That tight black apron he'd pulled out from his backpack suited him. 'I know. The Christmas thing started with ...' He stopped, suddenly looking unsure of himself. It was sweet.

'My mum,' she finished.

'I'm sorry. I heard about the accident. But don't feel you have to talk about it.' He gently put down the cloth he was using, as though she was an animal that might bolt.

'And Rosa.' The name just popped out, even though she

rarely let it. 'She was my little sister. I don't ...' She gulped down a sob and groped across the counter for a tissue. 'Urgh.' She blinked a few times and dabbed the corners of her eyes, the mascara soaking onto the tissue in ashy smudges. 'I don't mention her much. Easier not to.'

The loss of little Rosa had almost hit her harder than losing her mother, but that too was a guilt she didn't share. How could she? There'd been a horrific van accident with Rosa and her mum. Gretel hadn't even been there. Her mother had died at the scene. *On impact.* Those were the words. They'd been keen to reassure Gretel that she hadn't felt a thing. But how could an *impact* not hurt? Wasn't that the point in the word?

It had all been so instant, and her soul would have floated off somewhere lovely, with clouds and twinkly starlight. That's what Nell had promised her. Dear Nell.

But Rosa. For a few days they'd thought she had the tiniest fighting chance. But they were wrong. It had been like losing everything twice. And worst of all, the heaviness of it had collapsed onto Gretel's chest like it was all her fault. Her mum had floated away and entrusted her precious sibling to *her* and she hadn't been able to save her. In that stark, beeping hospital room, Gretel had promised Rosa this. That she'd live every day for her, with the childlike joy and wonder that Rosa had taught her. It had been just before Christmas – Rosa's favourite time of year. The time when her eyes were even brighter and her glee simply radiated.

Somehow that promise had morphed into this surreal world where she couldn't let go of cute penguin jumpers and the promise of Christmas. She was stuck here, unable to pack her memories away and move on. How had it got so out of hand? Yet how could she wave off her innocent wonder when dear Rosa had never even got to finish her childhood?

She shook her head and looked up, realising Lukas's arm was around her shoulder and she was shivering. 'I'm sorry, I . . . got lost for a moment. That's why it's better not to talk about it. And other people find it hard to deal with too. The death of a child. They don't have the words and they back away, frightened they'll say the wrong thing. Worried you'll cry. But people need to cry, don't they? It's only for themselves that others don't want you sobbing.' She took a deep breath. 'But I understand that. I'm rubbish with people too and I don't want to burden anyone. Maybe that's why it's easier to be the Christmas weirdo and keep people at bay. Can you pass more mulled wine?'

Lukas gave her a doubtful look and gently took her glass. 'Maybe you need a mug of hot chocolate.' He moved away and filled the kettle, keeping an eye on her as though she might break now he'd let her go. 'And please don't apologise or feel like you're a burden. You're not. If anything, you're the opposite. You're the most light-hearted, joy-loving pixie of a creature I've ever met. Disconcertingly so, deely boppers and all.' He gave her a cautious grin. 'This poor Christmas hater can barely work it out.' He fixed her with one of his pensive looks which seemed to last an age. Why was it so hard to breathe when he did that? Then he turned away and busied himself with the kettle. 'But it's OK not to be OK, as the saying goes. And I mean that. If you ever want to talk . . .'

'Thank you.' His kindness was disconcerting too. She blew her nose loudly into a fresh tissue. It felt strangely OK to be herself whilst he was in this rare mood of his, even if them spending time together was only going to be temporary. He had bigger, Michelin-sized stars to chase, and she was no more than a blubbering mess when she spent too much time with humans.

'I've had my fair share of *not* being OK, if that makes you feel any better; but that's a story for another night.'

What was his story? Something inside her danced at the thought of there being *another night*, even though she tried to ignore it. Then suddenly, she felt like she did want to talk; about the good things, at least. Christmas Day wasn't meant to be a soggy tissue pity party. She had some happy memories that were wriggling to be shared. It had been so long since she'd had the chance to let them out . . . so why. not?

She jumped down from the worktop and together they began to create order, chatting as they went.

'We loved Christmas, the three of us.' Gretel smiled as she remembered her little family, as tight knit as their festive winter woollens. 'We lived it. Mum's main income was from working the Christmas markets around Europe, so we spent a large chunk of our year making Christmas decorations in preparation.'

'Stained glass?'

'No, actually. The stained glass was something I picked up later. Learning a new craft and getting lost in it helped me escape, after . . . ' She shook her head. 'Anyway, Mum was into less fragile crafts. Creations that were built to last, ironically.' She gave a sad smile. 'Knitting, hand-stitching, felting. Things that wouldn't break on our travels in that crappy old van. We travelled a lot and we didn't really settle until we came here when Rosa was born. I think Mum found it too hard to bounce from place to place with two of us.' Neither of them had ever met their fathers. 'So when Mum discovered Mistleton during one of those wintery February fairs they used to hold here, we stayed and rented. She said the ever-present Christmas tree outside on the lane was a sign that this was our place. Our lives were so interwoven with that time of year, and as an Austrian, Christmas trees were always extra special to her. They're such a huge part of the Christmas tradition, even if we weren't often in Austria to embrace it. Then we met Nell. And how could Nell not be your person? Her spice-infused hugs and warm gingerbread. She was like Mother Christmas every day of the week.'

'Wasn't she just.' The skin around Lukas's eyes creased as he grinned. 'She certainly became a safe space for me when I was younger. Hell knows there were times when I needed one.'

She looked at him, her eyebrows raised in question, but he shook his head and waved her to continue.

'Then after the accident . . . I was just *lost*. Like my flock had disappeared and I was destined to be the stray one. As if I wasn't already gawped at enough. The girl from the Austrian family who'd made Christmas decs all year round and whose mum had knitted her jumpers.' She smiled to let him know she was OK with that. 'The only person I really had left was Nell. The few college friends I had became distant. They didn't know what to say and I didn't want to be a pain. I soon realised the only place I felt warm and safe was in Nell's Gingerbread Café, where it was always Christmas. I could wear festive woollens and eat Christmassy treats without any awkward questions. And I kept the Christmas decorations up in our old flat too, long after winter was done. Life just felt cosier that way, like I'd created my own sanctuary.'

The warmth of his eyes told her he understood, even though Christmas was probably never going to be his thing. 'And you've lived in Christmas ever since?'

She laughed. 'No! Even I know that would be pretty weird. I've had plenty of phases where I've tried to snap out of it. I've packed it all away and attempted to get on with things. I even started counselling a few times, and then made my excuses and bolted. Every time I pack the festive things away it feels like Mum and Rosa are slipping away from me. And *talking it out* seems like a terrifying pathway to wiping out their memory for good.'

'Wow, it must have been tough for you. Especially these last few weeks after losing Nell too.' She could sense him treading carefully. It was sweet, but she didn't want to be an eggshell.

She dropped her cleaning cloth into the sink. She'd already said too much and she didn't want to be *that person*. The one who weighed people down with sad stories and talked too much. 'Anyway! Your dough must be nicely chilled by now. Shall we?'

She moved to the fridge and he followed her.

'You know, I always find baking therapeutic when I need to switch off from things,' said Lukas. 'Let me guide you through how to roll out and shape the *Vanillekipferl*. As you work, I might even give you my trade secrets on making the best lebkuchen, just like Nell's. She would have liked that.'

Chapter 20

After getting through Lukas's impromptu Christmas Day baking lesson without causing chaos or wanting to murder anyone, Gretel was sure she deserved a break.

'More hot chocolate?' she asked.

She poured two mugs and they moved into the dark café. Gretel lit a few candles and dared to switch on a string of fairy lights, whilst Lukas plumped up two cushions on one of the comfy leather sofas. They sat together, the only background noise the soft, squeaky snore of a ferret.

Maybe sipping hot chocolate was even more intoxicating than drinking wine, because curled up on the sofa with Lukas's warm body enticingly close to hers, something inside Gretel was almost melting; and it wasn't just from the heat of her drink.

'Would you miss this place if we sold it?' she heard herself ask.

'I didn't think so, but ... ' He shook his head. 'Anyway,

I've had my heart set on opening up my own restaurant in Lower Paddleton one day. I'd call it Knight in the Mill. You know. After my surname, and the old mill building I want to buy.' Lukas had barely touched his hot drink, yet his face suddenly looked uncharacteristically warm. Was he blushing? She wanted to lean over and press her hands against his cheeks. But then she'd be almost on his lap and what if she toppled? Her face would be dangerously close to his, and then ...

She shook her thoughts back to the present. As much as she was enjoying the direction of her unexpected lap-tumbling vision, it was a tad rude to fantasise about your guests.

Gretel cleared her throat. 'Knight in the Mill. It's ... lovely.' She tried to ignore the sad twinge which reminded her that Lukas getting his dream meant selling The Gingerbread Café and Gretel losing hers.

Gretel had been strangely transfixed by Lukas's smoky grey eyes since they'd been lounging on the sofa, but suddenly they were almost aglow. 'I still want to lead the team at La Carotte Rôtie to get that Michelin star. But the bigger dream has always been to have my own place, where I create everything – not just the menus. The whole vibe. The ambience. A place where people want to be, like a true celebration of food. Right from the paintwork to the napkins, I want to make those tiny decisions that make the experience complete.'

Lukas gesticulated with his hands as he spoke, and now it wasn't just his eyes that were glowing. It seemed like his whole body was ablaze with a passion for his work. She could feel herself leaning towards him as though his zeal was magnetic. Was he leaning too? With every inch of her she hoped so. Before she could think it through, she was stretching her body over him to put her mug down on the table next to him, even though she had table space of her own. Was that obvious? In that moment, she didn't seem to care.

Her hip lost its balance on the soft sofa cushion and her secret tumbling fantasy started to play out.

'Woah.' He grabbed her waist to stop her falling fully into him, even though she'd definitely wanted to.

She turned her upper body to face him, still held gloriously in those solid hands. The hands of a chef with the strength of a knight. How hot they felt against her jumper dress. She bit her bottom lip. She wanted to kiss him. The fire in his eyes told her he felt something too. So what was stopping them? She sensed her lips moving slowly towards his, testing the air between them. Tasting it, almost. It was . . . spicy, sweet, smoky. He was beginning to look hazy . . .

And then he pulled away and winced, the split-second panic in his eyes sending a jolt of mortification straight through her. Lukas lowered her back to safety on the sofa and then stood up quickly, coughing into his hand. 'The biscuits – they're burning. Blasted oven timer must be on the blink. I sensed this place was getting way too hot.'

What did that mean? But Lukas was off towards the kitchen and she reluctantly pushed herself up to follow him. Didn't he know burning everything was just part of baking? Well, he was clearly a man of priorities. It was obvious he'd rather stick his face into a red-hot oven than get it close to hers.

As she heard him swearing from the kitchen, the embarrassing reality of the last few minutes sank in. She'd been stretching across him like a keen cat and that was clearly the last thing he'd wanted. She would never understand people.

When Gretel made it to the kitchen to inspect the oven's offerings, her heart sunk. 'They're burnt to a crisp.' She poked the tray with a wooden spoon and realised the universe was trying to tell her something. 'Even with a trained chef on hand, I still managed to incinerate the biscuits. What does that say about my chances of running The Gingerbread Café?'

'I'm more worried about what it says for my chances of leading my kitchen to secure that Michelin star,' Lukas replied. 'This is what happens when you lose focus. When you let yourself get distracted by . . .' He ruffled a hand through his hair and she guessed he was thinking of the *nearly kiss*. A million embarrassed butterflies died a death in her stomach.

Then his face dropped even further. He raced to his backpack and pulled out the watch he'd taken off when he'd started baking. 'Shit. I'm late for my shift! I'm never late for work.' He looked at her, like she was in charge of time. 'You see?'

He huffed in frustration. It wasn't quite as mean as his usual sternness, but after the almost, sort of truce . . .

'None of this is a good idea,' he said, as he moved around the kitchen, grabbing his things.

None of what? Cooking? Being nice?

'I've got to go. I ... ' He raked a hand through his hair. Was he about to apologise? 'I've got some *real* cooking to do.'

Gretel felt something inside her tighten. Heaven forbid his pretentious diners should go without their dark chocolate on a pigeon, or whatever it was. She folded her arms, waiting for him to leave.

When he'd gone, even the sight of the snow settling outside the window didn't bring her any cheer. She had stupidly let herself begin to warm to him. But his behaviour had pushed her back out into the cold.

Chapter 21

It was two weeks since Christmas had passed and Lukas was still being evasive. The *nearly kiss* had been a humiliating mistake and Gretel was telling herself she was happy to forget it. Who needed people, anyway?

Keep Calm and Bake Gingerbread, as one of Nell's old metal signs would have said. So she was doing just that. Although she'd come to see it would be much easier to keep practising the baking tips she'd picked up from Lukas if she lived somewhere with a proper kitchen. Her maisonette was barely suitable for microwaving a strudel and she was fed up of traipsing backwards and forwards to the café and leaving poor Angel Gabriel at home.

That was how she came to be standing nervously at the fresh white door of Nell's flat above The Gingerbread Café, clinging to her oversized artificial Christmas tree. She was moving in. Now it was just a matter of getting the damned tree through the door.

After some deliberation with no one in particular, she decided against the face full of needles option, and instead settled on going in butt first and dragging the tree after her. There. Didn't she sound like the wise, successful café owner she was about to transform herself into?

She smiled and unlocked the flat door with the key she hadn't dared to use until now. Then, rescuing the leaning tree by the trunk, she took up her reversing position and used her bum to push the door open. She leaned her weight backwards, hoping it would encourage the awkwardly wide branches to twang through. After a few tense seconds and not much twanging, she pulled harder. And at last ... *thuuuuud*.

'Bloody ow!' Gretel crash-landed onto her back with the prickly tree on top of her, cheap baubles clattering around her like giant coloured hailstones. Well, at least she'd had the sense to take off her handmade stained-glass ornaments and pack them carefully in boxes. She was basically a grown-up. Now, how would an adult get themselves out of this bristly mess?

'Girl, whaaaat?'

Gretel tensed, before realising it was Amber's voice. And there was her thinking it was usually Lukas who wasn't far behind a festive tree disaster.

'I dropped by to say hey and noticed the back door was wedged open with a box. I tried shouting for you ... ' said Amber, attempting to wrestle Gretel free from the awkward heap of branches.

'I guess I didn't hear you,' Gretel wheezed, hauling herself up and dusting stray needles from her snowman tank top.

'If you'd said you were doing this, I would have been straight here. Are you OK?' Amber was patting her down as though checking for broken bits.

'Oh, I'm fine. I don't need any help.' Gretel waved a hand.

Amber's eyes widened. 'Clearly.' She picked up Angel Gabriel's cage, which was near the front door. 'Come on, I'm here now. Stop being such a one-woman island.' Amber nodded towards the flat, which had a short corridor and then a closed internal door. 'Did you take a look yet?'

Gretel screwed her eyes shut and groaned.

'Hey, what's up?' She felt Amber's hand on her arm.

'It's nothing. I . . . ' She exhaled sharply. 'I haven't been brave enough to check this place out yet. Nell and I spent all our time together downstairs in recent years, even on special occasions. I haven't been up here for ages. And I'm guessing the place is still filled with her memories.' She clamped a hand over her face, partly to suppress a sob and partly because she knew if she breathed in too deeply, she might smell Nell's gentle fragrance of honeysuckle and baking.

When Gretel had had a short burst of dutiful messages with Lukas to let him know she was moving in, he'd told her he hadn't got around to clearing out Nell's things yet. She'd sent a curt message back telling him not to dare. It had been bold by her usual standards, but she was still reeling from his behaviour on Christmas Day. He knew how to ruin a girl's favourite time of year.

'We can always have a clear-out,' Amber said gently.

'Get rid of all those . . . *memories*?' Gretel could feel herself starting to shake.

Amber shrugged. 'I suppose you'll want to treasure some stuff. But aren't memories mostly things we keep in our heads? You don't have to live in a museum.'

Museum. It was an odd word when you said it too many times. Hypnotic, even.

'Woah, you're wobbling. Let's get you inside.'

And with a caged ferret in a Rudolph jumper under one arm and a sniffling Gretel lassoed with the other, Amber guided them both down the short corridor and let Gretel open the internal door.

When Gretel opened it, she remembered what Lukas had said in one of his messages. *It's not what you'd imagine.* He was right.

She'd expected it to follow the same Christmassy theme as the café, with reds and greens and glittering fairy lights. Hadn't it been like that the last time she'd been up here, several years before? The tiny maisonette Gretel was leaving was certainly a shrine to Christmas. She'd thought she'd be moving to a home from home, but with more space and the chance to use the money she'd been spending on rent to breathe a little life into the café. Business had been eerily slow since Christmas and she couldn't keep ignoring that either.

'It's . . . beautiful,' said Gretel.

She stood for a moment, taking it all in. The main living space in front of her was large and airy, with wide casement windows dressed with sweeping white voile. In fact, the whole room was a sea of white with touches of dove grey and the palest lavender. A coffee table took pride of place in the

121

centre of the room, decorated with a vase of silk eucalyptus which seemed to emanate calm from its silver-blue leaves. Other than the slight issue of the dust, it seemed the whole room was inviting her to relax and inhale.

Gretel slipped off her snow boots and tiptoed across the light wooden floor, letting every element of her new surroundings soak in. The comforting fragrance from the bunches of dried lavender strewn across the white dresser. The softness of the cloud-coloured rug she bent down to touch. And the sound of ... *peace*.

'This place is incredible,' Amber breathed, as though sensing the tranquillity too.

They moved to the kitchen, which was just as light as the living space, with modern white cupboards and gadgets in shades of cappuccino. More pots of silk eucalyptus leaves were dotted around on shelves and the white wall tiles shone brightly in the January sun which bounced off the frost outside and streamed through the windows.

'Lukas redecorated the flat for his auntie a few years ago,' said Amber. 'I mean, so I heard. You know, gossip or whatever.' She darted back to the main room and busied herself finding a spot for Angel Gabriel, as though she'd said too much.

Gretel got the feeling she wouldn't get anything else out of Amber, even if she did know more. Perhaps one day she'd get to the bottom of Amber's strange secrecies.

Had Lukas done all this work for Nell? And if so, had Nell really chosen these invitingly neutral shades for herself ... and what did that mean? Maybe she *had* been getting fed up of living Christmas every day, like Lukas had once suggested. Would she have reinvented the café downstairs too if she hadn't fallen ill? Nell had kept quiet about her illness as well. Perhaps there were some things Gretel would never know.

At least she and Lukas had already agreed on one thing. They wouldn't be redecorating the café downstairs, or the sign that promised *Festive Cheer All Through the Year*. Lukas had said there was no point in spending money if they were selling up, and Gretel couldn't imagine being able to bear that level of change. So at least some of her memories would be safe. For now.

Amber returned with Gretel's box of food. 'Here we go.' She placed it on the counter. 'You sort some cupboard space and I'll find your other kitchen boxes, if you like. Then it's surely time for hot drinks?'

'That's my only kitchen box,' said Gretel.

Amber inspected its contents and frowned. 'You live on doughnuts and Nutella?'

She shrugged. 'I don't mind carrot sticks or the odd strawberry fondue. I'm not a total child.'

'Obviously.' Amber giggled. 'Will you promise me you'll grab something vaguely nutritious and vegetable shaped from the local grocery store, and soonish? I love a chocolate spread as much as the next person, but I feel you need to vary your food groups.' She had her hands on her hips like a younger version of Nell, but she was being good-natured.

'We can't all dine on pan-seared whatevers with a quenelle of fancy mash, even on a boring Tuesday,' said Gretel. 'Like a certain pretentious chef.' Now she was giggling too.

'You're just repeating random phrases from *MasterChef*, aren't you?' Amber smiled as she grabbed cups and dumped spoonfuls of instant hot chocolate into them.

Gretel imagined that Lukas would have measured them with military precision and then sampled the liquid with his funny two-headed tasting spoon. But it was time she stopped imagining Lukas. She had plenty of new things to be getting on with and she surely wouldn't be needing him at all.

Two hot chocolates and a packet of doughnuts later, Gretel and Amber had hauled the last of the boxes from downstairs in the café up into Nell's old flat.

'I'll take this stuff in here,' said Gretel. She'd drawn the line at sleeping in Nell's old room and had instead chosen a spacious double. It was painted in fresh white with hints of grey and buttercream yellow, with a large vase of silk daisies on the dresser. It was yet another room that emanated serenity and gave her the feeling she'd have space to breathe, even if she hadn't known she needed it.

When she went back into the living area, Amber was coming through the flat door with another box of her stained-glass ornaments. Gretel put on some lamps now the day was darkening.

Amber placed the box on the floor. 'It will be so handy for you running the café and living up here. I think you've made a great choice.'

'Thanks. Although it's only temporary,' Gretel added quickly. 'Until we sell. But I needed a proper kitchen and this way I can focus on improving things in the café until then.' She bent down and rifled through her stained-glass ornament boxes, trying to calm her thoughts about her uncertain future. She plucked out a family of glass gingerbread people and began hooking them onto the tree, along with a few glass candy canes and stars.

'It has been spookily quiet since Christmas.' Amber nodded, cocking her head as she watched Gretel fiddle with the ancient tree lights.

Gretel knew most people probably took their tree down in January. But Gretel wasn't *most people*. She gave the fairy lights one last rejig before plugging them in and flicking the switch.

Popppppp. The two table lamps flashed off and threw the room into semi-darkness. Gretel winced. Her dodgy lights must have tripped the main switch, but it was absolutely not an omen.

A solitary glass star had fallen to the floor but somehow hadn't broken. When Amber bent down and passed it back to her she wasn't sure whether to laugh or cry.

'Not that I believe in signs,' said Amber cautiously. 'But maybe all of this is a message to try things differently?' She waved her arms around at the non-Christmassy flat, now infiltrated by the bedraggled exploding Christmas tree.

Gretel felt herself bristle at the mention of change. 'Keep Calm and Find the Fuse Box.' If it wasn't yet printed onto one of those motivational signs, it should be.

Though Gretel had to admit, she did need a plan. 'I know the café has been quiet, but I'll think of something.' She absolutely had to. Although she knew from experience that creative ideas didn't come when you summoned them.

Gretel went to put the stray ornament back onto the tree, then realising it reminded her of a silly Michelin star, hid it inside a box.

Amber squeezed her arm. 'Inspiration will come. And if it doesn't, we'll get out there and find it.'

Chapter 22

'Amber?'

Gretel was sure that was her – she was pretty distinctive with that flame-red hair and rebellious black lipstick. So why had she just darted around the other side of the aisle in the local grocer's as though she was hiding from her? Just as Gretel was trying to work out the correct etiquette when someone was unmistakably trying to dodge you in the world's smallest food shop, Amber reappeared as though they hadn't just eyeballed each other.

'Oh, hi, G!' Amber waved a casual hand. 'Fancy seeing you here.'

Had something about the girl changed since two moments ago? Gretel scanned her black and white skirt and shirt combo, which Amber always passed off as her work clothes, even though she changed the subject every time Gretel asked where she officially worked. Something was amiss.

'Just grabbing snacks.' Amber held up a fistful of Freddo chocolate bars. 'You?'

She seemed a little caught out, but Gretel knew how it felt when you didn't want to talk about something. She wouldn't butt her nose in.

'I need to grab some ingredients for my baking experiments. And you did warn me I needed to branch out and eat something that wasn't a doughnut.' She held up a bag of carrots and gave a shy grin.

Gretel had never been inside Gordon the Grocer's before, usually opting for the small shop near her old maisonette for her own shopping. Officially, she was meant to order stock and ingredients for the café from the big wholesale shop outside the village and save the receipts, but Lukas didn't need to know quite how much she was wasting.

Amber craned her neck to look at the ingredients in Gretel's basket. 'I'm not sure vegetables count as one of your five a day if you turn them into carrot and ginger cake.'

'I'm not!' Gretel protested. Although it wasn't the worst idea. 'The carrots are just for me, but I'm trying to bake lebkuchen biscuits, a bit like Nell used to make. Lukas tried to show me on Christmas Day, and then ...' She felt her cheeks redden.

'Oh yeah?' Amber raised her eyebrows in a way that Gretel absolutely did not appreciate.

This was why it was better not to have actual friends. They had a tendency to be nosey and go around grabbing wrong ends of sticks.

'You and that chef were doing some spicy baking?

128

From the colour of your cheeks, I'm picturing it like the touchy-gropey scene in that movie *Ghost*, but with dough instead of clay.'

'Haven't seen it,' Gretel lied, keen to put a stop to any more chat about groping. 'Anyway, it was the opposite of that. I burnt everything and he walked out in a strop.' Amber didn't need to know about the awkward bit where she almost planted a kiss on his face.

Gretel hurried to the counter and Amber followed.

'Zekia!' The jolly, rotund man behind the counter was greeting a lady who'd just walked in. 'How's it going?'

Gretel thought she'd seen the brightly dressed woman ambling up and down the street before, but like most people, Gretel didn't know her.

'Things are slow in the shop again,' the lady replied, grabbing some fruit and a large bag of plantain chips. 'Kingsley has sent me for supplies to keep his boredom at bay.'

The man behind the counter shrugged. 'That's the way it usually is outside of Christmas.'

Gretel tried to ignore the way Amber was trying to signal a *did you hear that?* at her with her eyebrows, as the grocer man was serving them.

When Gretel and Amber stepped out onto Green Tree Lane its cobbles were still wet from the rain they'd had that morning. The low January sun tried to dry the damp needles of the Christmas tree in the street's centre. As the people in the shop had been saying, it was deathly quiet. And by all accounts, it would probably continue.

Seeing the café so empty since Christmas had been

surprisingly frustrating, even though Gretel could have sworn she was a fan of peace and quiet. Maybe calm was lovely as a customer; but when you were paddling hard to keep things afloat, *quiet* was strangely terrifying. The money Nell had left to help get started was fast running out. At least if Gretel could get her head around this baking, she could stop spending a fortune on the upmarket gingerbread she'd taken to sneakily buying in, whilst she struggled to make a decent batch of anything. Not that there'd been anyone around to eat the stuff.

She also felt terrible that Amber kept coming in to help, yet there were rarely any customers to serve. No wonder she still wouldn't accept payment. Then there was the small matter that Amber wouldn't let her tell Lukas about her. She shook her head. Now wasn't the time to wallow in all the things she was getting wrong.

'So, you're still thinking up ideas to get more customers?' Amber asked, as they paced towards the tree as though it had an unspoken gravitational pull. 'Sounds like you're not the only one who needs them.'

Gretel sighed. It did sound worrying, although she could barely deal with her own issues right then. 'Yes, I'm still thinking. Although I haven't got any further than *bake better gingerbread*. Not exactly *Dragons' Den*, is it?'

'Hasn't Scary Lukas got any ideas? He's meant to be jointly responsible, isn't he?'

'If he ever showed up.' Since Christmas Day she'd seen more of planet Neptune than she had of Lukas. And she'd never seen that at all.

130

'Well, stuff him,' Amber concluded. 'We can come up with something creative.'

They reached the tree and Gretel tickled her fingers along one of the branches, like she'd done since she was young. It made her feel grounded to know it was the very same tree her mother had once loved and helped decorate each Christmas after they'd decided to settle here. At least some things were fine just as they were.

'I know you'll go off on one if I suggest trying anything outside of your comfort zone.' Amber waved her frog-faced chocolate wrapper at her. 'So what are you already good at? What are your strengths?'

Gretel scratched her head. 'Erm. Crafting? Making ornaments out of stained glass?'

'Yes! Those little glass penguins are actually pretty cute. I'd love to know how you do all that stuff. Maybe you could ... teach people? How about crafting sessions in the café to get people in? Sit and knit used to be all the rage. You could make it your own.'

'Like sit and solder?' Gretel imagined a group of locals cosying around over warm drinks and gingerbread, learning how to use a soldering iron to create their own sparkling stained-glass decorations. The vision was a lovely one, apart from all those *people*. Who was she to pretend she was good at being sociable or leading the flock? 'No, it wouldn't take off.' There were surely easier ways to fill the café than putting herself quite so *out there*.

Amber narrowed her eyes. 'Is this one of your *I'm not good with people* hang-ups?'

'No.' Gretel pouted. Damn, that girl was good.

'Because, newsflash, I'm nobody's first choice of bestie. I have pretty much no mates at … work.' Amber fiddled with her chocolate bar. 'Maybe you've got to trust that if you be yourself, you'll find your people. And the rest can just piss off.'

Did Gretel sense a certain bitterness in Amber's last sentence? But she couldn't help her burst of laughter. 'That's one way of looking at it. But I'm still not sure …'

'So let's ask people,' said Amber, decisively biting the head off a Freddo. 'Like market research or whatever. Who says business is just for grown-ups who watch *Dragons' Den*?' she mumbled through a mouthful of kids' confectionery. 'Here, let's speak to some shop owners and see what they reckon. They might even agree to put a flyer up for you if you get off your arse and make some.'

And with that, Amber marched towards a quirky little shop called Phoebe's Chakra Healing before Gretel had the chance to argue that she absolutely didn't want her bits and bobs healed.

Chapter 23

What exactly were chakras? And why did they smell so funny?

As Gretel and Amber piled into Phoebe's Chakra Healing, the first thing that hit Gretel was the aroma. It was a kind of smoky, spicy smell that was actually quite soothing. That was until Gretel hit her head on the windchime that was hanging near the door and the clattering made the shop lady jump out of her skin.

'Shit! I mean, *namaste*. Welcome, gorgeous souls.' The woman scrambled up from her cross-legged position on the floor and put the orange crystal she'd been cradling back onto a shelf. It reclaimed its spot with a collection of similarly orange crystals, on a wall that looked like a rainbow of gemstones arranged in colour order on their own special shelves. 'Sorry, I wasn't expecting anyone.'

'In a shop?' asked Amber.

'It's always so quiet.' Did the woman's smile look strained?

Maybe meditation wasn't so calming after all. 'I was clearing my chakras to attract abundance.' She took a deep breath and tried a more natural smile. 'And here you are! I had a feeling the universe would send you my way soon enough. Isn't that strange?' She gave Gretel an extra-long look which she didn't understand. 'I'm Phoebe. It's lovely to meet you.'

Phoebe must have been in her late twenties with long golden-brown hair that looked unkempt in a free-spirited way, floaty boho clothes and bare feet. A whole lot of crystal jewellery and bangles twisted themselves around her arms as though she needed to be anchored.

'You're clearing your *what*?' asked Amber, once the introductions were done. 'Seriously, I've got zero clue what a chakra even is, so give me the tea.'

Gretel knew this had nothing to do with getting a relaxing cuppa – Amber was ready for the lowdown. Phoebe guided her to a poster on the wall which showed a person in a cross-legged sitting-down pose that Phoebe called the lotus position. A rainbow of coloured dots was arranged along the figure's spine, from their red root up to their purple crown.

'These are the seven main energy centres in your subtle body,' Phoebe was explaining. 'Even though they're in a different realm to your physical body, each corresponds to a major bundle of nerves or organs inside you. It's important to keep them clear, balanced and spinning happily for your physical, emotional and spiritual wellbeing.'

Amber pulled a confused face. 'So chakras don't exist?'

'I don't think Amber has a *subtle body*,' Gretel muttered apologetically.

Phoebe pasted her smile back on and tried again. 'You know sometimes when you feel a bit crap and maybe you're not even sure why? Like something's just ... *off*?'

'Totally.' Amber nodded, hoicking up one of her over-the-knee socks.

'Then your chakras probably need a good MOT. They need harmony for energy to flow.' Phoebe looked at Amber with her eyes half closed as though trying to see something hidden. Then she moved Amber towards the display called Tumbled Stones, where smaller versions of the larger gems seemed to live. She pulled out a small, shiny, dark blue stone flecked with grey and pressed it into Amber's palm. 'Lapis lazuli. Carry it with you to help balance your over-active throat chakra, girlfriend, for the sake of yourself and all others. This one's on me.'

Gretel held her breath. Had Phoebe just called Amber a big mouth? But for the first time she could remember, Amber actually looked touched. She ran a gentle finger over the stone.

'For inner awareness and wisdom,' Amber read from the sign on the display.

'To keep your runaway mouth in check.' Phoebe smiled with a floaty innocence that was surprisingly endearing. 'You give *hashtag no filter* a whole different meaning.'

And she's met her match, thought Gretel, as Amber gave a firm nod in appreciation of Phoebe's honesty.

As Amber was *getting the tea* on her new lapis lazuli, Gretel took the opportunity to explore the shop. It was full of fascinating things she'd never heard of, from herby-smelling bundles of sage which you could burn to cleanse energy – whatever that meant – to Tibetan singing bowls which you could apparently use to make a ringing sound during meditation. If she'd been braver, she might have ventured inside before, but it always looked so mysterious from out on the street, and the thick net drapes stopped people from seeing the wonders within.

'Anyway, girls, this is cute,' Gretel heard Amber pipe up, with a clap of her hands. 'But we're here on business. My friend Gretel here is in charge of The Gingerbread Café, and she has a plan.'

Whilst Gretel was busy trying not to blush that Amber had just called her a *friend*, Amber explained to Phoebe about the proposed crafting sessions in the café. And before Gretel could stop her, Amber and her cheeky throat chakra were letting slip their worries about Francesca Whimple.

'She'll be gobbling up the café like a Christmas turkey and turning it into something soulless if we don't drum up some trade. Just saying.'

'I love the idea of stained-glass crafting sessions,' said Phoebe. 'Crafting is so mindful.'

'Though I guess you're already good at being zen,' Amber replied.

Phoebe's eyes flitted around the room as though keeping her mind in one place wasn't always that easy. Then she moved behind the counter and pulled out a black and gold business card, the initials FW gleaming on the front like a set of wonky gold teeth. 'Look, if I'm honest, Miss Whimple has been sniffing around here too. She offered me a fairly reasonable sum to buy the shop, and it's just so tempting when the place is eerily quiet.' She let out a tense puff of air. 'I've only been here a couple of years, but it's such a struggle. We only seem to get busy around Christmas. Even then, I've heard the village isn't thriving like it used to be. And can you believe this – not many people even want their chakras healed? Although goodness knows, most of them need it.'

Amber clapped Gretel on the back. 'G, it looks like your mission just got bigger.'

Gretel blinked. Mission? She wasn't even sure she wanted a mission. Teaching a café full of strangers when she wasn't even a mingler was a frightening enough thought. Had she even agreed to that bit? Was it too late to back out? 'I don't know anything about chakras!' she blurted, her palms starting to feel sweaty.

'Not chakras, you doughnut. Nobody knows what they are. No offence.' Amber gave Phoebe a quick apologetic grimace. 'Your mission to make this street good again to keep the golden Fuckwit out of town.'

'Woah, I'm still working out how to bake gingerbread. Please give me a break.' Gretel discreetly rubbed her hands down her corduroy pinafore dress. 'I've just never been the sort of person . . .' She knew she was rambling, but why was Phoebe giving her that spooky, eyes half closed stare she'd given Amber earlier on?

'Come on,' said Amber, pulling Gretel's arm. 'This just got interesting. We've got more market research to do and I want to know where else Francesca Whimple has been flaunting her flashy card. And if we want to round up more troops for your crafting sessions, we won't do it by hanging around here healing our chakras. Anyway, I bet once we get people through that café door and hooked on gingerbread and hot chocolate, they'll be flocking in all the time.'

'Did I mention I still burn everything?' Gretel mumbled as Amber dragged her towards the door.

Phoebe followed them, stopping off at her Tumbled Stones display and holding a hand over it as though waiting to be guided. Gretel couldn't help being somehow enchanted by her.

'Red jasper,' Phoebe shouted above the commotion, fixing Gretel with a knowing look. 'Keep it close to help heal your root chakra where those insecurities lie. Red is the colour of passion too.' She winked. What was all that about? 'And the third bonus? Warriors used to carry this stone for courage against the bad guys when they were heading into battle. Good luck!'

The stone looped through the air towards Gretel and she surprised herself that she actually managed to catch it. But passion? Battle? Gretel took a deep breath. These two had some crazy ideas.

'We'll keep you posted about the crafting.' Amber gave Phoebe a salute. 'Might even bring some flyers in, or something old school.'

'Lapis lazuli,' Phoebe reminded her. 'Keep it close!'

'Yeah, yeah. And Pheebs? What is that weird smell in here?'

Phoebe sighed, as though she didn't have enough crystals in the shop to sort out some people's throat chakras. She pointed to a little smoking pot on a shelf behind the counter. 'I'm burning some resin. It's frankincense.'

'Woo, now that's weird, isn't it? Because if Amber is like gold, and you're all about frankincense ... then I know exactly where we need to go to find our third wise woman. Let's complete our market research hat trick.'

Gretel had no idea what Amber was twittering on about, but she guessed she was about to find out.

Chapter 24

'Mystic Myrrh Flowers.' Amber pointed down Green Tree Lane at the next shop on her hitlist. 'If we've covered gold and frankincense' – she waved at herself and then back to Phoebe's fragrant chakra shop – 'it's surely a sign.'

Gretel shrugged. 'I've never been inside. Anyway, I'm sure we've done enough market research for one day.'

'Are you running scared again? If I'd let you, you'd go and hide away in your little festive grotto.'

'Not at all! It's just . . . '

'Yeah, yeah. You're *rubbish with people.* You'd rather hang around with your ferret and make no bother. Did you just witness how bad I am with people?' She gestured to Phoebe's shop again. 'And yet I just let my inner weird hang out and it went OK. Well, she gave me a funny blue stone and didn't want to charge me. No wonder business is crap for her, by the way. I'm no guru, but I'd guess that's not how to keep a shop alive.'

At least her honesty was refreshing. Although even if there was no particular magic to being a people person, it had always been so much easier not to be.

'I'm pretty sure my *inner weird* is off the scale compared to yours,' said Gretel.

'Nuh-uh. I don't have all the answers, but I still reckon we just have to find our people.' Amber pulled Gretel towards the flower shop.

Her people had a tendency to shuffle off and die on her – that was the problem. How she missed darling Nell. At least going through this excruciating embarrassment might help keep the café alive, and if she could just channel some of that wonderful way her mum and Nell had had with people …

'If you think you're odd, you'll be right at home here. I've heard this woman specialises in funeral flowers. And guess what? The gossip says dead people talk to her and tell her what foliage they want for their big send-off. Kooky, huh?'

It sounded tempting and terrifying all at once. 'No, I think I'll just …'

But Amber had linked her arm firmly through hers like two besties in a playground, and Gretel was almost intoxicated by the friendly closeness.

They reached the outside of Mystic Myrrh Flowers, which was distinctly lacking in flowers and strangely uninviting. The flaking paintwork and signage were black and dark purple and reminded Gretel of one of those funeral director places where you went to say goodbye to loved ones lying ghostly pale in cold, dark rooms. She shivered and pulled away, a wave of sadness rushing upwards in her throat.

Amber squeezed her arm with hers and guided her forwards. 'Gretel, I've got you. I won't let her weird you out. Anyway, we're here on non-funeral-related business, remember? Sometimes our mission is more important than the madness. And maybe this will do you good.'

Gretel swallowed her melancholy and lifted her chin, then inched her way through the door of the flower shop.

The woman working on an island in the middle of the shop looked up as the pair tinkled in. Her flower arranging fingers stilled and she blinked a few times from behind her retro green cat-eye glasses, as though not used to live customers. Gretel guessed the woman was in her early sixties, although she wore it well with her edgy purple bob and stylish black and white flowery shift dress. An expensive-looking purple shawl was draped around her slim, tanned shoulders and a dinky cup of clear tea sat to the side of her, a small white flower bobbing in the liquid. Thinking about it, Gretel had definitely seen this woman around, although like Gretel, she wasn't one to stop and chat. Gretel would never have linked her to this shop, from its dingy external facade.

The woman tilted her head to one side. 'Yes?' Although she seemed perfectly self-assured, she had a feline cautiousness to her which tied in with her soft purr of a voice.

Amber was already poking around the shop and Gretel watched her nervously, hoping she wasn't getting ready to deliver more truth bombs. This stranger was already exuding an unexplainable *something* that Gretel felt compelled towards.

'Awesome flowers,' Amber said, as she walked around.

Phew, that lapis-thingamy throat stone must be working its magic already. But Amber was right. The inside of the shop was so much lovelier than the outside would ever suggest. Gretel was rubbish with names of flowers, but there were even more colours rippling through the shop than Phoebe and her rainbow of crystals, and the smell was almost heavenly. If rose petals and honeysuckle decided to make gorgeous flower babies, they would absolutely smell like this.

'But we're not here for flowers,' Amber clarified.

'Yes, I know,' the lady said simply, as though she knew *all the things*. For some odd reason, Gretel didn't doubt it.

Amber flashed Gretel a wide-eyed look which said *I told you she was psychic*.

'People only come here for flowers of remembrance these days, and I'm one of the first to know if anyone's passed on.' The woman gave Gretel a slow apologetic nod.

'Because the dead people tell you?' Amber asked, with a genuine, puppy-like interest.

'Lapis lazuli,' Gretel barked into her hand, trying to make it sound like a sneeze. But it was too late. If the woman had fur, it would definitely be bristling.

She put down the white flower she'd been arranging into a wreath and looked over the rim of her glasses at Amber. 'What was it you said I could do for you?' Her glance moved to Gretel, as though imploring her to tame her badly behaved pup.

'Have you ever thought about crafting lessons?' Gretel blurted out, at approximately the same time as she heard Amber ask:

'Have you heard of Francesca Fuckwit Whimple?'

Gretel winced.

'Stupid swingy black hair, dumb trainers that don't even match her suit?' Amber continued, with the determination of a Labradoodle in search of a bone. She was even doing a hip-swingy-hair-swishy walk which was actually not a bad Whimple impression.

Much to Gretel's surprise, the flower lady pushed her glasses back up her nose and gave a faint smile. 'If I didn't recognise the name, I'd at least know that mincing walk. But unfortunately I *do* know the name.' She moved her wreath away and got up from her padded wooden stool, moving to a drawer in her flower-covered dresser. She pulled out Miss Whimple's black and gold calling card and placed it on the island between them. 'I think I need more jasmine tea.'

Within minutes the lady, who'd introduced herself as Eve, had moved her flower arrangement to safety and brought a pot of sweet-smelling tea and more dinky cups. The trio sat around the white marble-topped island and eyed each other.

Is this what *finding your people* felt like? Gretel wondered. She was enjoying this adventure round the shops much more than she'd ever thought possible.

'Why do you enquire about Miss Whimple?' Eve asked, her cautiousness returning.

Gretel took the less frightening route and explained they were mainly finding out whether locals would be interested in stained-glass crafting over hot drinks and treats at The Gingerbread Café. 'Not that anything's definite yet, but, you know . . . ' Gretel felt almost silly asking this talented woman to come and mess around turning bits of coloured glass into penguins. She seemed far too poised and glamorous to hang around with the likes of Gretel in a café themed like Santa's grotto.

'It sounds intriguing,' Eve replied, before letting her raised eyebrows move to Amber as though waiting for her to *spill the tea* on all things Whimple.

Gretel sighed; it seemed there was no avoiding it. At least she had her funny red battle stone from Phoebe.

'The real beef is that if Gretel doesn't get some customers through the door, the café will only be fit to sell to Franny Whimple's family, with their queue of Quickie Café-type tenants. Once she gets her hands on one shop, the rest are more likely to give up and sell.'

Eve nodded sagely and Amber ploughed on.

'We were just up the road talking to Phoebe from that chakra place. You know her?'

Eve stiffened slightly and shook her head. 'I don't tend to socialise around here. Too many ... *questions*.'

'Totally,' Amber agreed. 'Same in Lower Paddleton. That's why I chill around here where people don't know me and don't stick their noses in.' She tapped hers like she was the wisest of the three wise women. 'Phoebe mentioned the Whimple had been flashing her business card and offering to buy *her* shop too. So I'm guessing it's a thing.' Amber shrugged. 'I reckon Phoebe's tempted to sell because no one even knows what a chakra is, as if trade wasn't slow enough.'

Eve fiddled with her cup, swishing the liquid so the jasmine flower bobbed like a tiny boat in danger. 'Francesca

Whimple sniffing around Green Tree Lane like a fleabag on heat. Yes, it's a thing.' She gave a sad laugh. 'Although business is actually fine for me. Blooming, even. Most of my customers seek me out online. They've . . . heard things, and the novelty of what I offer has become extremely popular.' Her lips closed tightly like a purse, but Gretel could see them twitching. More words were dying to escape, if only she'd let them.

'So you don't want to sell up?' Amber asked.

Eve put her cup down, eyed them both, then exhaled a long breath. 'Actually, I do.'

'Oh. Why?' said Gretel. Was it OK to ask?

'Because sometimes, darling girl, we let ourselves get trapped in old habits that don't serve us, like clothes that no longer fit. And it's time to shed them and move on.'

As the words hung in the air, Gretel couldn't help wondering if they were meant for her too. But how could they be? Eve hardly knew her.

'How do you even know when it's time to shake off your clothes?' Amber pulled a confused face.

'When your soul doesn't feel good, nothing fits. It might be that something's missing or even that you need a total revamp.' Eve rearranged her shawl.

'Your outfit actually looks OK.' Amber nodded at Eve's dress like that was a winning compliment. 'So what's missing for you?'

Eve blinked a few times and then stood, tidying the empty crockery towards her. 'Oh, nothing much, dear girl. Maybe it's just time I took the money and got out of here.

Goodness knows, this street has become as lifeless as most of my customers. Maybe it's a job for a woman called Whimple.' She flashed another smile that didn't meet her eyes. 'I don't think my soul has got the energy for a revamp.'

The word *revamp* sounded ghoulishly frightening to Gretel too. And yet could anything be more terrifying than the alternative – a street where Miss Whimple and her fancy trainers reigned? Gretel had been hoping to make The Gingerbread Café great again *and* keep it just like it was – Christmassy all year round. If she changed things, it wouldn't be the same café she'd known and loved with her mum and Rosa, and it wouldn't be Nell's festive gingerbread sanctuary. Would she still feel close to them if she wiped out those memories?

Chapter 25

'So we're making stained-glass Christmas trees. In January?'

Trust Amber to say it how it was. It was Gretel's first stained-glass crafting session at The Gingerbread Café, and her insides were already wriggling with nerves. She wasn't used to having so many people around her, let alone being in charge of teaching them stuff. But if the café was going to survive, she had to give this her all. Having no customers was not an option.

'It's a festive-themed café and this is Green Tree Lane. I thought it would be perfect.' Gretel tried out the woman-in-control smile she'd been practising in the mirror, conscious she looked not unlike a coniferous tree herself in her green knitted dress with berry patterns. Surely someone would back her up? She looked at Phoebe from the chakra healing shop who was sitting next to Amber, but she was too busy munching hungrily on Gretel's gingerbread cake to notice.

'Mmm, now this is heavenly. Why did I never venture in here before? It's exactly what my chakras ordered.' Phoebe licked the crumbs from her lips and grabbed another slice, her crystal bracelets clinking in agreement. 'You'll have to give me the recipe.'

Gretel blinked. People really liked her cake? She'd given up trying to recreate Nell's old masterpieces and had instead dabbled in something simple of her own. Perhaps the cappuccino calm of the kitchen in Nell's old flat, free from the flashing demands of Christmas decor, *was* doing her good.

Her gaze bounced to Eve from the flower shop, who was sitting opposite Phoebe. She was busy rummaging in the box of coloured glass offcuts on their table, but she hadn't touched her cake yet.

Keep Calm and Get on With It, she could almost hear Nell and one of her retro signs warning. This was no time to start obsessing over cake.

'Anyway,' said Gretel. 'The triangle shapes for Christmas trees shouldn't be too fiddly for you to cut. At least we're not making holly!' She tried to sound upbeat, hoping it would mask the slight wobble in her voice. She could do this.

The haunted jukebox burst into the opening chimes of 'Do They Know It's Christmas?' and Gretel tried not to be put off by the surprise on some people's faces.

'I didn't realise the café stayed Christmassy all year long,' said a lady named Bea, who owned a shop down the road called Lavender & Honey. She was probably in her thirties and had seemed timid on arrival, but the cinnamon hot chocolate Gretel had spent all afternoon perfecting was clearly warming her up. Her keen eyes, which were a golden nectar colour like her neatly tied hair, were appraising the artificial Christmas tree that Gretel had dragged down from the flat and decorated with stained-glass ornaments. Who knew it would be so difficult to buy a real Christmas tree at this time of year? 'I can't remember the last time I came in here or even got close enough to read that bit on the sign that says *Festive Cheer All Through the Year*. You often overlook the places right on your doorstep, don't you?'

There was a rumble of agreement from the others.

Gretel had chosen a Sunday evening to run the crafting sessions, so at least the shop would be officially closed to other customers. She knew stained-glass crafting could be messy and noisy, what with breaking and filing glass, and using soldering irons to join the sections of glass together. In fact, if Lukas found out, he would probably have one of his grumps and veto the whole thing. But as he was still avoiding her since the Christmas nearly kiss, she hadn't bothered to update him about the classes. At least his absence had given her some freedom to find her way, even if she oddly missed his grumpy face. She'd even sneaked in a certain ferret, who was happily sleeping under Amber's table in Gretel's crochet bag.

But like quite a few of the shops on Green Tree Lane, The Gingerbread Café was closed on a Monday so she'd have plenty of time to clean up before the café opened again on Tuesday. Lukas was probably busy at The Rotten Carrot, and he'd stopped doing his annoying stroll-bys. She'd send him a message about the craft nights at some point. She just didn't want to be shot down before she'd even started.

'You're right there, girl,' an older lady called Zekia agreed from across the room. Gretel recognised her from that morning in the grocer's. Zekia wore eye-catching purple which complemented her richly dark complexion and ran a shop called Rum & Raisin with her husband Kingsley. 'We've been in the street for nearly a year and we still hardly know anyone. You're all so quiet!'

Jane and Jayne, a couple in their forties who ran a small art gallery and shop in the street, both nodded. 'Same here, although we've been here for years. It used to have more of a community feel,' one of them said. They both had lots of pretty piercings and wore paint-stained overalls, and with the similar names, Gretel wondered if she'd ever remember which was which.

As Gretel looked around the room she was honoured that so many people had turned up after her and Amber's flurry of leaflet dropping and accosting people in the street. Her first course was fully booked out by shop owners and residents of Mistleton and she could only hope they'd love the place enough to come back between classes and tell their friends too. It felt strange that they'd been sharing the same piece of world for so long, yet Gretel hadn't known most of their names until tonight. That was the price of resolutely keeping people at bay. Even selling her crafts had been an online, arm's length affair. She had a lot to get used to.

'I know most people.' Gordon the Grocer shrugged. He was the man who'd served her and Amber in the shop the other day. 'Your Nell was a lovely lady.' There were a few sad *mmms* from around the room. Gordon leaned back in

151

his chair and rested his hands on his belly like a pregnant lady. He was still wearing his dark blue shop-owner money belt, although it appeared to be empty. 'But admittedly, the street has let itself go in recent years, and we all seem to have retreated behind our closed doors to have a quiet sulk about it. I don't even bother to put any fruit and veg out the front any more. Easy to let things slip.'

'We don't do much sulking,' Zekia replied. 'But our place never gets a whole lot of customers. My Kingsley's homemade rum used to go down a treat when we lived in Peckham, and you should have seen my rum and raisin fudge and chocolates flying off the shelves. But here? The only time we've been busy was Christmas.'

'The street used to be buzzing all year round,' Eve said, having arranged a selection of glass offcuts into a flower shape on the table in front of her. 'Although nowadays you might be better off selling some of your goods online. Footfall isn't what it used to be.'

Phoebe nodded. 'I do some live crystal sales on Instagram to try and make ends meet, but still. It shouldn't be that way. I invested in my own shop because I want to see real people. To feel their energy, their vibrations. I want to make a difference.' She pulled another slice of cake onto her plate. Was that her third? Her chakras really must be out of sorts.

'Told you your mission was bigger than just breathing life into one little café,' Amber called across to Gretel as she was handing out safety equipment. She noticed Amber was wearing a short black and red tartan dress tonight instead of her usual black skirt and white shirt combo, and the extra colour suited her. 'Should we ask them for their take on FW?'

Gretel plonked a pair of safety specs and a dust mask down on the table in front of Amber and hoped it would soon be time for her to wear the latter. At least she hadn't shouted out her usual swear word nickname for Miss Whimple in front of all these nice new potential customers. Although Gretel had to admit the nagging worry that a collection of business owners whose own businesses weren't thriving probably wouldn't be dropping by to spend a fortune on gingerbread between classes. And if the shops in the street weren't busy, the café would surely suffer from a lack of shoppers stopping by to refuel on tasty treats. Maybe focusing only on the café's problems would be like trying to patch up a serious fracture with one of those cheap, not very sticky plasters. Gretel exhaled. For now, the mission of getting through tonight as a non-people person in charge of a rabble felt quite overwhelming enough.

Chapter 26

As the evening of Gretel's first stained-glass crafting session progressed, she noticed how difficult it was to keep everyone on track.

Trying to disguise her trembling hands, she'd set up her demonstration table at the front of the café so she could show them how to create their first Christmas tree. It had been unnerving having all those eyes on her, but somehow she'd managed to talk them through making the templates for each section of the tree and tracing around them onto glass, just like she'd rehearsed. She'd shown them how to score and break the glass and how to file it smooth. She'd even been brave enough to nip from table to table, helping them with the tricky process of wrapping their pieces with copper foil tape and soldering them together. Her heart had soared; she'd been proud of herself.

What she hadn't accounted for was that she was dealing with creatives. Gretel had hoped to see a room full of shiny green, uniform trees by the end of the session, but what she was faced with was a mish-mash of colours and shapes, most of which looked nothing like any sort of tree.

After her final inspection, Gretel walked to the front and put her hands on her hips, because taking up extra space would surely make her look more authoritative. It worked for Lukas – not that she was thinking about him.

'Ahem.' Gretel looked around the room, waiting patiently for the class to notice her. Should she have done that more loudly? Or was clapping better? She tapped on her demonstration table and winced as she saw Angel Gabriel's head poke out of her bag. To her relief, he sleepily popped it back in. He belonged upstairs, but it felt mean to leave him on his own all evening.

At last the class took the hint and looked at her.

'So. Who has a lovely green Christmas tree to show me?' Gretel asked.

A couple of the residents waved their hands and she nodded at them, thankful that at least some folk were listening to her around here.

'I made a rainbow of colours to represent the chakras,' Phoebe confessed. 'Too much green was making me feel unbalanced.'

'I think I'd be unbalanced if I was on my fourth slice of cake,' said Amber. 'I don't know where you put it.'

'I made a stem of eucalyptus,' Eve cut in. 'It just doesn't feel like Christmas in January, once my decorations have come down. I did use green, though.' The florist looked at Gretel apologetically through her cat-eye glasses, and as

Gretel noticed how similar her creation looked to the silk stems in Nell's flat, she made a mental note to ask her if she'd helped Nell choose them.

'I made a tree, but I chose a pretty lavender colour,' said Bea. 'I hope that's OK.' She looked a little sheepish. 'It almost matches Eve's hair.'

'It is beautiful,' Gretel admitted. As much as she wanted to tell her class off for not following the brief, she was impressed by their creations, even if most of them were a little wonky and there was an awful lot of broken glass. 'And do you know something? I'm starting to realise that sometimes you've got to do things your own way. Once you've worked out what on earth that is.' She looked around the café, with its holly wreaths in the window and the plastic Christmas tree she'd tried to decorate to look like Nell's. It all looked wonderful, but the consensus tonight had been that Christmas all year didn't work for most people. And if she was brutally honest, her own Christmas-obsessed life had been far from jolly for a while.

As though someone somewhere was agreeing with her, the sound of a guitar twanged through the silence. The jukebox had broken into the jittering intro of 'Time Warp', sending a wave of goosebumps across Gretel's pale skin. She rushed across and pressed the override button before Amber could burst into a spooky rendition. Since when did that interfering machine contain any tunes that weren't Christmassy? Maybe Lukas was right about the wiring.

'So next week can we design and make something of our own choosing?' asked one of the Jane and Jayne duo, bringing Gretel back to the present. 'Because my creativity feels stifled when I'm working to someone else's template. You know?'

'We'll see,' Gretel replied. They had a point, but all this changing of plans was disconcerting. She'd mapped things out meticulously in the hope it would feel less frightening that way. People couldn't just start going off script.

Amber had stood to clear a few things away and reheat the hot chocolate pan, although Gretel suspected from her curious jumping and hip shaking that she was demonstrating that dance from 'Time Warp', in case Gretel wasn't taking the hint. A few of the others got up to help pack away and shimmy along too, even though they only had Amber's loud humming to accompany them now Gretel had halted the jukebox. What would be next with this lot – 'Do the Conga'? But once again, as much as Gretel wanted to feel cross with them, she couldn't help smiling. She felt warmed by their bustling, the laughter and the sense of warmth and community that had been bubbling around the room all evening. Was she silly to have cut herself off from real life for so long?

Bea shimmied over to her and squeezed her arm. 'You've done a great thing this evening in bringing us all together. I sensed it wasn't easy for you, but it's what's been lacking around here for far too long. People are like bees – we need community, even if we don't always know it. Maybe this will be the start of us trying to communicate properly. Who knows what else will come of it if we keep putting our heads together? We're a creative bunch.'

'Maybe you could teach us how to bake too? You're the

master at gingerbread cake,' said Phoebe as she wiggled past with her empty plate.

'Oh yes, girl. I second that,' Zekia piped up. 'Tell us your secret.'

There was a chorus of agreement from around the room and everyone turned to look at Gretel, their awed faces sending a wave of pride straight through her.

'Your baking is divine,' Eve agreed. 'Nell would have been impressed.'

So she had known Nell, Gretel briefly registered, as her cheeks flushed. She was over the moon that she'd baked something of her very own that people were actually enjoying. It was spurring her on to want to try more. In this nurturing, creative bubble, it felt safe to admit a few things. Perhaps this community could help her. If she wanted to succeed in this café, maybe she did need to let people come ashore on her one-woman island.

'Can I share something?' Gretel asked, tentatively. 'Tonight's gingerbread cake is the only thing I've managed to make without burning or making a total mess of.' She was still sneakily buying in most things, and she knew it wasn't cost-effective.

'So you're getting somewhere,' said Zekia, her voice always so warm and reassuring.

'But I'd like to bake more,' Gretel continued. 'I mean, if I don't create and sell from the heart, I may as well let a chain take over. I might not get to keep this café for much longer, but while I get the chance I'm determined to give it a personal touch. I always felt so at home here and I want others to feel that too. That would be the perfect tribute to Nell. Creating a cosy, cherished space was what Nell was all about.' Gretel scratched her head. 'And yet trying to copy everything Nell used to do hasn't worked for me. Tonight's success is surely proof that I need to keep branching out in my own direction to stand a chance.'

'At last, she's ready to do it her own way!' said Amber, triumphantly, still bopping around like she was in *The Rocky Horror Show*, giving Gretel a life-sized, wiggling reminder to break free from her time warp.

Gretel found herself nodding. 'I think.'

'So what is your way?' Phoebe asked. 'Because the universe is absolutely telling me I need more gingerbread in my life. Don't go depriving me now.'

'Oh, there will be gingerbread,' Gretel reassured her. 'It will always be The Gingerbread Café. At least, while it's in my care.' She gave a sad smile. 'But I seriously struggled to recreate Nell's old recipes and I've all but burnt her kitchen down trying. It's surely a sign, but I'm so confused about what I should bake to make it my own.'

'Signs are definitely a thing,' Phoebe nodded, finding her plate a home in the dishwasher behind the counter and topping up her hot chocolate. Was that a sign she felt at home here already? Gretel hoped so.

Gordon the Grocer was holding his rebellious stained-glass apple in front of his face and peering at Gretel through it, his cheeks looking even redder than usual. 'Isn't it obvious?' he asked. 'Not that I know a lot about biscuits with my fine figure,' he chuckled. 'I'm the poster boy for living a

159

healthy, fruit and veg-fuelled existence.' He gave her a rosy wink. 'But what about trying those gingerbread biscuits with the coloured candy windows in the middle? You know, the ones that look kind of glassy.'

'Stained-glass ginger biscuits.' Amber nodded, like she was a girl who knew *everything*. If she did, it had taken her long enough to mention. 'Yeah, that would be totally you, G. If you just pretend you're crafting a piece of art, rather than baking ...'

Gretel winced as she remembered Lukas's Christmas Day lecture about treating cooking as a science before you got all artistic. But his advice hadn't got her far enough.

'Talking of community, I could bring you some fresh lavender. You could try baking it into a gingerbread recipe. I'm sure the flavours would work,' said Bea.

'We've got plenty of rum if you're brave enough!' Zekia's laugh bounced around the café.

'I reckon you should go seasonal,' said Gordon. 'Always works in the world of fresh fruit and veg. Come and see me for your spring rhubarb, summer berries, your autumn pumpkins ...'

'You had me at rhubarb,' said Phoebe, sprinkling extra marshmallows onto her hot chocolate. 'Very cleansing, and great for your root chakra.' She pointed at Gretel. 'Goes perfectly with cinnamon and ginger if you're wondering.'

'Sounds like you're already placing your orders,' Gretel joked, as she joined in with cleaning the tables, trying her best not to emulate any of Amber's dance moves. This lot were already kicking up enough glassy dust with their antics. Thank goodness she had tomorrow to do a deep clean.

'Why might you not get to keep the café for much longer?' one of the residents asked.

As Gretel explained that her co-owner may want to sell after the legal bits were sorted, Amber nudged her, hissing at her to quiz the other shop owners about Whimple & Sons. At least Amber had had the good grace to keep her naughty throat chakra under control and not bark out her thoughts. But Amber was right. The room felt like a snug space to discuss things, and everyone here seemed to care about the future of Green Tree Lane, even if nobody knew how to fix it yet.

'That Miss Whimple and her family will be the death of us all,' said Eve, through tight lips, once Gretel had told the others the woman had been pushing to buy the café and after the other shop owners had admitted they'd had the same insistent visits. It seemed they all knew how the Whimple family's interference had ruined the cosy feel of the neighbouring village and how its main shopping street had become a soulless home of ugly franchises once they'd bought up most of the buildings. It looked like the family had put Miss Whimple in charge of doing the same in Mistleton.

'It's a good job you can get chatty with the afterlife,' said Amber.

Eve blinked a few times, then turned away. Gretel noticed Phoebe narrowing her eyes in that curious way she'd seen her do before, as though trying to focus on something that wasn't plainly visible.

'So how can we improve Green Tree Lane so nobody needs to give up hope and sell to her?' asked Zekia, not one to skate around the issues. 'Because I'm working on a rum and raisin ice cream that will blow your socks off. I don't want our adventures in the Cotswolds to end before they've begun.'

'Francesca Whimple can get stuffed,' said Jane and Jayne in unison, one of them banging on the table and sending glass dust flying, the other gasping and trying to catch it with a cloth.

'Oh, you two are trouble,' said Zekia, doubling over with laughter and using an unsuspecting Gordon to help her balance.

The extra commotion signalled the end of Angel Gabriel's napping and he wriggled out of his bag, darting towards the closest patch of cake crumbs.

Ding diiiiiing. And Lukas Knight had to choose that moment to do one of his post-work stroll-bys, when she hadn't seen the guy since Christmas. Couldn't he even read a *closed* sign?

As he stood in the open doorway in his chef's whites with a backpack over one shoulder, the bell still ringing over his head and his eyebrows raised, Gretel wished the ground would open up and swallow her. With a ferret on the loose and the café full of dangerous-looking tools and glass dust, she was sure she was in for the lecture of her life about food hygiene and other boring rules.

Luckily, her crafting students seemed to sense the swift mood change and began grabbing coats and making excuses. Well, he knew how to clear a room.

But did he almost look a little sheepish as he moved out of the doorway to let the masses leave?

'Thank you for tonight – it's been exactly what I needed. See you next week.' Bea expelled a puff of air as though a weight was beginning to lift, and stepped out into the night, the others giving a quick wave and barrelling out behind her, the joy of the evening still buzzing around them.

Gretel noticed Amber taking extra care to stay in the middle of the ruckus, presumably not wanting to be seen by the man she called *scary*.

'Next week?' Lukas muttered to himself.

Gretel gulped. She knew none of this looked good. So why was it that every time he blew in like a cold wind, she still felt so inexplicably hot?

'We need to talk,' he said, closing the door to the rest of the world behind him.

Chapter 27

'Nice backpack.' Gretel signalled to the bag Lukas still had slung over one shoulder as he stood just inside the doorway of the café. It was the first time she'd seen him since the Christmas nearly kiss and she had no idea what else she was meant to say. The awkwardness sizzled between them.

Lukas nodded, as though acknowledging that in their tricky situation, it was as good a place to start as any.

'So are you going to tell me what this mess is about? Please say you sorted out extra insurance to cover this.' His eyes moved around the room, the café tables still bearing witness to an evening of broken glass and semi-dangerous tools.

'I'll look into it,' Gretel muttered as she scanned the floor for Angel Gabriel.

'It's just easier if we don't have customers suing us for slicing off their fingers with a cutting tool. That's if Environmental Health don't shut us down first.'

Gretel could tell Lukas was scanning the floor for her ferret as he rubbed his temples and exhaled. For all his lecturing, he didn't have his usual fight. He seemed different. Deflated, almost.

'Are you OK?' she couldn't help asking.

'Rough shift at the restaurant. Some days the place gives me a headache.' He rolled his shoulders. 'I left early.'

'Oh.' That didn't sound like him at all.

'And . . . things have been playing on my mind. I behaved badly on Christmas Day. I'm sorry. That time of year is never easy for me, but . . . ' He was rubbing his head again, as though it might get his thoughts in order. 'That's no excuse,' he concluded, simply.

Gretel felt some of the pressure lifting. She sensed there was more to be said, but it was kinder to wait until he was ready. As though he had no time for getting serious either, Angel Gabriel popped his head up from behind the counter and made his adorable squeaky toy noise – meaning it was play time. Gretel winced. She may have got away with him sleeping unobtrusively in a bag, but a ferret behind the counter was pushing it. She dared a look towards Lukas, but his face was surprisingly soft.

'I should knit him a candy-striped apron so he can serve coffee,' he said. And then registering the look of surprise on her face, added quietly, 'Nell taught me to knit.'

So he *did* have a soft side. Imagining him trying to master a pair of knitting needles amid a sea of colourful wool, she couldn't help but smile.

Though it wasn't time to discuss knitting patterns. Gretel

165

moved to the rear of the counter and picked up her delinquent ferret. 'I know this looks bad.' She nodded towards the various piles of tools and glass dust that the class had been in the middle of tidying before Lukas interrupted. 'But it was a really enlightening evening. It was surprisingly good to meet some of the other shop owners and I feel inspired to attempt a few different things.' She held her chin up, determined to try and stay brave. If she was braver still, she might suggest he had a go at some stained-glass crafting to ease his tension. No. She shook her head.

'New things? I'm intrigued,' said Lukas, nudging his bag under a table with his funny chef-clogged foot. He crossed the café and joined Gretel behind the counter, searching for a cloth. Gretel felt her skin tingle as his shoulder brushed against hers, but before she could settle into the fizzy sensation he was off around the café with his cloth and spray.

'Please don't tidy away my demonstration table,' she warned. 'Those are my special tools.' She didn't need to tell him she might need the comfort of quietly creating something later, after her first daunting experience of running a class. She would clean up her mess.

He considered it for a moment and then shrugged, as though he understood the importance of some things being sacred.

She watched as he cleared and cleaned each table with military precision, as if he found the restoration of cleanliness and order cathartic. There was something mesmerising about the efficient way he moved, not to mention how endearing it was to see him mucking in. When he froze mid-wipe to look up at her with those magnetic grey eyes, Gretel's heart skipped a beat. Well, that would be the embarrassment of being caught gawping. She cleared her throat and busied herself fussing with Angel Gabriel, who did look particularly cute in his sprout Christmas jumper.

'So are you going to tell me?' Lukas asked.

Oops. What had he been saying before all the staring? 'Erm.' She must rein in her unruly thoughts. Even if they'd once almost kissed, he'd pulled away and walked out on her, and he still hadn't properly explained himself. And he hated everything she lived for. He'd ruined her Christmas Day. And yet . . .

'Gretel?'

She dared to look up from her lengthy inspection of her ferret's sprout jumper to see Lukas's quizzical face. She shook her head. 'Sorry. I mean . . . I'm just surprised at you helping out, that's all. I know you're a fancy head chef or whatever.' Her oddly bouncing heart suggested that wasn't all, but he didn't need to know everything.

'A head chef doesn't just float around the kitchen tasting things with a shiny spoon.' He pulled his double-headed spoon from his back pocket and waved it. 'We have to work our way up the ranks. And even when you get to be in charge, the buck stops with you for a whole lot of things. Staffing, supplies, costings. Quality, safety, regulations. Complaints.' He clunked the spoon down on the table in front of him and rubbed his temples again. 'And that's before you've pulled some creatively spectacular menu out of your magical arse, and made sure the whole damned restaurant is running like clockwork in the vain hope of securing a Michelin star. It's no wonder a guy gets a headache.'

Gretel blinked in surprise. 'Oh.' So that's what was eating him. That and turning up to find the café he didn't even want was causing him an entire list of extra troubles. 'Hot chocolate?'

Lukas sank down into a chair and exhaled. 'I'm sorry. I actually stopped by to apologise, but seeing the place happy and bustling caught me off guard. Now I've done nothing but moan. I'm getting this all wrong, huh?'

Gretel placed Angel Gabriel tentatively down on a chair next to Lukas, willing them to make friends whilst she went to grab drinks. When she joined him at one of the wooden café tables she brought a freshly lit candle, remembering the cosy flicker always cheered her up. She waited for him to speak.

'About Christmas Day,' he finally said, as he poked around at the marshmallows on his hot chocolate in a way that was strangely endearing. 'I shouldn't have ruined a nice moment by getting arsey with you about being late for my shift. And I absolutely shouldn't have bolted and avoided you for most of January. It was dickish of me.' His gaze drifted up to meet hers. 'Which you may think is my standard behaviour. But it wasn't always.'

'So why?' she asked. She was glad to have marshmallows to distract herself with too.

'If I'm honest, I was enjoying myself way more than I was ready for. It spooked me. Especially at Christmastime.'

'What bothers you so much about Christmas?' she asked softly.

'None of this excuses my behaviour. You deserved better. But ... a few things.' His forehead furrowed as though he wasn't sure where to start. 'The most recent being my ex-wife, Mirabelle. She walked out on me three Christmases ago. Didn't I say Christmas was like a pressure cooker?' He let out a small laugh that didn't sound jolly. 'But my distaste for the festive season was already deeply scratched in before my wife opted to trade me in for the accomplished *Eduardo*. If only life was that simple.'

Gretel leaned across the table and squeezed his arm, before feeling self-conscious and pulling it back. She cleared her throat. '*Eduardo*. Why did you say his name like that?'

'Because really it's Edward Pickering, but when you own three high-end restaurants, *Eduardo Picante* apparently sounds better.'

They looked at each other and laughed.

'Does his fake name suit him?' she giggled, thankful for the lightened mood. 'Does he look like an *Eduardo*?' She pulled her fingers outwards from her lips in a pinching motion, like she was tracing the shape of a long, waxy moustache. 'A true *Eduardo* should surely sport dramatically twiddly facial hair?'

'He looks more like a Homer Simpson than anything – he has a chef's gut and approximately three strands of hair. But it seems my ex-wife opted for deep pockets in the end. I should have listened to Auntie Nell on that one.' He gave an apologetic look to the sky.

'Well, I hope none of his restaurants have a Michelin star,' said Gretel.

'Actually, one does. Which is a joke, really. Even you deserve a Michelin star more than that guy. Cooking comes from the heart, so surely it helps if you have one. In fact, so many things lately are making me wonder if all of that really means anything. It's just all so ... argh, I don't know.' He took a long gulp of hot chocolate.

'Wow, do you want to talk about it? Because I thought running a restaurant and getting one of those shiny Michelin stars was your dream?'

Chapter 28

'Getting a Michelin star was my dream. I mean, it is.' Lukas sighed and turned to ruffle Angel Gabriel's fur. The ferret squeaked happily and jumped from his own chair at the café table onto Lukas's lap. 'So many of my old gang from culinary school are smashing it. Marcus Spooning's restaurant has just been awarded its second star, lucky bugger. But . . . oh, I don't know. Do you ever feel like you're trying to fit into someone else's shoes and no matter how hard you try, they just won't fit?'

Gretel raised her eyebrows as she craned her head in the direction of Lukas's strange rubber chef's clogs.

'Very funny. They're extremely practical in the kitchen if you prefer not to slip over and face plant the floor. You should get a pair.'

'Didn't you just say trying to squeeze yourself into the wrong shoes was a bad thing?' She gave him a small smile. 'And yes, I'm beginning to see that no matter how lovely someone else's shoes are, we need to navigate the path in our own.' She looked around them at the café which had always filled her heart with joy. 'I'm never going to be Nell, but that doesn't mean I can't find success in my own small way. Whose shoes are you struggling to fit into?'

He expelled a slow stream of air. 'Long story.' Then suddenly he stood, taking care to cradle Angel Gabriel safely against him as he moved across the café. After a slight hesitation which Gretel guessed came from his obsessive desire for cleanliness, he deposited the ferret gently down on one of the blankets which was scrunched up in the lap of an armchair.

'I'll clean it,' Gretel reassured him.

She was surprised to see Lukas grab a basket of spare glass crafting tools and make his way to her demonstration table. She'd wanted to suggest he try it, but she'd feared he would brush her off.

'Can I?' he asked. When she nodded, he put the tools down, his brow furrowing for a moment as he took in the set-up on the table. 'So I ... decide on a design and draw a template?'

'Mmm hmm.' She couldn't help feeling pleased at the uncertainty in his voice.

'As though I was making a template to cut pastry.' He seemed to be giving himself a pep talk now.

'That's right.' She stayed where she was as he sketched, not wanting to interrupt his flow.

'Your question about trying to fit into the wrong shoes,' Lukas continued, almost absent-mindedly. 'A dad who never achieved his culinary dreams and made everyone's life a misery because of it probably didn't set me on the right path.' He rubbed his forehead. 'Now I'm confused about the direction of my own career too. At La Carotte Rôtie I feel like my creativity is stifled. The owner wants things a certain way and maybe that doesn't feel right for me any more. I'm making food that ties in with their name and ethos, rather than my own. And now I'm not wining and dining in pretentious circles with a certain ex-wife's unrealistic expectations weighing down on me, maybe I'm mellowing.'

Wow, she'd been seeing the mellow version? Yet his story sounded difficult.

'Anyway, enough of that.' He seemed to remember himself. 'What next, teacher?' He held up his simple sketch.

Gretel blinked. 'Is it The Gingerbread Café?'

He nodded, like he hadn't been expecting it either. 'This place.' His gaze landed on her for a few beats longer than usual. She felt a rush of heat. 'It's reminding me that Nell and this café were why my love for baking began. It was Nell and her gingerbread recipes that ignited that fire in me. Baking with her was so rustic, so homely.'

Summoning the inner tutor who'd made her first nervous appearance that evening, Gretel moved to his side. Such lovely words. He deserved her help. 'Next, you choose your glass.' It felt strange, telling him what to do. Yet sensing his uncertainty re-emerge as he peered into the box of offcuts, something inside her rose up, rallying to support him. She felt her shoulders straighten. 'Don't feel jittery. The glass will sense your fear.' Had she just given him a cheeky wink? Well, now she was blushing.

He smiled and picked carefully through the box before

pulling out his first piece. She instinctively guided his hands to hold the coppery brown glass up to the light.

'It's beautiful,' she agreed. 'But watch out for those air bubbles. You don't want too much weakness.' She pointed to a stronger part of the glass and he took her direction.

She watched as he drew around his templates onto his chosen fragments of glass, looking up at intervals for her encouragement. She enjoyed his sharp intake of breath as she showed him how to score the glass, the high-pitched scrape of the shard weakening beneath his hands unnerving him.

'Just wait until you have to break it,' she teased, before passing him her running pliers.

His creased forehead softened as he caught sight of her favourite tool. 'You stuck googly eyes on. Really?!'

'Hey, don't knock it. It makes life easier. Nobody wants to use upside-down pliers.'

He let out a laugh. 'I'm surprised you haven't knitted them a reindeer jumper. Well, you're a natural at putting people at ease. I can see why that lot took to you tonight.'

He could? And had they?

Their hands touched as she showed him where to position the pliers to break the glass, a gentle shock running through her.

It was time to deflect some heat. 'Erm. So why did you stop baking gingerbread?'

'You can imagine what my father, the cordon bleu chef, thought of me icing *girlie gingerbread biscuits*.' He sighed. 'When I went to culinary school the snobbery was much the same. So I changed direction.'

'And now you cook rotten carrots for a restaurant owner who sounds about as fun as your dad?' she asked gently, as she helped him to squeeze the pliers. The glass cracked. The break was perfect, and she sensed Lukas's shoulders untightening.

'Trust me, my boss could never be that bad. And I have been trying to move things in a more unique direction. The owner appreciates that if we want to be noticed for a Michelin star, we've got to stand out.' He inspected the break and nodded, preparing to try the next edge on his own. 'My boss does respect my need to do some things my own way. The flavours I've been working with in the restaurant are like a French Moroccan fusion, so I'm playing with those warm spices like ginger, cinnamon and nutmeg that were the heart of everything for me. Because what is food without warmth? Or a restaurant, for that matter.'

'You feel like La Carotte Rôtie is lacking warmth?'

He continued to break glass, with her careful direction. 'There's nothing unusually cold about it for a place with that sort of price tag. A high-end restaurant brings in more affluent diners with big expectations, and sometimes a surprisingly low standard of manners. The owner is all about crisp white tablecloths and serious sommeliers. But surely good food is about connection? It should be shared around a table with warmth and love.' He inspected his final shapes as though he knew they needed something more. Was he debating his next words? 'La Carotte Rôtie is lacking in soul and I'm partly responsible.' His voice was lower now, like his gaze. 'I bark out orders like a man on the edge, then go home to scoff my sad Pot Noodle for one. The head chef is the centre of everything. If the centre is cold and uninspired ... what hope is there?'

He turned to her, his eyes the greyest she'd ever seen them. Keen to reach out but unsure what to say, she passed him her filing stone.

'But you ... ' He moved his hand to take the tool. Another brush of fingers. Another jolt. 'It seems you did an outstanding job tonight. Mess aside.' He gave her a fleeting smile. 'From what I saw, you created more laughter and community in one night than I've managed in five years at La Carotte Rôtie. You stood up there bravely and showed people your heart. Nell would have been proud of you. I guess I am too.'

She pinched her lips together and gave a quick nod, turning away so he couldn't see the tears forming in her eyes. When had she last heard somebody say that? Maybe she'd spent too many years blending into the furniture.

Under the spell of this strange, out-of-hours truce, they worked together to finish Lukas's piece. Gretel felt her confidence build with every new skill she helped him explore, from the buzz of the glass grinder, to the smoothing of copper foil around the edges of glass, to the heat of the soldering iron. It was touching to see him off balance and looking to her for support. It had been a role reversal she absolutely wasn't expecting.

When Lukas finished polishing his piece, he held it up to the light, mirroring where he'd started earlier that evening. Gretel felt herself leaning in. When he turned his face towards hers, their noses brushed. They blinked, their faces still almost touching, before they both slowly pulled away. Gretel didn't know what Lukas was thinking, but she was sure she recognised a flicker of regret at moving backwards. But for her it was too soon to risk another rejection.

She cleared her throat and turned her attention back to his glass creation. 'You've done an impressive job.'

He shrugged. 'It was mainly you.' He looked around the café. 'Like a lot of things. You should have more faith in yourself.'

She now wished she'd had enough faith to kiss him. Would there be another chance?

'Why did you choose those colours?' she asked, keen to understand him more. The real Gingerbread Café was a honey-coloured Cotswold stone, the paintwork all reds and greens. Lukas's version was in shades of copper, ginger and brown, like a gingerbread house. Though she was sure she was scared of looking at things differently, it worked.

'I don't know. Maybe the current look is too festive. Or maybe I see it evolving, somehow?' He shook his head. 'Not that we'll be here to . . . ' He stopped himself.

She was glad he'd left it there. Just for tonight.

As the twinkle of Gretel's battered plastic Christmas tree caught her eye, it was as though a light had just been switched on in her mind. The poor tree had been around the block, up the stairs and down again; and it showed.

'Could I . . . ask you for your help with something?' The question was out before she'd had the chance to think about it. Yet somehow she knew it was the next step, and she was eager for him to stay a little longer.

Chapter 29

It didn't take as long as Gretel thought to take the Christmas decorations down. Suddenly, on that intimate evening, it had felt like the right thing to do. After all, she'd just managed to stand up in front of a whole room of strangers and share her precious craft with them, when a few weeks before she would have ducked to avoid a hello. She'd even managed to work with Lukas to create his own stained-glass piece, when she would previously have sworn he was the most difficult man on the planet.

In fact, she'd go as far as to say she'd enjoyed her evening, with her rebellious class and their talks of embracing every season. And perhaps Lukas's re-creation of The Gingerbread Café, without its usual festive colour scheme, had been the final sign that it wouldn't hurt to try.

So with a heart full of courage from conquering the near-impossible, there had felt like no better time to take the next daunting step. And just like pulling off a plaster, once she'd decided, she knew it was better to get on with it. Sometimes having a Christmas heckler on hand was a useful thing. Or maybe there was just something about Lukas that made Gretel look at things differently.

'There are spare boxes and old papers in the storeroom,' Lukas said, as though packing away Christmas was the easiest thing in the world.

'I'll grab some tissue paper for the delicate bits,' Gretel added, like they were simply making a list. One item at a time. One foot in front of the other. People did this every year.

'Talking of tissues,' Lukas said softly, pulling a box from behind the counter and arriving at her side.

She hadn't even noticed that tears had begun quietly falling, but she knew they were no more than a gentle release. An evaporation of emotions that were ready to take flight.

And once they'd gathered their packing materials – the things which would ensure the safe keeping of Gretel's memories – they set to work, like two unlikely elves.

'I won't miss this tinsel,' Lukas joked lightly, as he stood on a chair trying to coax the foil garlands from the ceiling.

Gretel remembered him batting away an unruly strand that had tried to attack him when they'd met Mr Birdwhistle (Junior) at the café just a few weeks before, and tried not to giggle.

Lukas and Gretel seemed to have silently agreed to begin with decorations which would cause the least emotion to pack away. Tinsel, which lived out of reach and didn't have a face, seemed like the perfect start.

Once they'd done that, the artificial holly wreaths in the windows felt easy enough.

'They're actually quite spiky,' said Gretel, as she tried to arrange them neatly inside a box.

'No good can come of decor that tries to attack you,' Lukas teased, giving the packed box of tinsel the side-eye.

'The windows do look quite bare now.' Gretel scratched her head. 'But I'll think of something.'

'You're creative,' Lukas agreed.

Gretel nodded as she skipped towards the kitchen to collect something she'd already created. When she returned, placing her stained-glass version of Nell outside a ginger-bread house in the café's bay window, they both smiled.

'She loved a good nosey,' said Lukas. 'That's the perfect place for her.'

Together they took down the snowflake lights which dangled from the ceiling, but agreed that a few sets of warm white fairy lights should stay.

'And I'll always make room for tealights on tables,' Gretel reasoned. 'We still want to keep the cosy atmosphere and that lovely spicy fragrance.' It danced around them right then and made the air feel enchanted.

'The log fire will still be great when it's chilly,' Lukas added. 'But maybe not in July.'

They looked at each other, their mouths unable to resist a smile. She was grateful for his humour to lighten an occasion she'd feared would be dark, and for the soft tinkle of non-festive piano music which the jukebox seemed to have selected for them.

And before she even realised it, she was packing away her glass ornaments too. As she wrapped each one in tissue paper she said a small goodbye. The little figures had become like old friends, after all. But she focused her thoughts on the new friends she was making. Real-life ones. And she could still carry memories in her head, couldn't she? Just like Amber had said.

'It's not so much *goodbye* as *see you soon*,' she whispered, knowing that Christmas would be back. She just had to hope she could wait until December to unwrap them.

In the meantime, there was still plenty of winter left. Lots of time for snow and hot drinks and woolly scarves, without the reindeer. And then spring would come, and she'd embrace that too.

She could sense Lukas was nearby as she spoke soft farewells to her glass creations – a solid support through this delicate journey. But he wasn't intruding.

'I'm not sure this feels quite right,' Gretel mumbled into a tissue, as she tried to pack away Brigitte. 'She symbolises my mum. Somehow she shouldn't live in a box.'

Lukas put his hand on her arm. It was warm and stable, and the touch seemed to fill her with something that made her feel safe. 'Then we'll think of something.'

Gretel nodded and closed the lid. Just for now. Because she trusted that they would.

Once they'd put Gretel's plastic tree and the other carefully packed boxes into the store cupboard, Lukas enveloped her in a hug and kissed her softly on the cheek. As though pulling away would be too hard for them both, he held his lips against her skin. She noticed with a thrill that they'd been touching for far too long for it to be passed off as simple friendship.

In that moment, she felt almost like a glass fairy being gently wrapped in tissue paper too. Only somehow, her wings were getting stronger.

And when, together, they came up with another idea involving the big tree on Green Tree Lane, she sensed a part of Lukas was changing too.

Chapter 30

'Crisis talks around a Christmas tree? So this is new.'

Gretel rolled her eyes at Amber. 'It's not a crisis talk, it's a planning session. And I'm beginning to think this doesn't have to be a Christmas tree.'

Amber placed her hand over Gretel's forehead. 'Do we have a doctor in the street?'

Gretel had called some of the shop owners and residents of Green Tree Lane to gather around the street's central Christmas tree that bright, late January morning. The air was crisp and frost still twinkled on the hills in the distance, but it was a brand-new week. Most of the shops in the street were closed on a Monday. Time was theirs.

Gretel noted with a wriggle of delight that her whole crafting class had turned up. Chakra healing Phoebe and Eve from the flower shop were there, who, along with Amber, made up her tentative trio of wise women. Although Gretel still felt nervous being in charge of things, she was getting used to it, and her friends had coaxed her into arranging the meeting.

It warmed her heart to see their newer comrades Bea from Lavender & Honey in her light purple mac and Zekia from Rum & Raisin, who always seemed like the life and soul of any party. Even Jane and Jayne from the art gallery and Gordon the Grocer were there. They stood around the tree brandishing the stained-glass lambs and daffodils they'd made at one of their crafting sessions, even if they did look a little confused.

'So what's happening?' asked Zekia, through a mouthful of spiced rum fudge which she'd been handing out from a brown paper bag on the insistence that people needed sugar. 'I hope it's something special if I'm missing a Monday lie-in with my scrumptious Kingsley.' She gave Bea a nudge and the dainty woman blushed.

Gretel looked around at the crowd of expectant faces and tried not to feel overwhelmed. Phoebe had already wrangled a piece of brown and yellow stone called septarian into her pocket and had promised it would help her communicate her message. She had no idea about that, but the friendship it symbolised was worth more than Phoebe could know. 'Erm . . .'

Phoebe gave Gretel an encouraging nod and patted her pocket by way of reminder. Amber giggled and shimmied her top half, jesting at Gretel's refusal to keep it in her bra like Phoebe had suggested. At least Amber wasn't patting anyone's boobs. Eve shushed the pair and gave Gretel a quick rub on the shoulder. She took a deep breath. This was a good idea and she could do this. It wasn't like she wanted to chop the tree down, or anything crazy.

'We've kind of touched on this before in class. It's just an idea and you can tell me to get lost if you don't like it. But I think we all agree that business isn't exactly booming in the street, other than a flurry at Christmas.' Gretel took a deep breath, her fist clamped around the shiny stone in her pocket. 'So maybe it's time we embraced every new phase of the year, to try to encourage trade all year round. We could decorate the tree, the street and even our shopfronts with different themes depending upon the calendar.' She raised her gaze and looked tentatively at the sea of faces. To her surprise, she saw a wave of nods.

'Well, it works inside my shop,' Gordon the Grocer nodded. 'Seasonal produce to keep things interesting and fresh. No reason we can't make a thing of it outside too.'

'Like a year-round celebration.' Bea nodded. 'Is that why we're out here with our January daffs?' She held up her glass ornament to the light before attaching it by its ribbon to a branch of the tree. 'It makes sense. It's such a shame for the tree to be bare for most of the year, other than the sad lights which have got more broken bulbs than working ones. Even at Christmas, we don't decorate the street like we used to. It hasn't felt worth the investment. So let's change that.'

The others followed suit, hanging their happy yellow flowers in different places on the tree. Gretel shook off the fearful pang that they were somehow disrespecting the very essence of Green Tree Lane. This was fruitful progress, wasn't it? And surely embracing every new phase

185

didn't mean forgetting that her mother, Rosa and dear festive Nell had never existed. And even if the inside of The Gingerbread Cafe would be moving with the times, at least they'd be keeping the café's sign, with the tagline that promised *Festive Cheer All Through the Year*. Even Lukas had mumbled something about it being a waste to change it.

'Still looks a bit bare,' said one of the Jane and Jaynes. 'We'll have to conjure up more ideas if we want the street to turn heads.'

Gretel nodded; they were right. The street deserved to be loved whatever the time of year. 'It would be great if shoppers had a reason to visit all year round. If we could make a real spectacle of every new phase, somehow.'

'Sounds totally doable with so many crafters and creatives,' said Amber, pulling her waitress notepad and pen out of her bag. 'So hit me with ideas. And once it's in writing, there's no backing out.' She threw everyone a firm look from beneath her quirky short fringe and Gretel was touched at her efforts, even though the group didn't seem to need her scare tactics.

'I'll decorate the street with pots of whatever flowers are in season,' said Eve. 'I love that daffodils symbolise rebirth. For January, I'd do pots of snowdrops and ginger alpinia. Ooh, and winter jasmine for community and inspiration.'

Amber pointed at Eve with her pen. 'Gooooooood.' She tapped the pen against her nose whilst she thought. 'And your shop always looks kind of miserable from the outside. No offence.'

'None taken,' Eve muttered, rearranging her cat-eye glasses.

'So could you put some buckets of colourful flowers outside your shop too?' Amber continued. 'Just so people are clear it's not actually a morgue.' She flashed Eve a winning smile and by some miracle she seemed to get away with it. Eve agreed, as long as the weather wasn't too chilly for her precious blooms.

'In which case,' Gretel added, 'maybe you could start putting your seasonal produce outside your shopfront again too, Gordon? I do miss seeing all those lovely colours.'

Gordon shrugged, in a *why not* gesture. 'Rhubarb and radicchio.' His loud voice reverberated around the street, reminding Gretel of a market trader. 'Crunchy pears and kale so curly it looks like a perm.'

Amber pulled a face and wrote something down on her pad.

'We'd love to do some artwork to brighten up the street,' said one of the Jane and Jaynes after a brief whisper between themselves. 'Maybe we can paint A-boards for everyone, in glorious seasonal colours?'

'That would be brilliant. Thank you!' Gretel beamed, her heart warming a little with each thoughtful contribution. Before she knew it, Amber's pad was filling up with all sorts of promises of help. It turned out Zekia was a whizz with a sewing machine, so she offered to throw together some winter flower bunting. Bea wanted to get ahead and knit spring flowers and honey bees for next season. And most of the group wanted to make ice-white snowdrops at their next stained-glass crafting class – with the exception of Gordon, who wanted to try his hand at glass Brussels sprouts.

'Let's start now,' Zekia clapped. 'You've coaxed me out of bed, so we may as well skip to it. I might even get Kingsley to serve up a tipple of rum at lunchtime. Got to keep the workers toasty and in good spirits.'

And suddenly everyone was milling around, collecting produce and materials from their shops and darting back to gather things from their nearby homes. Jane and Jayne set up a makeshift paint station on dust sheets around the tree. Others sat on thick blankets, cutting out bunting shapes from Phoebe's swatches of rainbow materials or attempting to knit. Gretel handed out warming cinnamon hot chocolate and spare knitted scarves. Eve fussed with flowers and Amber took photos of everything, offering to set up their own Instagram profile, even though she usually wrote off social media as *sooooo basic*.

'Maybe we could get some media interest too?' Gretel heard herself suggesting, as Amber took a close-up of a bunch of perky yellow daffs. 'You know. Local papers and even the radio. Perhaps they'd be interested in our regular makeovers.' It was refreshing to remind herself that winter had so much more to offer, beyond Christmas.

'Why limit ourselves to local press?' Bea's usually quiet voice piped up. 'The whole street coming together like worker bees to turn the place around is a tale everyone would love. And we did used to get trade from all around the country in our better days. We should let them know we're back in the game.'

Amber pulled a face. 'Is a bit of bunting and some pretty chalkboards enough, though? Or do we need something bigger to grab their attention?'

'Like what?' Gretel scratched her head, feeling a little deflated. Perhaps it wasn't much of a story after all. Maybe the world wouldn't even care about a few glass lambs and the promise of a Brussels sprout.

Before Gretel could ponder it further her thoughts were invaded by the deep growl of an engine followed by an aggressive screech of tyres. There were outraged gasps as the group looked up from their various positions around the tree to see a sleek black and gold sports car invading their peaceful space. The window rolled down and a woman's head thrust out, its black hair swinging.

Gretel gawped. There was only one bob that swung quite so annoyingly, and probably only one person with the cheek to speed around a pedestrianised street making pedestrians feel like they were in the way. Francesca Swingy Bob Whimple.

Chapter 31

'What's the party?' asked Francesca Swingy Bob Whimple, peering down from her sports car window at the shop owners who were gathered on cosy blankets around the Christmas tree. 'Are you, like, knitting or something? Why aren't your shops open anyway?'

Zekia began hauling herself to her feet, clearly not impressed with being looked down upon by the woman she'd once referred to as *that scrawny pipsqueak*. Some of the others followed, and before Gretel knew it Eve was dragging her up too. But where was Amber?

'You shouldn't be driving down Green Tree Lane. It's pedestrians only.' Zekia pointed to a road sign, which had admittedly seen better days.

'And we don't answer to you round here,' said Gordon.

'Not yet,' said Swingy Bob, with a sickly sweet smile which she seemed to think passed as genuine. 'And it scarcely matters about the no-cars thing.' She waved a hand.

'It's not like you ever get much of a crowd to run over. Maybe you could do with some more popular shops.'

Gretel could hear Phoebe taking deep breaths at the side of her, and then felt her tapping her on the pocket. It was her cue to test out this yellow and brown communication crystal Phoebe had plunged into it. Change might feel uncomfortable, but it was a hell of a lot less terrifying than letting Francesca Whimple get her way.

'Our shops are fantastic and we will have decent crowds,' Gretel heard herself saying, even though her voice was shaky. 'We're working on attracting new visitors to our street right now.'

Swingy Bob raised her eyebrows. Even her hairdo kept still for a moment, in anticipation of some gossip. 'How so? With knitted bumble bees and vegetable bunting?'

'They're honey bees,' Bea mumbled. 'Bumble bees barely make any honey, which you'd know if you were genuinely interested in my shop, like you said you were.'

Eve rubbed Bea's shoulder and scowled at Miss Whimple, who still didn't seem to realise she was actually being rude.

'This is just the warm-up,' said Gretel, still not sure where these words were coming from. Warm-up for what, for goodness' sake? They hadn't planned anything, beyond a bit of decorating and a few pics for Instagram. That much had felt huge enough, but now that their cute bunting was being sneered at . . .

'Coolio. What are you warming up for?' The bob was back in full swing, as though shaking its head in disbelief even though its owner was fake-smiling.

What was there to do in winter, once Christmas was

packed away? Gretel raided her memory banks for an answer. She could picture something. What was that? 'The Mistleton February Fair!' she blurted out. She remembered it from her childhood, but the village hadn't had one for years. 'We're bringing it back and it's set to be the best winter event in the Cotswolds.' Woah – was it? What was she saying? She should give Phoebe's funny stone back. Things were far safer when she'd just clung on to glass fairies for moral support.

Swingy Bob was quiet for a moment, presumably chewing over her thoughts. 'Great, save me a ticket. Maybe I'll drop by with some potential tenants and reassure them this place is showing signs of improvement. It's super handy that you're doing the legwork for me.'

'You don't own anything around here to rent out,' Gordon growled, one arm steadying his angrily wobbling belly.

'Like I said, not yet.' Swingy Bob swung her head towards Gretel. 'But that charming café should be up for grabs soon, and Lukas and I go way back.' She gave Gretel a wink. 'Lukas is always game.'

Was he? And why did the insinuation make Gretel's stomach churn?

'Anyway, I've gotta shoot.' Miss Whimple waved a hand. 'See you later, peeps. And keep up the hard work. I appreciate you.'

With that, the car window rolled back up and Miss Whimple reversed at speed and swung back in the direction she'd come from. The group tried their best not to cough in the dust her tyres spat up as she zipped away.

Gretel rushed around the tree to look for Amber. She was there, inspecting her black-painted nails as though she hadn't darted off at the first rumble of Miss Whimple's engine. There were still a few mysteries about Gretel's new friend, and it wasn't like headstrong Amber not to sound off about the rule-breaking sports car.

But before Gretel could quiz her, she heard footsteps coming towards them across the cobbles, in the opposite direction to Miss Whimple's dust cloud. Gretel's heart did a little shimmy as she saw Lukas striding towards them in worn jeans and a slim fit blue jumper, his backpack slung over one shoulder.

'It's Lukas,' she whispered to Amber, for the sheer joy of saying his name.

Amber flinched and did a quick check over her shoulder. 'Shit, you're right. Erm. I'll leave you kids to it.' Amber moved quickly around the tree, grabbing her black canvas satchel. 'Keep hold of the pad with the list, yeah? I'll see you in the café tomorrow.'

Gretel darted after Amber as she marched away, towards the main road and her bus stop back to Lower Paddleton. 'What's going on with you today?' Gretel asked. 'First Swingy Bob Whimple and now Lukas. He's honestly not that bad! And anyway, I know you wanted to be an unofficial employee at first, but isn't it time we told Lukas about you? I'm hoping the café will get busier again with our efforts to rejuvenate the street, then I can take you on for more hours and actually pay you ...'

'No! Don't mention me to him or that Whimple woman. Not at all, OK? Just, please.' Amber shot her an imploring look, then checked her watch. 'I shouldn't be here anyway. But shh, yeah?' She dipped her head and scurried away.

'OK,' Gretel agreed to Amber's quickly disappearing rear

view, her heart feeling heavy. She hoped her friend was all right; plus she was reaching the stage where she didn't want to keep secrets from Lukas. She'd get to the bottom of this at some point. But for now, she'd keep her word.

'Something I said?' Lukas stepped up behind Gretel, his warm breath tickling her ear and sending a ripple of delight down the side of her neck and across her shoulder. As though he knew the effect he was having, he placed a steadying hand on her arm. Gretel sighed. It was probably just as well. Who knew where that errant ripple would have ended up without some gentle guidance?

Gretel felt her eyes close momentarily as the warmth of Lukas so close against her back made her insides jiggle. Since their intimate evening of stained-glass crafting together and the way he'd opened up to her, she was melting. 'Nothing you said,' Gretel replied with a gulp, suddenly realising that in that moment, just about anything he said would make her liquify like solder. The depth of his voice, those tiny vibrations across her skin, his closeness.

Then, as though sensing the air between them was getting far too heated in front of all these strangers, he backed away. The space behind her felt cold.

'I don't think you've even met her to offend her,' said Gretel with feigned breeziness, trying to regain some sort of composure as she turned to him.

'She seemed familiar,' he said absently. 'That striking red hair . . .'

Gretel felt a burst of jealousy shoot through her, and then instantly disliked herself for it. Amber was surely too young for Lukas and he hadn't meant it in that way. Gretel knew what was really setting off this odd envious streak was Miss Whimple's suggestion that Lukas was *game*.

'Your friend Francesca Whimple was just here.' She blinked at him, hoping she didn't seem like a needy, green-eyed weirdo. He could be *friends* with whoever he wanted, but something inside her was nagging to know more. 'God knows why she was driving her silly flash car down a pedestrianised street, but she enjoyed mocking our efforts at trying to breathe some life into the place.'

'She probably wondered what you were up to.' Lukas shrugged. 'I'm wondering the same. What *are* you all up to?' He held her gaze for a moment before turning around to take in the various crafting huddles. Lukas had helped Gretel come up with the idea of redecorating the central Christmas tree the other night in the café, when he'd helped her take down the decorations. But the ideas to decorate the whole street with bunting, painted A-boards and more welcoming shopfronts had only taken shape today. Gretel explained their new plans to Lukas.

'And then I blurted out to Francesca Whimple that we were bringing back the Mistleton February Fair.' Gretel laughed into her hand. 'I have no idea where that came from, but the idea's growing on me.'

'The February Fair?' Lukas mussed his light beard. 'We haven't had one for years, but it's a brilliant plan. I remember those warming winter-spiced soups and hot rolls, although you're probably picturing toasted marshmallows and extra thick hot chocolate.'

Well, now she was. She smiled, before remembering something was still bugging her.

'Though Miss Whimple basically said whatever efforts we made, she'd still get her hands on The Gingerbread Café, because you and her go *way back*. And that you're *game*.'

Against all logic, she just wanted him to hold her and take her strong feelings away, even if he wasn't hers to be jealous about and even if her new friends would be right there gawping and giggling.

As her eyes began to seek out the floor in embarrassment, Lukas put a gentle hand under her chin and lifted her gaze back up to meet his. 'Is that a flash of envy I see in those striking green eyes of yours?'

He leaned his face down, his sweet spiciness tickling her nose, his lips teasingly close.

'I hope so, Gretel, because quite strangely, I like it.'

She'd always wondered what love stories meant when they talked about quivering lips, but now she knew. Hers were trembling mid-air as though they'd forgotten how to speak and just wanted to yelp *kiss me*.

'Well now, is this that hot chef of yours?' The unmistakable sound of Zekia's voice approaching broke the moment.

Lukas jumped backwards and raked a hand through his hair, looking a little awkward. He turned to face Zekia and the others, who were now quickly gathering like bees to the honey, and was soon introducing himself with a confidence that made Gretel wish they could get back to that chat about her *striking green eyes* very soon.

Chapter 32

'Mmm hmm, Mr Hot Chef. You can join us more often.' Zekia licked her lips as she sampled one of Lukas's gingerbread muffins, the sweet apple sauce centre oozing out gloriously. 'Just the right amount of spice for me.' She gave him a friendly poke in the chest, just as her husband Kingsley came by serving up his spiced coconut rum in small yellow glasses.

'Woman, keep your hands to yourself!' Kingsley laughed, his bright eyes shining and his white beard shaking with his chin. 'Give the other ladies a chance.' He winked at Gretel, who'd been trying her best all day not to look too *into* Lukas. Clearly she was failing.

Lukas followed the trajectory of Kingsley's wink and Gretel felt her cheeks flush. She busied herself with her dinky glass, pretending it was just the heat from her rum.

'You've got a fine lady there, Kingsley.' Lukas patted the older man on the back. 'They're not easy to come by.'

Lukas continued his rounds dishing up lunchtime muffins

to the crafters around the tree, taking time to talk to them and find out what they were doing, and sharing his own creative suggestions as he went. Gretel pretended to busy herself rearranging the new decorations on the tree, but really she was marvelling at this interesting new side to him. She rarely saw him with people, although she knew he led a team in the kitchen at La Carotte Rôtie. Her early impressions had been that he was stern, obsessive and moody, so she'd imagined him to be the same in a group. But either she'd got him all wrong or he *was* beginning to mellow. Perhaps it was a bit of both. Being around so many lovely people was certainly warming her own reluctant heart.

And yet . . . She shook her head. She didn't want to feel guilty about enjoying people's company, but she kept getting the suffocating panic that the more she opened up to new people and things, the less often she thought back to old ones. Was she slowly losing those vivid memories of her family and Nell? They used to be right there with her every day, in the fabric of festive woollens and the glint of a fairy's wing. But now . . .

'Penny for them.' Eve arrived at Gretel's side with a couple more pots of daffodils to place around the tree.

'I can already tell exactly what's on her mind. Or who.' Phoebe arrived at Gretel's other side, armed with a watering can and a packet of rose quartz chips. If only it was that simple.

Phoebe had been sprinkling the tiny crystals around Eve's flowers to give them loving energy. Her bracelets jangled as she popped a few into Gretel's pocket, where once upon a time she may have kept a gently wrapped glass fairy. Well, at least it was somewhere safe.

'Although word has it you're the psychic one?' Phoebe looked at Eve, who still hadn't given much away about the rumours that she received messages from the deceased about which funeral flowers they fancied.

'Like flowers, we often grow in new directions,' Eve said, putting down her pots and standing to rearrange her purple bob. 'And letting our roots grow into the soil whilst our shoots branch out and explore new climbs should be encouraged. Change is a wonderous thing.' She pushed her glasses back up her nose and swished off towards her shop to collect more pots, her flowery tea dress billowing out behind her.

Gretel put a hand to her throat and tried to swallow a lump that was rising. Whatever Eve had meant, her words had been beautiful. Yet the thought of new things blossoming always reminded her of the people in her life who'd never had the chance. Was she ready to move on from them?

As though sensing her thoughts, Phoebe squeezed her arm. 'It's OK if change feels scary. Even a snake gets anxious when it sheds its old skin. But when the shiny new version emerges it's worth all of the discomfort, because finally everything fits.'

Gretel nodded, letting a few silent tears fall before wiping her face with her sleeve.

'Better out than in,' Phoebe reassured her. 'Talking of positive change, look. The front of Eve's shop seems to be changing for the better. Shh, don't tell her, but I found it a bit dark and eerie before. She's pulled out that fake foliage that was crammed inside the window. It looks more inviting already, don't you think? She's inspired me to take down the drapes in my shop window for a more welcoming vibe. I'll never heal the world's chakras if I can't get people through the door.' She nodded over to the blankets where some of the artwork was taking place. 'And guess what? Jane and Jayne said they had heaps of spare paint, so Lukas offered to help repaint some of the shopfront window frames to brighten things up. He's making superfans already.'

They looked over to where Lukas was crouched down by Jane and Jayne in their paint-splattered shirts, appraising their A-boards and dishing out more muffins. They giggled like a pair of schoolgirls at something he said and Gretel got another sense of just how magnetic he could be. Jane and Jayne usually reserved their lovely dark eyes only for each other.

Kingsley came around pouring out more rum, this time with a honey flavour. Gretel noticed Lukas only ever had one, which was probably a sound plan with the strength of it. Bea loved the idea of using honey in almost anything and suggested she and Kingsley should try her lavender honey too. Gordon wanted Kingsley to make a ginger and pear spiced rum for the February Fair, which everyone heartily agreed with. Gretel wrote it down on Amber's pad, hoping by then her friend would be beyond doing a runner every time Lukas turned up or the day would quickly become comical. But despite the strange little mysteries, it was magical to see creative ideas flowing.

The rest of the afternoon continued in the same vein, and the street was filled with inspiration, laughter and even more cake. Gretel watched Lukas as he continued to support and delight her new group of friends. He mucked in with everything from cleaning shopfronts to hanging up bunting. He even winked at Gretel when Bea tried to teach him how to knit a bee, letting her reign as the expert when Gretel secretly knew he was a whizz with his *knit one, purl one*. But though Lukas kept trying to swing Gretel's way with a variety of excuses to be near her, she tried her best to stay out of his magnetic field. She knew that once she got too close it would be near impossible to encourage herself away.

'Got you.' Lukas grabbed Gretel lightly by the waist as he finally managed to catch up with her. They were by the Christmas tree as she was putting up the stained-glass lilac flowers she'd spent the afternoon working on.

'Be careful! They're made of glass, you wally.'

'I'm learning to tread more carefully. Look, I haven't even got my clumpy chef's clogs on today.' He waved a trainer-clad foot. 'And you've broken free of your festive snow boots. What's the world coming to?'

'I know – flowery pumps in January. I'm feeling pretty adventurous!' She waved a foot back at him, conscious that it probably looked to the others like she was showing off her leg in her short denim pinafore dress, even if she did have woolly tights on. She was sure she heard Gordon give a low wolf whistle somewhere behind them. She put her foot back to the floor and coughed, wriggling away from Lukas's waist hold, as much as she wanted to sink into it.

'Great . . . pumps,' Lukas replied.

The sun was setting now, throwing shades of deep orange

across the sky and silhouetting the shop owners as they packed away for the day. Gretel watched as her stained-glass lilacs spun gently in the evening breeze, their petals chinking lightly against the fragrant needles of the tree. Lilac for renewal, Eve had said.

It always smelled so good standing right there, but that evening, instead of worrying about things slipping away, she would try to focus on the extra sprinkle of spice that had joined the mix. She inhaled deeply, hoping Lukas didn't guess quite how intoxicating his presence was becoming.

'There's still something missing, don't you think? On the tree, I mean.' It wasn't the time to get too deep. Gretel looked upwards, trying to work it out.

'I do think. And soon enough we might just have the answer, so don't stray too far.' He gave her shoulder a quick squeeze and disappeared to help the rest of the group take their final bits of equipment back to their shops before they locked things away for the evening.

She wasn't sure how much time passed as she stood peacefully by the tree, but before she knew it Lukas was patting Bea on the arm and thanking her for something, and she was waving goodbye to her friends as they walked off towards their nearby cottages. Soon she would see smoke from their log fires puffing through chimney pots into the night air, making the village smell like a wonderful bonfire. She wondered absent-mindedly what Lukas was up to. Did the others know? She was sure she'd sensed excited whispers earlier, but she was too engrossed in her quiet moment at the foot of her favourite tree to worry about it. She sighed, her warm breath on the chilly air fogging up the petals of a lilac decoration. Wiping it off, she realised her glass creations were beginning to glint in the light of the moon which had just peeped its silvery crown over the tops of the distant roofs.

'You would have loved this.' She reached out and gently spun one of the stained-glass lambs. 'Especially you, Rosa. You had so many smiles for everything, as though your joy was endless.' She pulled her hand away. 'But it wasn't, was it?' She felt a quiet tear tickle her cheek, followed by another, but she allowed them to fall. Sometimes you had to let things go. It wasn't moping, simply shedding. Releasing emotions that needed to be felt so they could pass. Clinging on wasn't fair, to herself or to the poor souls she was clinging to. She didn't know anything about what happened after you were gone, or if she believed in things like hearing deceased people's voices. But she knew it wasn't healthy to carry on living in the festive shadow of a life that was never to be. It was surely OK to say goodbye to Christmas and wave hello to each new occasion with a grateful heart. To celebrate the passing of time rather than trying to freeze it in a snow globe of snatched memories. She didn't have to feel guilty.

Tears are how the heart speaks; that's what her mum would have said. She gave a small laugh as she yet again wiped her face with her sleeve, realising her mum would also have said always carry a tissue and don't make such a mess of your jumper. She was usually quite good with the tissue part. Dear Nell would have said the same, though she would have pulled a fresh hanky from her candy-striped apron. It would have had a gingerbread man embroidered into the corner.

Gretel wondered if Nell had taught Lukas to embroider as well as knit.

She was giggling softly at that thought as Lukas arrived again at her side.

'Are you OK?' he asked, his voice low and gentle as though she was as fragile as one of her glass creations. For a long time she had been. But day by day, with the friendship and warmth from her new community, she felt her cracks trying to fuse. And didn't they say you were stronger where your wounds had healed? Like the shards of glass she soldered together to make beautiful things. Phoebe even swore she could see rainbows in the cracks of her crystals. Maybe that was true.

'Yes, I'm aiming for OK. Thank you.' Gretel turned to him slowly, taking in every inch of him in the inky moonlight. His slate-grey hair and eyes looked like they were made for the glow of the moon. And that manly stubble ... She shook her head. 'I mean, being OK is an ongoing process. I'm not fixed just yet, if that's even a thing. But right now I'm not wearing Christmas deely boppers or a single item of clothing featuring penguins. And call me wild, but I think I kind of like it.'

He laughed tenderly. 'You're right, you're wild. Which is why I hope you won't think this is too extreme. Listen.' His eyes screwed shut for a moment as though he didn't dare look at her reaction.

And then she heard it. A loud, mechanical rumbling coming towards them from just around the bend. Was this the surprise he'd been talking about? What was going on?

Chapter 33

'I had no idea it was cherry season.' Gretel laughed as the machine drove into view.

'It isn't,' said Lukas. 'That's why all respectable cherry pickers are on standby for more pressing tasks, like helping local villagers put the perfect decoration on top of their non-Christmassy Christmas tree. Care for a ride?'

Gretel looked upwards to the end of the machine's long arm where a stout man, who looked not unlike a Ribena berry in his purple overalls and straw hat, was up in the cradle controlling it. 'With him?' She didn't realise you could drive the thing from up there, but he was doing an impressive job.

'You can go up with Farmer Wilbur if you prefer. But I think he'd rather nip off to the pub to meet Gordon and leave us to it. He's Bea's kind of eccentric dad,' Lukas explained.

'Ahh, so that's what you were thanking Bea for earlier.'

'Friends in high places.' Lukas gave her a nudge as he looked up to Wilbur in the cradle, clearly pleased at his terrible joke.

It turned out Wilbur ran the local lavender farm, amongst other peculiar projects that generally made poor Bea roll her eyes. He parked the cherry picker next to the Christmas tree and after a bit of a demo with the controls he was off on foot in the direction of the pub, promising to return after his pork scratchings and shandy.

'A cherry picker with fairy lights,' Gretel mused, as she admired the cradle, which was festooned with glittering lights, not unlike the solar lights which lived on the tree, even if most of those needed replacing. The ones that worked were twinkling now too. 'Farmer Wilbur must be an old romantic.'

Lukas shrugged. 'He's in charge of the Christmas decorations and general tree maintenance, even if both could do with some love. Maybe he found a spare set lying around. He has specific approvals to use his machine here, so he's promised to fix the dud tree lights soon too.'

She could tell from the smile Lukas was trying to hide that he may have put in a few special requests. The thought warmed her on an evening that was beginning to get quite chilly. She suddenly noticed she was shivering. Lukas stepped to grab his backpack, pulling out his coat for her. It was the green parka with the furry hood that he'd been wearing on Christmas Day when she'd bumped into him up the hill.

She'd sensed even then that there was something about being around him that made once-dormant parts of her begin to shimmy to life. Now there was no denying it. Against all her carefully laid plans to keep feelings of closeness at bay, she was falling for him. Did he feel something too? The toasty green coat he was draping around her shoulders as he helped her step into the fairy-light-strewn cradle told her he might, and that was scarier still.

'But what will we put up there?' She turned to him with a quizzical look as he stepped into the cradle behind her.

'Ahh. That's lady's choice.' He dug into the bottom of his backpack and pulled out a carefully packed cardboard box. 'I swung by the café earlier and picked something up. But there are a few options in the bag, in case I've done the wrong thing.' He ran a hand over his stubbly face as though he was genuinely nervous. 'Look, I know today must have been difficult for you, even if most of this was your fantastic idea.' He nodded to the street around them as shadowy bunting fluttered in the night air and the tree at their side bowed abundantly with lovingly made offerings. 'You're doing a brave thing.'

She huddled further into Lukas's coat. 'Maybe things lose their sparkle if you don't give them the chance to rest.'

'Well, I felt your huge reluctance to pack your favourite glass fairy away the other night when we cleared away the Christmas decorations at the café. It's the one you were making when I barged into you with the spiky end of a Norway spruce the Christmas before last.'

Gretel remembered the scene when the fairy had gone flying, but he'd somehow caught it. 'She's called Brigitte. It was my mother's name.'

Gretel took the box from Lukas and opened it, gently peeling back the tissue paper to reveal Brigitte. As she held her up by her purple ribbon, the light from the moon flickered across her iridescent wings like she was preparing for flight. 'She adored being outdoors and she belongs here. Thank you.' As they huddled there, a memory came to her. One that must have been lost for a while. 'Mum will love getting a great view of the February Fair. I remember sharing our first cinnamon hot chocolate there, cosying up outside Nell's café, little red-cheeked Rosa tucked up in her pram. She'd be excited to see the fair returning. They both would.' Gretel lifted her eyes to the sky. This wasn't all about losing things.

Lukas rubbed her back gently and she took a deep breath. When she was ready, she nodded and he pressed the controls so the arm of the cherry picker moved up towards the top of the tree. As they rose serenely, the mechanical buzz sending a mellowing vibration through them, Gretel held the angel to her chest. *You can watch over us all*, Gretel told her silently. *It's what you always did best. I don't need to grasp on to you until your poor wings break.* Gretel knew that later she would find a space on the tree for her little glass Rosa too. They belonged together.

Lukas operated the machine deftly without disrupting her thoughts. When they reached the top he stopped them gently and turned away to give Gretel privacy, but she pulled him back. 'It's OK, you can help me. I want you to.' She kissed the angel's small face and then, balancing carefully, reached over and used the ribbon to tie her to the top of the tree. She expected to feel a wrench when it was time to let go, but it was the opposite. The simple gesture felt freeing and right. *Gute Nacht, Mama.*

And then something told her it was time for her to rise too. Just a little. So she pressed the foot switch like Farmer Wilbur had showed them and moved the controls until they were gliding up above the tree, interrupted only by Lukas's surprised laugh. When she stopped them safely she realised he had one arm around her waist as though he was keen to help anchor her. She liked that thought. They turned together slowly, taking in the magnificent view. Every part of her body felt exhilarated, her mind almost dizzy with mischievous joy.

They were as high as the chimneys which puffed in the distance, the dark hills standing guard around them. Above, the stars shone brightly on this clearest of nights, as though bathing them in their blessing. Then she noticed that Lukas's jaw was tight where he was trying not to shiver. Of course. Without cloud cover it was cold if you'd given your coat away, even if your colouring did look magical by starlight.

Before she could overthink it she turned to face him and opened the front of the coat, which was rightfully his, and beckoned him in. He paused briefly to check she was sure and then moved in closer, his arms slipping around her waist and finding the warmth of her back, his cheek brushing against hers. Her skin tingled as he exhaled, releasing a shiver that could have been cold but somehow seemed like more. When he pulled his head back to look at her his eyes were like silver as they caught the moonlight. She felt almost breathless.

And yet . . .

'Are you OK?' He smoothed a few wisps of blonde hair away from her face to get a better look. She might not understand him yet, but he seemed to know when she needed to talk. 'Is something troubling you?'

She sighed, conscious he'd feel her every breath against his skin. She wondered if he could even make out her quickening heartbeat. 'What if all of this comes to nothing?' He'd probably assume she meant their hard work to turn Green Tree Lane around, but she was also terrified this absurdly romantic moment would fizzle out to nothing more than another awkward blunder.

'Is this about Franny Whimple again? Because you know your misplaced jealousy was doing strange things to me this morning.' He gave her a cheeky smile.

'Are you *game* for her?' She felt silly even saying it, but isn't that what Swingy Bob had said?

'I'm game for you.' As he pulled her in more tightly to his firm chest she lost sense of whose rapid heart she could feel beating.

'That wasn't the question.' Was now the time to be pedantic? But if she was going to let her fragile heart keep falling, she wanted to feel sure where it would land. 'Would you let her win?'

'The café, or my heart?' His eyebrows knitted. 'Franny is misunderstood, Gretel. Most of her behaviour is driven by others. But trust me, I definitely don't think of her like that.'

Gretel pulled away, freeing herself from his embrace. 'But the café is still fair game.'

He raked a hand through his hair. 'Look, I don't have all the answers, OK? But I do know something is changing in me. Today has been one of the best days I've had since I don't know when. Being around you and becoming part of this community you've created felt incredible. It's like you're giving me something I didn't even know I needed. And I know already that it feels addictive. *You* feel addictive.' He took a tentative step towards her and she didn't stop him. It was almost as though she couldn't. 'Like you, I still have broken parts to fix. I can't promise how I'll feel in a few months' time about the café or the future life plans I'd always thought I wanted. So if you want to put your foot on the pedal now and manoeuvre us back to the safety of solid ground, I'd understand. We'd never have to mention this.' He took another small step in, his grey eyes fixed on her in a way that was making her melt. 'I know your world is fragile. And yet . . . ' He closed the gap between them, his body fitting snugly against hers once more. 'If you're willing to take a chance, I want to be gentle.'

Before she could stop herself she lifted her arms upwards, grabbing the back of his hair and pulling his face towards hers. 'Not too gentle,' she whispered into his mouth as their lips met in a kiss that stirred every part of her.

Chapter 34

'And you two did *what* in a cherry picker?' Amber was sitting on the worktop of the downstairs kitchen in the café, swinging her legs with glee. Angel Gabriel was curled up on her lap.

'Nothing! We just kissed, that's all. And I started it.' Gretel's cheeks felt hot as she arranged the ingredients for her stained-glass gingerbread biscuits on the worktop.

'Ooh, well, I didn't know you had it in you. Living your best life right up there in the sky for the whole village to see.' She put her fingers over the ferret's ears. '*And* you were wearing that short denim dress. I bet that was handy!'

'I had very thick tights on! And it was just a kiss,' Gretel repeated through gritted teeth, wishing she'd never mentioned it. But somehow she'd been bursting to share it with someone and Amber now seemed like her closest friend, even if they were the unlikeliest pair.

'As if you wouldn't have had a bit of a poke around. Always

good to check the produce.' Amber gave her a wink as she yanked up one of her over-the-knee socks. She was wearing an electric-blue dress with little skull patterns tonight, rather than the usual black and white combo that she insisted was for her *other waitressing job*. And was she sporting less of her severe black and white make-up and Biro arm etchings? She definitely looked lovelier, even if her sassy mouth hadn't changed.

Somewhere out in the empty café one of the Jackson 5 burst into 'I Saw Mommy Kissing Santa Claus', and as Amber sniggered Gretel made a mental note to unplug the stupid wayward jukebox until at least Christmas. It was nearly February, and its cheek had outstayed its welcome.

'So where is he tonight, anyway? Busy at the restaurant?'

'Yes.' Gretel nodded as she popped on the oven and began lining her trays with baking parchment. 'He works so many shifts there. It seems stressful.' Gretel hadn't seen him for a few days since the cherry picker kiss and she'd been jittering for another moment like that.

'He'd surely go mad if he caught you with a ferret in the kitchen, anyway, being a fancy chef.'

'He loves Angel Gabriel now,' said Gretel, a beam on her face as she remembered the way Lukas had fussed over him on the night of the stained-glass crafting.

Amber raised her eyebrows, but Gretel was positively skipping around the kitchen as she prepared her ingredients. She didn't have time to worry about anyone's funny looks.

'Well, just make sure you keep your feet on the ground, now you're not whizzing around in a cherry picker. Scary

Lukas still wants to sell this place, doesn't he? I don't want him nicking your heart and trampling all over your dreams.'

Gretel waved a hand. 'He's not that scary when you get to know him. I'm sure everything will work out, one way or another.'

There was a knock at the back door, followed by a chorus of *cooees* and two eager faces fogging up the glass. Gretel was glad of the interruption from Amber's doubtful look.

'The fam,' said Amber, as Phoebe and Eve swanned in. Gretel still wondered who Amber's real family was. She never wanted to talk about her Lower Paddleton life.

Phoebe was wearing one of her floaty gypsy skirts with a knitted jumper that even Lukas would have been proud of, and Eve looked her usual immaculate self in a flowery shift dress that wouldn't have seemed out of place at a wedding.

As they gave hello hugs and made a fuss of Angel Gabriel, Gretel dusted flour off the stools and apologised for the mess she was already making. She'd come to learn that her baking could still turn out well, even if she'd never be as meticulously tidy as Lukas. She smiled as she put a flame under the hot chocolate that was waiting on the stove.

'I'm so happy you're here,' said Gretel, impressed at the effort they'd made to pop around and watch her try out her first batch of stained-glass gingerbread biscuits. 'It's great to have your support.'

'Well, of course,' said Eve, washing her hands and putting an apron on. 'We believe in you and we can't wait to try your edible art. That's what friends are for. Look at the wonderful things you've done for us too. Our shops are all looking brighter thanks to you inspiring us, and that vegetable bunting is going down a treat.'

Gretel felt her cheeks colour at the compliment. 'We'll have plenty more to plan and do for the February Fair as well. I can't say I'm not nervous, but if we pull it off ...' She searched the cupboards for her favourite mugs and lined them up side by side. 'It will be the best!' She couldn't help a little happy bounce as she said it. She hoped it was true.

'Of course we'll pull it off,' said Amber, jumping down from the worktop to continue gathering Gretel's list of baking equipment so Gretel could concentrate on the mini marshmallows and hot chocolate. Angel Gabriel was stowed safely in the front pouch of Amber's dress like a baby kangaroo.

'Having a wonderful, wintery fair was a fantastic idea, Gretel. We all can't wait to bring it to life,' said Phoebe. 'Just from the January makeover we did this week we've seen an influx of trade. Word's getting out thanks to Amber's Insta pics. I had a brand-new customer booking in for a course of chakra healing sessions today, and somebody even bought crystals. I'm pretty sure the universe is telling me to celebrate by eating some gingerbread. What have you got?' She pulled her purse out from her bag.

'Put that away,' Gretel insisted. 'I probably owe you a fortune with these beautiful bits of rock you keep shoving into my pockets.'

Phoebe held up a finger. 'That reminds me.' She put her purse away and rummaged in her bag, pulling out a heart-shaped shimmering white crystal flecked with black. 'Moonstone to help you open up to love and affection.'

'Oh, she doesn't need much encouragement,' said Amber, plonking down the electric hand whisk like a girl who enjoyed a good stir. 'Just wait till she tells you what she got up to in that cherry picker, by the light of the moon. I think she needs a crystal to help her keep her pants on.'

'I did keep my pants on! And they've heard all there is to know.'

Phoebe raised her eyebrows and placed the crystal gently down on the worktop. 'It's there whenever you need it,' she whispered.

Angel Gabriel, apparently fed up of the smut talk, made a series of his clucky-squeak noises and leapt from Amber's pouch onto the worktop. He made a dive for the crystal and began pushing it along with his nose as though trying to make off with it.

'Somebody doesn't want you opening up to any more love and affection on top of Farmer Wilbur's boom lift.' Amber giggled as she pulled the ferret back into the safety of her arms and put the heart-shaped stone into Gretel's bag.

'Ferret basically means thief,' Gretel muttered, choosing to ignore Amber's jesting. 'He keeps running off with the crystals you've been giving me, Phoebe.'

Phoebe nodded as she rubbed the green crystal pendant around her neck. 'We often seek out the crystals we need. Have you ever considered that his chakras might be unbalanced? I have a lady who buys crystals for her dog, Cedric. He's got such a problem with loneliness. He wears black obsidian in a bandana around his neck . . .'

'Has he tried getting actual company?' asked Amber.

'His owner's often on retreats.'

If Phoebe was the huffy sort, she probably would have huffed. Gretel knew she wanted to.

Eve butted between them with a soapy cloth and began wiping the worktop where Angel Gabriel had made his mad dash. 'So, Gretel. Apart from the fact you're probably breaking rules about ferrets in kitchens, why haven't you invited your hot chef to help you with your baking experiments tonight? Are they running him into the ground at that restaurant of his?'

'Told you she was psychic,' Amber winked.

Gretel handed out the drinks and popped a selection of Lukas's latest chewy choc chip and gingerbread cookies on a plate, wondering absent-mindedly when he'd get over his hang-ups and just make some cute gingerbread people. 'He is really busy. But also . . . ' She picked over her words.

'Eve will tell us what you're thinking even if you don't.' Amber shrugged. 'You may as well spill the tea.'

Angel Gabriel squeak-clucked his agreement and Eve shot them both a look.

'You're welcome to share your thoughts with us,' said Phoebe, moving over to squeeze Gretel's arm. 'We're your friends now, like it or not. And having a new friendship group is a novelty for all of us. In a quiet village like Mistleton you don't get many people wanting to talk to the funny chakra lady.'

'Or the girl with skulls on her dress and the woman who chats to dead people,' Amber added. 'Believe me.'

'Maybe I'll make a lapis lazuli bandana for a certain

person's throat chakra,' said Phoebe in her serene voice that always balanced out Amber's cheek.

On the plus side, Gretel realised that anything she said was likely to be less outrageous than Amber's outpourings. So as she began weighing out her ingredients and grating her spices into little bowls like she'd seen Lukas do, she felt moved to divulge a few truths to her unlikely group of friends, even if her thoughts weren't yet fully formed.

Chapter 35

'I do love having Lukas around,' Gretel confided. Just the thought of him filled her with a fizzy, warm glow. 'But he *is* a trained head chef. My baking has been going well and I want to prove to myself I can do this. These stained-glass gingerbread biscuits are brand new to me and trickier than anything I've tried before. It would be incredible to have a few signature bakes I can call my own.' The delicious scent from the cinnamon stick wafted up as she pushed it against the grater.

Phoebe nodded. 'It will do wonders for your growing confidence, although I definitely have some crystals for that.'

If Gretel could succeed with these eye-catching biscuits, with their melted boiled-sweet centres that looked like coloured glass, she would feel even more positive about her preparations for the Mistleton February Fair. She had a whole lot to live up to.

'Not to mention you don't want to place all your delicate

eggs into one man's rickety basket,' said Eve, as Gretel cracked a large free-range one and congratulated herself that she didn't lose bits of shell. 'You want to know you can stand on your own two feet. Putting so much trust in one person can be terrifying. And I hope none of you discover how it feels to have your fragile trust trodden on by someone you thought you loved.' The last sentence came out as a whisper and Gretel wasn't sure the others had heard it. Eve looked out of the window into the dark night, not seeming bothered when her hot chocolate misted up her wise-woman glasses and hid her eyes from view.

'Cooking is just about confidence, so my ... flatmate always says,' said Amber, before Gretel could ask Eve if she wanted to talk. But maybe Eve's thoughts had been private.

Gretel nodded. She did feel more self-assured tonight. Her hands were moving deftly like an artist's, preparing her materials ready to create. Maybe with these small steps she was finding her feet, even if she sometimes felt unstable without the comforts of Christmas and guilty that her memories might be fading.

'Are you even old enough to have a flatmate?' Phoebe narrowed her eyes at Amber.

'Yeah, obvs,' Amber replied, thrusting another cookie onto Phoebe's plate. 'Now feed your cake-hole chakra.'

If it was a distraction technique, it worked. After a calming breath, Phoebe took a bite and groaned. 'Mmm, I think I'd be anybody's in a cherry picker if they could bake like this. So what else is eating you? Because instinct tells me there's still something.' She was narrowing her eyes again in that way that made Gretel wonder if she had X-ray vision.

Although she hadn't realised it, Amber's caution from earlier had been playing on her mind. And now Eve was warning about trust too. 'When it comes to the café, what if Lukas is still Team Whimple? Business is business, and he might still sell it to that monster,' Gretel heard herself admit.

Amber pulled a face. 'Yep, that bit still sucks. But I've told you to think about buying him out if he's so desperate to sell.'

Gretel placed her cubed butter and sugar into the mixing bowl and began to whisk, the electrical whizz churning up her thoughts. Did Amber have a point? Because now she was finally getting her head around baking, the process wasn't so frightening at all. The preparations were systematic, and when you got to the hands-on bit it was actually quite satisfying. Maybe if she approached all scary life goals in that way ... 'One step at a time,' she shouted to Amber above the din, before she could get carried away with herself. 'The café doesn't make much money yet, so buying anyone out could only ever be a distant hope. And Lukas would have to be willing to wait for me to build the funds and to put his own dreams on hold.' She switched off the noisy gadget. 'It wouldn't feel right asking him to do that.'

'Sometimes dreams change,' said Eve, simply.

After just witnessing her ingredients turn from impossibly rigid to light and creamy with a few spins of the whisk, Gretel dared to wonder if that could be true. And as she added her once delicate egg she noticed that when she mixed it with care the transformation could be almost as smooth as silk. Soon she was sprinkling in her freshly zested clementine and fragrant spices and realising that it really did take all sorts to bring something magical together.

For once Gretel resisted her impulse to ignore the suggestions in her recipe and race on. Instead, she let the dough rest in the fridge, like she'd learned to do, whilst she and her friends moved around the kitchen, tidying, cleaning and flouring the surfaces ready to roll and cut out the shapes. Gretel was going to make winter flowers and use boiled sweets in happy shades of yellow to make the stained-glass centres. She would hand-craft daffodils and winter roses in intricate shapes and if things went well, she might even ice them in different shades. She had a steady hand and a determined heart, so surely it was worth a shot?

Gretel planned to make larger ones to hang in the café window on different lengths of ribbon to replace the festive holly wreaths. She and Lukas had taken them down and packed them away the other night when she'd decided it was time to start moving away from Christmas, but what she would replace them with had been troubling her. In fact, the whole café seemed sparse now, although her three wise women had told her not to panic when they'd talked about it yesterday over Amber's newly created gingerbread and cocoa latte. Together they would think of something. 'It takes a village,' Eve had kept saying, as though the idea was only just dawning on her. Gretel liked the sound of it.

As well as the larger biscuits for the window display, Gretel would make a batch of smaller and less intricate ones for the four of them to try, with some spare for the café if they were in any fit state for public consumption.

'It's chilled,' said Gretel, pulling her dough out of the fridge.

In front of her eager audience she began cutting out her shapes using cardboard templates she'd made, exactly like she did when she was preparing to cut glass. She'd guessed that bringing her glass-cutting tools would have been a step too far, but she worked determinedly with the sharp knives she'd chosen and the process felt similar, other than that there were no satisfying snaps of glass, and if she went wrong, she could just re-roll her dough and start again. That part was a blessing.

Gretel's creations were soon lined up on trays ready to go into the oven, which she'd made everyone check to make sure it wasn't on the blink after some of her previous burning disasters.

'It's all good,' Amber confirmed.

With a joint prayer to the universe or whoever was listening, Gretel put the trays in the oven and four women and a ferret cheered and squeaked as appropriate until the oven door was slammed shut and the timer set.

Amber and Phoebe shuffled off through the café to use the toilets, even though Gretel had offered them use of her bathroom upstairs. They were whispering about something and Gretel left them to it. Eve took charge of the washing-up whilst Gretel dried and put things away, in the hope that busy hands would distract her from worrying about her bake.

'I'm determined not to burn them,' Gretel said to Eve as she pointed to the oven. 'I know they're only biscuits but they've taken me hours of careful planning and preparation, and the more you put your heart into something, the more it hurts when it all goes wrong.'

'Isn't that just the truth, darling girl,' Eve replied, with a strange sadness. 'But we already know these biscuits will be a work of art. You created them from your soul. You researched the recipes, you crafted each piece with loving care, and you showed that dough who was boss tonight. Any kind of creation starts with confidence, just like Amber said. You didn't let it smell your fear.'

That last bit reminded her of Lukas.

Within no time the oven was beeping and the four women, minus a sleeping ferret, gathered around the oven for the big reveal.

'I'm too scared to look.' Gretel pushed the oven gloves into Amber's hands.

'No wonder you used to burn everything if you faff around like this instead of opening the oven and getting on with it,' Amber replied.

Eve grabbed the oven gloves. 'She doesn't burn everything any more.' She pulled the oven open and received a face full of hot steam, then passed the gloves to Gretel so she could demist her glasses. 'They're your babies, Gretel. Save them!'

Gretel thrust on the gloves and went in hands first, hardly daring to peep at the contents of each tray as she pulled them out and lined them up quickly on the worktop.

'Drum roll . . . ' Amber tapped out a beat on a biscuit tin.

Phoebe moved her out of the way. 'Wow. I can officially confirm they look bloody delicious,' said Phoebe, dancing around the trays.

'Then gimme a whoop for the best new baker in town,' said Amber.

Gretel's three friends cheered as she peeked at the trays through nervous fingers, letting out small sobs of joy as she realised that the biscuits looked pretty damned perfect, even if she had no idea what they'd taste like. They were like something from one of those fantastic baking shows where contestants got all tearful in tents. There were no broken off bits or burnt edges, and they could probably pass as small pieces of edible art.

With all the clapping and congratulating, Angel Gabriel woke up and decided he was off. He jumped out of Gretel's crochet bag, making a bid for freedom across the floor and through the door which led to the café, which was accidentally still ajar after Amber and Phoebe's trip to the ladies' room.

Gretel jumped as she heard a scream from the café, her hand flying to her mouth. 'What the . . . ? Who's out there?!'

Chapter 36

Gretel could feel her heart pounding. Who was out there in the dark, closed café – and what were they doing with her ferret?

Phoebe and Amber looked suddenly guilty and Eve grabbed Gretel's arm. 'It's OK, it's the others. We invited them to join in with your baking success because we knew you'd do brilliantly. Don't be cross with us.'

'We sneaked them in when we popped to the loo,' Phoebe admitted, looking sheepish.

'The others?' asked Gretel, leaning against the worktop to try and stop her head spinning.

'It's just the gang.' Amber shrugged, like it was completely normal for intruders to come and celebrate your biscuits.

Phoebe linked arms with Gretel and the four of them moved towards the partly open door where Angel Gabriel had escaped. Eve carefully collected a tray of the smaller stained-glass gingerbread biscuits as they went.

When they got into the café their friends from the street were all there, huddled around a table by candlelight. Angel Gabriel was stretched out luxuriously across Gordon the Grocer's large belly like it was a king-size ferret bed.

'Surprise!' Their voices seemed conscious they'd given away the *surprise* bit.

'Sorry about the scream,' Bea said quietly. 'I hope I didn't scare him.' She pointed to Angel Gabriel. 'I wasn't expecting something small and hairy to accost me in the dark.'

'Clearly doesn't have a boyfriend,' said Gordon, Angel Gabriel wobbling with his belly laughter.

'So how did those biscuits turn out?' asked Zekia, pushing herself to her feet, her long wildly patterned purple and yellow dress bustling around her. 'Will that hot chef of yours be licking his gorgeous lips?'

Gretel turned and took the tray from Eve, her stained-glass gingerbread biscuits still lined up on brown baking paper like flowers in a field. There were carefully shaped daffodils and winter roses, each with their transparent yellow centres made from melted boiled sweets. Her heart soared when she put them down on the table and received a round of applause.

'They really are like mini works of art,' said Jane, who Gretel now knew definitely wasn't Jayne. Jane without the Y had slightly darker hair and was a little shorter.

'Absolutely,' said Jayne.

Gretel waved a hand. 'The larger ones which I made to hang in the window are more detailed and I'm going to ice them too.'

'They'll be showstoppers,' said Eve, with a confident smile.

Whilst Gordon offered to buy the batch with the contents of his money belt and Gretel insisted they didn't need to pay to be her guinea pigs, the others began pulling out various items from under tables and inside bags. Gretel paused to watch them. What were they up to now?

'We noticed your café was a little bare since you bravely took down the Christmas decorations,' said Bea. 'We're so proud of you.' There were nods and claps. 'And we know you'll probably have your own ideas and you're much better at crafting than us. But we wanted to help you brighten the place up with some bits we had left over. Let's hope this is the first of many fun, regular makeovers for this place and the whole of Green Tree Lane.'

Bea held up a string of bunting with colourful triangle flags interspersed with knitted gingerbread hearts. 'It'll be Valentine's Day before we know it.' She blushed. 'My dad and my little boy Xander have been helping me with the knitting. They're working on some bumble bees for spring too – they're better at knitting than me.' Gretel remembered that Bea lived on the local lavender farm with her eccentric dad, Farmer Wilbur, and her son, and that her shop on the street was stocked with produce made with their lavender and honey. 'I can hang it up if you don't think it's too terrible?'

'Can't be as dreadful as tinsel and reindeer all year long.' Gordon chuckled, apparently having appointed himself comedian for the evening. What was tickling him lately?

Jane and Jayne showed her a new chalkboard they'd made her for behind the counter, edged with little painted gingerbread people frolicking amongst snowdrops, and Eve had got Gordon to carry over some small pots of orange and white crocuses for joy which they dotted around the tables. Gretel had noticed Gordon hanging around Eve's flower shop more and more over the past couple of weeks, under the premise of *helping out with a few odd jobs*. She wasn't sure why anyone would wear smarter shirts than usual to do messy DIY, but Eve hadn't made any complaints.

When Zekia pulled out a bright yellow apron she'd made for Gretel from material left over from her latest dress, Gretel thought she might sob. It had frills around the bottom like the edges of a daffodil, and it wasn't that she didn't love it. But how could she explain that the step of taking the Christmas decs down had been hard enough? Changing the way the café had always looked already felt like some kind of betrayal to Nell, her family, her memories ... How could she stand to actually *replace* them? Breathing new life into things was a wonderful idea, in theory ...

As though sensing something, Eve was quickly at her side. 'Nell would have loved this,' she whispered. 'I hear she took such pleasure in choosing flower themes for the flat upstairs. She especially loved the daisies for fresh starts. Maybe she'd have changed things down here too, if she'd had the energy.'

'You advised her on flowers?' Gretel asked. She hoped she meant when Nell was alive.

Eve winked. 'Eucalyptus for inner and outer strength, and

lavender because it's calming and it smells nice. She may have dropped by.'

Amber noticed Gretel fiddling with the apron. 'Need some help?' She rubbed Gretel's arm and discreetly turned her away from the others, lowering her voice. 'Moving on can't be easy. But as great as you look in candy stripes, no one would expect you to live in hand-me-downs for ever.'

'It's not just that.' Gretel couldn't control the wobble. 'It's just so hard to remember things as they were when things are changing. My memories. Mum and Rosa ...'

Amber pulled her into a hug and she let the tears fall. When Gretel was ready, she pulled away.

'I never knew your family,' said Amber. 'But if they were half as joy-lovingly daft as you, they'd have been bouncing with delight to see giant gingerbread and knitted bunting all over the place. Am I right?'

Gretel gave a snotty laugh and nodded, allowing Amber to loop the apron strap over her head. Eve arrived with tissues and Phoebe grabbed Angel Gabriel and stowed him in the perfectly ferret-sized front pocket. Not that she'd ever get away with serving food with a mustelid on her person under Lukas's watch, although that was probably fair enough.

'Thank you, everyone. You've done a lovely thing. I'm just ... overwhelmed.' Gretel smiled through her slightly less tear-stained face.

'Can we eat some ruddy biscuits now?' asked Gordon, clearly oblivious. He straightened himself and tucked in his belly when Eve went over to swat him. 'Just the one for me, obviously. Got to keep this fine body ship shape.'

Gretel laughed, happy for some normality to resume, even if her new normal would always be worlds apart from the old one. She busied herself with passing around the tray, glad of the sense of purpose. Amber went behind the counter to rustle up a pan of her new gingerbread and cocoa latte.

'Woo, girl,' Zekia said through a mouthful of gingerbread. 'Your hot chef had better give up the day job right now. There's a new cook in town.'

Now Gretel was definitely laughing. As she tasted one of the biscuits she had to admit it was good, but it would never be up there with a Michelin star-worthy cheesecake with a fancy *roux jus*, or whatever they called their funny sauces. Which was absolutely fine. The café would be about tasty treats made with love, for as long as she had her say in the matter. She tried not to think about the soulless cheap coffee chains Swingy Bob Whimple would sooner crowbar in.

'Taste test passed with a rainbow of flying colours,' said Phoebe as she tucked into her second. 'I'll check a few, though, just in case.'

'And the guinea pigs are happy,' said Amber as she lined up tall latte mugs along the counter.

They milled around, munching on biscuits and grabbing themselves lattes, Amber taking photos for the new Instagram profile she'd set up just for the café. She'd apparently picked up some winning tips from a social media whiz called Lexie, who'd bounced into the café one day with her blonde pixie cut and sunflower jumpsuit, grabbing a cuppa with her sister Sky. The advice was working wonders.

'You know, I can't wait until the autumn,' Bea confessed.

'Can we have pumpkin-spiced hot chocolate and ginger-bread shaped like squirrels and autumn leaves?'

'Blackberries, apples, cavolo nero.' Gordon counted off autumn produce on his fingers.

Jane and Jayne pulled faces as they hammered up nails for the new blackboard. 'You can keep your cabbage-spiced gingerbread, Gords, if it's all the same.'

'And anyway, you've missed out a whole bunch of seasons,' said Jane, balancing on a chair with a nail between her teeth. 'What are we doing about resurrecting this wintery February Fair?' she lisped.

Gretel plonked herself down next to Zekia, who was having a lively chat with Phoebe about flavours for a warming autumn rum. 'Do you know what? Now I've made a reasonably respectable batch of gingerbread, and I've seen what the café can look like with the help of you lovely people, I feel like we might just have a shot.'

'Amazing! I'll grab the official brainstorming pad,' said Amber, making a dive for it. 'Let's get some ideas on paper.'

The residents who remembered the days of the fair, before it had fizzled out for reasons no one could pinpoint, shouted out the things they had loved about it. *Warming winter soups. Friendly market stalls. Hot chocolate.* The newer residents added their own ideas, like *art trails* and *baking competitions.* And just as Gordon got a friendly swipe around the head from Eve for suggesting a range of games from *pin the tail on the Whimple* to *bash the swingy bobbed rat*, Gretel heard a key turn in the café's front door. There was only one other person with a key. And there was only one person who made Amber duck and sit behind the wide expanse that was Gordon, grabbing his flat cap to hide her conspicuous red hair.

The bell tinkled and the door opened, a small, white-blossomed tree appearing in the doorway in a scene not unlike Norway Spruce-Gate from the Christmas before last. Except this time Gretel was ready for him, and Lukas's head popping gingerly around the side of the spindly branches rather than barging in spike-first told her he was treading more carefully too.

'Did anyone order a winter-flowering cherry tree to replace that sorry plastic thing with the deathtrap lights?' Lukas asked, with a grin.

'No.' Gretel sniffed, trying not to look impressed but knowing that her face was giving her away. Her insides were doing a Maypole dance at the sight of him, and the gorgeous potted tree was melting her heart.

He took a small step inside, reminding her of his tentative steps towards her on the night of that first and as yet only kiss.

'Wow.' He took a deep inhale. 'Somebody's been doing some gingerbread baking and I don't smell burning. Do I get to try?'

'Don't worry, chef, I saved you one,' said Zekia, whipping a biscuit from the small mountain on Phoebe's plate.

'Knew I could count on you, Zee,' Lukas replied.

Well, check him out, on nickname terms with her new gang already.

And as everyone moved around to accommodate him,

other than Amber who'd fled out the back way at the first chance, it looked as though he was in to stay, at least for that evening. There was nothing like getting your feet under the coffee table. After that, who knew? He'd have to continue those tentative steps and Gretel would see how far she trusted him to tread.

For now, they had a winter fair to plan. Because as pretty as blossom was, its presence was fleeting. Gretel knew it was a reminder that life could be short and when petals fell, it was OK to begin again.

Chapter 37

Lukas's next tentative step was not quite as cautious as Gretel had imagined. And as embarrassing as it was, she really had spent the rest of the week bouncing around the café like a love-sick puppy in a daffodil apron imagining his next advance.

Not that she was incapable of making advances of her own, of course. But in the great game of dating chess, if Lukas was a Knight, she was curious as to what his next mysterious move might be. Could it get any stranger than the night of the cherry picker kiss?

As she was about to close up the café that Friday teatime, Lukas poked his head around the front door and made his opening gambit. 'Spooning on the River. Fancy it?'

Gretel stopped mid-step, her bunch of café keys swinging in her hand. 'Excuse me?'

'Tonight, if you're free. I could pick you up around seven?' His eyes were twinkling.

'For spooning. By the river? Like ...' She attempted to contort her body into a spoon shape like people did when they were snuggling on a bed. But then realising she was just sticking her bum out and pulling a confused face, she cringed and straightened herself. 'I'm not sure what you mean.' By the friendly smirk on his face, she was definitely getting the wrong end of the spoon.

'It's a restaurant in a nearby village. Marcus Spooning's place. Remember I told you it had just been awarded its second Michelin star? Well, he's throwing a private banquet and as an old culinary school mate, I'm invited. Want to be my plus one?'

'Me?' She scratched her head.

'Yeah, Gordon the Grocer goes to darts on a Friday and Zekia keeps insisting she's happily married, so ...' He gave her a playful wink. 'Of course you, silly. You're top of my list.'

'For Michelin-starred food when I'm happy with hot chocolate and a biscuit?'

'So let's go wild.' He shrugged. 'Try a mangetout or something.' He moved in through the door and closed the short gap between them. His grey eyes simmered as they held her gaze. 'Please, I'd love to have you by my side. Not for spooning. Unless you want me to add that to the menu for later.' That cheeky smile again.

As he leaned down and touched the tip of his nose against hers, she knew it was checkmate.

Lukas picked Gretel up at seven o'clock. She'd never eaten at a place with Michelin stars before, and who even knew what a banquet entailed? Lukas had at least promised there'd be no pigs on platters with apples stuffed in their mouths, or anything garish. In fact, Marcus Spooning's restaurant was exclusively vegetarian, which is why Lukas thought she'd like it. Not that she was a big fan of vegetables – she just couldn't stomach the idea of eating her animal friends.

'You'll steal the show,' he told her when he arrived, kissing her lightly on the forehead. She'd chosen a knee-length powder-blue dress from her limited selection of non-Christmassy items, which she couldn't remember ever having worn. He swirled her around like something from one of those ballroom dancing shows she used to watch with her mum, even if neither of them had really been able to dance. She slipped on a fluffy coat and some ballet pumps, and out into the fresh spring night they went.

As Green Tree Lane was pedestrianised, Gretel had suggested they walk the short trip to Lukas's cottage just outside the village, to grab his car. She knew a stroll in the fresh night air would help shake off her nerves, although she secretly wanted to have a nosey at where he lived. Gretel had never been inside Lukas's cottage, and as she gave it the discreet once-over from the outside, she wondered if and when she would. It was modest yet beautiful, with its slightly squiffy Cotswold stone walls and ornamental vines sneaking above the doorway. The old wooden door was painted heritage green to match the window frames. It wasn't showy or pretentious at all.

Gretel knew it wasn't the house he used to share with his now ex-wife Mirabelle, before she'd traded him in for

Eduardo. Lukas and Mirabelle had lived somewhere modern outside of the village, so he'd said, with too many glass surfaces, and large rooms that made him feel chilly.

'*Starry Knight*.' She read the name on the slate plaque by the door. 'It's a stunning cottage.'

'I'll show you around someday,' he promised as he opened the car door for her, his arm brushing against her shoulder and sending tingles through her body. She really hoped he would, but for now, she was wriggling with excitement for their first proper date.

Chapter 38

Twenty minutes later they walked arm in arm into Lukas's friend's restaurant, Spooning on the River, which overlooked the water. Gretel couldn't help noticing the resemblance to the building Lukas had his eye on for his own restaurant in Lower Paddleton. Despite Lukas's body heat, Gretel felt herself shiver as they stepped inside. For all its exterior charm, the restaurant was the opposite of cosy. It had so many mirrors Gretel felt like there were twice as many heads staring at her – and as for that humungous central chandelier . . . She dared a look upwards. No, it wasn't going to fall on them at any moment.

'Knighty.' An intimidatingly large man in chef's whites came over to clap Lukas on the back, slightly too aggressively in Gretel's opinion. 'Glad you could make it, old chum.'

Old chum? Who even spoke like that? Gretel glanced at Lukas to see if he thought so too, but he wasn't giving much away.

'Wouldn't miss it, Marcus,' said Lukas. 'Huge congratulations. You deserve it.'

Well, at least he hadn't called him Spoony.

'Let's hope you get a move on with your own Michelin star, hey, boy? Are you still cocking about at La Carotte Rôtie, or have you sorted out a proper plan?'

'It's all in hand, mate,' said Lukas, clapping Marcus on the back in the same excessive fashion. Gretel secretly hoped it was payback, although from Lukas's amiable smile she couldn't tell.

'Anyway, make yourself at home, Knighty boy. Come on in and see how the big chaps do it.' Marcus gave Gretel a sleazy wink that made her want to go home and have a good wash.

Could she manage to feel at home amongst those stiff white tablecloths she'd be terrified of spilling something on? And what was the point in so many confusing knives and forks? It seemed as though even the cutlery was a test of who belonged and who didn't.

The banquet was to entail sitting at long tables whilst well-dressed youngsters scurried around serving them identical fancy-looking food that they hadn't even chosen. There were some more private tables up on a mezzanine VIP area, but Lukas and Gretel were apparently not Michelin-starry or important enough for one of those.

As she looked around, Gretel tried to shake off the weight of disappointment. She'd been expecting a candlelit meal at a table for two, rather than having to make small talk with a party of strangers who seemed so well dressed and grown-up compared to her. She wouldn't even be able to quiz Lukas on what he thought of it all. Although from the way he smiled and greeted other old friends and their partners with ease, maybe it was his kind of thing.

'Let's sit,' said Lukas, placing one hand on the small of her back and steering her lightly towards their seats at the long banqueting table.

From the moment they sat down at the table with all its gleaming glasses, she felt like a klutz. Although at least she could partially hide herself under the tablecloth.

'Have I worn the wrong thing?' she whispered to Lukas, feeling her shoulders droop as she took in all the glitz at the table. Gretel had put on the smartest dress she could find, but compared to these women with their long fitted velvet ensembles and sparkly jewellery, she just felt plain. Were these the people she'd socialise with and the types of places they'd go to if she spent more time with Lukas? She shook her head because she was surely being silly. Lukas wouldn't be in charge of everything.

'I'm a little disappointed that you didn't wear your deely boppers or that Christmas tank top with the snowmen,' Lukas replied. 'But apart from that ...' He squeezed her hand and she felt a little brighter, even if she was still looking forward to leaving.

'Celeriac risotto with garlic confit and dehydrated beet-root powder.' It was a statement rather than a question, Gretel noticed, as a young waiter slid a fancy plate of rice in front of her. She didn't dare argue. She turned to Lukas to ask him what *confit* meant and whether it would be rude to ask for ketchup. But Lukas was having a hearty *old chum* chat with the man next to him, who was appraising the food rudely with his mouth full, spilling beetroot powder on his white cummerbund. Instead, Gretel amused herself by imagining Gordon the Grocer's face when she'd tell him about the dehydrated beetroot. At least she knew her new friends back in the village would find it funny.

A sommelier came around describing and pouring wine with a twisty armed flourish, but Lukas put a hand over his glass and signalled for sparkling water. Gretel mustered a smile and accepted wine, partly because all of this might be less painful with a splash of alcohol, and partly because she didn't understand how anyone could stomach water that tasted like a gassy burp. She didn't know how Lukas could drink it.

Yet when Lukas rested his hand on Gretel's arm as the waiter swept away her plate and announced the next wobbly dish to be a 'tri-colour vegetable timbale, madam,' the reassuring warmth of Lukas's touch made her feel instantly grounded.

Lukas leaned in gently towards her. 'It's called a timbale because of its drum shape,' he whispered into her ear.

'Why can't they just call a drum a drum?' she asked, guessing it was another bit of code in the *fancy-grown-ups-only* club.

But as Lukas's lips brushed against her earlobe in a soft laugh making her want to close her eyes and be devoured by him, she realised she didn't care about trivial differences like gas-belly water. Before she could stop herself she'd slipped a hand onto his leg under the table, the firmness of his thigh under the shine of his suit trousers feeling like support on slippery ground. She used her other hand to fight the blancmange-like tri-coloured whatsit on her plate.

Lukas reciprocated by sliding a hand onto her thigh. The closeness of his bare skin to hers through the thin chiffon of her dress sent an electrical pulse through her that felt like a firework fountain.

Gretel took a deep breath. Maybe this wasn't her kind of night out, but with Lukas by her side she was going to get through it. As she noticed him watching Marcus Spooning do the rounds like the king of the show, she wondered if Lukas was picturing himself in that starring role one day. She ought to feel proud that he had big dreams.

'What do you think is for pudding?' she asked him, her stomach still rumbling after the tiny morsels of food she hadn't much liked the taste of. 'I could kill for a huge bowl of comfort food and custard.'

'Do you know what?' asked Lukas, grabbing her hand. 'I can sense you don't feel at ease, and I doubt we'll get anything as wholesome as custard. Shall we get out of here? I can rustle up whatever you fancy back at mine.'

'Do you know how to make apple strudel?' Gretel asked, trying not to sound too keen.

'With my eyes closed,' said Lukas, standing up and holding his arm out for her. 'I'll even add rum and raisins if you're good.'

Well, who could say no to that? Gretel could barely get up quickly enough and they were soon giggling like kids on the run as Lukas bundled her fluffy coat around her shoulders. As they hotfooted it towards the exit, a voice hissed down from the mezzanine.

'Lukassssss.'

They looked up to see Francesca Whimple, wearing a black designer-looking cocktail dress with her trademark black and gold trainers. She gave them an annoying finger wave as she peered down at them, her sleek bob swinging.

'Didn't see you down there. You should have said!' The Whimple's voice was sickly sweet, as always. 'I could have wrangled you a place in VIP. Hang on, I'm coming down.'

Gretel heard Lukas grumble under his breath, but it was too late. The squeak of Miss Whimple's trainers was already on its way.

'Erm.' Gretel tried to think of an excuse not to face the pesky Francesca. She'd had enough trouble holding her chin up tonight, without having to put up with that woman's over-zealous niceties, which she now knew were entirely artificial. 'I need the loo. Won't be long.'

Gretel loitered in the ladies' for as long as she could without it seeming odd, and then reluctantly made her way back towards where Lukas and Francesca Whimple were now chatting. Gretel hung around behind a coat rack, hoping for their conversation to come to a natural end and for the Whimple to squeak back up the steps where she came from, without Gretel having to say hi. What was taking them so long?

'This vegetarian food's a load of shit, isn't it?' The Whimple was giggling. Lukas didn't appear to be joining in.

244

'I can't wait to get out of here and grab a burger. It's nothing like the incredible food you create.'

Lukas shot a look over his shoulder and Gretel ducked.

'Mmm.' Lukas's reply seemed non-committal.

'How much longer until probate is sorted with the café and we can arrange the sale?' Francesca asked him.

He exhaled. 'Not sure. At least a few months.'

Francesca put a hand on his arm. 'I can see the place is weighing you down. I can move my tenants in early if you want. Take the pressure off you.'

Gretel held her breath.

'I still need time to think,' said Lukas, after what seemed like the longest pause. 'We're trying to turn the place around. Things are up in the air right now.'

Swingy Bob gave a little snort. 'Oh, come on. That café will never make the kind of money your own Michelin-starred restaurant will bring. It's not even a viable business in its current state. You're made for bigger things.'

'Maybe,' he replied.

Just as Gretel was wondering why he wasn't standing up for The Gingerbread Café, she saw Lukas shake off Miss Whimple's hand, which had been snaking up his arm in a way that could almost have been flirty.

There. That rebuff surely meant Gretel's hopes for the café still had a fighting chance. It was normal that he was still thinking about the restaurant he'd always wanted and it was too soon for Gretel to start pushing him about it. She wasn't a bossy Francesca Whimple type.

As the irritating woman said her goodbyes and strode

off in search of fresh meat, Gretel decided she wouldn't mention what she'd overheard. It was weird to be hanging around behind coat racks, and parts of the evening had been strained enough. She and Lukas had just been getting back into their usual, fun dynamic and she wasn't going to spoil that with jealous talk. After all, they had a delicious apple strudel and custard to look forward to at Lukas's cosy cottage, and Gretel was all but ravenous.

Chapter 39

'Strudel. It means *whirlpool* in German. Isn't that fascinating? It's because of the swirl of filling and pastry you can see when you cut a slice.' Lukas closed the oven on his freshly made dessert and set the timer. 'But I'm sure you know that already.'

Gretel nodded. 'I was raised speaking German with my mother. Well, Bavarian. It's a German dialect.' He already knew she grew up eating strudel, and so many other warm and sweet delicacies from the festive markets where her mother had often held a craft stall, although she had more English tastes and traditions now.

'Tonight felt like a bit of a whirlpool,' Lukas admitted, as he looked through his cupboards for the ingredients to make hot chocolate.

They were back at Lukas's cottage, Starry Knight, after what had been a pretty odd first date at his friend's restaurant. Gretel was glad to get away before dessert, especially after Francesca Whimple had shown her interfering face. Gretel was trying not to get too hung up on what she'd overheard about Lukas being unsure of the café's future. It was normal that he was still mulling things over, and at least he'd shrugged off the Whimple's encroaching hand. She could trust him.

'A whirlpool in what way?' Gretel asked, cosying up in the soft cream loveseat in the corner of Lukas's kitchen, a knitted blanket she'd swiped from the front room covering her legs. The whole cottage had a warm and charming feel, with its low, oak-beamed ceilings and the orange glow of lamps. Now Lukas had lit the open fire and the logs were beginning to crackle and smell like a bonfire, Gretel could imagine herself here toasting marshmallows through the winter.

'Like when two worlds crash together and send everything into a spin.' He poured milk into a pan, broke off some rich cooking chocolate and began stirring over the heat. 'It took me by surprise. I hadn't realised quite how much I don't fit with my old crowd any more.'

Gretel felt herself releasing a quiet sigh of relief. She hadn't felt comfortable there either.

'Some of the things I used to worry about, like impressing my pretentious peers with the perfect lobster bisque, just seem pointless. I'm not even sure I want to cook the kind of food that would get the seal of approval from people like Marcus Spooning or . . . '

'Your dad?' She said the words gently, remembering what he'd told her before about the mean cordon bleu chef.

Lukas nodded. 'Always so many rules with him. In his

248

own eyes he'd failed as a chef and he was damned if he was going to let me embarrass him and do the same. But he'd forgotten what it was to cook for the sheer joy of it. To create the sorts of things that would put smiles on people's faces or bring families together. And in trying to please him, and my ex-wife Mirabelle, I forgot how to bake for the joy of it too.' He sprinkled grated chilli and cinnamon into the hot chocolate as he stirred. Gretel went to protest about adding too much heat, but then decided, once again, to trust him.

'Do you still speak to him? Your dad, I mean.'

Lukas scoffed. 'No. Can you believe I'm still trying to impress a man I don't even like and no longer speak to?'

She watched as he poured out two mugs of thick hot chocolate and accepted hers with a small smile.

'I guess he was the root of my Christmas hating too,' he said, perching on the edge of the loveseat next to her.

She moved along to make space and patted the seat to let him know it was OK. He shuffled up slightly, but she could tell he wasn't ready to relax just yet. Something was playing on his mind.

'You don't have to say any more, but you're welcome to offload if it will make you feel lighter.' She blew the top of her hot drink, watching the flecks of red chilli dance. 'I'm beginning to find that a problem shared . . .'

He exhaled sharply. 'I don't want to dump my past onto you, but it doesn't feel right to hide it from you either. Especially when you've been so open about yours and mine probably sounds stupid in comparison.'

'It's not a competition.' She placed a hand on his shoulder.

'As much as you love one of those.' His body felt nearly as warm as her drink, even though he was just wearing his smart trousers and a white shirt with his black cooking apron over the top. Not wanting to break the bond, she let her hand slide down and rest at the bottom of his back. His muscles were firm and inviting and she tried her best to resist the urge to start squeezing the poor guy when he needed a friendly ear.

'Christmases were hard when I was growing up.' His shoulders dropped a little. 'Dad took it as his cue to drink even more than usual, and he could get nasty. Mum and I were always creeping around him, like he was an untamed beast that might fly into a rage at any minute. He had an evil tongue and sometimes he could get violent. Though, of course, in public we had to smile and pretend Christmas was just fantastic. Couldn't let the successful crowd get wind of it.'

'I'm sorry,' said Gretel again, the words somehow feeling woefully inadequate.

'Don't be. These things just become part of our stitching, don't they?' He turned to her and rearranged the blanket so it fitted more snugly around her lower body. It was a thick grey cable-knit pattern and she wondered if he'd knitted it himself. She could guess what his mean and *manly* dad would have said about that. Not that a real man, or any decent human, would behave like that.

'The worst thing was, Mum stayed with him for all those years out of a misguided sense of responsibility to me. She thought a strained family was better than a broken one. She left him as soon as I went off to culinary school. Took herself to live in the Scottish Highlands – pretty much as far away as she could without crossing water. She rarely keeps in touch, although maybe she just has too many bad memories of those years.'

'Hmm. That's tough.' Gretel rubbed his back. She hadn't seen her mum at all since her teens, and yet was it somehow worse to have a mum who was still living but chose not to return? Lukas's mum was Nell's sister, although she couldn't remember ever meeting her.

'So Christmas never felt like a thing to be celebrated. It was a pressure cooker of life's worst emotions and each year I couldn't wait for it to bugger off. Mum used to try so hard to make everything jolly, with her homemade Christmas puddings and her collection of gaudy flashing decorations. But it was like the harder she tried, the harder he threw her efforts back in her face. And the more it hurt her.' He put his hot drink down on the wooden farmhouse-style kitchen table next to him. She hadn't seen him take a sip.

'Was Nell there for you?'

'Nell had no idea what was going on, but she always welcomed me in with open arms and gingerbread whenever I needed her. No questions, just comfort. It was cathartic to just turn up and bake with her in my younger years, before Dad began mocking too much.'

'And when you married?'

He raised his eyebrows as though asking whether she wanted to hear all this. She squeezed his arm and nodded.

'Mirabelle got completely fed up of me trying to avoid

Christmas. She'd dress the house up like a Harrods shop window in the hope she could turn me around, and I'd slink off to work just to avoid the place – not that a restaurant full of festive drunks was much better. It was one Christmas when she finally gave up and left, although we'd been growing apart for far too long. We'd been suited once and I'd enjoyed the challenge of living up to her ideals for a while, but people change.'

He seemed matter-of-fact about it, as though he was over any sadness. Then his head jerked up, as though he'd thought of something. 'Actually, can I share something else with you, while we wait for the strudel to cook? I'd really value your opinion, and you deserve a break from me waffling on.'

When he looked at her, that cheeky glint was back in his eyes. Who was she to refuse?

Chapter 40

'They're only leftovers, really.' Lukas looked almost bashful as he pulled a selection of storage boxes from his fridge and arranged them on a coffee table near the loveseat where Gretel was sitting. He'd said the word like it held a certain melancholy. 'Nice to share them for once. They're just a few recipes I've been experimenting with. Want to try?'

'You had me at leftovers.'

As Lukas took lids off the various containers, Gretel's stomach began giving in to a hunger she'd forgotten was there. She'd barely touched the tiny morsels of pretentious food at Lukas's friend's restaurant that evening. Fork now in hand, she was secretly thrilled Lukas had done away with the formality of plates. She was ready to dive in.

'Mmmwoooow,' she mumbled through a mouthful of cheesecake, throwing off any guilt about gobbling so much pudding before bedtime. That part of her never planned to grow up. 'What is this? It's heaven in a box.' She closed her eyes as she let its lightness tease against her tongue. It was like a heady mix of creamy silk and biscuity spice and it was all kinds of delicious. She never wanted it to end.

'Just something I threw together earlier today. A few ideas have been playing on my mind lately.' He cleared his throat and gently lowered himself onto the loveseat next to her. 'This one's a white chocolate cheesecake with a ginger crumble topping. You honestly like it?'

She opened her eyes slowly, as though rousing from a luscious slumber. 'You couldn't tell?' Her voice came out several octaves lower than she'd expected and she felt her cheeks glow, conscious she was almost moaning. Being around him was already sending her senses into overdrive, but now he was staging an attack on her tastebuds too? She'd be defenceless.

His pupils dilated as he watched her, his eyes drinking in her movements as she sampled his desserts, which all looked so homely and inviting, and smelled like a sweet and spicy dream. There was a summer berry and gingerbread ice cream cake that made her feel both warm and shivery all at once, and a plum and five spice tart with a ginger custard that was surely made with the milk of angels.

When she next looked up from her taste-testing he was almost on the edge of his seat.

'What?' She wiped her mouth in case she had pudding around it. But as she searched his keen eyes she realised what he was waiting for. 'Oh. You want my formal approval? Like me getting lost in a binge-fest wasn't enough of an answer?' She treated him to a smile through her sugar-induced haze. It was adorable that he was hanging on for her endorsement, even though he was an accomplished chef and she was still wearing her baking L-plates. 'The desserts were perfection, all of them. But ... what are they for? I'm guessing they're too homely for La Carotte Rôtie. Are they for your new place? The restaurant with the mill?'

She tried to sound casual about it, as though she wasn't holding her breath.

He looked away and shrugged. 'Perhaps.'

With the taste of his exquisite desserts still on her tongue, she couldn't help remembering Francesca Whimple's words that evening. Lukas's talents *did* deserve bigger things than a café serving hot chocolate and gingerbread. Was she being selfish, trying to tether his finances to the café? Perhaps she should be more supportive of his dream to sell the café and buy his own restaurant, even if it was in direct conflict with her own.

Or maybe there was a middle ground. If the February Fair boosted trade in the street and things stayed buoyant, perhaps she could look towards buying Lukas out one day. Would he wait that long? She blinked herself back to the present because she was getting ahead of herself. There was no way she could mention that sort of crazy plan yet.

'Though maybe ...' Lukas chewed his mouth. 'Maybe we could try these desserts at the café. For a while, at least. Would you be up for serving them if I have time to bake more? No pressure if you have your own ideas. You're doing remarkably well without my moody interference.' He gave her a shy smile.

Her heart swelled at this tantalising nod towards commitment. 'I do have some more recipe ideas brewing, especially with all the inspiration from the other shop owners. I could incorporate Bea's lavender and Gordon's rhubarb . . . Maybe you could help me bring these ideas to life at some point.' She returned his timid smile. 'But I do love your creations. Gold star for you, Mr Knight. I'll make room under my glass cloches for your bits and bobs.' She winked. 'I'll need all the extra sweet treats I can get if we'll be feeding the masses at the winter fair.'

He squeezed her hand. 'We *will* be feeding the masses. Which reminds me.' He jumped up and paced to the Welsh dresser, pulling a sketchpad and pencil from a drawer. 'Because do you know what kept occurring to me tonight?' He was gripping the pencil like he was about to do something triumphant. 'I kept thinking the restaurant was packed out with Marcus's so-called friends. But much like if I opened my own place and invited the same contemporaries and hangers-on, they'd just be there to brush shoulders, compare notes and scurry off to try and do one better. I didn't feel any love in that room. Did you?' He waited for her to shake her head. 'There was no sense of community or camaraderie like you've created in The Gingerbread Café. No real connection. No sense of in-it-togetherness. Just people turning up to show off, bitch about the food and hobnob their way upwards. Building something successful and special isn't about getting bums on seats and it's not about gathering a room full of disconnected people. It takes . . . ' He scratched the side of his head with the rubbery end of the pencil.

'It takes a village,' said Gretel, remembering Eve's words which she was sure were part of a saying about something or other.

'Exactly!' He pointed the pencil at her. 'So screw what anyone thinks about *real chefs* not faffing about with *silly gingerbread men*. If I let stupid thoughts like that dictate my life, I'm as small-minded as them. So I'm not just going to make gingerbread folk. I'll make a whole goddamn village. Shops, people, cottages with tiny smoking chimneys. The flipping lot, made of gingerbread. Care to join me? By the time of the Mistleton February Fair we'll have it looking like the best work of foodie art the Cotswolds has ever seen.'

Gretel let out a surprised laugh, but when she looked at Lukas it was clear he wasn't joking.

And suddenly, the passion in his dark eyes was too strong to resist. Gretel put her drink down, pushed the blanket aside and leapt up, rushing towards him across the kitchen in her stockinged feet. Throwing down the sketchpad, he was already on his way. Their bodies met in a flurry of excitement. She pulled his face in towards hers, their lips meeting and moving together in a rhythm that just felt right. She tiptoed backwards, pulling him with her, until their eager bodies tumbled down onto the loveseat with Lukas gently but firmly on top. She wrapped her legs around him, knowing that it felt too soon to turn the loveseat into a lovemaking seat, but imagining exactly how that could work when they were ready.

As the oven beeped to let them know the strudel was baked, Lukas groaned into her mouth that it could wait, as their lips moved together in a whirlpool of their own.

Chapter 41

With the excitement of planning and preparing for the Mistleton February Fair and creating their gingerbread village, it was the end of February before Gretel knew it.

Things had been moving along nicely between her and Lukas. They'd had a couple of less pretentious dates and some cosy nights in, but despite calling themselves a couple, they had been taking things slowly. With her string of short-lived relationships, Gretel had never been this up close and personal with a man before. But with the romance of Valentine's Day still in the air and the closeness she'd felt over their weeks of creating the gingerbread village together, she sensed she was welcoming in a new level of intimacy. She almost couldn't wait for what would be her very *first time*.

'I can't believe the fair is tomorrow,' she said to Amber, as she carefully iced the roofs of the gingerbread houses with white icing and stuck colourful gummy sweets on top.

'Yep, the *February* Fair,' Amber replied. 'So why have you got festive tunes on in here?'

Gretel stopped and blinked. 'Have I? The radio must have slipped onto that all-year-round festive station or something. Weird.' She leaned over and flicked it off.

Amber was raising her eyebrows, but then she did that a lot.

They were in the kitchen at the back of The Gingerbread Café, which she'd closed for the day on Lukas's insistence, to get ready for tomorrow. What with the café's new window displays and improved menus, and the whole street bustling with the interest in the seasonal decorations, the place was always so busy. There was no way they could juggle it all. Gretel would definitely need to talk to Lukas about taking on some *official* staff, although he was sneakily borrowing a few from the restaurant for her tomorrow. She still felt dreadful that Amber wouldn't let Gretel tell Lukas about her.

They'd been organising and making the decorations for the tree and the street all month and now Gretel was keen to see it come together.

'Anyway, it's not fair you've been keeping me inside all day when I'm desperate to see how the street's looking.' Gretel sensed a subject change was in order, to encourage Amber's eyebrows back to their normal level.

'We want the final touches to be a surprise for you, nosey. And Eve's got something up her sleeve with her shop, so don't finish decorating her gingerbread shopfront until you've seen it.' Amber was using her phone to take close-up photos of the gingerbread village to share as teasers on the Instagram profiles she'd set up for the street and the café. Her Insta tips from Lexie with the pixie cut had been going down a storm, but people would have to come to the fair to see the full, impressive display. Amber had also been busy decorating the inside of the café with the stained-glass bunting and edible stained-glass biscuits that Gretel had made, and swirling meringue buttercream frosting onto Lukas's ginger peach cupcakes. Adding artistic flair was turning out to be Amber's thing.

'Why all the mystery? Eve's been hiding her shopfront with sheets for the past few days so she must be planning a big reveal.'

'Yeah, it's about time she branched out from making sad-looking wreaths for dead people.'

'Amber!'

'What? I say it with love, but it's true. Anyway, Eve's definitely looking a lot brighter since Gordon the Grocer has been round there with his power drill.' Amber looked up from her phone to give Gretel a wink. 'Now we just need to fix up Phoebe's lost heart.'

I say it with love was something Phoebe had been encouraging Amber to say to mitigate her wild mouth, although Gretel wasn't sure you could plonk it anywhere and still blurt out whatever you fancied.

Gretel put her piping bag down. 'Oh. Do you think Phoebe's lonely?' Gretel had never really considered it. Phoebe always seemed so zen, and not everyone felt the need to be paired off.

'Totally. She's always going on about her heart chakra, and have you seen how much gingerbread she can get through for one small human? Something's missing in her world, and it's not just the latest rose quartz unicorn.'

Gretel sighed. Her own life had been so much lovelier since she'd found this unlikely collection of friends, even if she often felt a huge guilt that her memories of her family and Nell were fading, and she sometimes awoke in a blind panic that she was doing the wrong thing. But having Lukas to cuddle up to in the evenings and to share some of her thoughts with had so often soothed her. She hated to think of Phoebe missing out on anything her heart longed for.

'*Keep Calm and Trust the Universe.* It will bring you what you need,' Gretel heard herself saying, as she tested the little lights in the gingerbread village. Now, that was definitely a sentiment that Phoebe would get behind. She tutted as she noticed the light wasn't working inside Phoebe's gingerbread chakra healing shop. Why hadn't she noticed that before? It meant Phoebe's little stained-glass windows weren't illuminated like the others. But now Gretel had noticed, she'd do her best to make it right.

Lukas and Gretel had spent the last few weeks drawing up templates, baking gingerbread pieces and carefully fusing them to make an edible replica of their village. They'd also been busy with intricate icing and adding colourful details for the perfect wintery scene. She'd decided to decorate the front of The Gingerbread Café in less Christmassy colours in this gingerbread version, a bit like the stained-glass piece Lukas had once made. As she'd admitted to Lukas, festive reds and greens suddenly felt a bit much all year long. From the pretty pots of snowdrops outside the shops to the

Christmas tree decorated in February blooms, Gretel hoped the final gingerbread village would be spectacular; although it would break her heart if anyone dared to eat it.

She'd tried to argue with Lukas over that bit, but he'd insisted that food, however beautifully created, was meant to be eaten. After their heart-to-heart that night in his cottage about the real reasons he shied away from Christmas, she was hoping if they kept talking, he might be feeling festive enough to make a brand-new gingerbread scene with her when next Christmas came.

Gretel fiddled with the wiring but Phoebe's shop still wouldn't light up. Feeling the frustration, she stepped away. She'd break something if she got too jittery around the delicate village. She grabbed a gingerbread biscuit from her box of broken bits and hopped up onto one of the high stools, chomping down onto the biscuit with excessive crunch.

'What's eating you?' asked Amber, as she fiddled with her photos for Instagram.

Gretel let out a huff, small crumbs spraying into the air, which she desperately batted away from the gingerbread village. 'Urgh. It's just so much pressure, isn't it? I mean, what if it all goes wrong? What if nobody comes to the fair, or if one week later everyone's forgotten about Green Tree Lane and the shops go quiet again? Or if the gingerbread village collapses in a sorry heap, or . . . '

The kitchen door squeaked open and Angel Gabriel scarpered across the floor, skidding across the tiles and crashing into the metal bin with a loud clang.

'Or a ferret scoffs all of the cakes in the village baking

competition,' said Amber, putting a hand over her mouth to stop the guffaws.

Gretel bashed her palm against her forehead. She must have left the kitchen door ajar by accident. 'You see? He shouldn't even be in here. My brain's not used to juggling so many things. And the press will be there tomorrow too. All those eyes on us – it's terrifying.'

Now she'd tasted Lukas's desserts and seen his passion to create such star-worthy recipes, Gretel felt an extra pressure to make the fair a success. If the event could give the street positive publicity and a lasting boost to trade, she secretly hoped the café would really take off. If it did, there was an outside chance she could build towards buying Lukas out one day, so he could follow his bigger dreams.

Amber rescued Angel Gabriel from the floor and gave his fur a ruffle before placing him back out in the closed café in his cosy ferret basket. When she returned she washed her hands and grabbed a biscuit, hopping onto a stool next to Gretel.

'What does this represent?' asked Amber, waving her broken biscuit at Gretel.

Gretel cocked her head. 'It was meant to be Zekia. She was going to stand outside Rum & Raisin looking cheery with Kingsley, but her head fell off. We had to start again.'

'No, silly. I mean, what does the box of broken biscuits represent? Because you could just chuck the duffs in the bin like most people.'

Gretel gasped. 'No! I promised myself I would always keep a box of misfits and I'm proud of them.' The penny was starting to drop, but Amber finished the sentiment for her.

'You said you keep it to remind yourself it's OK to make mistakes. And that even when stuff doesn't go as planned, something good can still come of it. Like afternoon snacks!' Amber waved headless Zekia at Gretel, and Gretel couldn't help laughing.

'Actually, Zekia two came out much better. Don't you think?' She waved her arm towards the gingerbread village, where a brightly decorated Zekia stood smiling next to her bearded husband.

'Exactly. And is it your job to make sure the fair is so awesome that it breaks the freaking internet and all the shops in the street make a fortune from now until for ever?'

'No.' Gretel shrugged. 'But I feel I owe it to Nell to make a success of things here for as long as I can. And if together we can keep the wolf that is Francesca Whimple from our doors . . . '

'Together,' said Amber, grabbing her hand. 'Exactly that.'

There was a knock at the back door and Phoebe popped her head in. 'It's time!'

'Hooray!' said Gretel. 'Can I finally come outside?'

'Time for Eve's big shop announcement?' asked Amber.

Phoebe held up a hand to silence them. 'Yes, but wait. Ooh, there's such good energy in here.' She narrowed her eyes at Gretel in that odd way she sometimes did.

'What?' Gretel asked, brushing her face with her hands. 'Have I got crumbs?'

'No,' said Phoebe, stepping inside. 'I'm just noticing a change in the colours of your aura lately,' she replied. 'In a good way.'

'And there was me thinking you were homing in on the biscuits,' said Amber, grabbing the tin of broken bits and waving them at her. 'Since when do you read auras, anyway? You're as kooky as Eve and her chats with the afterlife.'

'Eve doesn't have psychic abilities,' said Phoebe, as though it was obvious. 'I've never seen indigo or violet in her aura.'

'Riiiiight,' said Amber. 'That purple hair had me fooled.' She was clearly jesting, but Phoebe just smiled. 'So what's going down with Gretel's aura? What's the change?'

'It's been getting a tinge redder,' said Phoebe, grabbing a handful of broken gingerbread. 'In a good way. She's definitely more grounded and in control of life than she used to be, and she's becoming more courageous too.'

'I'm not sure if I feel any of those things today,' whispered Gretel, her eyes flitting to the broken light in Phoebe's gingerbread shop, hoping she'd keep her special X-ray eyes away from it.

'But you are,' said Phoebe, with a gentle shrug. 'I didn't even bring you a crystal today. The universe told me you've got this.'

Amber jumped up and high-fived Phoebe. 'You talk a lot of sense for a gem nerd. I'll let you read my aura one of these days if you like. One-off treat. Now let's get out of here.'

Amber pulled on the baseball cap she'd taken to wearing when she thought Lukas was likely to pop up, and Gretel noticed that her make-up was looking less pale again. The warmer make-up suited her, even if the cap wasn't quite her look. She wondered absent-mindedly if it would show in a person's aura if they were hiding something – because Amber definitely was.

Chapter 42

After being cooped up all morning in the café's kitchen, Gretel was surprised at what a crisp, bright February afternoon it was outside. To her huge relief, Green Tree Lane looked as pretty as a picture. Amber and Phoebe had linked arms with her and they made their way towards Eve's end of the road.

'The tree,' Gretel gushed, when she caught sight of it, rushing over to take a closer look. It was laden with the decorations they'd been making at their café craft evenings, which had become far more regular and had expanded to include all sorts of their favourite crafts. She spotted knitted winter roses and stained-glass hearts, with dried flower garlands looping around the tree and giving off a gentle perfume. 'It's beautiful,' she said to Phoebe and Amber, who'd eagerly followed her over. As Gretel looked around, everything was. The street was well and truly wearing its winter fair coat, and was a world away from the unloved-looking ghost town she remembered of recent years.

Bea stopped to give her a wave from next to one of the lavender pots she'd dotted around the street. She'd told them English lavender was the only one of her dad's varieties hardy enough to be out in the February chill. Gretel could imagine that if they held a summer fair one day, Bea would be in her element.

'What do you think of the street so far?' Bea called over. 'I know some of it's impractical for the weather.' She pulled her woolly coat around her. 'But we couldn't resist!'

'I love it,' Gretel called back, her voice catching as she said the words. She couldn't see glass angel Brigitte at the top of the Christmas tree from where she was standing, but she knew she would be up there, whatever the season; unless there was call for another foray in a cherry picker, at least.

'Well, that's a relief,' said Zekia as she sashayed over, strings of bunting made out of wintery tree material draped around her neck. 'Because there's no time to change it before this fair of yours. I've still got to make my winning sweet potato, rum and raisin cake for the baking competition.'

'It's not just my fair,' Gretel said kindly, although she could feel the pressure beginning to rise again. 'It's everybody's fair.'

'We're in it together,' Amber reminded the others.

'Too true.' Zekia nodded. 'In which case, who's seen that stepladder to hang up my bunting? I'm too top-heavy to be getting up that high. I need one of you spritely types,' she chuckled.

'I'll go up the ladder for you,' said Jane, who was coming over to join them, a collection of framed sketches under one arm. 'When Eve's done with the stepladder.' She pointed to Eve's shop, where Gretel had already spotted the tall stepladder, probably ready for someone to climb up and pull down the dust sheets when it was time for the shopfront reveal. 'But someone will need to help Jayne lay out the pictures for the art trail. Amber? You drew some of them.'

Jane held up the sketch on the top of the pile, which was an intricate mish-mash of wintery things, from speckled starlings to snow-capped hills. Gretel knew Amber had offered to help with the artwork but she hadn't realised just how good she was. Although when she thought of it, some of the birds were like the black Biro drawings she used to see on Amber's arms, which had begun to disappear over the months. Perhaps they'd all been slowly changing.

'Yep, I'll help.' Amber nodded from beneath her baseball cap, taking the stack of pictures from Jane. Was she blushing under there?

'Your drawings are incredible, Amber,' said Gretel, aware that her comment would probably add to Amber's embarrassment, but not willing to let her talents go unnoticed. 'Did you do art at school?'

Amber waved a hand. 'School was ages ago. Whatevs.'

'Whaaaaat?' cried Zekia in disbelief, putting her hands on her hips.

'Showtime!' Amber shouted, pointing towards Eve's shop as the florist came through its front door straightening her purple bob, Gordon the Grocer following behind her. Amber gave a loud wolf-whistle which Gretel guessed was another distraction technique.

Gretel had never seen Eve looking so radiant, in her winter pansy patterned dress which bobbed happily on top of its netted underskirt, a thick shawl wrapped around her shoulders. Even her purple bob looked shinier, and was finished off with an oversized fresh flower tucked behind her ear. Eve gave everyone a little wave as they gathered around.

'Thank you for taking a few minutes out of your day to come over,' said Eve, giving an extra-long smile to Gretel. 'I know you're busy. But I wanted to do this today as I didn't want to steal any limelight at our grand fair tomorrow, and perhaps this feels too personal for all those ears. I wanted to share it with you special few.'

Phoebe and Amber were either side of Gretel, and Phoebe squeezed her hand. Gretel caught Amber checking over her shoulder, presumably on Lukas watch. Gretel knew he'd be on one of his split shifts so he'd probably drop by to help out soon. Gretel had already decided Amber's ducking and diving was getting ridiculous, and she was going to have things out. If nothing else, they'd both be at tomorrow's fair and it would be so much easier if Amber wasn't always scurrying off.

'Anyway, I'm not one for long speeches, but spending time with you all and working together to bring our street back to life has made me realise just how barren Mystic Myrrh Flowers had become. Yes, I still had plenty of online orders, but I'd marketed myself as the go-to woman for funeral flowers, to the exclusion of all the things I used to love. Like wedding flowers.' Her voice dipped slightly with the final two words.

'She once told me myrrh is a tree gum used for embalming *bodies*,' Amber whispered.

'But when I've seen so many of you adapt, grow and even lay your own pasts gently to rest, I knew it was safe for me to do so too.' Eve flashed her eyes towards Gordon. 'Because if you're too busy living in the shadow of past ghosts, how can you be fully present and enjoy smelling life's roses?' To everyone's surprise she kicked off her kitten heels, moved Gordon out of the way and climbed the stepladder. When she was as high as she could safely go she tugged the sheets which were draped over her new shop sign and they floated to the floor like redundant spectres.

'So welcome to Eve in Bloom,' she said with a flourish. 'Flowers for all seasons and every occasion. Especially weddings!'

As everyone cheered and admired the new-look shopfront with its rosy pink shades and pretty new sign, Eve climbed down and came to speak to Gretel, Phoebe and Amber.

'You've done a beautiful job,' said Gretel, and they all joined in with congratulations.

'But seriously, spill the tea,' said Amber. 'Did you really talk to dead people to get their funeral flower requests?'

Gretel winced but Eve just smiled.

'There was a rumour I did, many years back. And when people started believing it, funeral flower orders were soon flying in.' She shrugged. 'So I went with it. I used to wear a lot of black and a melancholy face back then, so the rumours almost suited me.'

'You, wearing a lot of black?' asked Amber. 'What were you feeling dark about?'

Eve looked over her shoulder and lowered her voice. 'When I was just a slip of a girl, I was stood up at my own wedding by a man I thought loved me. Can you imagine? *He'll be here any moment*, the panicked vicar kept saying, before sending my wedding car back around the block. But I could tell from my mother's pursed lips and my dad's tightening fists that he wouldn't.' She gulped and Gretel placed a hand on her shoulder. 'My parents had always said I was too young and he wasn't right, but I was headstrong. And the worst thing? One month later, his heavily pregnant wife turned up on my doorstep. I'd unknowingly been messing around with a married man.'

'Oh Eve, you poor thing,' said Phoebe.

'What a dick.' Amber tutted and shook her head.

'I'd only just finished my apprenticeship in floristry, but after that turmoil I couldn't face making another wedding bouquet. Or christening flowers, for that matter. Suddenly my world felt dark and the only art I wanted to make with flowers was in memory of times gone by. When my father died not long after I became obsessed with seeing a clairvoyant, and before I knew it people in the small village where I lived were saying I spoke to the departed. Then the idea quite caught on.' She gave a little laugh.

'You're a true entrepreneur!' Amber rubbed her arm.

'It has paid the bills so I can't pretend it didn't serve me well, but it's time to move on. I've spent a lifetime mourning something that was never meant to be. Pushing people away

271

for fear of more heartache. The excuses I've made to keep friendships at bay.' She grabbed each of their hands in turn. 'Oh, I've been so silly.' She sniffed back her tears.

Gretel fought a few of her own as a wave of recognition washed in.

'Feelings aren't silly,' Phoebe reassured her. 'But we're glad you're ready to move into a happier space now. I'm here for you.' She looked at Gretel and Amber too. 'All of you.'

'Right back at ya, soul sisters. I've needed you more than you know.' Amber scooped them into a curiously long hug. 'But hey, don't ruin my eyeliner. I've got work to get on with.' She pulled away and signalled to the assortment of artwork she was cradling, before hurrying off to see Gordon about placing the first piece of art for the art trail in his shop.

When Lukas arrived, slipping his arm around Gretel as she took a quiet moment to contemplate Eve's new shop-front, she was surprised to find herself imagining a new look for The Gingerbread Café. Had Eve just shown her that making that final break from the past didn't have to be that terrifying? So why was she still holding back?

'Can I guess what you're thinking?' Lukas asked, interrupting her thoughts. 'Are you wondering if we should do the same at the café?'

She shrugged. 'I guess there's no point if you're still undecided about its future.'

'That's true,' he said quietly, although did he sound less sure than he had before?

No, she was imagining it. She wriggled away. 'Anyway, it would be too scary. Too final. I think I've dealt with enough change for one season.' She tried on her brightest smile, unsure whether she was disappointed with herself or with him for not showing any fight.

As Kingsley arrived with celebratory rum and Zekia brought up the rear with cake, Gretel's heart swelled again. She may have been on edge about tomorrow's fair. Making sure it lived up to memories of fairs gone by and brought in new crowds for the future felt like a lot of strain, even though it wasn't only hers to bear. But as Lukas and her new friends cosied around chatting, she couldn't think of a lovelier bunch of people to help settle her pre-fair jitters.

Chapter 43

'It was only meant to be a small village fair,' Gretel whispered, watching through the café window as the crowds descended upon Mistleton, wrapped in big coats and bobble hats. The weather was fresh and the morning frost had cleared. It was the perfect kind of day to warm your hands around a mug of Gordon the Grocer's winter veg soup.

But Gretel was too nervous for that, even if they were *good* nerves. 'I never even thought I was a *people person*. Should we hide? I mean, they'd manage ...'

Lukas arrived behind her, his arm slipping around her waist. She was wearing the bright yellow frilly apron that Zekia had made for her, on top of a heart-patterned jumper dress she'd knitted especially.

'You're a natural with people, even if it does still feel new. And you did want the fair to make a difference. It's even been getting press coverage.' He nodded to yet another reporter with a fancy-looking camera slung around her neck. 'Prepare to go viral.'

'Wow, really?' She tried not to sound terrified.

Because everything would be *just fine*. The street was looking incredible. She'd been busy with the whole gang since the crack of dawn, putting up gazebos, setting up Phoebe's tumbled-stone tombola and making sure everything was ready for the various contests and activities.

'The only thing we ought to be afraid of are those alien-shaped vegetables in Gordon's misshapen veg competition. Did you see that parsnip with two legs and a whiskery manhood? That'll give me nightmares for years.'

Gretel giggled. 'Vegetables are overrated. I'll stick to the baking competition if it's all the same with you. My money's on Bea's lavender and honey cake, but only because you didn't enter.' She turned around to kiss him, hooking her arms around his neck and disappearing into the quiet moment of magic before it was time to open the café.

'Come on.' Lukas gently teased her out of her peaceful haze. 'People will be banging the door down to try our new gingerbread waffles and *lebkuchengewürz* hot chocolate.'

Lukas had been showing her how to make her own gingerbread spice mix and it really made her favourite drink pop. Gretel sighed and looked over her shoulder. 'Life *is* always better with a bit of spice.' As the winter sunlight caught the new heart-shaped glass bunting that festooned the café's bay window, she felt like at least one person up there was agreeing with her.

Lukas had arranged for a couple of his kitchen apprentices

from La Carotte Rôtie to serve with him in the café for the day so Gretel was free to wander and soak up the atmosphere of the fair, and help out where she was needed. *This is your day*, Lukas had insisted. *Enjoy every moment.* She couldn't help feeling he was being too kind; it had always been a team effort. But she wasn't going to argue with the chance to roam free and experience the fun of the fair.

She did a last lap of the café, rearranging the bright new cushions Zekia had helped her to sew at one of their craft classes and lighting the tealights on the tables, before walking out into the street. Some of the shops had opted to have small market stalls to bring more life to the street, and most shop owners had roped in family or friends to help run everything. Bea's son Xander came by with a group of children as he took charge of the gingerbread treasure hunt. Amber gave Gretel a wave as she zipped by on art trail duty, Angel Gabriel's little ferret head popping out of the front pocket of the skull and butterfly patterned apron Zekia had helped her to make. Even Bea's dad, Farmer Wilbur, of cherry picker fame was on hand in his purple Ribena-berry overalls, helping to judge the wonky vegetables, with his sister Elsie presiding over the cakes.

Jane and Jayne had built some makeshift wooden shelters to go around the tree, which they'd draped with fairy lights, just like Gretel remembered from February Fairs of years gone by. People were already huddling under them with hot soup and refreshments which they'd bought from the various shops or stalls. Gordon and his shop boy had even set up a turnip version of a coconut shy and had thrown down some potato sacks for the youngsters to bounce around doing sack races.

There was no doubt about it – Green Tree Lane was buzzing. There were smiles on faces and the chilly air was filled with laughter. Her mum and Rosa would have loved this. Nell too. It was the perfect mix of the old village traditions with a good sprinkling of new ones.

Gretel recognised all sorts of accents, from locals to further afield, and plenty of excited tourists. Better still, people were spending money. As Gretel walked around taking it all in she noticed that every shop or stall was bustling and the shop owners were in their element. She could hear Gordon with his market stall patter and Kingsley laughing heartily as he talked about the benefits of rum. Phoebe was trying to juggle her crystal shop and her tumbled-stone tombola. She also seemed to be in charge of her customer's crystal-needy shih-tzu, Cedric, so Amber and Jane were taking it in turns to be her extra set of hands.

'Fluorite!' Phoebe said gleefully, as she handed a clear green and purple stone to a prize-winning little boy.

'Keeps your teeth clean,' said Amber, with a cheeky grin.

Phoebe tinged her small bronze energy-clearing cymbals around Amber's head, whilst keeping her zen-like smile. 'It soaks up *aaalllll* negative energy,' she said in a sing-song voice, shoving a spare one into Amber's pocket.

Gretel smiled and kept walking.

Seeing Mistleton alive with people filled Gretel's heart with joy, even if all the people taking photos and the press attention was making her stomach quiver. Amber promised it was great if people were sharing photos on social media. When Jane and Jayne had made the painted A-boards for each of the shops they'd added hashtags for visitors to use, to encourage them to share their pics. As Amber explained, it was free marketing and it *couldn't go wrong*.

As Gretel finished her circuit of the street she landed back outside The Gingerbread Café, keen to feast her eyes on their gingerbread village that was on display on a trestle table outside the café. But her eyes were accosted by an infinitely less welcome sight. She tried not to audibly groan. There was only one person around there who'd turn up to a village fair in a businessy trouser suit and customised trainers. And why was she taking such a keen interest in the dainty gingerbread shops and houses?

'Gertrude! Well, mwaaaaah.' Francesca Whimple grabbed Gretel's shoulder with a grip that might leave imprints, delivering exaggerated air kisses nowhere near her face.

'It's Gretel,' she corrected her, through gritted teeth. Not that Gretel didn't call her Swingy Bob when she was out of earshot, but still. At least she made an effort to get her name right when she was listening.

'Gretel. Absolutely! And what a fantabulous job you've made of this fair. You've even started to give the café a new look.' She pointed to the edible art hanging in the window. 'The prospective tenants who are coming to the fair later will just love it.'

If the street wasn't so busy with happy customers and nosey reporters, maybe Gretel would have had it out with her about what she'd overheard her say on that rainy day in Lower Paddleton. Or maybe she'd never be that brave.

Gretel had a quick look around to check no camera lenses were pointing their way. 'We haven't even decided we're selling yet. And if we are, to whom.' She crossed her arms. It was still a serious conversation she needed to have with Lukas, but she'd had enough to get her head around with planning for the fair. And she was still hoping the fair would change the café's fortune for the better.

Swingy Bob raised her impossibly thick eyebrows. 'Riiiiiight.'

Why did she say that as though she knew more than Gretel? Just as she was resisting the urge to shove the woman's annoying head into one of Gordon's dusty old potato sacks, her thoughts were interrupted by more visitors approaching the table.

'This gingerbread village is really quite something,' said an older lady with a big furry hat. The two younger women with her, who could have been her daughters, nodded their less furry heads. 'Look at that darling florist's with the tiny flowers.' She pointed at the gingerbread replica. 'And here's that lovely Lavender & Honey with the sweet lady waving outside, and that yummy flavoured rum place. Everything lights up too. How enchanting.' She straightened herself and smiled at Gretel, who was relieved she'd got all the lights working, including Phoebe's, the night before. 'Yes, what a marvellous village this is. I'd quite forgotten. Well done for brightening the place up and bringing this fair together.'

Gretel felt her cheeks redden. 'I can't take all the credit . . .'

'Shh now,' the lady replied. 'Everyone says wonderful

things about you. Your hard work will be all over the news-
papers soon enough.'

Gretel tried to smile.

'We're from Lower Paddleton.' Hat lady shot a harsh look
at Swingy Bob, and her daughters followed suit. 'It used to
be a charming village too, before our independent shops
were bought up and those ugly chains and franchises took
over. Dreadful business. It's lovely to see such a unique
café. Don't get me started on the dishwater they serve up
in Quickie Café. Perhaps I don't fancy my *coffee in a jiffy.*'

In the distance Gordon's turnips crashed to the cobbles
in a crescendo of cracks. A crowd cheered.

'Not everyone can handle progress,' said Swingy Bob,
talking to Gretel as though the other women didn't have
ears. 'But I can see you're coming around to it. Thanks for
jazzing the place up a bit.'

'You never did like a *festive puke disaster*,' Gretel
said sweetly.

Even though Swingy Bob looked completely confused,
Gretel felt silently triumphant.

'Look at that meerkat thing in that girl's apron pocket,'
said one of hat lady's daughters, pointing at Amber in the
near distance.

'That's a ferret,' said the other woman. 'And doesn't she
go to Lower Paddleton High with our Kasey? Ember, is it?
No, Amber?'

Miss Whimple shot her head around to look, her hair in
full pendulum swing as she gawped at Amber disappearing into the crowds, her red hair partly disguised under a

baseball cap. 'Since when did she hang around this place? And why the hell is she wearing an apron?' She turned and strode off in the direction Amber had gone in, her annoying black and gold trainers squeaking across the cobbles.

What on earth?

'What's the uniform at Lower Paddleton High?' Gretel quickly asked.

'Black skirt or trousers, white shirt, black and white tie—'

'Black satchel,' Gretel finished, taking a wild guess. Not unlike a waitress, apart from the tie. Or maybe she should have more faith in her friend. She couldn't be at school if she was hanging around here in the week so often, could she? Though if she was at school, Gretel would surely be in all sorts of trouble for having her cleaning tables when legally she should have been in class.

A sack race of children bounced by, giggling and barging each other, sending Gretel's thoughts into a jumble.

Whatever the story, much like her conversation with Lukas about Situation Whimple, it was a discussion for another day. Gretel just needed to get through this one without anything unravelling, especially in front of all of these eyes and cameras. *Keep Smiling and Carry On* was the mantra that would have to get her through.

Gretel took a few deep breaths and looked over to the top of the Christmas tree. It was a good few metres high, but she knew in the right light the low sun would dance across the iridescent wings of the fairy-turned-angel who represented her mother. She was sure she caught a glint of something. Was it a sign everything would be OK?

Chapter 44

Bea walked by arm in arm with her son Xander, leading a troop of children on the gingerbread treasure hunt. They all waved madly at Gretel. Xander had been so excited when Gretel had come up with the idea and his enthusiasm had reminded her of little Rosa. Rosa would have been skipping along after them with glee.

Gretel recognised some of the children from the café as fans of the gingerbread people she'd been making. Some days it still felt surreal to be in charge of things, but maybe she was making a small step in her mum's more sociable shoes after all.

Gretel moved out of the way as two people came out of the café, raving about the new menu and how wonderful the place looked. Gretel still felt Lukas's Michelin star-worthy desserts deserved a better showcase, but he was in his element making them and was thrilled when people enjoyed them. And as the bustle of her community continued around her, Gretel hoped that despite the strange events with the swingy bobbed woman, all would be well.

Gretel shook off her unease as Eve approached.

'Look at this street. It's buzzing! I couldn't resist bringing over this pot of dwarf daffodils for you as a little thank you for coming up with the idea. They match your apron so well.'

'Wow, thank you.'

Gretel noticed how Eve's flowery gardening gloves matched the green and white kimono wrap dress she was wearing under her big shawl. She looked brighter and more glamorous every day. 'Anyway, I'm proud of you, Eve of Eve in Bloom. The array of flowers outside your shop today would put The Chelsea Flower Show to shame. And don't think I haven't noticed how impressive Gordon's fruit and veg are looking. I wonder who's inspired him to scrub up his sweet potatoes and sing songs about purple sprouting broccoli?' She gave Eve a nudge. 'You both seem jolly.'

'We do?' Eve pushed her cat-eye glasses back up her nose. And was she blushing the shade of one of her pretty pink roses? 'Yes, I guess we do. And I would never have picked him out as my type, although I've been busy telling myself *no one* is. But sometimes people surprise you when you get to know them. Don't you think? Or maybe you just surprise yourself about what you really need. Thank you for coaxing me out of my cave and into this wonderful community.'

Gretel held up her hands. 'It was teamwork.'

'It takes a village,' Eve nodded. 'Even your Lukas seems to be accepting it.' She looked towards the gingerbread village, which the whole gang had been cooing over that morning before the fair. 'Although it takes a special someone to bring everyone together. I'm sure Nell used to be good at that too, in her day. It's the secret sauce of a café owner.'

They both turned instinctively to look at the stained-glass version of Nell outside a gingerbread house, which sat on the windowsill in the bay window of The Gingerbread Café. She'd always loved a good nosey. Gretel didn't know what the long-term future of the café would be, but for now, she was willing to believe Nell would have been proud.

Eve took her gloves off and put an arm around Gretel's shoulder. 'You've got the sauce, darling girl. Don't doubt it.'

As they smiled in the sunshine the sounds of happy chatter from the market stalls hummed around them.

'Why did the gooseberry go out with a prune? Because he couldn't find a date! Ha ha haaaa. Grab your gooseberries here, madam. We only regret the gooseberries we didn't take.'

That one could only be Gordon. Eve rolled her eyes and Gretel burst into laughter.

'Now, talking of gooseberries. There was something interesting going on at Phoebe's tumbled-stone tombola when I walked by. Care for a look?'

'Absolutely.'

Gretel and Eve walked along the street, past the Christmas tree where visitors were huddled with steaming hot chocolate and bags of Zekia's best rum and raisin fudge, and landed outside Phoebe's chakra healing shop. The shop was definitely more open and inviting without its thick net drapes, and Phoebe had set up a little stall outside, with crystals of different shapes and sizes arranged in colour order like a beautiful rainbow.

But what was even more striking was the vast smile on Phoebe's face as she chatted to a man Gretel didn't recognise. There was something alluring about him with his mysterious harem pants and dark hair twisted into messy dreadlocks. Their eyes and hands danced as they spoke, and Gretel noticed that Phoebe seemed to have forgotten about her tumbled-stone tombola. Meanwhile, Cedric the shih-tzu was making friends with the small black and brown crossbreed who seemed to belong to the man with the harem pants.

Gretel nudged Eve. 'Cedric's heart chakra seems to be on the mend. He's found himself a friend, and perhaps one for Phoebe too.'

'I yam what I yaaaaam,' Gordon serenaded passing customers in the background. 'I know, I know, madam. I'm such a fun-gi!'

They chatted for a while before Eve realised she ought to rescue Jane, who'd been looking after Eve's shop. Amber seemed to have disappeared, as had Swingy Bob Whimple, although nobody was missing *her*. And just as Gretel made her way back to the café, realising how much she was missing the warmth of Lukas's hugs, he appeared through the throng.

As though sensing something on her face, Lukas opened his arms and she bundled in. She loved the way her head fitted snugly under his chin.

'Nell would have loved this,' he said.

She heard his voice catch as he said it, which set off a few silent tears of her own. 'I know,' she murmured into his chest.

As she unravelled herself to take it all in, Gretel had to admit that this was perhaps her best memory since her mother and Rosa had passed away. And wasn't it OK to make new ones?

People bustled in and out of shops, grinning and carrying bags. Children played, villagers gathered in gazebos laughing at wonky vegetables and judging cakes. Winter flowers bloomed, grocers sang and love was blossoming all over the place. Even the contemplative nods of journalists and the clicks of their cameras felt like a gentle applause. Things had gone pretty well today and nothing could take that away from them. Green Tree Lane was officially back in business.

The fair continued to buzz, and before Gretel knew it the sun was setting on what had felt like an almost perfect day. The crowds had gone, Zekia had been crowned the fair's star baker and everything from the gingerbread village to Phoebe's pretty crystals had been packed away. Gretel and Lukas cosied up together in one of the wooden shelters at the foot of the Christmas tree, laughing as the whole thing wobbled when they sat.

'Do you ever get the feeling that everything might just be OK?' Gretel heard herself asking, as she marvelled at the wisps of orange cloud that trailed across the sky.

'Not often,' Lukas admitted. His arm was around her shoulder, filling her with a warmth she needed as the sun was saying goodnight. 'But perhaps right now.'

He turned to look at her, his eyes seeming to drink in every detail of her face as though she was infinitely more fascinating than any sunset. His lips were teasingly close and she felt torn between touching her own against them and hearing more of his reassuring words. She studied them, trying to make her choice. In the golden light of the retreating sun they looked so soft and kissable.

'And is it just me, or is the enticing possibility that everything could really be OK actually scarier than when you're sure everything's going downhill?' Gretel asked.

A light danced across his eyes as those tempting lips twitched into a smile. She watched as they parted as though getting ready to kiss away her insecurities. Or was that just wishful thinking?

'Gretel, it's absolutely terrifying. Because the more I think about it, the more I know my future isn't what I'd been working towards. Although it scares me to say it ... I want my future to be with you.'

Her heart felt like it would soar. Those words were *everything*.

His eyes fixed her with that magnetic look which always drew her in – but this time his mouth was in on it too. And who was she to resist?

She moved her head towards his, stealing the last bit of air between them before their lips met in a kiss which swept some of her fears away. As their bodies twisted towards each other, Gretel realised that she was ready for a whole lot more than she was willing to give under a Christmas tree in such a public place.

'Can we go back to yours?' she mumbled into his mouth as the kissing became deeper.

'Are you sure?' he groaned back, in a *please don't say you're teasing* kind of way. His apparent aching need for her brought even more heat to her body. She needed some of this clothing off.

'You'd prefer to carry on here?' She giggled.

This time his moan was edged with something that sounded like the thrill of him wanting to. 'What are you doing to me? You're right, we need to move.'

He rose quickly, the shed shaking as he pulled her up with him like he needed her body to hide his arousal. It certainly felt like he did. Gretel felt an excited laugh bubble up. But then he stopped and held her hands, pinning her again with those stunning eyes.

'I mean, are you sure you want to go somewhere where we'll be completely alone, whilst we're both feeling so ... excitable? You get to change your mind at any point, but now would be a kind time to let me down gently.'

Her eyes flicked cheekily to certain parts of him that were certainly not *down*. 'That's good to know. Are you ready?'

He kissed her again, more slowly this time, his lips soft and warm against hers like a glorious *I'm ready*. She couldn't wait to get back to Starry Knight cottage and get wrapped up in Lukas until the moon took over from the setting sun.

Chapter 45

It was the morning after the Mistleton Fair and Gretel felt like she was in a dream. She was snuggled up in Lukas's bed at Starry Knight cottage after the best night she could remember.

She lay alone, luxuriating in the memory of it, the hollow next to her still warm and smelling of him. After a delicate morning hug he'd kissed her gently and had gone downstairs to make fresh waffles. She could get used to waking up with a chef. A smile crept across her face as she remembered last night's hurried walk home, full of excited whispers, anticipation. And promises.

She'd been acutely aware it would be her first time, as had he. Yet everything had felt instinctive.

They'd rolled together on his bed, learning their way around each other's bodies, the sheets soft and fresh like they'd been waiting. She'd savoured every delicious moment. When they'd finally brought their willing bodies together under the twinkle of the stars through the shutters, fully protected and safe, it had felt like utter bliss.

And right now, she was missing him already. What was taking him so long? She would surprise him and go to help. He'd taken the only dressing gown, so she pulled her jumper dress over her naked skin and crept down the stairs in bare feet. She stopped on the bottom step as she heard Lukas talking. Just one voice. She guessed he was on the phone. As she turned to retreat to the warm bed, not wanting to interfere, she thought she heard him say a name. Franny. *What?*

She shook her head. It didn't really matter if he was speaking to Francesca Whimple, did it? Well, it was way before breakfast time, so that was kind of weird. But the woman was all about business. She probably never slept.

Yet what *business* would Lukas have with the Whimple now? She and Lukas had talked about it last night – they were keeping the café. Together. After the success of the fair, the café's incredible takings and the sense of achievement they'd both felt, they were giving it a go. Perhaps he'd need to let Miss Whimple know that. It was only polite. But as she tiptoed up another step, she couldn't help overhearing. His voice sounded animated. He was excited about something.

'I can picture it now – a proper place to call my own. I'd completely redo it, obviously. It would be a disaster as it is. Totally the wrong look. But I'm imagining a really intimate vibe and top-notch cuisine. Great table linen. The best desserts in the Cotswolds.'

Gretel froze, her hand clutching the handrail for support.

What on earth was he on about? His own place? With top-notch cuisine? But he'd said . . . Her chest tightened. Had he wanted to turn The Gingerbread Café into a stupid fancy restaurant all along?

'And the views up there are amazing.'

She blinked. What views? From the café, you could just see out onto the street. Oh God. He still wanted to buy that swanky old mill building, didn't he? That stuff he'd said last night about keeping the café had been a bunch of lies. But why? Her hand flew to her mouth. To get a naive virgin into bed?

'No, of course I haven't told her.' He scoffed.

She'd heard enough. She tore down the stairs and into the kitchen, marching barefoot across the hard floor, not sorry she accidentally shoulder barged Lukas in her rush. Luckily her shoes and bag were still by the back door where she'd dropped them, though he'd have to keep her underwear. She wasn't coming back.

'Gretel.'

As he was busy scratching his head she unlocked the door and ran out into the cold, grey air. His gravelly path felt like tiny knives on her feet, but there was no time to put on the shoes she'd grabbed. At least she could use them as missiles if he dared come after her with his absurd excuses.

But what was there to say? She'd heard everything.

She made it around the side of the cottage to his front gate, which in their excitement to get inside last night, they hadn't even closed. Her stomach lurched.

Once she was off his property, she made a run for it, the

chill burning her lungs. Was that his voice? But she wasn't stopping. Not until she was somewhere safe. Like she'd always known, people weren't to be trusted. Especially not Lukas Lying Knight.

She was nearly on Green Tree Lane before her lungs began to give up. She was puffing hard and her feet were probably bleeding, but she was nearly home. *Home*. Where the hell was that? She'd given up her crappy rented maisonette. Now it was clear she couldn't stay at The Gingerbread Café. Things were crashing down around her.

She managed to turn the corner, the Christmas tree coming into view. At least she would always have that. Her pace slowed as she gasped for breath, the world dizzying.

'Gretel.'

Oh God, was she hearing things? Or had he come after her? She ploughed onwards as quickly as she could with aching lungs, the cobbles slippery under her feet.

'Gretel!'

She spun around. 'Yes, I know what my bloody name is.' If these were her last breaths, she did not want to waste them on this idiot. She tried to turn and scurry, but he'd caught her wrist. The momentum spun her back towards him. She glared down at her wrist then back up at him. 'How dare you. Get off me.' Her voice was a wheeze, but she'd never been so hot with anger.

His eyes widened. 'I'm sorry.' He pulled his hand away.

'Sorry for what? Lying to me? Sleeping with me? Chasing me down the road and manhandling me?' The words were flying from her mouth and she couldn't stop them.

'No! I mean, I'm sorry if I hurt your wrist; I definitely didn't mean to, but ... what? Gretel, what's going on?'

Oh, he was good. What a showman. No wonder she'd been fooled. 'I heard your conversation with Swingy Bob Whimple.'

'Who?'

'Sorry, *Franny*.' He was trying to wriggle out of this already.

'Right, well, I was just telling her ...'

Why was he hesitating? She wasn't giving him the chance to make up another lie.

'Telling her that you're a stuck-up twat of a chef who can't wait to have his own proper restaurant with *top-notch cuisine* and *great table linen*. What kind of complete nob gives a shit about table linen?'

He laughed. 'No, you've got it all wrong.'

He laughed. She was standing out here at the crack of freezing dawn, bleeding bare feet and without any knickers on, and he was *laughing*? After she'd given herself to him so trustingly? And after everything she'd just heard him say?

She was not sticking around for this.

Her feet took over and she marched towards the tree, desperate to reach The Gingerbread Café on the other side of it. She needed to close the door on this madness.

But there he was, rushing after her again. She turned towards him. 'Stop following me! Don't you think I feel foolish enough already? I fell for everything you told me. I fell for *you*. I believed that you were changing, that you weren't some pretentious, grumpy-faced sod. I thought you cared about me, about Nell and the café. And all along you were just trying to win me around so you could get your own way. In the café and *other places*. You probably still think gingerbread is beneath you.'

He reached for her arm again, but she pulled away.

'And you're a bully. Maybe you're not so different from your horrible dad after all.' She heard her own sharp intake of breath as soon as she'd said it. And as she looked up she saw the hurt in his eyes.

He turned his back on her and began striding away.

She took a step backwards, getting ready to bolt in case he changed his mind, but her back hit something hard. She dropped her shoes and turned, her flying arms pushing the thing in panic. It was rough against her hands – a makeshift wooden shelter from the fair. The one they'd kissed in last night. It had been unstable then too, and just like her it was falling hard.

And then she heard it. *Thwaaaaack*. The shelter had toppled and hit the Christmas tree. The tree lurched forwards, its branches shaking. Flower petals and glass ornaments showered down like confetti mixed with ice. *Ching ching ching*. The glass broke into shards as it hit the cobbles.

Gretel shot a look to the tip of the tree, where Angel Brigitte wobbled for her little glass life. Would the tree hit the floor? No. Its roots were firmly planted. But with its new angle, the angel struggled to cling on. The tree's tip vibrated. Gretel's mouth opened in the shape of a slow-motion wail, but there was no sound.

She tried to drag the shelter from the tree, but the action made the branches shake harder. The angel was hanging by a thread. Gretel gasped and ran around the tree, her feet slipping against the cobbles. She flung out her arms as she saw Angel Brigitte breaking loose. But Gretel wasn't fast enough.

The angel crashed down onto the cobbles, splintering into more pieces than it would be possible to fix. Gretel felt the crack as though it had happened deep inside her core. As though it was the sound of her own soul breaking.

Just when she thought that was it, little glass Rosa fell from another branch and cracked like an eggshell next to Angel Brigitte.

Gretel felt the tears pouring out of her, hot and furious. This was a sign. No, this was a great, glaring omen. She should never have stepped away from her Christmas sanctuary. Turning her back on her memories, putting her fragile heart on the line. It had been reckless.

Her shoes still lay strewn. She shoved them into her bag, before collecting what she could of her broken glass angels. Her feet were collecting more cuts, but she didn't care. They were already bleeding from her run. Now her hands would be too.

She limped towards the front door of The Gingerbread Café. At least it was too early to be seen. And from the looming clouds, it looked as though the impending rain would wash away any stains on the cobbles. The way her skin was crawling, she needed a serious shower too.

But more than anything, she needed to be alone. To get away from this. Because her heart had never felt heavier. Without a doubt, this was the worst mistake of her life.

Chapter 46

'What a bloody noise,' Gretel complained to Angel Gabriel as she harrumphed down the stairs from her flat to the café in her mince pie slippers. Obviously it wasn't Christmas, but she was past caring about that. The sooner she could get back to her cosy old festive life, the better. She just had to untangle herself from this one first. The universe would send her a way, because much like this excessively loud postperson, the universe always delivered. She just had to look out for the sign.

In fact, whoever had just posted whatever it was had made such a racket, it was as though they'd been hell-bent on letting her know something had landed. It was probably just as well, as she'd overslept. Not that she felt like opening the café today. Not one little dot.

It was the day after her Monday morning row with Lukas. She'd spent yesterday hiding inside the café and obsessively cleaning after the mess of Sunday's fair, and everything that had followed. Curtains drawn, doors locked, as though her life had needed a good old scrub.

Her mind hadn't stopped chewing over the events with Lukas and regurgitating them in different shapes. She barely knew what to think, other than she felt humiliated and furious. She wasn't proud of her actions. Like an out of body experience, she'd felt dangerously out of control. Her flight instincts had taken over and who knew what had happened to her mouth. She'd accused him of manhandling her, which she unequivocally knew he hadn't. It hadn't hurt when he'd taken her wrist and she hadn't felt unsafe. And the thing she'd said about his dad had come from nowhere. She'd never even met the man.

Yet when she weighed it up against what Lukas had done . . . Making her trust him, fall for him, even sleep with him. Pretending he cared about her and even saying they could keep the café together, when all along he was still mapping out his Michelin-starred dreams, down to the detail of the *great table linen*. Had the lies just been to keep her on side, so she'd agree to anything and sign whatever legal documents he put in front of her? Was Swingy Bob Whimple in on it too?

She wondered with a sickening pang whether he'd always had designs on stealing away her *first time*, or if that was an extra bit of sport. He knew how inexperienced she was. She'd been honest with him. She'd always struggled to feel close enough in any of her previous, extremely short relationships. Why on earth had she dared to change that?

To top it off, Lukas hadn't even bothered to get in touch.

She felt utterly miserable. So much for doing things differently and trying to be brave. She'd dared to step out of her snow globe, but she hadn't been strong enough for the storm. Life could be cruel. And now much like her precious glass angels, every part of her felt smashed.

She landed at the bottom of the steps with a thud and switched the café light on.

'And where's Amber? Did you scare her off?' She held her ferret at arm's length. He wriggled and shook his head. 'No, of course you didn't. I bet I can guess who's responsible for that.'

She hadn't seen or heard from Amber since the fair when Swingy Bob had chased after her. Who knew what had happened or whether the rumours about her still being at school were true? Amber had left Angel Gabriel with Jane and Jayne, and she hadn't been around at the end of the day when they'd tidied the street.

'Maybe friendship isn't all it's cracked up to be either, huh?'

Angel Gabriel squeaked.

Well, one thing was clearly true: happy bubbles invariably burst. Gretel sighed and put Angel Gabriel down on the wooden café floor. He scarpered towards the front door's low letter box, where a newspaper was hanging sadly onto the bristly doormat.

The newspaper that had been rammed through appeared to be the *Cotswold Crier*, although it now read the *Cot Crier*, thanks to being shredded on delivery. She hadn't ordered a copy, although perhaps someone wanted her to see the write-up about the fair.

Angel Gabriel sank his teeth into the paper and tugged at it, tearing off the *Cot* part and running away with it gleefully. She exhaled. She couldn't face looking at the write-up yet.

She made her way behind the counter and opened the tall fridge, pulling out milk, and finding chocolate and spices in the cupboard. She threw things into a pan, put the heat on and began to stir, the whirlpool of liquid trying to swallow her thoughts.

As she leaned across to put the milk back and slam the fridge shut, the draught made the papers stuck to the fridge door with magnets flutter. Something fell to the floor. She reached down to grab it. If she was quick, she'd only have to leave the stove and stop stirring for a second.

It was a photograph – an old one. Had it been hidden? She squinted to get a look at the blurry image, taking a few moments to register. It was her as a teenager, with her mum and little Rosa. Here in the café, next to one of Nell's real-life Christmas trees. Smiling, like nothing mattered. Happy, like they always had been.

Why had it taken several blinks to work that out? Were her memories fading? Their faces used to be etched into her mind so vividly. With her daily, in everything she did. Talking to her when she was lonely, guiding her when she felt lost. But where had they been these past few weeks? Since she'd packed things away and let herself start moving on, they'd barely been here. Had they moved on too? Were they cross with her for getting rid of Christmas, their special time of year?

A memory of smashing glass rang through her ears. Two

falling angels breaking on the cobbles. She hadn't been able to save them and now they were gone. To be replaced by what? No Lukas. No Amber. She hadn't seen the others since the fair. She had a café to open and she couldn't even be bothered with that.

Gretel gulped as a sob rose inside her from the depths of who knew where. Her loss was as painful then as it had always been. At least that bit hadn't faded. She pulled a tissue from her dressing gown pocket and let the tears flow. It was normal to cry. Maybe she was overreacting. She'd been getting stronger, hadn't she? And that had to be a good thing, even if some days she would still feel like crap.

As she took some deep breaths and blew her nose loudly, she heard an angry hissing from the stove. Her hot chocolate. She'd forgotten to stir it, which was rule number one of keeping things together. The smell of burning chocolate scorched the air. Gretel rushed over, flicked off the gas and took another deep breath. A burnt drink was the least of her worries.

'Woah!' Gretel jumped as Angel Gabriel reappeared at her mince pie-slippered feet, the word *Cot* still clenched between his teeth. 'Oh God, let's just read this damned newspaper.'

She whizzed through the paper's inky pages and landed on the double-page spread that called itself *Mistleton Fair Scandal – Gingerbread Café Plagued by Vermin.*

Her jaw dropped as her eyes homed in on the photos. Where the hell had those come from? That wasn't even possible! Was it? They were pictures of Angel Gabriel throwing shapes all over the gingerbread village and running around on the café's kitchen worktops, although she could have sworn he looked more like a rat. She shook out the creases in the paper as though the simple action might straighten things out. But all it did was waft a toxic inky smell up at her.

Amber had been looking after Angel Gabriel all day on Saturday. Hadn't she? Gretel had trusted her not to let her precious little ferret man out of her sight. Yet there was the proof. Lukas would blow a fuse, if he had any left to blow.

Rat-a-tat-taaaaaat. The firm knocking at the café door made Gretel jump. It was too early for hopeful customers. Who was out there? She shot a look at her tired dressing gown with the festive wreath patterns, wincing as she thought of her tear-stained cheeks and her eyes that were probably red and puffy. Whoever it was would have to get lost.

'Gretel. Are you in there? I can see the lights are on.'

Gretel felt her body stiffen. It was Lukas, and he did not sound impressed.

Chapter 47

'Gretel!' Lukas's stern voice outside the café door was not going away.

Gretel bent down to scoop up Angel Gabriel and huddled him close.

'Look, I've got my key,' said Lukas's disembodied voice. 'Fair warning – I'm coming in.'

Shit. Shit, shit, shit. Gretel made a bid for the stairs as she heard a rattling of keys, but she knew it was futile. He didn't live far out of the village and they shared a bloody café. It was barely a day or so since they'd shared the same bed. He was going to catch up with her at some point.

Gretel stopped at the bottom of the stairs and turned around, her forehead sweaty, the soggy hand that was strangling the *Cotswold Crier* now muddied with ink. Lukas strode through the door and let it bang shut behind him, the bell giving a loud jangle in case she'd missed his cacophonous arrival.

He put his hands on his hips in that *I'm the boss around here* stance that she remembered and hated from the early days of their café conundrums. And was that a rolled-up copy of the *Cotswold Crier* in his vice-like grip? Urgh. Well, she had plenty to be cross about too, even if she did *not* want to talk about it.

She jutted out her chin. 'You were looking for me?'

'What's this?' He waved the paper in front of him. 'Have you seen the report?'

'I don't know where those photos came from.'

'Does it matter?' he barked. 'Your bloody ferret was running amok all over this café and you know the rules. That was completely irresponsible. You'll get us shut down.'

She had not missed this side of him. The side that was rude and obnoxious, and made her feel two feet smaller.

'You and your team took control of the café on Sunday.'

'You were in charge of that ferret. One job!'

And she couldn't even get that right. She felt her chin dropping.

'Imagine how embarrassed I was to have Franny Whimple hammering on my door first thing this morning, brandishing this paper. I had to stand there in my boxer briefs whilst she divulged news about my own café that I didn't even know.'

'Being the last to know when everyone's laughing behind your back. Imagine.' Gretel snorted, which sounded about as sexy as her greying dressing gown looked. 'Why aren't I shocked that you paraded yourself in front of that mean woman in your man pants?' she muttered. 'You seem to take these things lightly.'

'Maybe I'd thought it was someone else.' He raked a

303

hand through his hair. 'Anyway, who's this *source close to Gretel Rosenhart* who filled them in on the story? Apparently they're saying vermin in food preparation areas is a regular thing around here. We've *specifically* talked about this.'

'None of my friends would have said that! And I only have one waitress ...'

'So now you have secret staff? Who else works here – Santa Claus?'

'Angel Gabriel is *not* vermin. And he only sneaks into the food kitchen when I forget to shut the door. It's not like he jumps into the mixing bowl and dances the hoola to the tune of "Jingle Bells". He's not even that keen on gingerbread.'

'Gretel. Rules are rules! Why do you have to be such a child about everything?'

Bloody ouch. 'I'm twenty-six, you twat. And I'm bored of you suggesting I can't behave like an adult.' She pouted, which was admittedly not her most mature face.

'Why do I get the feeling you're never all in on anything? At first it was the café, then with saying farewell to your crazy twelve months of Christmas.' His eyes scanned her festive dressing gown and mince pie slippers. 'Then you sleep with me, storm out and throw insults in the street. Now this.' He flapped the paper again. 'Maybe you're not the person I thought you were.'

'*I'm* not the person you thought I was? Just get out.' She could feel her whole body trembling but she was not backing down.

'Understood.' He dropped the newspaper to the floor and began to turn away.

The haunted jukebox broke into the bom-bom-bom-ooos of 'Lonely this Christmas', and Gretel's teeth gritted. She'd switched that damned thing off for the gazillionth time, she was sure of it. She did not need the likes of Mud to tell her things were going downhill faster than three fat reindeer in a toboggan.

'Christmas again in your world, huh?' Something in his voice sounded like it was out of fight, as he turned and walked through the door.

She ran a hand through her messy blonde plaits, realising they were probably now stained with the *Cotswold Crier's* black ink. She exhaled. 'Close the door behind you,' she said pointlessly, determined to have the last, childish word.

Real life was messy when you stopped wearing festive deely boppers and dared to put your heart on the line. Now hers was officially broken. What she wouldn't give to be curled up in her tiny old maisonette in her reindeer onesie. She'd given this café and Lukas her all. But all she'd done was cock things up – for herself and for the whole of Green Tree Lane. The village fair had been tarred with her vermin scandal. She was a failure. And as soon as the universe gave her a fast-track back to her old life, the better.

Chapter 48

If Gretel had wished for a helping hand back to her old life, what she'd received had been more like a shove. Which was fine. A girl could take a hint.

Not long after Lukas had stomped out of the café yesterday, Mr Desmond Peabody from Environmental Health had wombled right in with his copy of the *Cotswold Crier's* vermin scandal and his clipboard. She'd barely had time to get out of her dressing gown and half-heartedly open the place up when he'd arrived. As customers had started piling in, Mr Peabody had begun poking around. It turned out he'd received an official complaint and he took an unhealthy pleasure in carrying out his inspection.

It also turned out Angel Gabriel was taking a snooze in an open tin of biscuits that Gretel had left out in the kitchen. Who wouldn't want to sleep somewhere that smelled delicious, with great mid-nap snacks?

But Mr Peabody hadn't seen her point.

Instead, he'd slapped a big, ugly *close this dump down* notice on her forehead, right in front of her customers. At least, that was what it had felt like. Fortuitously, Franny Whimple had been right there sipping her Quickie Coffee takeaway and offering to buy the place from her and Lukas cheaply.

Well, Gretel was damned if she was going to watch Swingy Bob Whimple do her black and gold trainered victory dance all over the cobbles. Gretel had told her to bugger off. She was doing this her own way instead.

'So step one of getting back to my old life begins today,' Gretel now told little glass Nell, who stared back dispassionately from the bay window of the café. 'I'm sorry I've let you down, but I'm seriously not cut out for this. And pretending that I am is bloody exhausting.'

Gretel let the words hang as though somebody might dispute them. How ridiculous. Because there *was* nobody. As another wave of sadness hit, she swallowed her tears and spun towards the café's front door.

She marched through it and locked it shut behind her. Even though it was Wednesday, the café's sign said *closed*. As far as she was concerned, it would say so indefinitely. Pulling her shoulders back, she strode up Green Tree Lane with purpose, Angel Gabriel hopping along behind her on his lead.

'Not long now, boy. Off we go.'

Angel Gabriel looked a picture in the dandy ferret waistcoat and gingerbread patterned bow tie that Zekia had made for him at one of the café's craft nights. Not that there would be any more of those. Gretel took a deep, steadying breath.

She'd break it to them at some point, but this morning there were more pressing matters. She'd booked an appointment at the offices of Duckman & Birdwhistle Solicitors on Bell Lane, which was a few streets away. She hadn't told Lukas, not least because they still weren't speaking. But if they had been, she wouldn't want him to talk her out of this.

The last couple of days had brought one disaster after another, and it was more than she could bear. How much energy was one woman expected to have? It was easier when it had just been her and her memories. Her hand twitched to the old photo of herself, her mum and Rosa which was now in her pocket. She wasn't going to keep forgetting their faces.

Anyway, this was absolutely the right thing to do. She pulled back her shoulders again, mildly annoyed they wouldn't just stay in place. She'd done her best for the café and Green Tree Lane, and her new friends could take things forward from there. They didn't need a condemned café dragging their reputation down. It was better off closed and off her hands for good.

'Miss Rosenhart,' said Mr Birdwhistle (Junior) with unnecessary gusto when she was finally sitting in his office. 'Pleased to make your acquaintance again. You're here for an update with regard to the estate of Eleanor Ellbridge, I presume?' He pushed his glasses up his nose and squinted at her from behind his large leather-top desk.

'Not really.' She shrugged, not caring if she came across as an immature grouch, because that was exactly how she felt. She was also over telling him her friend had called herself

Nell. It wouldn't be her problem soon enough. 'I'm here to give my half of The Gingerbread Café back. I reject it, or whatever the fancy legal term might be. I don't want to play any more.'

He raised his eyebrows.

'You don't want to play,' he repeated. 'Interesting. Well, if you mean you want to disclaim the gift, I'm afraid it's altogether too late. You've already accepted the legacy and probate is well underway. It's not possible to disclaim your share at this point.'

Gretel huffed. That sounded completely ridiculous, but she ought to have known these things would be complicated. 'OK, so I'll give my share away to a good cause or something. Are ferrets' homes a thing?'

Angel Gabriel squeaked his approval from his perch on her knee and Mr Birdwhistle grimaced. He hadn't been impressed when she'd insisted on bringing her pet into the office, but she hadn't come here to impress him, even if Angel Gabriel was wearing his best bow tie.

'If you give your share away, Miss Rosenhart, you will still be liable to pay inheritance tax, which will equate to a substantial sum. Do you have the funds?'

Gretel fiddled with the hem of Angel Gabriel's waistcoat. 'No,' she muttered.

Mr Birdwhistle sighed, which was a sound Gretel was becoming accustomed to. 'It's not my place to advise you, of course. But if I were in your position, I'd be minded to sit tight for a short while longer. When the probate comes through and legal title for the property is transferred to yourself and Mr Lukas Knight, I understand he's keen to sell. If you're both now in agreement you want to move on, you can find a swift buyer, pay your dues, then donate the surplus to whichever charitable ferret establishment tickles your fancy.'

She gave him a tight nod, picked up Angel Gabriel and stood.

'Although, Miss Rosenhart, my mother always used to say this. *Charity begins at home.* So before you steam ahead trying to avail yourself of the inheritance Mrs Ellbridge was so keen for you to benefit from, I would urge you to consider what *you* want from life.' He sniffed and rearranged his papers. 'Use the funds to do whatever makes you truly happy. Scandal aside, I hear you did an outstanding job of orchestrating the February Fair and turning the café and the street around. I'd be surprised if anyone could excel at such projects if they didn't find any joy in them. I'm sure Mrs Ellbridge saw that potential in you. Don't go frittering your opportunities away.'

She didn't know much about frittering things away, but if a fritter was something that had been battered and deep fried, that just about summed up how she felt. All she needed was for someone to stick a fork in her and wrap her in yesterday's newspaper, then she was absolutely done. She brushed down her skirt, said her goodbyes and left the office, Angel Gabriel tucked under her arm.

As annoying as it seemed, some of Mr Birdwhistle's words had rung true. But when she factored in the cruel words of the *Cotswold Crier* and the downward spiral of events that proceeded, it was too late to claw her way back to joy. She would just have to take the solicitor's advice on the *sit tight for a short while longer* plan.

Only she had no intention of sitting tight in or above the café. It would be too painful. It was time to cut the apron strings, whilst she still had a shred of dignity.

Chapter 49

Gretel's old maisonette in Holly Road had always been a bit on the chilly side. That was why it was perfectly sensible to be wearing her elf jumper dress and candy-striped tights that cold March evening. Nobody liked to get goosebumps on their legs, after all.

Besides, who was going to see her? Precisely nobody. And Angel Gabriel couldn't judge because he was wearing his little elf jumper too.

'Life is officially cosier when you live inside Christmas,' she explained to him, through a mouthful of apple strudel. Who knew it would still be at the bottom of her old freezer exactly where she'd left it, just a few months ago? Or that her landlord wouldn't have managed to find another soul willing to rent the place whilst she'd been gone. It was clearly their loss.

It had been a busy few days. She'd spent them reclaiming her old, rented maisonette and then sneaking all of her stuff out of Nell's old flat by the back door, so as not to cause a scene in the street. She'd ignored everyone's frantic knocks on the café's front door.

Gretel watched Angel Gabriel as he bounced around the threadbare carpet, careering into things. She'd set up his usual ferret playground of tubes and boxes, but somehow she had an overwhelming sensation that nothing seemed to *fit* any more.

'Has somebody shrunk this place?' Not that it had ever exactly been spacious. She shoved a box out of the way with her foot to make floor space for her empty plate.

She assessed the situation from her hollow in the sofa, which really did need new springs unless she'd eaten *a lot* of gingerbread since she'd last sat here. Hmm. Perhaps it was all this extra stuff that was making her old maisonette look like it was bursting at the seams. Was her life fuller than it had been before? Even her plastic Christmas tree in the corner was sagging under the weight of all those additional decorations. *Don't worry, we'll soon have everything exactly like it was*, she'd reassured Angel Gabriel when she'd put it back up. For a ferret, he'd been surprisingly good at disbelieving looks.

Then once the tree was up, she'd made a big show of putting the decorations back on it, as though she needed to make a point. Not that anybody was watching. Though if she could just reconstruct the walls of her old life, perhaps she could forget all of the treacherous mistakes that existed beyond them.

'I've still made room for a few glass daffodils,' she reasoned, with nobody in particular. Even Angel Gabriel had wandered off and was trying to forge himself a nest with the colourful cushions Zekia had made for the café.

Well, she was damned if any new café owner was having them, and they may as well be here whilst the place was closed. The same went for the knitted bunting that Bea had made for her, and that lovely gingerbread chalkboard that Jane and Jayne had painted up. And between her donations from Phoebe and Angel Gabriel's stealing sprees, they had somehow amassed an impressive collection of small crystals too.

'We really must give those back,' she conceded. 'It's not like you'll need crystals for loneliness with me back under your feet.' She laughed, trying to ignore how hollow it sounded. They wouldn't be lonely rocking around the pokey maisonette together again, would they? There was barely enough room to be alone.

Or would they? Because when they'd lived here before, they hadn't had a busy working life full of creative ideas and beautifully budding friendships to compare it to. And there hadn't been Lukas. She looked at the empty apple strudel carton which was balancing on top of a box turned coffee table. There was a small mound of used tissues next to it, because inexplicably, eating a strudel without him had made her cry. She'd told herself the tears were for nearly having lost her memories of her mum and Rosa. But she had the sneaking suspicion she was telling herself a lot of things lately. She was beginning to lose track of how many of those things were true.

Another wave of tears swelled up through her body, desperate for a release. The pressure mounted behind her eyes and she grabbed a soggy tissue, letting the tears flow. They'd been arriving too often over the last few days and she was getting fed up of them. Moving back in here was meant to be making things easier, not harder. She was trying to ignore the nagging thought that she was now lacking in purpose. Out there in the real world she'd been building things instead of merely existing. Friendships, community, a life.

Yet over the last few days, it had felt as though all of that was falling apart too. Squashed back into this maisonette, she'd never had more stuff. But she'd never felt emptier. There was no reason to get out of bed at any given time. No café to open. No gingerbread men to accidentally burn and then ice back together. Not even an annoying jukebox to reprimand.

And by her own efforts at ducking and diving, she hadn't seen the people she'd been starting to call friends. She hadn't bothered to hunt down Amber and sort out that whole schoolgirl debacle. She'd avoided Eve and Phoebe. In fact, they were probably both busy with the new men and dogs in their lives to even worry.

From her furtive comings and goings she'd seen Jane and Jayne with their stepladder, putting the street's tree back in place and saving as many ornaments as they could. Gretel still had the remnants of Angel Brigitte and little Rosa in a glass jar in the cupboard, next to her jar of instant hot chocolate that would never taste as good as the stuff she used to make in the café.

'Well, there's no point in making a pan of the real stuff just for me,' she explained to Angel Gabriel, in case he'd been wondering. Though he didn't seem bothered.

Another sob broke free. People talked about being bored to tears, but she was becoming bored *of* them. It was as though they were never-ending. The more she cried . . . well, the more she cried. But she'd surely get used to things again. And then life would be just fine.

She collapsed back on the sofa and pressed a few buttons on the remote control, hoping she'd find something to bring back her festive cheer. To her surprise, the ancient DVD player fired up and a familiar, blond-haired boy appeared on the TV screen. Well, who knew? Her old copy of *Home Alone* was still in the machine. At least she wasn't alone in having made everyone disappear. Wishing for some peace and quiet to wear outrageously bad knitwear and scare off life's baddies was clearly a thing. She imagined setting up an obstacle course of blowtorches and tarantulas to keep Swingy Bob Whimple from The Gingerbread Café, and couldn't help a tiny chuckle.

'Oi, runaway. Open the door. I know you're in there and you'd better not be eating mince pies and sulking.'

Gretel momentarily froze as the voice came through her letter box. There was no mistaking it, although Amber was a fine one to talk about runaways. Gretel jumped up and kicked an empty jar of rich fruit mincemeat under the sofa. Not even she could find mince pies in March, and she'd been in no mood for baking.

'I can see you, you know.'

As Gretel turned to the front door, trying to calculate how long it would take to go and wriggle into something that wasn't an elf jumper dress, she saw Amber's wide hazel eyes staring through the letter box. No wonder her maisonette was so chilly if her landlord had no respect for draught exclusion.

It was a novelty to have someone who cared enough to kneel down on her doormat and poke their eyeballs through the brassy slot, as much as she ought to have been annoyed about it.

From somewhere behind Gretel came a rattling of gunfire. 'Jeeeeesus!' The letter box twanged shut. 'Are you firing shots at me like that kid from *Home Alone*?' There was a break in the barrage and the eyeballs reappeared. 'Oh, you're actually watching *Home Alone*. Well, lemme in, woman. I've always got time for a little dude in a bobble hat sledging down the stairs, even if we are nearly hitting spring.'

Gretel sighed. She did need to find out what was going on with Amber, and her heart was having an unexpected sing-song at the thought of company. She'd missed Amber's no-nonsense wonky throat chakra, even if she was a bit confused about what had gone on.

'Yeah, yeah, I know I'm in trouble,' said Amber, as though she was reading her mind. Or maybe that was the thing about friends. They just knew. 'But I'm on my knees here, and this scratchy-arsed mat is ruining my new fishnets. Give a girl a break.'

Even though there was barely room left in the maisonette to swing a cat, if anyone would be so despicable, Gretel had a strong sense she would always make space in her world for Amber. She was beginning to realise Amber was one of the people who'd been making her once empty life almost complete. *One* of them.

Chapter 50

Even though Gretel was now pretty sure Amber was just a schoolgirl, standing there on Gretel's doorstep that evening, Amber suddenly looked the most grown-up she'd ever seen her.

Amber was still dressed for rebellion, and probably always would be. Gretel couldn't think of anyone else who could pull off a riot of red, black, netted skirts and fishnets with such sass. But she'd softened on her usual thick white make-up and black eyeliner so that her face looked rosy and sincere, almost like she was ready to be seen.

Only Gretel hadn't fully realised how much Amber had been hiding.

The skin on her friend's arms wasn't etched with the complicated Biro bird patterns which had seemed to come and go either. And, thank goodness, she wasn't hiding her stunning flame-red hair under an uncharacteristic baseball cap, just to avoid being spotted. Was she finally allowed to be here?

'So let me in. I don't want to miss that scene where Kevin gets his shit together and defends his house with Micro Machines and cling film.' Amber pointed over Gretel's shoulder to the crappy old TV, where *Home Alone* was still playing. Gretel noticed her smile was only lifting at one side. What was weighing it down?

Gretel grinned through her tear-stained face and stood back to let her friend in, but instead of inching past her to fight her way through boxes to the sofa, Amber flung her arms around Gretel and gave her the tightest squeeze.

'People. Need. Air,' Gretel managed to say, from inside Amber's keen clinch.

'Erm, people need to stop doing crazy stuff, like moving out without telling anyone. What the hell are you up to?' Amber moved her grip to Gretel's shoulders and held her at arm's length. 'And why do you look like crap? It's as though you've been crying for days and I'm not even going to ask about that elf dress. Sit down, G. This feels like one of those situations when grown-ups would make a cup of sweet tea and eat biscuits. I'll put the kettle on.'

Amber guided Gretel back to the sofa, gave Angel Gabriel a quick fuss, then climbed across the mess of the maisonette to the pokey excuse for a kitchen in the corner of the living room. She clattered around like a girl on a mission, any earlier awkwardness thrown aside in honour of the emergency cheer-up situation. When she handed Gretel hot tea and plonked herself down on the saggy couch next to her, Gretel just wanted to sob with relief at having a trusted human close. She'd scarcely realised the extent of her loneliness until that moment.

'Wanna talk?' Amber asked. She manoeuvred herself into a cross-legged position facing Gretel and released the half packet of Ginger Nuts she'd been clenching under her arm.

And for the first time since for ever, Gretel actually did. Between tears and bargain biscuits, she shared some of the less private events of the last few days with Amber, and Amber soothed and got outraged for Gretel in all the right places.

Then Amber cleared her throat. 'Look, I've got some confessions to make and you're probably going to kick my arse about some of this. But hear me out.'

On the TV, little Kevin applied aftershave to his delicate face and let out a scream.

'You're still at school, aren't you?' Gretel knew she might as well dive straight in.

'Erm, yeah.' Was Amber blushing?

'Shit, Amber. Shouldn't you have been in lessons most days? You let me think your black and white outfit meant you were a waitress! You could have told me the truth.'

Amber exhaled sharply, her body sagging like the sorry brown couch. 'The truth being that I'm sixteen and I should have been yawning my face off in some dumb Business Studies class? Yeah, because that would have gone down well.' She looked up meekly.

'So you don't like school?'

Amber picked her nails. 'It wasn't just the classes that were bothering me.'

Gretel blinked a few times as she tried to compute.

Amber was avoiding her gaze now, her usual bolshiness slipping as though she was letting Gretel in.

'The other students?' Gretel asked softly. She almost couldn't imagine anything fazing Amber, and yet she was still so young in the scheme of things. Nearly the same tender age Gretel had been when she'd lost her family. That terrifying point when you're stuck between childhood and becoming a woman and you're not really sure who you're meant to be.

Amber nodded, her eyes still firmly fixed on the black nail varnish she was now scratching off. 'Yeah. School has never been great, because, you know.' She gave a small smile and waved her hand around herself. 'It's not easy when you dare to be different. But over the past couple of years there have been a few girls . . . ' Amber's voice caught and she stopped, as though she didn't have the words.

'Who've made it extra hard for you?' Gretel finished, grabbing her and squeezing her tight. Her heart felt like it would sink right down to the core of the earth.

'Look, seriously, I'm on top of it now. My sister came in to school to report it with me earlier this week. And man, people don't want to mess with my sister.' She gave a small laugh.

'Your sister?' Gretel asked. 'You've never mentioned her. Or any of your family, to be fair. You've always avoided my questions.'

'Yeah, that's the second thing. And you're not going to like it.' She paused, as though working out the best way to break it. Was that a tarantula crawling across the TV screen? 'My surname's Whimple.'

321

Gretel's mouth dropped open. 'As in ... *Whimple?*' Seriously? She gulped in a deep breath. Part of her wanted to kick and scream and make an almighty fuss. What was it with people lying to her? And why did it invariably link back to that swingy bobbed monster? But she could see from Amber's contorted face that she was suffering enough. 'So Francesca is your sister?' Well, it explained some of the ducking and diving. She guessed Francesca would go mad to hear of her sister skiving school to support The Gingerbread Café, and Lukas must know Amber is a Whimple too, if he and Francesca went *way back*.

Amber nodded.

'I won't even ask why you didn't tell me that.'

'I know, I know.' Amber jumped up and began tidying messy plates, as though they were still in the café. 'I've always hated her too. More than most people. My brothers and dad are no better. But that's not the worst of it.'

Gretel exhaled sharply. What could be worse than all of that? Even Angel Gabriel had gone into hiding. 'Go on.'

'Francesca saw me at the fair. She'd had no idea I was hanging around in Mistleton and supporting you all. She was fuming. But I hadn't even seen her arrive. When I popped to the loo and left Angel Gabriel with Bea's son, Xander ...'

Gretel stood up swiftly, cold tea and biscuit crumbs flying. 'She took those photos of him in the kitchen and all over the gingerbread village, didn't she?'

Amber grabbed a cleaning cloth, her eyes wide. 'I'm so sorry. She staged and edited the photos then passed them to the papers with a fake story, before reporting you to some bloke she knows at the Environmental Health Department. I had no idea until last night when I overheard her bragging about it to Dad. She's desperate to buy out the café to try and impress him. It's actually pretty sad.'

'But Lukas wants to sell it to her anyway?'

Amber looked blank. 'No, I don't think so.'

'I overheard him talking to her.'

Amber tried to scrub tea from Gretel's elf dress. 'Look, I can ask her. Let me try and sort all of this out. I feel terrible. I swear, I've always been on your side and I only hid the truth because I couldn't stand people knowing I'm related to her. I knew I'd be rejected if I did, and I hate what the family business does.'

Gretel closed her eyes. Her mind had been so busy trying to unpick lies lately, she barely knew what to believe. As Kevin got his crayons out to make his battle plan, her thoughts became clear.

Finally, she pulled Amber into a hug. 'Thanks for being honest with me. I believe you. But speaking to Francesca Whimple is something I need to do for myself.'

Chapter 51

Gretel had never been on a road trip with friends before. Packed into Eve's new flower-patterned delivery car with Eve, Phoebe and Amber, it felt momentous. They were giving her a lift to the Whimple & Sons office so she could confront Francesca about the fake vermin story she'd leaked to the *Cotswold Crier*.

'Thank you for this,' Gretel said quietly. Despite being angry about what the swingy bobbed interferer had done, Gretel was still a bag of nerves about confronting her.

'We couldn't let you sit on that freezing Lower Paddleton bus by yourself,' said Phoebe.

The car felt toasty with them all squashed in. She'd missed their warmth.

'The way this one packs up her life and disappears when we're not looking, I'll be putting a tracking device on her elf-dress-wearing arse,' said Amber.

'I'm not wearing anything Christmassy today,' said Gretel.

Amber whooped.

If she was going to look brave in front of the Whimple, festive eight-year-old would not be a strong look. Though as the recent snow glinted at them from the tops of the surrounding hills, she'd allowed the comfort of her fluffy coat and snow boots.

'I think we *all* need a reminder that we're here for each other,' said Eve gently, looking at Amber in her rear-view mirror.

Amber ruffled Angel Gabriel's snowy fur. He was dozing on her lap, in a makeshift car harness. She'd been overjoyed to be allowed back in charge of him. 'You know, I'm pretty much the coolest kid in school now. Since I helped organise the Mistleton Fair and the social media, I'm like some kind of influencer. Fickle, huh? I'm going to start charging them to hang around with me.'

'I'm proud of you for getting back to school, courageous Amber.' Gretel pulled her into a side hug. They'd picked a Saturday so Amber could join the moral support road trip, but Gretel was absolutely facing Francesca Whimple alone. 'Sometimes we've got to show those mean girls who's boss.'

'You know it,' said Amber, her voice catching. 'You gals are my people. You gave me a sense of purpose and showed me I'm worthy of having real friends. We're the most unlikely bunch, but I kind of love ya.'

Gretel dabbed her eyes with a tissue. 'Yes, that.' She sniffed. She still wasn't great with a speech.

'And Lukas?' asked Amber.

The windscreen wipers swished away the odd snowflake

that was still falling. But like the roads, her mind was slowly beginning to clear. Despite everything, she'd missed him with every inch of her.

'We'll see,' Gretel concluded. For now, it was the best she could promise.

'Ooh, will you need a crystal for Operation Whimple?' Phoebe asked, leaning over from the passenger seat with two hands full.

'Here's the bit where she makes you put rocks in your bra,' Amber giggled.

Gretel shook her head. 'I've got this.' Although she had no idea if that was true.

Gretel hadn't booked an appointment with Swingy Bob Whimple. Amber had sneaked a look at her diary and confirmed her sister should be in the office. The woman didn't deserve time to prepare her story or disappear.

As Gretel stepped through the door of the garish office on Penny Road, she noticed they were too modern for a tinkling overhead bell. How would anyone know she'd arrived? The reception area was empty, other than a few stray Quickie Café cups and the smell of bad coffee.

'What the fuck did you do that for?'

Gretel jumped. It was a loud male voice, coming from a room behind the reception area. Shouldn't people at least shut the door if they were going to have a row?

'Why fucking wouldn't I?' came the reply. It sounded like Francesca Whimple, although she seemed quieter and less sure of herself than usual. At least it was clear where she got her swearing from. 'Someone's got to stand up for the kid.'

'By declaring to the whole world that the Whimples get bullied? We run this sodding village. We'll be a laughing stock.'

'Someone needed to tell the school about it. I thought I was being helpful,' said Francesca, her voice still unsure.

'We deal with family business *ourselves*.'

'What, by doing some more bullying? Suddenly it doesn't seem so clever.'

'Argh, you girls just haven't got the backbone, you know that?'

There was a silence. Even Gretel felt a pang of sympathy for the swingy bobbed woman.

'Yeah, you mentioned,' came Francesca's deflated reply.

Gretel jumped again as she heard a scraping of furniture. Somebody was on the move. Gretel scurried towards the front door, but didn't make it through before Swingy Bob Whimple stomped out into reception. When she caught sight of Gretel, her jaw dropped.

'And have you managed to get your useless foot in the door with any of those shop owners in Mistleton yet?' the male voice shouted. 'You said that café was nearly sorted.'

Gretel felt her stomach plummet.

Swingy Bob regained her composure and grabbed a take-away Quickie Café cup from the reception desk. 'Have you come to sell me a café?' she asked Gretel. Her voice, through gritted teeth, didn't sound that hopeful.

Gretel straightened and shook her head. 'I've come about this.' She pulled a rolled-up copy of the *Cotswold Crier* from her bag and waved it. 'And I deserve an explanation.' She doubted she sounded nearly as scary as the bellowing man, but she was definitely determined.

Swingy Bob pointed to the front door. 'Let's go.' She stiffened her shoulders and marched towards the exit, Gretel scurrying along behind her.

Chapter 52

With the random patches of icy snow that hadn't been cleared from the pedestrianised shopping road in Lower Paddleton, it was slippery in places. Gretel guessed that was what happened when a street became unloved.

'Erm, where are we going?' Gretel shouted after Swingy Bob Whimple, doing her best to catch up.

'I need some air.' Swingy Bob shot Gretel a look over her shoulder as she puffed on her vaping thing.

Maybe looking backwards was perilous after all – because it was then that Swingy Bob lost her footing.

Her arms circled like propellers, but they didn't do much to save her. She squealed, her polystyrene Quickie Café cup flying from her grip. Gretel instinctively moved in to grab her, just about stopping her from diving face-first into the street's central fountain.

'Who put that fucking thing there?'

Was it the time to explain the stagnant and now

sleet-covered fountain had been there for decades, if only anyone had still cared?

Swingy Bob's cup landed in a patch of snow with a milky brown splat.

'That stuff tastes like piss water anyway.' The Whimple flattened down her blazer and cleared her throat. 'Thank you,' she muttered in Gretel's general direction. 'Now, what was it you wanted?'

Gretel took a deep breath. 'I'm just going to come out with it.' She was glad her words sounded firmer than her quaking legs felt. 'I know you nicked my ferret on the day of the fair and staged photos so he looked like a rat stealing food, then shared fake news with the *Cotswold Crier* and Environmental Health. Miss Whimple, you've done some terrible things.' Gretel put her hands on her hips, remembering Lukas's stance when he wanted to *look in charge.*

Miss Whimple shrugged. 'Can't be so fake if they inspected and shut you down.'

'They caught me on a bad day.' Gretel pursed her lips. Her ferret wasn't *always* sleeping in a biscuit tin, and he was never a rat.

'Well, no publicity is bad publicity. If you sell me the café, I'm sure my new tenant can turn that around.'

'I don't want The Gingerbread Café to have that sort of publicity! And I've got no intention of selling the place to you.'

Miss Whimple rolled her eyes and puffed on her vaping thing. 'You and Lukas are a pair of thorns in my arse.'

'What do you mean?' asked Gretel, trying to sound casual and not at all like she hadn't spoken to him for days.

Miss Whimple narrowed her eyes. 'You still don't know, do you?'

'Of course I know.' What did she know? She tried not to look suspicious or fidgety.

'Ah, what the hell.' Miss Whimple threw her arms up. 'I'm going to break free from Whimple & *Sons* as soon as I can anyway. My dad's a shit and my brothers do screw-all but twat around in their boat shoes having *business lunches*. I'm the one doing the hard work and getting hated for it. And I've apparently still got no *backbone*.' Her cheeks looked flushed, as though she was aware Gretel had overheard that bit of her dad's telling-off. 'If that's what it turns you into, I don't freaking want one. Dad's outrageous stance over Amber is the last straw.'

To Gretel's surprise, Miss Whimple picked up her poly-styrene cup and chucked it in a bin. 'Wanna walk?'

Gretel nodded, and they continued their pace along Penny Road, away from the Whimple family's office.

'So the thing you were going to say about Lukas?' Gretel said quietly, taking cautious footsteps in the snow. She did feel a bit sorry for the woman, but she wasn't here to massage her wounds or praise her work ethic.

Miss Whimple screwed up her face as though her brain cells were having an argument, before giving up with a sigh. 'Lukas told me the day before the fair that he was falling for the café and he didn't want to sell it to me. Or to anyone. That's what pushed me to take those photos of that mole of yours, although to be fair, the thing was quite happy to run around nicking gingerbread when I let him.' She shrugged like her actions were perfectly acceptable. 'I thought a few leaked pics to the papers and Environmental Health might persuade Lukas he was onto a loser with that place.'

They passed a couple of boarded-up shops and Gretel's heart felt sad.

'But I heard you speaking to Lukas on the phone, the morning after the fair,' said Gretel. 'He was telling you about the restaurant he was planning and the fancy food he wanted to create. How is he going to pay for that if we don't sell the café? Or is he planning to gut the café and turn it into a Michelin-star-seeking place?' The very thought of it turned Gretel's stomach.

'Seriously, it's not my idea to share. When I spoke to him he was like an irritating, excitable puppy, but he was embarrassed to share it with you so soon into your *thing*.' She wrinkled her nose. 'It's more of a longer-term concept. But he's not planning on selling or gutting the place. Weirdly, he wants the two of you to keep the café and let it evolve however feels right. His idea doesn't affect any of that, and actually, you'd probably like it. It's annoyingly ingenious.'

Gretel blew out a long breath. 'Oh gosh, really?' If Miss Whimple was telling the truth, it sounded like she'd got completely the wrong end of the stick when she'd overheard that conversation. The way she'd behaved. The things she'd said to him. She put a hand on her spinning head. She'd have some serious making up to do – though she had no idea what Lukas's grand plan could be, or if he'd want anything to do with her after their arguments. 'But why would he tell you that stuff?'

'We used to be mates in high school. We both had shit dads, so we had plenty to rant about. Though he's been a hell of a lot less ranty lately. Maybe someone's cheered him up a bit.' Miss Whimple gave a small laugh, as though it was hard to believe.

'And why are you telling me this? You've never liked me, and aren't you more likely to get your hands on the café if Lukas and I are rowing?'

Gretel moved to avoid a man coming out of the 99p shop, laden with bounty. When he saw Miss Whimple, he ducked to avoid her.

'Like I said, I'm out of there. And you can bet Whimple & Sons won't be arsed to put in the hard graft to talk the shop owners in Green Tree Lane into selling. That village has become as tight knit as one of your weirdo festive jumpers. No offence.' She waved an apologetic hand.

The motion made Gretel slide on a patch of ice and Miss Whimple grabbed her arm. Gretel nodded a thank you, and they continued their walk.

'As much as you used to annoy me, you were there for Amber when she was going through some difficult stuff at school. None of us realised, or knew she was skiving. She reckons you didn't either. But you created a safe space for her when she felt she had no one to turn to.' Was Miss Whimple's voice actually wobbling? 'I feel dreadful that I wasn't decent enough to be that person, and even worse that I've been turning into a freaking bully to impress an idiot who's no better. Sodding family, hey? Sorry. Not to be ungrateful or whatever.'

Gretel tried not to be offended. She could tell the woman

was trying, even if it would take a while for her to morph into a fully reasonable human.

They came to the end of Penny Road, which forked off in two directions.

'Right,' said Gretel, awkwardly. Despite their chat, she still felt nervous about asking this. 'Francesca, I still need you to do something for me. In fact, you ought to do this, to put things straight.' She fiddled with the sleeve of her coat. 'I want you to admit to the newspaper you were spreading fake news and to tell the truth. Get them to print a new report. The fair was a success, and it's not fair to the village for the whole thing to be overshadowed by bogus scandal.' Even in the chilly weather, Gretel's palms were sweating. But she wasn't backing down.

Miss Whimple kicked at a patch of snow with her black and gold trainer. 'Tell the papers I made the whole thing up? That's pretty embarrassing.'

Gretel shrugged. 'You said no publicity was bad publicity. I'm sure you can spin it into something useful. Maybe you can tell the world you've changed and start off an anti-bullying campaign or something. You're a clever woman, aren't you?' It didn't hurt to massage her ego a tiny bit, if it meant getting her to fix things.

'Yeah, I am pretty clever.' Miss Whimple nodded her gratitude. 'And you know what? Now and again, you show a bit of promise too. For someone who used to dress like one of Santa's little helpers, obvs. I mean, you managed to bring that dead old café and street back to life. Maybe you're a people person.'

Gretel wasn't sure she was ready to believe that. 'So you'll do it?' she asked, trying not to hold her breath.

'Not sure I'll name and shame myself, but I'll make sure the paper knows it was fake news and I'll get them to print a retraction. If you promise to keep being there for Amber, that is.'

It sounded like an easy enough deal. Gretel stuck her hand out like she'd seen businessy people do on telly, and they shook on it, before stepping off in their separate directions.

And after that small victory, it was time for Gretel to fix a few more things.

Chapter 53

Gretel jumped back into the car, where her three wise women were waiting. There was a hopeful pause before Gretel's face broke into a grin, and all four of them began bouncing in their seats and cheering, the little flower-patterned car rocking around like a dinky toy. Gretel filled them in on her chat with Swingy Bob Whimple.

'So what next?' Amber asked.

Gretel scratched her head. 'Have you still got your trusty brainstorming pad?'

'Damned right I have.'

'Then it's time to make our *Home Alone* inspired battle plan.'

As Eve drove them back to Gretel's maisonette in Mistleton, Gretel passed around the bag of lebkuchen she'd successfully made that morning, using a jar of her homemade *lebkuchengewürz* spice mix that may have slipped into a box as she'd been fleeing the café. Well, they'd need sustenance if they were going to work out how to fix Gretel's mess.

'Perhaps you need to start with the Christmas stuff,' said Phoebe, gently. 'You can't continue to live in that clutter. It's blocking the flow of good energy.'

'She needs a massive clear-out,' Amber agreed. 'Starting with that poor plastic Christmas tree. If any of that festive shit is sparking joy in March, I'll eat Marie Kondo's sunhat.'

Why hadn't she seen that Amber was related to Francesca bloody Whimple? But she meant well. Gretel smiled and gave her an accidentally-on-purpose elbow.

Then Gretel considered Amber's suggestion. Her mind swam back to a few days ago, when she'd been sitting on her crappy rented sofa, surrounded with festive junk and stuffing her face with apple strudel. She had felt lonely. Because if she was honest, Christmas wasn't about *stuff*. It was about *love*. And hope, and friendship and spreading cheer. Her heart skipped back to the Christmases she remembered with her mum and Rosa, and all the joyous festive spirit that had twinkled around the log cabins of the *Christkindlmärkte* and set her soul alight. She couldn't recreate that feeling in March by wearing a penguin jumper and putting deely boppers on her head. Some things only made sense at the right time of year. If she tried to drag out Christmas all year long, it simply lost its magic.

'Put *Christmas clear-out* on the list,' said Gretel.

Eve gave Gretel a supportive glance in the rear-view mirror. 'I agree that's a great place to start. But perhaps the situation goes beyond a bit of feng shui. Gretel, darling, we need to make sure you feel strong enough not to hide from the world and escape back to Christmas when life gets tricky.'

Gretel nodded. She also needed to help herself believe that letting go of Christmas didn't mean forgetting her memories of her family and Nell. They would always be there, with or without a sad plastic Christmas tree.

'Have you thought about counselling?' Phoebe asked, reaching back to give Gretel's arm a squeeze. 'It can help to talk about things.'

The hilly scenery that Gretel loved passed by through her window. The huddles of trees, the quaint little church. Even Bea's dad's lavender farm. Yet with its light blanket of snow, everything had a special newness.

'I've tried counselling in the past, but ... you're right,' Gretel conceded. 'I've never stuck with it. I owe it to myself to try again.'

'Looking after your mental health is totally a thing,' said Amber. 'Or we can set you up with Phoebe and her chakra healing.' She winked. 'And Gretel doesn't look like she's got room for many more crystals.'

'OK, *enquire about counselling*. Put it on the list,' said Gretel.

'So now we just have to get you back into the café.' Amber shrugged as though that bit was easy.

'And patch things up with a certain Mr Knight. The poor man must be heartbroken that you've disappeared and not told him where you've gone,' Eve added. 'I've seen him searching the street like you might appear from behind a string of bunting.'

Had Lukas really been looking heartbroken? She hardly dared to believe it. 'The way I behaved when we had that first row.' Gretel shrank a little in her seat. 'I might have totally cocked things up.' If she was honest with herself, there'd been a big, lonely hole in her heart since the moment he'd walked away. She couldn't live without fixing this, or at least trying.

'If he's got any sense, he'll love the pants off *all* of you. Not just the sparkly, having an awesome day bits,' said Amber.

Gretel nodded again. She had a feeling she loved all of him too.

She nibbled the chocolate off a lebkuchen biscuit whilst the mental image formed. 'Right, I've got it. Add these things to the list. I'm not going down without a particularly quirky fight.'

Just over a week later, the battle plans were well underway.

Once Gretel had created headspace by gifting some Christmas excess to charity and booking her first counselling session, she was ready to tackle the café, and the mess she'd made with Lukas. With a buzz in the air as her friends rallied around to support her, Green Tree Lane felt alive with possibilities. It was café front makeover time.

Her friends had suggested a Monday when the shops were shut, so they could be on hand to help with the makeover part. But first Gretel would also have some *making up* to do. And that was a leap she had to take without them.

She'd been busy with preparations all week, including jumping through Mr Peabody's hoops. Her equipment was in place, apart from her showpiece. And after a heart-stopping pause, Lukas had replied to her message to say he'd meet her outside the café at the suggested time.

'We'll lay this out under the café window.' Jane and Jayne

carried a paint-splattered dust sheet between them, like a hammock. She thought back to the ghostly sheets which had been thrown over the café's tables when she and Lukas had first met Mr Birdwhistle there. She hoped with a pang that she wouldn't see those returning.

'Thank you,' she told them.

'Here, I brought you this.' Bea was at her side, pulling a cotton sachet from her pocket. 'It's dried lavender. It's symbolic of serenity, grace and calm, although I just sniff it when I need a moment.' She giggled. 'Keep it on you just in case.'

It really did smell calming. Gretel swallowed a lump in her throat and nodded her thanks to Bea, remembering that Nell had loved lavender too.

'Kingsley and I will be back later with our new passion fruit and ginger rum.' Zekia bustled past and rubbed Gretel's arm. 'I'm sure you'll have a few things to celebrate.'

Gretel hoped she was right. As she busied herself rearranging pots of paint around her borrowed stepladder, Amber, Eve and Phoebe hurried over too.

Eve was holding a bunch of pale blue flowers and some hair grips, and with Gretel's nod, Amber began weaving them through her hair. They matched her new woolly jumper perfectly. 'It's a bit early for cornflowers, but it's handy when you know a florist.' She winked. 'Cornflowers are delicate, but oh so courageous. Their little flowers stand up to the elements when so many others would flail.'

Gretel gave her a hug.

'And I know you probably don't need this, but I couldn't not give you something.' Phoebe pressed a small crystal into

Gretel's coat pocket. 'It's the tumbled stone I intuitively picked for you the first time you came into my shop. Red jasper – the stone warriors carried into battle. And it's the colour of passion.'

Gretel could definitely feel her cheeks burning red. 'Is it normal to feel this bloody terrified?' She was painfully aware that even with all her wild efforts, Lukas may still tell her to get stuffed.

Eve grabbed Gretel's hand. 'Sometimes you've got to take a chance, even though it's scary. We only regret the gooseberries we didn't take, as a wise grocer once said.'

Angel Gabriel squeaked his approval from the front pocket of Amber's dress as Gordon waved at them from across the street.

Phoebe checked her watch. 'It's nearly time. Are you ready?'

'As I'll ever be.' Gretel balled her fists.

She knew her new friends would be back later to gather around with paintbrushes and gingerbread, if she could only pull this off. There was even promise of a newspaper reporter, ready to scoop a fresh story. She prayed it wouldn't be another disastrous one.

But now, this moment was for her and Lukas, whatever the outcome may be. The others hugged her and rushed away as they saw him coming.

Gretel's breath caught in her throat when she saw him. Just like it had on their first real encounter in The Gingerbread Café, when he'd barged into her life with a Norway spruce. She remembered the electricity she'd felt when their hands had touched as he'd passed back her glass creation. The one he'd saved. In that moment, she'd been so cross with him she could have poked his eyes out. She only hoped he wasn't feeling that way about her now. What a journey it had been.

Lukas looked up at her as he walked across the cobbles. Other than a dusting on the tops of the surrounding hills, the snow had melted now, and the winter sun bounced off his slate-grey hair. His chest wasn't quite as puffed out as it often was, but still enough for his fitted cable-knit jumper to pull tight. No chef's whites or funny rubber clogs today.

As he got closer, she could see his eyes held a questioning look. He stopped in front of her. Her mouth opened but she didn't yet have the words, so they held each other's gaze. Her heart was pounding at all the things she wanted to say and do. At the sheer joy of seeing him. At how good he looked, even though she could see tiredness under his eyes and his stubbly beard looked unkempt. She wanted to touch him. Was he feeling something too?

Teasingly, he stepped towards her – but she could sense it wasn't yet an invite. His posture was open, yet they both knew there were things to be said.

'I'm sorry.' Though her voice was quiet, she hoped its weight would convey how deeply she felt it. God, she'd missed him. 'After that night . . . ' She tried not to blush as the memories floated between them. 'I overheard you talking on the phone and maybe I got the wrong impression. I thought you wanted to sell the café.'

He raked a hand through his hair. 'We'd already talked

about it, Gretel. I'd told you I was ready to keep it. To run it with you.' There was a gruffness to his voice.

'I know, I'm sorry. In my fear of trusting people, I guess I thought you'd lied. I said some *horrible* things. And I really didn't mean them. I don't even know where they came from – they just flowed from me like hot fury. At the thought of losing you, I went into an uncontrollable panic. I'm working on that.' She hoped her small smile would be enough.

He nodded. 'You took me by surprise. I should have known how fragile things were, been quicker to explain myself. We both could have handled things better.'

She wasn't sure he'd done much wrong, but she was touched at his offer to share the burden. Though there was still more she had to know.

'Did you see what happened to the Christmas tree?' she asked. 'Just after that first argument?'

He glanced over to the street's central tree, his face confused. He cocked his head, trying to work it out, then paced towards it. She followed. Despite everything, the tree would always be one of her favourite places, rooted and constant. The villagers had done their best to straighten and redecorate it when she hadn't been able to face it.

'It looks different, somehow. What happened?' He looked to the top and saw Angel Brigitte was missing. 'Oh God.'

'It's OK,' she said quickly. 'I accidently knocked one of the wooden shelters into the tree when I was fleeing from our argument. A few ornaments fell. In some ways, I think it helped me. I was still afraid to let go of things, as though memories would fade and I'd be left with nothing. But I hadn't realised the importance of holding on to the present. I've created a new life, and I love every part of it. I don't have to feel guilty.' She knew Nell and her family would have wanted her to be happy. And in embracing different times of the year she'd been remembering new things about them too. Times they'd shared outside of Christmas, like the February Fair. She sensed there would be more.

She felt a squeeze of her hand. That electricity. It reminded her she was alive and that living felt good.

'I'm sorry I made you run,' he said. 'And I'm so sorry about the tree. I didn't realise. The thing I was talking about on the phone that morning . . . it's a longer-term idea. It felt too early in our relationship to spring it on you, but let's get it out in the open right now. No more fearing the future. And I swear it doesn't go against my promises to you. I meant them.' He exhaled a long breath. 'Still do.'

Her heart bounced in her chest. Had he really just said that? Did it mean things would be OK?

As he explained his tentative idea for the café's more distant future, Gretel's pupils dilated as she tried to imagine it. As her mind created the vision as delicately as though it was made of glass, she couldn't think of anything more perfect – for both of them. It would be dependent on so many other things, and there would be lots to plan. But she could see why he hadn't told her so early on and why they should incubate the idea between the two of them, like a fragile egg. It wasn't time for them to share this with the world just yet.

As she nodded in excitement he squeezed her hand and

turned back to the café, his eyes landing on the winter-flowering cherry tree that he'd bought her, which she'd placed outside the café's front door. Her friends had hung stained-glass gingerbread people from its blossoming branches. Did she sense a small smile?

This time she led the way back towards it. He was right behind her.

When he caught sight of the new sign she'd placed proudly in the window, he did a double-take. 'Since when do we have a five-star food hygiene rating? And are we back in business?'

She liked the *we*. 'Since I invited Mr Peabody from Environmental Health to come back and inspect. We're officially allowed to reopen, with a clean bill of health. Not quite a Michelin star.' She shrugged. 'But nice to get top score. And we never did have rats.'

His gaze lowered. 'Franny called me to confess what she did there. I'm sorry I doubted you and your stylish little guy. You've done an incredible job of turning this around.'

Her heart swelled at the compliment.

'And these pots of paint?' he asked.

'I thought it was time for a new look.' She paused. 'If you want to. I didn't make a start, just in case.'

He nodded slowly. 'What were you thinking?'

She picked up Lukas's first stained-glass creation, which had been hanging from the stepladder. It was the one she'd guided him to make that night in the café, as they'd worked cautiously side by side. A gingerbread house in biscuity shades from milky to rich dark chocolate, looking so delicious she could almost eat it. 'I love the colours you chose. If we decorated the café like this, it would remind me of a real gingerbread house, all cinnamon, ginger and spice.' She moved around, lining up various pots on the windowsill and pointing to the paintwork. 'I'm finally ready to say goodbye to the festive reds and greens. They just don't work all year long. What do you think?'

He bent down to inspect the shades. 'A while ago, I would have said festive colours even once a year was too much. But like a lot of things, they've grown on me.' He stood. 'Though you're right. It's time for a change and these are perfect.'

There'd been a time when the word *change* would have sent a bolt of fear straight through her. It would have made her think of losing things and memories fading. But the more she imagined the café's new colour scheme, the more it felt like the perfect blend of old and new. She could picture the coppery hues sparkling in the sunlight, radiating joy to everyone who visited.

'I think Nell would have approved,' said Gretel. 'It's still in keeping with the gingerbread theme, but we'd be adding something of our own too.' She hoped this was enough of a demonstration of her commitment to him and the café. That she really was *all in*.

'And the tagline?' he asked. 'Should we rethink *Festive Cheer All Through the Year*?' His voice was cautious, but there was that *we* again.

'I was thinking *Friendship and Cheer All Through the Year*.'

He looked up at the sign and cleared his throat. Was he blinking back a tear? 'It's perfect. Nell would have loved it.'

Lukas moved his gaze to Gretel. He stepped in, his eyes full of an intensity that made her once fragile heart want to burst. But the low growl she could hear wasn't from him. Her showpiece was on its way.

Chapter 54

'I know a cherry picker isn't strictly necessary for a café front makeover. But after everything we've been through, somehow a stepladder didn't seem enough.'

Farmer Wilbur had left them outside The Gingerbread Café with his prize machine, the cradle bedecked in fairy lights like the old romantic he was.

'This one does come with exceptional memories.' Those red cheeks on Lukas's usually cool face were adorable.

'I had quite fancied being up in the boom lift when you arrived, whispering my soliloquy of love like a *Romeo and Juliet* balcony scene. But you deserved a proper, face-to-face apology.'

'Care to go up there together?' He held out a hand, like he was offering his partnership in a dance.

She took it and they stepped into the cradle.

'Don't you feel a bit silly now?' She giggled as the odd passer-by craned their necks for a nosey. The cherry picker had seemed like a good idea at the time, but now she did feel a bit of a numpty. At least the last time they'd done this it had been dark.

'I was actually going to wear festive deely boppers and a flashing reindeer jumper to meet you today, so think yourself lucky.' He gave her a cheeky grin.

'What? Sensible, Christmas-hating Lukas, head chef at La Carotte Rôtie, dressed like a Christmas nerd?'

'I'd honestly rather not stay there if you'll have me in your kitchen.' He winked. 'I mean, I'm quite the catch. And you might just have flipped my thoughts on Christmas. It used to be a time of stress and high emotions for me. I couldn't look at a mince pie without coming out in hives.' He smiled and she poked him in the ribs. 'But somehow with you, every day feels like the best day of the year. With your childlike wonder and your crazy ferret, you make me laugh even when I'd rather be grumpy. So if Christmas is your time of year, I'm down with that.'

'Actually, you're in luck. On both counts. I *do* want you in my kitchen.' Right then, it wasn't the only place. 'And I am ready to have Christmas just once a year. In December. It turns out Christmas isn't about wheeling out the plastic tree whenever you fancy and hoping it will make you jolly. It won't. Not without love, and the people who mean something.' She grabbed a tissue to dry a tear. 'Lukas, I've missed you. Let's not fight like that again.'

He turned towards her and took both of her hands, as though he wanted to hold all of her delicate hope in his. 'I love that you came here with a cherry picker to fight for me, you daft thing. But Gretel, you'd already won.'

She let go of his hands and threw her arms around his neck, kissing his soft warm lips and laughing all at once, her body toppling into his and pushing him backwards. His foot landed on a pedal and suddenly they were rising upwards in the cherry picker's cradle. Past the sign that they would soon repaint, and the slightly dishevelled Christmas tree still planted firmly against life's knocks, and up beyond the roof of The Gingerbread Café. She'd missed the way Lukas made her feel grounded and safe, even way up here.

Epilogue

Nine months later

It was the week before Christmas, and for the first time in a long while, The Gingerbread Café was practically effervescing with festive charm.

Gretel had lovingly placed Nell's old holly wreaths back in the windows, the winter-spiced candles were scenting the air, and all manner of stained-glass fairies and snowmen spun gently from every possible hanging place. Even the street outside was dressed up like it used to be, with red and green lights strung between the old-fashioned lamp posts, and artificial snow fuzzing up windowpanes. Perhaps they could hope for another sprinkling of the real thing this year.

It was a Sunday evening, and Gretel and Lukas had invited all of their friends from the street for a special Christmas meal. The lights were dimmed, the logs in the fire crackled and the wayward jukebox had chosen to play

'Wonderful Christmastime', which for once seemed like a choice they could embrace.

'I think they've got something to announce.' Zekia elbowed Amber as they helped to lay the impressive run of tables that stretched the length of the café.

'Everyone seems to be announcing stuff lately.' Amber gave Eve and Gordon the Grocer a pointed look as they folded napkins, engagement rings glinting on both of their ring fingers.

Eve simply smiled. She did a lot of that these days. As did Phoebe, who spent increasingly more time with River, the dreadlocked guy they'd seen her chatting to at the February Fair, and his rescue dog, Squiffy. The three of them were sweet together. Phoebe also spent less time binge-eating gingerbread and weighing her bra down with crystals, and she swore her chakras were more balanced than ever.

'You've had exciting news of your own,' said Bea to Amber, as she set some of her handmade miniature lavender Christmas trees along the table. Their tiny baubles sparkled under the fairy lights. 'You'll have to book me in for one of those henna tattoos. They look spectacular.'

Amber and a couple of her new school friends had set up a small henna tattoo studio at the back of Jane and Jayne's art gallery. They took it in turns to work there at weekends, although Amber was still making time to lend a hand at the café, and was even helping Gretel promote her Sunday stained-glass craft stall in the corner of the café. Who said Business Studies had been wasted on Amber?

'My treat,' said Amber, squeezing Bea's arm.

They hadn't seen as much of Bea lately. Her dad, Farmer Wilbur, had been forced to slow things down for health reasons, so she was helping out more at the family lavender farm, and seemed slightly frazzled for it. Her younger sister had been covering her shop, and much like their dad, was quite a character. Gretel had missed having Bea around, but it was lovely to welcome in new friends too.

Talking of new friends, Sky, who was the sister of Amber's social media guru Lexie with the pixie hair, had recently moved into one of the empty shops on the street. With Lexie's help, she was turning it into an emporium for quirky upcycled furniture and chalk-style paints, as inspired by Lexie's own shop in Tewkesbury. Gretel had loved seeing a splash of fresh colour, and this exciting new business was a sign that Green Tree Lane was thriving.

Kingsley was busy polishing up some small glasses for his latest festive rum, his happy smile radiating as always. The rum was cranberry and candy cane flavour, and Gretel could already see Gordon hovering nearby to be chief taster.

Gretel moved around with a tray of lebkuchen she'd baked that morning, congratulating herself on her delicately iced hearts and stars.

'Ooh, you're a natural.' Zekia winked.

Nell and her mum would have been proud of the ginger-bread treats, and little Rosa would have been loading up her pockets, her smile a picture of innocence. Some of the sweet things Gretel had remembered about them over the year, as she embraced each season instead of merely existing in Christmas, had surprised her. One of her favourites had been a memory of Rosa's chocolatey cheeks after pinching Gretel's Easter egg one year. How Gretel had giggled with Lukas about that one.

Lukas's mum, Sally, was even staying in a nearby B&B for Christmas. With Gretel's support, Lukas was keen to fix some of his broken memories of Christmas, even if his tender new relationship with his mum was still in the early stages.

'Sorry we're late,' said Jane, as she and Jayne bustled through the door. 'But we come bearing gifts!'

'Babysitter issues.' Jayne beamed, her face always so delighted when she referred to the little girl they'd recently adopted.

Gretel felt a tear in her eye as they handed her a new chalkboard for behind the counter. This time it was beautifully hand-painted with festive gingerbread people and sprigs of mistletoe, and finished off with candy canes made from a child's messy fingerprints. It was Gretel's first tear of the season, and as she dabbed it with a tissue, she knew it was a happy one. Her counselling had been going well and this year she didn't fear her emotions, whatever they may be.

She thanked Jane and Jayne, and placed the chalkboard behind the counter, where little stained-glass Nell was presiding outside her gingerbread house for the festive season, together with the new stained-glass angel Brigitte, whom she'd made last week. She too would be carefully packed away in tissue paper for another year once Christmas was over. Gretel had created the angel in honour of her late mother, with Lukas on hand to pass the googly-eyed pliers.

But Brigitte, together with Rosa and her late friend Nell, would live for ever in her memory whenever she needed them. Saying *Gute Nacht* did not mean forgetting.

Gretel felt like she could watch this scene unfolding for hours. These friends, this tightly knitted community, filled her heart with joy and wonder every single day. This may have been the first time she'd allowed herself to unpack Christmas for a long while, but for the first time since she'd lost her family, the season actually felt special. It was filled with laughter, love, friendship … and a generous sprinkling of hope.

Even Angel Gabriel was curled up inside the ferret hammock in his mansion of a cage, with his new ferret friend, Spooky Lou. Gretel had rescued her from an animal shelter at Halloween, as Angel Gabriel had been pining for a special friendship of his own. The café was now officially pet friendly, although ferrets were to be kept strictly under control and out of mischief. And they definitely weren't allowed near the new wintery gingerbread village which took pride of place in the café's bay window, and which Gretel and Lukas had so lovingly created to mark the season.

In fact, there was only one thing missing from this scene. Well, two. She checked the time on the wall. Any moment now.

And as if by clockwork, the café door tinkled open and in the doorway appeared the tip of a freshly cut Norway spruce, wet with evening dew and smelling like a pine grove. Only this time the person carrying it knew to tread with care, even though Gretel was far less fragile than she had been two years earlier. Gretel thought back to that time when he'd brought in a tree for Nell and had nearly knocked Gretel off her feet. Or perhaps he had. How much they'd both grown.

'Hey!' Lukas's face appeared around the side of the tree before he took another step. 'Is it safe to come in?'

As the jukebox broke into 'I Never Knew the Meaning of Christmas', Gretel could have sworn his eyes were alight with Christmas magic. Much like her heart at the sight of him. His slate-grey hair was mussed by the damp night air and from wrestling with a tree, and no torso had ever looked as good in the cosy Nordic jumper she knew was hugging him under his parka. And were those the first flakes of snow caught in the fur of his hood? He'd been embracing Christmas with nearly as much fervour as she had, and whatever the spirit of Christmas was, she knew she wanted him right there to share it with her always.

Gordon the Grocer jumped up to pretend to be helpful with carrying the tree in, and before long the friends were decorating it with their latest craft-night creations.

As they gathered around the tree with gingerbread mince pies and rum butter, the smell of boozy hot chocolate dancing on the air, Lukas jingled the bells on a nearby Santa sleigh decoration to get everyone's attention.

'Announcement time.' Amber clapped.

'Shh, don't put them under pressure,' Phoebe whispered. She didn't try to ply her with any crystals for her throat chakra, but Gretel could tell she was thinking about it.

Gretel felt her cheeks colour, conscious of the sorts of news they might be anticipating. She was only just used

356

to sharing her world with one man and an extra ferret, so it felt too soon for any sparkly big newsflash. But this was the perfect next step for them and her heart jigged with the excitement of it.

She linked arms with Lukas, his warm, spicy scent making her headier than any festive drink.

'Do you want to tell them?' he asked her, his eyes relishing the last moments of their secret.

Gretel nodded, then turned to address the crowd. She cleared her throat. 'So. Erm, I'm going to be leaving the street.'

There were a few gasps, interspersed with knowing smiles.

'But don't panic, I won't be far,' she continued. 'We'll still be right here running the café. But I'm moving into Starry Knight cottage, with my gorgeous Mr Knight.'

The gasps turned to cheers, followed by hugs and back slaps. Glasses were chinked and hips shimmied in celebration.

Lukas jingled the bells again. 'That's not all.'

The room went silent again and Gretel blushed. 'No, no, not that.' She shook her head and held up her boozy drink as an alibi. No babies in mangers just yet.

'It's a different type of passion project,' said Lukas. 'We've got planning permission to turn the flat above the café into a cosy supper and pudding club.'

'With a ginger and spice theme!' Gretel added, barely able to contain her excitement. She'd been thrilled when Lukas had told her about his idea, the day of their second cherry picker kiss. It was the thing he'd been talking to Francesca Whimple about over the phone, the morning of their first argument. He'd been embarrassed to run it past Gretel at that early stage, as his perfect scenario involved her moving in with him, if and when she was ready, which would naturally free up the space. It would have been too forward to mention living together back then, even for Lukas. 'I'm delighted we can finally make this happen.' She knew Lukas didn't care about his pretentious old culinary world any more and he didn't miss the headaches of La Carotte Rôtie, but he was artistic and ambitious and he deserved to have his own space. 'It will be a true celebration of food like Lukas has always dreamed of, where there'll be no limit to his creative expression.' With a bit of teasing, she'd even helped him to choose *great table linen*.

As their friends gathered around them, sharing their congratulations and ideas and offers of support, Gretel felt the spirit of community and Christmas flowing around the café with renewed vigour. It really would be a 'Wonderful Christmastime'.

And what was more, she knew this feeling would continue long after she'd gently packed the season away.

Acknowledgements

Fabulous people, I'm thrilled you've taken time to read *The Gingerbread Café*! I do hope it brought you warmth, joy and plenty of giggles. (And if you've loved a book, authors always appreciate a kind review. Extra thanks if you're a review-giving bundle of gorgeousness!)

Now, I've made a list of the incredible people I'd love to thank, and we could be here for a while! So cosy up with a cinnamon hot chocolate and let's dive in ...

Thank you to my delicious readers. Your dedication makes all of this possible. If you've been with me since my debut novel *A Colourful Country Escape*, I'm even more grateful to you. (And if you haven't read it, do have a nosey! It's full of colour, fun and scary peacocks. It's the perfect escape.)

Ginormous thanks to my extremely patient husband Neil, who keeps me and our little boy alive whilst I hide in a quiet room and get obsessive over adjectives. Thank you for supporting me whilst I 'try and make it as a writer.' Oh, and for always laughing at my jokes. You're my soul in a bowl.

Thank you to my fantastic Commissioning Editor, Rebecca Roy. Your belief in me and my stories has changed my life and I'll never be able to thank you enough. This book was a huge team effort, so my deepest thanks also to Darcy Nicholson, Sophie Wilson, Ruth Jones and Lorraine Green for your superb editorial advice. Along with Bec, your creativity has given *The Gingerbread Café* great sleighfuls of extra Christmas magic. And thank you to Natasha Gill for your boundless energy and general loveliness. I know there are lots of others on the Little, Brown teams whose names I may never know. I'm indebted to all of you.

High fives to my wonderful agent Kate Nash and everyone at the Kate Nash Literary Agency. You all work so hard to support and champion us authors and to make the process much less frightening! Thank you for answering my relentless 'stupid question alert' emails.

Thank you to friends and family who've supported my writing journey with the buoyancy of a thousand pompoms. Between you, you've travelled hundreds of miles to celebrate my stories, showered me with flowers and peacocks and cupcakes, crafted gorgeous gifts, shared fun photos of my books, told your friends about me, lifted me up, cheered me on – and so much more. There aren't enough pages to name you all, but thank you to Mumsie and Dave and the rest of my adorable family, to Linda and Geoff all of Neil's fabulous lot. To Vic, Tamara G and Joe, Lauren (you read a book!), Jasmine (did you pull it out of the basket yet?!), Katie and her fab mum Janice Preston, Lara, Georgeta

Vlase-Harvey, Rashpal Panesar-Gipson, Florence Keeling, Cat and Nads, Rosie Owen, the Denmark Road High School gang, teams MOH and Zurich, and everyone who's extended a hand of friendship on this wild and wonderful ride.

To my online family in my Facebook group, Chick Lit and Prosecco, for your never-ending cheerleading. There are so many of you bookish superheroes, including Sue Baker, Karen Louise Hollis, Susan Buchanan, Jodie Homer, Henriette Trampedach, Bernadette Maycock, Sophie Neville, Bea Stevens, Rebecca Paulinyi, Grace Power and many hundreds more. Your kindness gives me wings. (If you're reading this and you haven't yet joined us, please do! Chick Lit and Prosecco is one of the most delightful bookish spaces I know.)

Thank you to the other Facebook communities I'm part of, including The Friendly Book Community, and some wonderful admins – Sarah Kingsnorth, Marie Harris, Adrienne Allan and Hazel Elkin. You're a true support to books and authors.

Thank you to the marvellous authors who read early copies of my books and provided sparkling endorsements and moral support: Pernille Hughes, Nicola May, Christie Barlow, Sandy Barker, Kitty Wilson, Bella Osborne, Samantha Tonge, Holly Martin, Katie Ginger, Jaimie Admans, Nina Kaye, Lynne Shelby, Leonie Mack and Isla Gordon. Please do Google-stalk them and buy their incredible novels!

Massive thanks to Christina Young and the magnificent Gloucester Book Club, Maddie Simpson at BBC

Radio Gloucestershire, Candia McKormack and Tracy Spiers at Cotswold Life, Helen Gadd and Jenni Phillips at Gloucestershire Live, Kathryn Goddard and Alex Morefield-Broome for their wonderful photography.

A big thank you to Gloucestershire Libraries, and to so many wonderful bookshops, especially Waterstones in Gloucester, Alison's Bookshop in Tewkesbury and Rossiter in Cheltenham.

Huge thank yous to the Romantic Novelists' Association and New Writers' Scheme for career-changing guidance and mind-blowing opportunities. I would not be here without you.

To all at St Catharine's Under Fives playgroup in Gloucester. To the staff for giving Luca the very best care so I could write my books, and the helpers and committee for showing me what true community spirit is all about.

And finally to my late friend, Gina Charlton. This book is dedicated to you. My heart soared at finding someone so full of love, light and sparkle. I wanted to keep you for ever. But so sadly that wasn't to be. You'd planned to write your own books one day, so this one's for you. If you look carefully, you'll see the dog with the crystal in his bandana, which you cheekily challenged me to include. And if I look carefully, I know I'll see you everywhere. You are magic. Xx